Daughters of Legianne

Realms of Covens

H.S. Sullivan

Edited by This Bitch Reads Media @thisbitchreads_

Hardcover: 979-8-9901349-1-1

Paperback: 979-8-9901349-0-4

Ebook: 979-8-9901349-2-8

Cover photo: Wolf Quillin

Cover design: HVS

hssullivan.com

Printed by Crocketts Point Press

For those who feel lost or forgotten.

Warnings

PROLOGUE

THE woods were dying. Not one that slumbered, awaiting to waken as spring sunk its roots into the soil. But one full of death and decay. It clutched at Róisín's chest, leaving her with that bone deep weary feeling of sickness edging in.

She breathed deeply, the foulness of it burning her senses, before stepping from her backyard and into the darkness. In the wake of each footfall, the earth sprouted green, and Róisín moved deeper, leaving a beacon to safety for anything left within.

The late April sun stretched out across the sky overhead, and pain radiated from the trees, the silence deafening. Her hands flexed at her sides, and she reached out with her senses, trying to locate the source, but found nothing.

A strong rancid smell slammed into Róisín as she stepped around a rotted stump with a black substance coiling up its base, bringing a sharp sting to her senses. Her magic of earth and life within began to weep in sadness causing her to struggle to keep her steps steady. She didn't fail to note how the yellow and orange rays of the spring sun failed to reach through the trees. How its warmth did not penetrate.

It had been like this through the entire town of Greens Glen, Maine. No longer was it the cozy small town, tucked away in the northwestern region of the state, with its tall maples, cedars, hemlocks, or pines. The once vibrant green landscape had become muted. When winter came, the gray of the season settled in and never left. Birds and wildlife fled, in their wake only silence remained.

She crouched low, her bare feet mere inches from a pungent ooze that seeped from the ground. The hem of the dress she wore brushed against the edges, immediately staining the spring green colored fabric black.

Inhaling again, she smelled more than the rot. The disease that caused evil tickled at the back of her throat.

"He drains us," a quiet voice said from the colorless brush on her left.

She rose, smoothing her dress, and turned. "Who does?"

"The humans call him Stewart, but that's only because of the face he wears," the voice replied.

"Madigan," came the response in soft whispers around her.

Fear. She could feel the fear here. Faint, but it reached for her, begging for help.

Alert and prepared, Róisín moved closer to the brush. After a moment, a small white rabbit carefully came through the bramble. Extending her hand, she waited, studying it. The rabbit hopped into her outstretched palm.

"We've been waiting for you," it said.

She tipped her head back, the bare branches stretched over them. "He's using the life here to build his power."

The rabbit's pink nose wiggled, letting her know she was correct.

"My grandmother..."

"Before the birds left, before they stopped singing, they sang Norah's song, feeling Aoife pass and Norah's magic release back to us."

Norah had been Aoife's mother, Róisín's great-grandmother. Nature embraced her the way she had embraced it with her elemental magic.

Róisín continued to absorb her surroundings, noting two tall cedars wrapped around one another like lovers, stretching for the sky. Their trunks were a swirling blend of blacks and grays. All that remained of the life within were the dots and splashes of umber.

"So much pain, so much fear, so much... everything." The dull throb that started in her chest when she stepped into the woods had become a sharp, piercing pain. She fought to keep her breathing even. She needed to hold in her power. Needed to remain hidden.

"It came slowly at first. We didn't know what was happening. Then the waters changed."

"Show me."

"This way." It hopped down and bounded around the sludge-like puddles.

With one last glance at the cedars, Róisín made her way deeper. She knew she was close, the stench overpowering. The elemental magic within her began to scream, begging to be released to heal and rebirth the wood.

She knelt on the ground at the edge of the small pond. Its water was green and murky. A red film floated at the top. The disease within reached out and grabbed at her so quickly, she reared back to avoid its grip and fell onto her bottom. Pushing her hair from her face, she narrowed her eyes at the pond.

"He's strong," the rabbit said.

"Madigan is an elder. He's—" She frowned, her pulse dancing just over her eye. "He's not supposed to be here." She choked on a breath and squeezed her eyes closed, fighting off the wave of power that came at her again. "He'll know I'm here soon."

"Then we must work quickly."

She staggered to her feet, taking the rabbit up with her. "We must get back to my house. It's protected. I'll be able to let the others know what I've found. We need to plan. Now that we've found him, we can finally do something."

The rabbit twitched its nose in response.

She made quick work retracing her steps back to where she had found the rabbit, pausing at the entwined trees. She laid a hand on the cedar bark, feeling the last traces of life deep inside.

"Save my love," the taller one whispered to her.

"I'm going to save you both." She soothed it with a stroke of her hand over the bark. Then she dug her fingers around the grooves of the trunk and closed her eyes.

Drawing her magic from her core and through her limbs, the warmth of her magic greeted and embraced her. It pulsed at her fingertips, and she pushed it outward. The ground around her greened with small flowers springing up, creating a carpet of purples, pinks, and yellows.

The rabbit scampered down from her shoulder to the lush ground now around them, its eyes full of delight at the sight.

"The stories were true." It bounced between the blooms, nose twitching.

Róisín pressed her other hand against the tree, and slowly, her power moved inward. Snaking coils of red spread up her arms. It slithered along her skin, moving towards her neck. She hummed *Caru Canu*, a song from her childhood about two dogs her father had taught her to help keep her focus.

Overhead, a hawk circled, calling out. Her power surged and the rabbit ducked its head behind a rock, shielding itself from the light that now broke free from her body.

The trunk became hued in shades of deep brown, its branches bloomed—leaves green and vibrant. A small release of air sounded, as though the two trees sighed.

Slowly, Róisín's skin drew in the coils, feeling the magic within her singe the darkness of them and healing its disease.

"You'll be protected." She stroked her hands over the bark. "He cannot harm you again."

The rabbit came to a rest at her feet. "What will you do now?"

"We'll go home and let the others know. We need to end this. And —" She looked up at the trees canopy, just as twined together as their trunks. "I'll keep coming back, when I can, to fix this."

"But..." The rabbit took one of its ears between its paws, rubbing the tip of the ear. "Can you do that? All that power?"

"I can try." She drew in a deep breath, nodding. "I can try."

Róisín bent to scoop the rabbit up and tried to quiet the rising voice of doubt within her. The power from the magic she'd inherited from her grandmother's passing months before was still new to her. It felt so much different from the magic she'd been born with. From her mother's. Not just the immense power of it, but it was like it'd been relieved to have found her.

Aoife's passing had left so many unanswered questions, especially the ones Róisín had about her mother, Brenna. Brenna had held secrets. Secrets that had impacted Róisín's life.

This, in Greens Glen, had been only sign of him over the last several decades of Madigan. He'd drained resources from the humans in efforts to cause illnesses and death. Slowly, painfully, siphoning the energy from nature and humans alike to expand his power.

They'd lost their tether to him as an elder witch of the Council when he severed it, and somehow he had cloaked himself so that even intense spell work could not locate him.

Until now.

Something about this place had held him there long enough for them to find him.

Róisín could only hope that they were not too late. That the council of the Covens could end this before there was nothing left in any of the realms.

CHAPTER 1

KINCAID McGrath stood with his arms crossed at the back of the packed gymnasium of Greens Glen High School. A steady, throbbing beat had begun at his temples and his ears rang.

He didn't want to be here, but Lina had tossed her hat into the ring for the new town select board members. Tonight was the night they would vote. So here he was, being a supportive older brother while she was determined to take a seat up for election, currently held by what the townspeople had deemed a "lifer."

Bill Smithfield had sat on the board for forty years and held the title as Chair for the past thirty. Despite the hammering of his gavel and his shouts for quiet, the volume level continued to rise in the room.

Bill was also the reason the volume level in the gymnasium was at screech, having suggested that before they vote on the select board seat, they vote on allowing the expansion of Munson Technologies on the outskirts of Greens Glen.

Caid rolled his eyes.

At six-foot-four, he towered over most of the people there, giving him a virtually clear path to find Lina. She'd pressed her lips into a thin line, her blond hair, almost the color of sand, tucked into a neat bun.

7

Her back was rigid, and her hazel eyes stared daggers at the other side of the room.

Stewart Munson sat quietly, a dark and ominous presence between his broad stature, black hair he wore slicked back, and deep slate colored suit. He wore a slight upturn of his mouth.

"We can't even drink our own water anymore! Why would we allow an expansion?" someone shouted.

"None of our problems started until he came and set up shop here." Another pointed an accusing finger at Stewart.

"Has anyone called the EPA to test what's seeping through the ground from the factory?"

"Bill will let us die just to make a quick buck for himself," another shouted from the far side of the room.

The heavy wooden doors to the room swung open, knocking against the wall with a reverberating clang. A cool gust of air followed, and Caid savored the feel of it in the sweltering gymnasium.

The entire room fell quiet with hushed whispers full of questions and unease. Every single resident, children included, had squeezed into the meeting that night, so the late arrival even had Caid quirking his brow.

A younger woman with hair the color of autumn stuttered to a stop. Her bright blue eyes were wide, and her throat bobbed when she swallowed hard, visibly nervous with all eyes on her.

She brought a hand up and rested it at the base of her throat. "Is this where the town meeting is?"

"Yes, yes, it is, little lady." Bill rose from his seat, hurrying around the long meeting table toward her. "And you are?"

"Róisín McKenna." She took his extended hand and shook it.

"Ah, yes, the young lady that moved into Kitty Lagree's house earlier this spring. Welcome." His eyes lingered on her, his smile edging toward a leer. "I'm the Chairman of the Select Board, Bill Smithfield."

Caid's hackles rose, and he clenched his sweaty palms—either from the heat of the gym or the way Bill gripped her hand and licked his lips while eyeing her.

Chairs scraped over the floor, pulling his attention from the pair. Several men and women rose and moved toward the aisle, eyes on Bill.

He clearly wasn't the only one with that feeling.

"Pleasure to meet you, Mr. Smithfield." She attempted to free her hand, but he wouldn't let her go.

"Give her some space, Bill," someone called out.

"She's half your age."

Another snickered.

Bill nodded his head. "Please, call me Bill, hon. Come." He waved a hand toward the rows of metal chairs, and the group of people watching them. "Join us."

She gave him a small smile, the discomfort clear on her features. He released her hand, then turned away from her, and her posture visibly loosened.

"Now is as good a time as any to take a ten-minute recess," Bill said when he returned to the table. "Then when we come back, we can hold the votes for the select board seats."

Caid went to wade through the people filing out and head toward his sister, but she waved over Róisín.

They exchanged a quick greeting and hug. He shook his head and chuckled. Of course, his social butterfly of a sister had already met her. Lina had never been afraid to speak to strangers, nor ask probing questions one shouldn't until they knew someone.

Shifting his weight, he leaned back against the wall and groaned. He was ready to get his vote in and get home. It'd been a long day and tomorrow looked to be even longer with his new hire starting.

"Caid!" Lina's megawatt smile flashed, and she picked her way through some of the crowd filtering back in. Róisín followed close behind.

Caid straightened and rubbed his palms on his jeans.

"You made it," Lina said, finally making her way to him.

"You said to be at the gym by seven or you'd egg my truck and T-P my house, of course I made it."

"He's kidding, just so you know." Lina flushed and offered a sheepish smile to Róisín. "I swear."

He hummed. "No, I'm not. She egged my last truck because I missed a birthday party. Her birthday party. That she threw for herself. For turning twenty-eight."

Lina let out a noise between a groan and a whine. "Caid. You'll scare her. Stop it."

"What?" He lifted an eyebrow. "Stop egging vehicles to get your way, and maybe you'll be less scary."

Róisín covered her mouth to hide her smile, looking between the two at their exchange.

They stopped and turned toward her, both their left eyebrows arched.

"I'm an only child, so I don't get to see this dynamic often." Róisín laughed.

"Isn't that lucky?" Caid pushed off the wall. "I'd give my left leg to be an only child."

"Oh, you love me, you know it." Lina pushed his shoulder.

"I do." He sighed, looking up at the ceiling. "I do. Lord only knows why, though." He offered his hand to Róisín. "Kincaid McGrath."

The smile she flashed to Caid was warm and friendly, unlike the one she gave Bill, and she reached her hand out to shake his. Their hands connected, and she inhaled sharply.

He glanced down, noting that goosebumps covered both their arms.

"Róisín McKenna." When she released his hand, she clasped hers together in front of her. "Lina said that you're in construction, and I know this is really an awkward time to ask, but I have a back patio door that not only sticks because it goes lopsided when I slide it but has taken to leaking more and more each time it rains."

"Smithfield said you're in the old Lagree house, right?"

"Yes. Mrs. Lagree's two sons handled the estate sale. They'd mentioned the door was old and may soon need replacing. I guess I just thought I'd have a bit more time."

He studied her for a moment. The way her hair, now that she was closer, shined with reds, burgundy, blond, and hints of purple. It contrasted with her bright blue eyes, the color of warm Caribbean water. A splash of freckles covered her nose. Caid blinked and mentally shook off the rest of the exploration just as he reached the curved line of the cupid's bow that shaped her top lip.

He cleared his throat. "I could stop by and look at it later this week, if that works for you."

She released a deep breath and her shoulders dropped. "Perfect, thank you so much. I work from home, so any time, any day works."

"In case something comes up, or it gets worse." Caid reached into his back pocket and pulled out his wallet to fish out a business card. "Here you go."

She glanced down at the card, then up at him, making no attempts to hide her scrutiny. It equated to a microscope. He was a sample on a slide, and she was the scientist picking apart his every cell, determining what, he didn't know. Whatever it was, it had him fighting the urge to look away, to hide from her attention, and sweat gathered at the base of his spine.

He cleared his throat, motioning to the card. "And don't thank me yet. You may just find out that you need to replace more than a door."

"I guess I'll cross that bridge when I get there."

"All right folks!" Bill pounded his custom engraved gavel to get everyone's attention. "Let's get this vote for the board started so we can get everyone home before tomorrow. We'll table the expansion vote, for now."

"It was nice to meet you, Kincaid." Róisín tipped her head to him, and Lina tucked her arm in hers. They made their way back to where Lina had sat before.

Some eyes in the room followed the pair, but the way Stewart Stewart watched Róisín with dark eyes unnerved him. Like watching a predator mark its prey. Róisín, if she was aware of Munson's watchful eyes, didn't let on. She kept her attention on Lina, their heads tucked together, whispering like old friends.

He shoved his hands in his pocket and tried to shake off the jolt that had wrapped around him, unlocking something inside, when he had shaken Róisín's hand.

Chapter 2

Stewart Munson. Something about the name was dark and uninviting. And fitting to what Madigan represented.

Róisín shivered.

She sat on her bed, legs crossed beneath her, blinds closed and lights on low. Her magic hummed its power against the wards around the house. The energy from it lifting the hair on her arms and smoothing some of the edges left from the remains of the energy that had slipped home with her after the meeting.

Touching Caid's hand had been a jolt through her system. Electrified tingles shot straight over her skin. She also hadn't failed to notice how he had kept his own attention on Stewart. The angry energy rolling off Caid when Lina had introduced them slammed into her, and, for a moment, she struggled to breathe. It had been that handshake that had shifted that energy into something else. Something new.

"I know he looks grumpy all the time, but he's just an introvert. Don't let his size intimidate you, he's really a giant teddy bear," Lina had said with a smile.

A giant bear in flannel and jeans that hugged those thighs just right. Róisín let out a soft sigh.

Róisín was tall, nearly five-foot-eight, but Caid had towered over her. He had the same sandy blond hair and hazel eyes as Lina, but that was where their similarities ended.

Róisín pulled her hair back into a ponytail, then focused on clearing her mind.

David hopped onto the bed, bouncing toward her. "Will we begin?"

The rabbit had stuck to her side since they found each other in the woods. He was her guide, her connection to the spirits of the woods who could reach and follow Madigan's magic.

"Can I sit next to Nanette? She sneaks me candies."

He sniffed the air, his whiskers fluttering, and she stifled a giggle. "Someone has a sweet tooth."

He pulled one of his long ears down between his paws. "Those caramel balls she carries are quite delicious. Have you ever had one? I imagine that's what happiness tastes like."

A smile bloomed on her face, and she held out her hands for him. "If Nanette will allow it. You may end up next to Lucius this time. But don't worry, he has a fondness for woodland creatures."

"Fond of eating them, maybe" David's nose twitched with little enthusiasm.

She rolled her eyes, huffing a soft laugh. "Lucius is a vegetarian. He won't eat you."

He made a small grunting sound. "Says you."

"Come on. Close your eyes, clear your mind. We need to go."

Moments later, David and Róisín sat around a circular mahogany table within the sprawling and towering stone castle in the realm of Alleyette. It had been the meeting place of the elders, the oldest, most powerful witches from each Coven, for over one thousand years. A neutral realm, with no permanent population, human or witch, Alleyette and the castle had represented a haven to all.

The first time Róisín had sat at the table, fear tried to swallow her whole. Aoife had brought her before the eight seats of the council to seek approval to transfer Brenna's magic to Róisín. Róisín hadn't known what was happening. Only that her mother's magic had never passed down to her after her death. Aoife had learned the council had placed it in the stone until they could meet and decide on where it would be placed.

A close vote. Brenna's power was Róisín's by just one vote. She knew from that moment on, the council would take care to watch her. Every step she took, every choice she made would be monitored. Any slight misstep, and her mother's power would be lost. Her own life could be forfeited.

The eyes on her now as she waited for the meeting to start reminded her just how closely she was being watched.

Egos sat with her at the table, egos with eyes. Those eyes were all on her, waiting.

The attention made the room seem unbearably cold, her body wanting to convulse with shivers to warm her. She tightened her muscles and clenched her jaw, fighting the chill. If she showed any sign of weakness among the realm leaders, she'd surely be taken from the task. And that would be an insult, a black mark. She would be a failure.

Instead, she focused on the ones at the table that didn't appear to want her to fail.

"You've been able to locate him?" Nanette Wallingsford asked, her hand slipping into her pocket. David's ears perked up. She sent him a wink and gave a slight wave of a finger from her free hand.

"Yes, he's known as Stewart Munson." Róisín set a stack of newspaper clippings related to what the humans believed to be mysterious illness affecting the vegetation, including aerial views of before Madigan's work had started. "Under the guise of a factory that makes solar panels, he is siphoning life from Greens Glen's forests, other lands, waterways and the surrounding area."

Nanette leaned forward and thumbed through the stack for a moment before turning back to David.

Róisín narrowed her eyes at the witch, then pulled out new images, ones she had captured herself of the woods on her property. "I've done some hiking through the woods behind my home and the damage is far-reaching."

The council members circulated her information around. Quiet murmurs filled the spacious carved stone room.

"Have you been able to make any repairs?" Lucius McArthur asked, his steel-gray eyes peered at her over his hands steepled before him.

"Some. I can't feel his connection, but I can feel his power. The town had a meeting tonight, and I felt him probing. Trying to access me, test my magic."

"I'd assume Aoife's teachings held fast?" Mildred Abel shifted, leaning closer to her. Mildred, a real-life version of a woods faerie with round grass-green eyes, pale, almost colorless hair, had been one of Aoife's longtime friends.

"It did. However, I don't think he'll give up trying." Róisín shuddered.

"Keep that shield up. If you need help with new wards, just reach out," Mildred said.

"What about the townspeople, do they suspect anything amiss other than it just being waste and ruin from this factory?" Lucius asked. "Has anyone gotten sick? Any associated deaths?"

Róisín slowly blinked at him, absorbing his questions.

"Apologies," he added. "I guess I should start with, what have you learned so far?"

"He does make the panels and dumps the waste from the product directly into the soil behind the building as a sort of sleight of hand. I've been there for a month, and I've yet to associate the few deaths in town in the last five years to him."

Nanette turned her attention away from David and looked at the six council members before her. "Do we have any evidence yet that this is, in fact, Madigan?"

Róisín swallowed hard, avoiding the empty eighth seat, the seat for the Aunellion Coven leader, for Madigan, and set an object on the table.

The stench of the dark magic and its power radiated from the petrified piece of wood. Those around the table recoiled, a sharp intake of breath came from every witch in the room.

There was no denying it was Madigan.

"Call back any witch not on assignment. There should be no dalliance. They need to be here or in their home realms as soon as they can," Lucius said, his tone brokered no room for argument. "Even without his connection to us, we need to cloak ourselves and ward our power when we are in Earth's realm. It's imperative for everyone's safety."

A murmur of agreement went around the table.

He turned to face Róisín. "Absolutely do not engage with him when you're there. Once more have returned, we will send help. Until then, I cannot stress enough to not engage."

"I understand." She would go to whatever lengths she needed to avoid Madigan. And Bill. "Shoot. He," she paused, rubbing at the back of her hand. "The current town leader is under his thrall."

"Are you sure?" Nanette asked.

Róisín had sensed the thrall Stewart, or Madigan, had wrapped around Bill before he'd reached out to shake her hand. "I could feel the grime of it when he shook my hand. That slipperiness trying to seep into my skin." She shuddered remembering the feel of it slithering over her neck.

"Shit," Mildred muttered, garnering a glare from council member Shasta Fierro. "What? It's just a word." She rolled her eyes.

"There's no way we can break it without revealing Róisín's power," Nanette said. "Hold on." She blurred into a dance of blues, yellows and oranges, fading out as she shifted from the room.

"I have runes for you to carry when you're working in the woods there." Shasta withdrew a small pouch, then waved a chestnut-colored hand, sending the pouch lifting from the table and over to her. "I've placed holes in some to be worn as charms when you don't have pockets. It will mask your power and keep your wards in place while you're working."

"Thank you." Róisín wrapped her fingers around the pouch, the power of the runes inside reaching for her, clinging to her fingers. The offer from Shasta was a rare one. She had been the one to keep the closest eye on her since the council vote over Brenna's magic. Sometimes, the attention was curious to Róisín. Sometimes, Shasta sat across the table from her with a stone face, unmoving, not even blinking. Other times, her eyes had a shine to them, her face and posture both tight, almost pained. Róisín could never make out what it meant.

"Here." Nanette appeared next to her chair. "Aoife gave this to me when I was your age." With a small, cloth-bound book, she leaned over Róisín's shoulder. Her long salt and pepper colored hair tickled Róisín's arm as it shifted over. "It'll be useful to ward and protect the people of the town. The town meeting you were at was to replace this town leader, correct? What of the potential of the new leader?"

"Yes. She's a pure heart."

"Good." Nanette smiled. "Protect her so that Madigan cannot take control of her as well. The less his power can touch among humans, the better."

"We will defeat him and restore balance," Lucius said.

"Aoife would kick our asses if we didn't." Mildred received another scolding look from Shasta and sighed.

"We'll meet again one week from tonight. By then we should have heard from everyone and have had most return where they are needed. If we let this rot fester any longer, it'll be the end of all of us, and we risk losing him again," Lucius said.

Shasta lifted her hand, her eyes on Róisín as she did so. "What timeline are we looking at? Alleyette week? Ely week? Earth week?"

"I'd prefer a Baijiolan week." The distaste for Róisín dripped from Henry Edevane's words, and he slid his glacier blue eyes from Lucius to her. He tugged the sleeves of his suit jacket down his tanned wrists, then folded his hands on the table before him. "It would give me far more time to gather my people."

"That's nearly three weeks earth time," Nanette sputtered. "Do you know how much he could accomplish? We may never get this opportunity again."

Henry lifted a shoulder, then dropped it. "I cannot guarantee my people then."

"Neither can I." Frederick Lunestran, who sat rigid next to Henry, dipped his head in a slight nod. Much like Henry, he wore a suit and tie. His obsidian black, just like the long hair he wore tied in a neat bun at his nape. His yellow eyes were cold, calculating, and his skin the color of milk.

The duo were always scheming, skirting the edges of the council laws. However, all witches knew Frederick was more dangerous than Henry. Whereas Henry abided by family and Coven tradition, Frederick only looked out for himself.

"A Shianshani week?" Shasta suggested.

"Ridiculous! That's just four Earth days," Henry nearly shouted.

Now it was Shasta who shrugged her shoulders.

Róisín sat quietly, the clear division of the council unraveling at the table. Her stomach danced with her nerves

Lucius lifted a hand to stop the bickering, his eyes dark, mouth a tight line. "We've located him, which means he's either comfortable and slipped, or we are running out of time. We cannot short ourselves." He looked at Shasta. "Nor can we afford the safety of time." This time, he shot Henry a fiery look. "We need to meet in the middle of all realms' time, which means one Earth week."

A bloated pause filled the room as they all looked at one another.

"Until the week," they said finally, in unison.

Róisín and David returned to her room.

She set him on the soft cotton comforter, then dropped heavily next to him. "I think Nanette may want to take you home when this is done."

"That is something I wouldn't dream to complain about. How do you feel about the meeting?" He hopped closer to her and rested his paws on one of her thighs.

"I…" She sighed heavily. "I don't do well with politics. Or asking for help. It feels like they all hate me."

"They cannot hate you. They need you. He wins without you."

She lifted an eyebrow. "I don't know what it's like to live as a magical, talking rabbit, but I can tell you, the only reason they fought like they did tonight is because there's a dislike there. Lucius aside, they've never trusted me once I received my mother's magic. This was a solid reminder of that."

"Shasta and Nanette gave you tools to help," he said.

She stroked a hand over the cover of Nanette's book. "That's true. And Mildred offered help should I need it."

He sat back on his haunches. "See? You think you're in this alone, but perhaps you need to shift your thinking of how people perceive you."

Before she could respond, he hopped from the bed and disappeared.

CHAPTER 3

Lina tucked yard stakes under one arm, a package of fresh markers between her teeth, and an armful of rolled poster board under her other. She used her bottom to bump her car door closed and turned to face Róisín's house.

A white, nineteenth-century farmhouse with yellow gingerbread gable pediments, shutters, and porch posts. Globe flowers, lily of the valley, primrose, tulips, and phlox spilled out of pots across the three-season porch. She gulped in a greedy breath, inhaling the scent of blooms, one that had become foreign in Greens Glen.

Lina made her way up the path to the front door and resolved to not only take advantage of Róisín's offer to help her make campaign signs, but to find out just what she fed all her plants to make them grow better than anyone in town currently did.

Greens Glen had been stuck in winter. The plants, the trees, the lawns, all had gone their dormant, muted shades of gray, yellow, and brown. When the snow fell, it was easy to forget. Life around them was supposed to be washed of color. But in these warmer months, when the air was supposed to be fragrant with blooms, pine, dirt, and freshly mowed lawn, there was nothing.

Shortly after the color fell away, so did the smell. It simply didn't exist anymore. She turned to look across the neighborhood. The sting of tears threatened at the sight. Would they ever get life to grow again there?

"Róisín!" She spun back to the door and pressed her nose to the screen of the wooden door, peering in. "It's Lina!"

"Oh! Hold on just a second, my hands are covered in flour," Róisín shouted.

Lina mumbled and shifted her goods to one arm. "I've got it, take your time."

She halted as she crossed the threshold into the house. The inside was not only vastly different from what she recalled in her years spent there as a child, but it was far from what one would expect with the cozy farmhouse exterior. The sitting and living rooms were now a deep shade of forest green, with accents around the windows painted so dark they were almost black. Varieties of houseplants filled the two rooms in pots along shelves hanging along the walls, or arranged near the cream-colored sofa and loveseat. The sitting room had a robin's egg blue lounge bearing stacks of ancient looking books.

Something aromatic and tasty tickled Lina's nose. She followed the smell into the kitchen.

"Oh, it smells delicious in here. What are you making?"

Róisín tipped her head. "Scones from a family recipe."

"You've even got them like wildfire in here," Lina took in the plants that filled the space there as well.

"What?" Róisín turned and her cheeks turned red. "Oh, those. I love plants."

"Don't be embarrassed." Lina waved a hand at her. "It's amazing how good you are at getting everything to grow. You're going to have to give me tips. I can't even keep a snake plant alive right now."

Róisín wiped her hands on a dishtowel, then set the timer for the stove and turned to give her undivided attention to Lina.

"I figured we go simple." Lina looked at the things she'd laid out on the kitchen table. "Bill will still have all those fancy signs he gets made every year he runs. I looked into it, and Thomas would kill me if I spent even half of that kind of money. Plus, on such short notice, they'd have to be expedited."

"I think simple is better," Róisín said. "They'll be expecting to see the fancy signs because that's what we're used to when people are running for office. To see a cut-to-the-point sign will probably catch more attention."

Lina chewed on her bottom lip. "I think you're right. What should we say?"

"What's the official title of the seat again?"

"Select Chair is what we've always called it."

"Lina McGrath-Commons for Greens Glen Select Chair?"

Lina held up a blank poster board, envisioning her name scrawling across. "I like it. Let's do it."

They fell into a comfortable silence and worked together, crafting poster after poster. They were nearly finished when Lina said, "Has Barb been over yet with one of her famous pies?"

"She and Clarence came over before my car engine was even cold on my first day."

Lina snorted. "That sounds about right."

"They've been very kind. Everyone has, to be honest. Well, for the most part everyone has. I've been a new person a few times, and it's always hard. It's nice when there's a few welcoming faces."

The tip of the marker Róisín held streaked across the poster board as she worked, spelling out the words for the campaign. Lina was grateful to have her support, for her to move to town at the unexpected height of her campaign. She'd only known Róisín for a little more than a month, but it had seemed like longer.

The air in the gymnasium had sizzled that night, growing warm the moment Caid and Róisín shook hands. Caid hadn't been able to take his eyes off her, and it had left her curious, and hopeful that maybe her brother could finally find someone to be happy with and settle down. Have what she and Thomas had since the seventh grade.

"What about my brother?" She leaned back in her chair, capping the marker she held.

Róisín's hand paused over her poster and her brow wrinkled with confusion. "Your brother?"

"You met him the other night at the meeting?"

"Well, yeah, I know who your brother is." She shrugged, then went back to writing on the poster board, this time with more care than before. "I just didn't know if you're asking if he's been nice to me or not."

"That. And didn't know if he looked at your door yet." Lina motioned to the patio slider behind her.

"Not yet," she answered. "I'm not really in a rush. The weather looks like it'll be dry for a stretch, so it's okay."

Maybe she'd read the situation wrong, and there hadn't been something there. "Still, he said the end of the week and here it is the end of the day on Friday. Which means the end of the week. I'm going to give him so much shit the next time I see him."

"Please don't," Róisín said. "It's really okay. He's probably busy."

Lina's shoulders dropped, and she frowned. "It's been hard for him. For anyone in town to get and keep help. Few want to stick around and fight Munson Technologies, and who wants to live where you can't drink the water, hunt to eat, or grow any vegetables, let alone flowers?"

"How long has it been this way?" Róisín asked quietly.

"A little over a year. It wasn't right away." Lina shook her head. "The water, the bad soil, that came a little after. A lot of us were quick to figure out what the cause was. I mean, it was right there, coming from a pipe at the back of the factory. We've had town vote after town vote to stop the expansions, to force him out. Nothing happens. Bill's power has gone to his head, and he's vetoed everything. We questioned his power to do it this past winter, but..." She sighed.

"Nothing changes."

"Not just that, but everyone—it's so chaotic. Everyone is mad at everyone. Every town meeting there's shouting and screaming at one another. When I told Thomas I wanted to run against Bill, he practically begged me not to. He just got a promotion with his job, so he's spending more time down in Portland. He wants to sell the house and for me to come with him."

"Would that be so bad?"

"It feels like I'd be throwing in the towel, just like everyone else has done."

Róisín tapped her index finger against her chin. "If you beat Bill?"

"We immediately hold a town vote to put a pause on any new

industry here and any more expansions of Munson Technologies. Then I meet with our lawyer to see how we can go about getting the factory shut down legally, so our asses are covered."

"Do you think the town would back you?"

Lina held Róisín's gaze with her own. "Everyone but Bill Smithfield, no matter the cost."

Róisín looked over their finished signs, around the kitchen, then to Lina, clearly warring internally with something. Her eyes shifted back to the table.

Lina sat quietly, waiting and curious. They hadn't known one another long, but she hoped that whatever had Róisín chewing aggressively at her bottom lip, she would trust Lina enough to share.

"You know you can count me in," Róisín said.

"Perfect." Lina beamed at her. "I should probably get going. Meet in town tomorrow to stake these up where we can?"

"I'll bring the coffee."

CHAPTER 4

———————

CAID had put off stopping by Róisín's house. He couldn't deny it, so instead, he sent every single call of Lina's to voicemail and kept himself limited to his house and current job site.

Climbing into his truck outside of the hardware store, he cursed as he knocked his elbow on the steering wheel, then tossed the bag of screws into the passenger seat. Exhaustion had worn him down to a bed-headed, grocery-bags-under-his-eyes, mess.

Lina's sport utility vehicle pulled in three parking spots up from where he sat.

He rubbed his elbow, trying to muster the energy to start his truck and head back to the site where he'd left his only employee and longtime friend, Wyatt. He released his elbow and yanked on the lever at the side of his seat, causing the back to fall with a thud against the backseat, and he hopefully dropped out of view.

There was a knock at his window. "Yoohoo! I know you're in there, jackass, I can see you."

"Go away." He lifted a hand and slapped it at the window.

"Kincaid James McGrath." Lina's tone turned serious. "Open the door."

"No."

He startled, jerking upright when she pressed her face against the window and blew a raspberry against the glass. "You're washing that off."

"Unlock the door."

He turned the key to the accessories on position, then tapped the button at the door. The window dropped. He aimed his best Big Brother Stare her way. "What do you want, pain in my ass?"

She scoffed and rolled her eyes. "How'd I get saddled with you?"

"As the older one, I think I'm the one that gets to ask that, not you."

"Why haven't you stopped by Róisín's yet to look at her door?"

He couldn't stop the strangled, choking sound that escaped his throat. Which did not go unnoticed by Lina, given the way her left eyebrow inched up. "I've been busy."

"Mm, you lie." She pointed a finger at him and shook her head. "And you're such a terrible liar, too."

"Is there a reason you're harassing me?"

The smile she gave him reminded him of the Cheshire cat. "Two reasons, actually."

"Oh, God." He pinched the bridge of his nose, squeezing his eyes closed. If ever there was a time to find a genie bottle, this would be it. His first wish would be to have a volume button for her. He'd have to do his best not to wear out the mute option.

"First, I want an actual answer about Róisín. You said you'd stop by, and you haven't yet."

"Leen." He dropped his forehead against his steering wheel and sighed. He hadn't lied when he said he was busy. With his new hire bailing already, he couldn't line up more work for him and Wyatt until he had a better idea of how much longer they'd be on their current site. With just two sets of hands, things took longer than they would if he had more.

"Have you been sleeping at all?"

When he lifted his head, Lina was almost right next to him, having climbed on the side step of the truck, leaning in through the window.

"Jesus!" He jolted away from her nearness.

She chuckled at him, then shook her head. "Caid. I worry about you. You do way too much."

"I'm fine. Can you scoot back a little? There's a personal bubble"—
he motioned a circle around himself—"and you're in it."

"I need your help."

Everything, work, Róisín, his crumbling hometown, his wish for
that mute button, it all fell away until it was just him and Lina.

"Move." He motioned for her to step back. He wound the window
up and pulled the key from the ignition, then joined her outside of the
truck. "What do you need?"

"Help to put up my signs."

He was the canary, she the cat, and she'd just snared him.

CHAPTER 5

STEWART Munson was drawn to the pretty auburn-haired woman pulling the yard signs from the trunk of a blue convertible parked in front of Greens Glen Cafe. The moment she walked into the gymnasium he could smell the magic on her.

Not like his, no. No one was like him. No one would ever hold his power. He'd learned over his centuries that nothing compared to dark magic. It was limitless. The more he embraced it, the blacker his soul became.

He shifted in the driver's seat of the sedan he drove. His tall, broad frame dominated the cabin, but he tolerated it, as it was only temporary. He rubbed a hand over his jaw, questioning the familiarity of the young woman. If he still had some connection with the witchkind, it would take moments to learn all he needed to know about her. Instead, he was reduced to acting like those disgusting humans.

Snooping around, asking questions. Socializing.

His skin crawled at the thought while he waited for a car to pass before pushing out of his car and crossing to her.

"Good morning."

A small noise escaped her, and she jumped, almost dropping the signs. "Oh, hi, good morning." She was slightly breathless as she smiled at him. "Róisín McKenna."

"Stewart Munson. Here, let me get those for you." He moved to take the signs. Anything to brush her hands, figure out just who she was.

"That's okay, but thank you. Lina is right there." She motioned toward a red SUV two spots over from her car. "We need to get these up this morning."

Could she feel his magic? If she could, she hid it well. He could sense just a glimmer of power—maybe her lineage was diluted with humans for it to be so weak.

Not wanting to give himself away and wanting to get to know just who this little witch was, he took a step back, keeping his eyes on her. He would play the cards right, bide his time.

"Well, it was a pleasure meeting you, Miss McKenna. I hope to see you around town again. I'd love to buy you a coffee, or perhaps lunch sometime."

She gave him another slow, half smile and nodded. "Thank you, Mr. Munson. It would be a pleasure."

And a pleasure it would be.

He stepped back onto the sidewalk, then made his way to his car, trying to play it casual. He raked his fingers through his jet-black hair, the sign of just another man turned away by a woman. Nothing more to see.

Róisín may have diluted magic, but power was power to him. And the power of even a weak witch was far more fruitful than the slow leaching he had done to the lands and humans around the realms.

CHAPTER 6

Róisín held a stapler in one hand, her other arm linked with Lina's. The connection grounding her, anchoring her from fraying into threads that could be carried away by the wind. She couldn't shake the sense of his eyes burning on her, from somewhere. Even the sounds of their footsteps had her senses on edge.

They walked just a few paces ahead of Caid, who they'd saddled down with two armloads of signs tacked to stakes. His eyes stared ahead, lips in a tight line. He had said no more than a handful of words to them, using grunts and head nods to communicate. But beneath the scowls, there was always a light, affectionate glimmer in his eyes when he looked Lina's way. A slight smirk tugged at his mouth when he'd shake his head in feigned annoyance as he hammered a sign stake into the ground. There was no doubt that he loved his sister, so it wasn't a surprise to Róisín when Lina had told her how she'd finagled Caid's help with their sign posting mission for the afternoon.

It made her think of Matthew. They weren't brother and sister, but seeing the dynamic between Lina and Caid, she understood how much like siblings she and Matthew truly were.

Róisín smiled. No, they weren't blood related, but they had grown up together and had been best friends much like she could see Caid and

Lina were. Róisín also didn't doubt that she could've easily duped Matthew into helping them, just as Lina had with Caid.

"But if you don't have gills, how the hell do you breathe underwater?" Lina's question brought Róisín from her memories.

"Simple, mermaids don't need gills to breathe. Their magic would allow their lungs to use water like we breathe air."

Lina's head swiveled to her, a brow raised. Róisín would love to tell her of the Trifoan mermaids. How glorious they were with their jewel toned fins and vibrant rainbow colored hair. But she couldn't. Her experiences with humans that learned there was more than the mortal world had proved heartbreaking. To other witches, it had been dangerous.

"Are we going to talk about mermaids all day, or are we gonna pitch some signs?"

The closeness of Caid's voice made them both jump.

Lina shrieked and spun around, lifting her arm as she did, almost knocking him in the head with the stapler that she clutched in her hand like a weapon.

"Don't sneak up on us like that!" She shook the stapler in his face, scowling at him.

He nudged her hand away from him. "Didn't stop you from climbing in my truck window earlier to get into my face."

Róisín took a step away from Lina and Caid to give herself space. Her heart and lungs squeezed together, like they had grown fingers, and the digits wrapped themselves together.

Madigan had reached for her with his mind again. It felt like insects and their small feet rushing along her spine, trying to burrow into the base of her skull. The probe this time was more desperate than in the gymnasium.

She took a steadying breath. Only two more days before the council met again. All she had until then was her own magic and training. She couldn't crack. He couldn't find out who she was or why she was there. Anything that could cause him to take action before they were ready or cause him to flee and disappear again would be damning.

She was safe. Her wards were up, the power of her magic cloaked. And she was with Lina and Caid. She looked around at the house lined streets of the neighborhood they walked, scanning the yards that looked as though their printer had been near run out of ink as they were made. Madigan was nowhere to be seen.

Lina pointed. "Fine, then let's put one here."

"Right here?" Caid pointed a stake at a section of grass. The day had grown warmer under the late spring sun and he had rolled the shirt-sleeves of his flannel shirt to his elbows. The sight of his forearms flexing with movement grounded Róisín in the moment, letting her finally draw in a full breath.

"To the left." Lina aggressively waved her index finger. "No, your other left."

"They let you build houses?" Róisín said.

Lina whistled low next to her. "Damn that was good."

Caid's head whipped up, eyes dark on her. Lina covered her mouth, trying to hold in her laughter, but failed, the sound bursting out of her in a loud, rolling noise.

"That was such a good burn." Lina lifted her hand for a high-five from her.

Róisín held up her hand for Lina. "A trick my father taught me." She wiggled her left thumb and index finger. "The left side makes the L."

"Are you paying attention to this, brother dearest?" Lina called over her shoulder to Caid.

With one more thwack of his hammer, sinking the sign stake several inches into the ground, he gathered the remaining signs in his arms and straightened to his full height. When he stepped toward them, Róisín fought the urge to take equal steps back.

How can anyone be so tall?

The panicked squeezing in her chest, remnants of Madigan's presence, released her heart from its vice and set it pounding again, pushing blood through her veins. Something close to ecstasy filled her. A rush of tingles and heat much like when her magic rose and released from her body.

With her feet rooted, she tipped her head back to keep her eyes on Caid as he approached. His hazel eyes landed on hers, then dipped down to her mouth where they tracked the movement of her tongue as she wet her lips.

The gold flecks flared briefly before he shifted his attention up her face. "Where are we putting the next one?"

"I thought maybe Boylson's Corner? I can't put them on private property unless I get permission, and I figured I could do that later this week." Lina's voice sounded muffled, like she was underwater when she spoke.

Caid's face dipped closer to her, ever so slightly.

Róisín's breath quickened. A buzzing closed in around her, making her skin tingle to the point where she became hyper aware. What was that sound?

"...and after Boylson's, maybe the end of Roberts' division? I just don't want to be in the car all day, so wherever we can post in walking distance..."

"I can do four more before I need to get back to the site and close up for the day. I need to be at Miss McKenna's first thing tomorrow to look at a door." He may have been speaking to Lina, but he still focused completely on her.

Lina came into her peripheral. "That's fine. We've already done more than I hoped to get done today. And I'm sure if you're saying first thing in the morning, you mean sunrise, so Róisín probably will want to get home and to bed, so she will be up."

He grunted. "And I'll make sure to use my proper left." He stepped back from her, breaking whatever connection that had been in place.

Goosebumps rose along her exposed skin in the absence of him. Swallowing hard, she made to follow them.

Chapter 7

Not long after the sun rose the next day, Caid's booted feet stopped just on the other side of Róisín's wooden screen door. As a peace offering for his behavior the day before, he brought a fresh cup of coffee from the cafe. He balanced his coffee with Róisín's in one hand and gently rapped his knuckles on the front door.

"Oh, shoot!" She said, muffled on the other side of the door. "Dangit. Just a second! Ouch," she muttered, sounding closer to the door now. It swung open quickly a moment later, she appeared, flustered, pushing the hair from her face. "Hi," she greeted him.

He handed her the coffee, an eyebrow arched from his curiosity. "Morning. Everything good?"

"Just not quite used to the funky layout in here yet. I keep stubbing my toe on the same corner of the wall when I walk out of the living room." She brought the cup to her nose, inhaling and closing her eyes. When she opened them, they were filled with amusement and curiosity. "Mocha and cinnamon, my favorite."

"I bugged Lina earlier to see if she by chance knew. A sort of..." He scratched his jaw, before rubbing the back of his neck and shrugged. "Peace offering for being rude, and having you up so early."

"Thank you." She placed her nose over the top of the cup again, inhaling loudly. He stood, riveted, when she brought the cup to her lips to drink.

He lifted his attention up and over her shoulder, to beyond her, his jaw clenching, and he tried to block out the sound of the small moan of delight she made as she sipped. The way her face lit up like a child's on Christmas made it worth the three rows of the heart-eyed smiley faces Lina had sent him earlier.

"Come on back." She motioned him in. "I started poking around on the internet, looking at new doors. If you hit me with the news today that I need to replace it, I have narrowed it down to a few I can show you. I just like to be prepared, no surprises." She took another sip of the coffee and used her tongue to clear the bit of whipped cream left behind on her top lip.

Needing a distraction, he set his cup on her table and went to the door to check around the casing.

"Can I?" He gestured outside.

"Sure, go ahead. Whatever you need to do." She waved him on.

He tried to shake off what it felt like being around her—almost electric, a hum over his skin. An invisible magnet tugging him into her space, demanding him to be closer. Caid gave her a nod and slipped through the door to check the backside of the house.

The expanse of green grass in the backyard, and the pots upon pots spilling over with flowers, vegetable plants, and vines, caught him by surprise. Not because she'd only been in town for a few months, or even that it was only mid-May in Maine. Seeing plants flowing so fully out of the pots was a sight he didn't believe he'd see around town again.

He slowly eased a piece of trim around the door to check behind it when she popped her head out and looked up at him.

"If you see a white rabbit hopping around out here, that's mine, so please don't shoo him away." She flashed him a smile, then was gone, withdrawing back into the house

So she was back to shy, reserved Róisín like the night he had met her. Yesterday, trailing her and Lina, hearing snippets of their conversations, witnessing their interactions, he'd witnessed her quick wit, and her mellow sarcasm that had drawn his sister in. They paired well together, even if sometimes it was at his expense.

He sighed, pulling out the small notepad he'd tucked into his back pocket when he had gotten out of his truck, and began making a list of repairs needed.

Moments later, sure enough, a white rabbit came bounding across the side yard toward the back patio. It hopped up into a chair just opposite where Caid stood, slack jawed.

The rabbit seemed to watch him, studying him. Its nose twitched, whiskers wiggling as it sniffed the air. Its small, black eyes on him.

Caid watched it for a moment longer before setting to work, taking measurements. The quicker he got this taken care of and out of there, the better. He still hadn't worked out what had possessed him to stalk over to Róisín and just stand there, towering over her like he had. Why had he just stared at her, mapping every inch of her face, charting every mark of it, and not said a word? Not even when he caught the way her pupils slowly dilated, or her lips parted ever so slightly. His body moved before his brain could catch up with it and when it finally did, he was lost in the ocean of her eyes.

Walking to the other side of the door, he came to a halt.

Róisín had an earbud in her ear and danced from the living room, into the kitchen. She'd changed from the oversized shirt and jogger combination she greeted him in, into a cropped tank top and tights. He tried to draw his attention back to his work, but something about her movements, about her, mesmerized him.

She eyed a glass of thick green liquid on the counter like she was a boxer getting ready to tap her opponents gloves before a match. Taking it in her hands, she took in a deep breath, eyes squeezing shut and her nose wrinkling, before downing the contents. Róisín quickly set the glass down and covered her mouth with her hands. Rapidly blinking her eyes, her body shivered before she removed her hand and let out a very audible gagging noise.

Shaking off the distraction, he quickly went back to examining the siding around the door trim.

The sound of the door sliding open had him turning back to the kitchen.

"I'm going for a run. Will you—" She gestured towards the door and the notepad he clutched so tightly in his hand, his knuckles were sure to be white. "I guess just send the details to me? I'd hate to make you wait around for me to come back, and if I slack off any more today, I will start making excuses to keep slacking and get nothing done."

He blinked, forcing himself back down to Earth, to the patio in her backyard. Clearing his throat, he looked up at the crumbling trim at the top of the door. "It'll probably be a bit."

"It's bad, isn't it?" She frowned at the house.

"It can be fixed," he said. "The stuff that can't be, we can replace. It's been leaking for a long time. The boys, I think the reason it sat so long before they sold, is because they wanted to hold on to it. A simple repair got the chance to deteriorate and get worse. I need to figure out how far the rot has moved from the door, which means some of this has to come off."

Those turquoise eyes followed his hands as he motioned to the siding at the rear of the house.

"If that's okay, I mean," he added.

She sighed, her shoulders slumping. "Whatever you need to do. I trust your knowledge and judgment on this."

He nodded, keeping his eyes on the house and off the way her top hitched up when she straightened, revealing the creamy white skin of her stomach.

"Okay. I need to get moving before I go put my sweats back on and find my butt on my couch with my face in a book for the rest of the day."

Once she'd disappeared around the corner of the house, he exhaled, running a hand through his hair. He froze in mid-movement when he noticed the rabbit had moved closer. The way its black eyes stared back at him, Caid swore it was a silent warning it conveyed to him. That if he even thought of overstepping with Róisín, the rabbit would act.

Shaking his head at that insanity, he went back to pulling the siding from around the door.

CHAPTER 8

Two days later, Róisín sat at a table in the sitting room of her Coven's designated suite in Alleyette. The suns had risen hours before, pulling her reluctantly from the comfort of her bed. Now, despite the warmth of them pouring through the floor-to-ceiling windows that lined the room's east wall, she huddled beneath her robe, her breakfast quiche before her. She had managed just one bite, the eggs tasting like ash. The result of the previous evening's council meeting stealing the flavors of her favorite dish.

Lucius had done as he promised and prepared to send a handful of the witches that had returned to Alleyette to aid Róisín with Madigan. However, the council demanded a vote.

Safety concerns, Mildred had said, Frederick and Henry agreeing with her. The only votes in her favor had been Lucius, Nanette, and Shasta. As it was Róisín requesting the assistance, she had to abstain from voting. Unable to break the tied vote, the line was drawn.

They wouldn't help her.

Róisín pushed around her now cold eggs on her plate. The betrayal from her community, especially Mildred, clung to her this morning.

She'd managed two and a half months in Greens Glen without Madigan knowing her identity, but he probed deeper every time their paths crossed. The day she and Lina posted signs, again just days later when she walked into the grocery store, when that tickle growing stronger at the back of her mind caught her attention.

Róisín rubbed the back of her neck, her stomach clenching tightly. She never had to ward herself so deeply, for so long. The relief had been immediate when she had arrived in Alleyette just days before. A small part of her dreaded returning to Greens Glen and needing to find the energy to bring it back up. It hadn't just been the exhaustion, it was the way her senses dulled when she had to cloak her magic. She couldn't feel things as fully, or deeply. She had always considered cloaking to be a sedative in that aspect.

Humanlike. The cloaking muted the heightened sense of smell, taste, and touch that witches had. Other witches noticed it in the slower way a witch moved, the longer it took to react.

A soft knock echoed through the empty room. She turned to the door, hesitating. Lucius had come to her the night before, assuring her there were other avenues they could try with the council and asking her to trust him. He was the only one in the castle that would find their way to her door. Had there been new news?

Róisín pushed up from her chair, zipping up her hoodie she wore as she went. Lucius or not, she was not answering the door in a camisole, braless. She popped the door open and all of her words left her at the sight of whose form greeted her through the crack.

Shasta stood, glancing up and down the hall, her dark hair braided and coiled around the top of her head, immovable even with the quick movements. She wiped her hands on her deep purple velvet dress, the Molennius wolf and mountain crest over heart highlighted by the light coming in from hallway the window.

Clearing her throat, she gave Róisín a small smile and stepped into the room.

Róisín finally moved and shut the door behind them and turned to where Shasta stood in the middle of the room, pulling free a book tucked under the velour skirts.

A door within Róisín's mind cracked opened. As though a memory, long locked away, long forgotten, reached for her, begging her to walk through.

Lavender and chamomile filled her memory. Her mother, sitting before the grand stone fireplace of their home in Ireland with the book in her lap.

"One day, my little rose, this will be yours and your world will shine new with the knowledge of our magic and its power," her mother said to her with a soft smile.

Róisín's eyes began to sting and ribs grew tight, her breaths shallow.

"That was my mother's," she whispered.

Shasta tipped her head to one side, her brows knitting together over her honey-colored eyes as she scanned Róisín's face. "Have you ever used it? Her magic?"

"I..." Róisín's shoulders dropped. "I can't."

"Sit. We need to talk." She sat at the table where Róisín's cold break-fast remained untouched. She placed the book on the table, her hands resting on top of it. "Aoife championed for you to have Brenna's power, but I think she feared it. You need to learn how to harness it, control it."

Her emotions rose like hands in her throat, its fingers wrapping around her windpipe, threatening to squeeze. Swallowing hard, she dropped into the seat across from Shasta. "I can't use her power."

"Tell me what happened."

"It was when I was with Alexandria in Molennius." The words spilled out of her before she could stop them. Her mind was filled with a fog that was struggling to clear. Something was there. Something about Shasta. Her magic yawned and stretched through her, its stroking fingers soothing and calming her, sending the unspoken message that Shasta was a safe place for her. But how? How did her magic know she could trust Shasta? The feel of a warm hand atop hers on the table drew her gaze upward.

"Breathe, sweetheart." Shasta's voice was soft and her eyes glittered with the tears that built in them. "Breathe."

Warmth expanded in her chest and she had a flash of a memory. A warm, amethyst and emerald colored kitchen. The smell of freshly baked cookies. Shasta's dress, amethyst, the color of her Coven. A new, unexplained sense of calm washed over her. She trusted her magic, and it was urging her forward. With a loud exhale, she took that step.

"We left late from a club. He was—" Her breath caught, and she wrung her hands in her lap. "He was right there in the darkest corner. Human, but he smelled like rot. He went for Alexandria first, but I jumped on him and when he pulled the blade, I didn't even think, didn't even weigh the risk of Alexandria asking questions. I just..."

"Acted on instinct to save you both," Shasta finished.

"Was it instinct?" The question had burned her still, decades later. "It just rose inside of me. Like it acted for me, like it felt my fear and used it, aimed itself at the source. It was nothing like how my life magic comes to me. And after—" She shivered. "Everything was suddenly squeezing in. The pain I felt every time my heart beat. Everything was muffled sounding, and I almost couldn't breathe. It was weeks before my power returned to me."

"We won't start working yet." She slid the book toward her. "I want you to read this first. Every page. If you fall asleep reading it, start over. This is important. Aoife should've taught you."

"She didn't have the time," she said, distracted.

The quiet whispers from the book pleaded with her to open the pages, consume its words. She smoothed a hand over the cover as she'd done so many times before as a child.

Róisín laid the book on the pale wooden table between them and blinked back the wetness forming in the corner of her eyes. Perhaps not touching the book would relieve the ache in her chest so that she could focus on Shasta and her words.

"She had over fifty years," Shasta replied. Her tone was dark and unfriendly. "More than enough time to teach you."

There had been no love or friendship lost between her grandmother and Shasta. They had only ever come together for the sake of their people, and that was it.

"Why are you helping me?"

"Your mother and I were very close for many years. I was the only one there when she married your father."

"But..."

"There were things." Her voice was rough, strained. She picked at the wrist of one of her sleeves. "There were things that Brenna knew from early on that changed things. No, I can't say that exactly." She shook her head, then closing her eyes, she fell silent for a beat.

Shasta sat stone still except for the steady rise and fall of her chest with each breath.

"Things were already changing, but once Brenna learned what she did, it all happened faster." She glanced at the book, then lifted her eyes back to Róisín's. "She shielded herself from Aoife. To live away from her, in peace. Then she met Stephen. For a time, she reconsidered letting Aoife back in, but there was..."

Róisín searched within for her earliest memories with her parents, the ones from when her father was still alive. Her father bringing her mother a bouquet of flowers that he had picked from her gardens, and she scolding him with laughter and a wide smile before letting him sweep her into his arms, spinning her around their tiny kitchen. She had none with her grandmother in those years. How had she forgotten? A quiet alarm sounded within her. First the recollection of her mother when she had seen the book, now this.

What else had she lost, and how?

"Aoife blamed me. She never liked that Brenna and I got on so well. She very much wanted to keep all relationships within her Coven."

Shasta's eyes shone as tears built in them.

"That's why you two never got along," Róisín murmured.

"I think that's why she fought so hard for Brenna's power to come to you after she passed. She could be a very spiteful woman. Even Nanette and Mildred cannot deny that."

Róisín lifted the book from the table. The soft crackle from the fire roaring in the river stone fireplace, the constant smell of freshly baked bread and chamomile, wrapped around her chest, hugging so tightly, it began to hurt. She wanted desperately to be home at that moment. Would she even recognize it if she went to Ireland? She tried to recall the shapes and colors of it, but failed.

She took a shaky breath and seized the opportunity of having Shasta before her. "Why did you vote against me?"

Shasta shifted her weight and bowed her head. "I knew you had no teacher. I knew Aoife would do nothing once you had it other than let it fester. Maybe even fade into nothingness. I wanted it to be returned to the stone, released to you when you were ready."

Róisín's finger trailed beneath the words on the first page of the book. As she read, the lines opened the door to the secrets of her mother's power.

To wield the power of death is to wield the power of fate in one's own hand. If one does not hold the balance of both light and dark, they shall be consumed and become dust...

Róisín swallowed hard and lifted her eyes to Shasta. "Why now?"

"I'll be honest, I still don't think you're ready. Brenna would agree. She often wondered if she was too over protective, doing you a disservice." Shasta pushed to her feet and stalked to the tall arched window that overlooked the castle courtyard. She stood so close to the glass that her warm breath fogged the pane. "I told her to always trust her gut. She knew Aoife better than any of us. Let that knowledge guide her in keeping you safe."

Róisín turned in her seat, dozens of questions swimming inside of her head. "There are things you're not telling me."

Shasta's nod was slight. "And it is not my place to."

Róisín rose and went to her side. "But you're going to help me?"

"We're out of time and Madigan is a very dangerous, powerful man." Shasta faced Róisín, her magic moved through Shasta's eyes in a swirl of soft browns, golden yellows, and bright greens. "You need to access all your power, and not have any fear of it. It'll leave you exposed to him, and he'll want what you have. Every drop. I will help you with this. Nanette will help you master the elemental powers from Norah's family. Lucius has given us the go ahead to do whatever we need to do to help you, even if the council has made the vote against it. And you already know he'll be there for you, whatever you need."

Róisín straightened. "You'll all get in trouble."

A dangerous grin spread over her face. "Living is the risk of trouble. I will not let them sacrifice you for this. Neither will Nanette or Lucius. We owe it to Brenna."

She chewed on the side of her thumb. "I just read this book?"

"Read it, then we begin." She crossed the room to the door, pausing halfway before turning back to her. "And Róisín? The Seer in Roidon can answer any of those questions."

Róisín drew her brows together, confused. Instead of explaining, Shasta opened the door and left.

Slamming the book closed, she rose and dressed quickly. She needed to be back in Greens Glen later that day to let Caid into her house. Which meant with how time moved in the realm of Roidon where the Seer lived, she had only a little more than two days to track down their Seer and learn what she could about her grandmother.

CHAPTER 9

Roidon was quiet when Róisín arrived. The air was fresh with human life--like freshly cut grass mixed with rain. Sweet summer blooms accented the scent, a sign of the witches that lived here. Trees topped with leaves, marigold, magenta, and deep blues filled the land-scape. The buildings were bold splashes of every color imaginable. The way the gilded dirt sparkled brilliantly under the suns always led her to believe that crushed bits of gold blended in the soil.

At the edge of the capital, the bright colors dimmed as she went. A thick forest of black, gnarled trees stood stretching toward the sky. The Dead Forest. The Seer's home sat in the middle, protected by the many tales of horror its darkness and snagging limbs created. Humans never dared to trespass, and witches did so with caution.

Róisín made her way through to the clearing toward where the Seer's home would be waiting should she make it. With each step she took, the trees shifted. Some reached forward, grasping at her with their branches smelling of acid and decay. Her magic rose, slowly seeping light through her pores and the trees recoiled as though they had been burned.

"I've been waiting for you, child." The Seer sat on a wooden rocker wrapped in a deep purple knit shawl on their porch. "You're late."

"Late?" Róisín hesitated at the bottom of the steps.

"You should've been here decades ago." The Seer's disapproval was rich in their scolding tone. "Come inside."

Frozen in place, blinking, dread crept along her spine and she worried that she'd made a mistake in coming. A wrongness lingered in the air, like the sludge at the bottom of an oil bin brushed against her nose, reaching to grasp her senses, trying to coil around them.

The Seer rose and ambled to the door. It swung inward with a high-pitched shriek.

The noise violated her ears, making her cringe.

"You don't have time to waste, child."

"This will be fun." She sighed and eyed the steps. They looked like something had chewed on them, jagged, and nearly black with rot. With each step, the weakened wood groaned, the rusted nails creaking. She came to an abrupt stop in the open doorway, speechless and taken aback by the casualness of her surroundings.

Róisín didn't know what to expect, but walking into such a common, cozy, decorated home wasn't it. The scent of freshly baked bread and the burning wood from the fire in the small stone fireplace in the sitting room cleared the sludge from her senses. A rack of neatly folded knitted throws hung on one wall. Several paintings of landscapes hung on another. Small knick-knacks littered shelves and tables around the room.

"Sit." They pointed to a seat near the fireplace before turning to leave the room.

Cautiously, Róisín lowered herself into the plush blue suede seat. To her left there was a faint clatter of cups, followed by the slow shuffle of footsteps coming near.

The Seer appeared in the sitting room clutching the handles of a silver tray, a tea set resting atop it. Despite the silver veil covering their face, the heat of their gaze burned her.

Her face and neck grew hot before she could reign her reaction in.

"You've come with questions about Aoife, about Brenna."

After setting the tray on a table between them, the Seer adjusted the veil, exposing a face wrinkled with time and milk-white eyes.

Róisín couldn't pull her attention away, and she took in every line, every shape. No one knew how old the Seer was, nor how old the Goddess or her daughters, the Sisters of Fate were. Even the history books of the witches didn't say.

"Your mother came to me when you were a small witchling."

The statement caused Róisín to startle, a slight gasp escaping her lips. A crawling, skittering thing ran along the skin of her arms. Why was she so surprised to hear her mother had come to the Seer? Most every witch did so at some point in their life

"Seeking answers, just as you are." They waved a hand in her direction when they passed by her to sit in the open chair. "The Sisters had come to her."

"Fate's Sisters?"

The Seer nodded, finally sitting in the matching blue seat across from her, then busied themselves with preparing the tea. The teapot and cups bore an intricate pattern of gold swirls and roses.

Róisín's eyes froze on the cups. Could the roses be symbolic of her arrival there?

Róisín leaned forward. "How much can you tell me?"

"I'm allowed almost everything, and only because our future demands it. Sugar?" They held up a cup of tea.

Róisín's mouth became a desert. She tried to speak, but the dryness trapped her voice. Instead, she shook her head.

"Aoife sought power. A power greater than any witch should hold on their own. It is why we have the council, our rules, our laws." They brought their nose to the filled cup, taking an inhale before giving a nod and passing it to her. "Oolong, to help clear that messy mind of yours. Where was I?"

They paused, looking from her to the tray. "Ah, the Goddess. She demands a balance, and once the balance tips on our side, it tips in the human world as well. If it should become far enough out of balance, all life will cease to exist."

The tea scalded her tongue and throat causing her breath to quicken. "Including ours?"

"All life, everything. Aoife saw that her own line was a direct threat to the power her dark soul craved. She knew as it expanded, she could not survive to gain the power she had wanted. She went against the

Sisters, the Goddess, and took it for herself. Her mother, the aunts, her uncle, the children."

Róisín gasped. "She... she killed them."

Was Aoife so malicious? Sometimes her words to Róisín were harsh or cold, but Róisín had always assumed it came from a place of just not knowing how to communicate with her after not having a family at her side for so long.

"She tried first to draw their power away from them while living, but she worried it would attract council attention. More?" The Seer gestured to her empty cup, and Róisín shook her head. "The Goddess worked feverishly with the Sisters to stop her. That was when she blocked them, stopped their interference. At least, not before the Sisters could take an action they hoped would cause her to change direction. A child."

Róisín's mother, Brenna.

"For a time, it seemed that it worked. The Sisters were unsure if it was Brenna's arrival, or if it was that Norah had moved on from life and Aoife finally gained a seat on the council. She could have a say in the control of the Covens."

"What about my grandfather? What about Bernard?"

The Seer's eyes shifted to black before shifting back to a milky white. "Bernard was no better than she. When she went against him, that was when they knew the child didn't change anything."

"That's why they went to my mother." Róisín's hands throbbed, causing her to look down. Her knuckles had gone white, the porcelain beneath her hands feeling weakened from her grip. She loosened her hold and moved the cup to the saucer on the table before she shattered it.

"Yes. They protected her. They knew you would come, a further extension of Aoife's Coven, distancing her from complete power."

Róisín covered her face with her hands, drawing in a breath, trying to keep her composure. Was Aoife the reason she'd forgotten so much?

This power-hungry Aoife the Seer spoke of could take memories, and Róisín suspected the Aoife she knew wasn't the one everyone else did. "Did anyone know? Did anyone suspect it?"

"You waste questions. You know the answer or you would not be here," the Seer snapped.

The votes against. The denial of frontline support.

"Mildred?"

"She was Aoife's right hand on the council, just as black a soul as Aoife."

"Fuck." She groaned. "Shoot. Sorry."

An amused smile tipped the Seer's mouth up. "You are much like Brenna. She had a choice to make, to right this wrong. It was not an easy one, but there was no other way."

"She didn't... I thought it was because she couldn't go on without my father?"

"I cannot say what the Sisters have sighted for the future, if they want you to know, they will come to you. They told Brenna what had to be done, what your Coven needed to shoulder in this future."

Anger sparked deep inside of her. The fire it ignited, scalded. It charred her insides, sending a choking smoke to her throat. Unable to speak, she shot to her feet, fists clenched tightly. Her magic frantically tried to wrap her in a cooling embrace, but she shoved it away and stalked toward a window. Her eyes burned with unshed tears as she stared at the twisting, bending trees that surrounded the house. Her life up to that current moment had been filler for *this* moment. She wanted to scream, to shout, that she was worth more than this, that she deserved more. Deserved to live, find love again, have a family.

Her heart clenched in her chest. Róisín pressed her molars together, hard. "I'm paying for my grandmother's sins. I'm going to lose everything because of her, is what you're telling me."

"No, child, no." The Seer motioned for her to sit down. "You will wipe your grandmother's sins from all the realms. You will make it right again."

She opened her mouth to speak, but the Seer shook their head. "That is all I can give you. It is time for you to return to Alleyette. Be careful with whom you choose to share what you learned here today. There are many who may appear to be with you, that you will find are not. Even in the highest of power."

CHAPTER 10

CAID hoisted his chop saw onto the lowered tailgate of his truck, then drew a hand down his face, letting out a heavy breath. He'd been sleeping like shit. Each night, a sensation like an electrical current running under his skin kept him from relaxing, and his mind discovered the magic of flight, taking off on some very scenic adventures.

The wooden screen door lightly slapped closed, and he pinched the bridge of his nose. It hadn't been Róisín's fault that just this morning his mind had taken one of those adventures, with his hands brushing along her bare skin, her body writhing beneath him.

"Get your shit together, McGrath," he muttered.

Shoving the chop saw into the bed of the truck, he gathered his brad nailer and case for his reciprocating saw, pausing when he saw Róisín lower herself onto the top step. Her eyes were on where the sun was sinking below the leafless trees.

He wanted more from her than this. He wanted to hold her in his arms as they swayed to quiet music. From the way her eyes lit and face glowed when she tended to her plants, or returned from a walk in the woods, had him wanting to show her all of his favorite trails, mountains, hidden ponds. Wanted to be the one to make her laugh every day. The one who got lost in her body every night.

But he couldn't.

He had dated, had even been engaged once. Love and he did not mix. Kate, his ex-fiancée, had pointed that out to him. Many times.

"Does your heart tell you every waking moment that it wants me? Or is it your mind telling you this is something you must do?"

Caid couldn't give her an answer. He'd stood, speechless, as she screamed at him until she had nearly lost her voice, then threw the engagement ring at him. She had been offered a job in Boston and wanted him to move with her. He'd asked for a little time, suggested he stay behind to take care of selling the house, then move after. In reality, they both knew it was his way of saying no.

Looking down at his feet, he gathered himself. Focused on his breath in and out, counting to ten. He slammed the tailgate closed and when she looked at him, he tossed his head toward the black, rust-stained roll off dumpster in front of the small garage. "Benny will be here first thing to haul that off and give us a replacement."

"There's more that needs to come off?" He could hear the panic in her voice.

The only love Caid knew and understood was the love he had for Lina.

Yet another strike against him when things fell apart with Kate, his relationship with Lina.

It had been him that had drawn the line there. He refused to walk away from his sister, and when Kate had told him that it was her or Lina, the choice had been easy.

He'd been okay with being on his own, keeping to himself. Until Róisín had walked into that gymnasium. Since then, it was almost like she consumed him.

Keep it professional, McGrath.

Wiping his palms on his thighs, the canvas material of his Carhartt's wicking away the sweat that had started there, he made his way toward the steps. Toward her. His heart pounding in his ears, he lowered next to her. "That's just the siding, sheetrock, and some insulation. I've got a material delivery coming tomorrow too that'll have the Zip Wall we need to get the rest of your outside wall out that's rotted. I didn't want to leave you with a gaping hole in the back of your house, so we had to wait for the deliveries to line up."

"Thank you." She clasped her hands in her lap, her shoulders dropping. "I've been meaning to catch you to ask about it all, but I've been so"—she released her hands and spread her fingers—"swamped with a work project."

Every day for the past two weeks, she'd been surrounded by stacks of books and papers at her kitchen table, or on the chaise lounge in the sitting room off to the side. Sometimes when he'd glanced through the patio door, that pull within him nudging to see her, she would pace, hands in her hair, eyes pinched, lips moving as though she tried to sort out an issue with only herself as a sounding board.

Caid didn't know what she did for work, he could only guess it had to do with history given the appearance of all the worn leather and canvas covered books always littered around, but sometimes he had wanted to pop his head in and ask if she needed help.

"Have you always been in construction?" she asked.

"Pretty much. Wyatt's dad, Ed, did it before he retired and headed south for Florida with Sandra. Once I could hold the hammer and pound a nail, I was his shadow. Taught me everything I know." His eyes trailed her index finger, following its motion as it rubbed along her bottom lip.

"You naturally just stuck with it? Never wanted to do anything else?"

Needing to reign himself in before he crawled up her, pinning her to her front porch, he cleared his throat and pulled his attention back to her front yard and the small subdivision that lay before it.

"Never really cared to do much else. I enjoy working with my hands." He squeezed his eyes shut the moment he said it. Felt her stare burning into him. He risked it, cautiously opening his eyes and looking down at her.

The left corner of her mouth tipped up, her eyes the color of the clear blue sky that day, glittered with laughter at him.

Quickly turning away so that she didn't see the way his cheeks burned with embarrassment, he held out his hands. "Something the simplicity of these as a tool, and using them to create, to build things for myself, or others is so... satisfying."

She hummed. "My job is sometimes like that, but it's more my brain that does the building and creating, so to speak."

"What do you do for work?"

"I'm a historian and researcher for auction and selling houses. I help locate specific antiquities that their larger clients are in search of, and often will help appraisers with value determination for upcoming auctions."

"Sounds smart," he said.

Kate had been smart, too. Her job in finance and ambitions for Wall Street had her climbing her corporate ladder like a firefighter racing to the top floor. He'd seen the paperwork she often had to take care of, and even with his being quick with numbers, he could never wrap his head around it all.

"You're too simple, Kincaid..."

He shook the memory from his mind and took a risk with Róisín. "Do you enjoy it? Sometimes I've seen you ready to rip your hair out or wear a hole through your kitchen floor."

She lifted her head, turning to him.

You idiot, McGrath, she'll think you're a creep. He had to fight his body's urge to wince.

"It has its moments," she said. "But I couldn't imagine doing anything else."

"I should probably get going." Caid shifted, ready to spring to his feet. "I don't want to keep holding you up."

When they stood, their shoulders bumped together from having shifted so close to one another as they sat. She teetered a bit, and he reached out to steady her. When his hands wrapped around her biceps, heat shot through him.

He couldn't find his breath, or his words. Needing to put distance between them, he politely told her goodbye and started toward his truck.

"Hey Caid?" she called down to him.

He paused with his hand on his door handle, turning back to her.

"It was nice getting to chat with you. Don't be a stranger, okay?"

It wasn't until he was in the safety of his truck, on the road, four houses down, before he vocalized what ran through his head. "I'm so fucked."

CHAPTER 11

Lucius found himself in the middle of Manhattan. Standing in a long, cream-colored hallway, facing a sunny, yellow door. He rocked back onto his heels, his loafers sinking into the plush green and blue geometric printed carpet, and sighed. Matthew had to know he was here by now. After thirty minutes, he had to know.

"You're being a foolish old man," Lucius muttered. He was a five-hundred-thirty-year-old grown man standing outside of his son's door, afraid to knock.

Taking a step closer, he drew in a breath and held it. He lightly rapped on the door. Barely a second later, it swung open, and he released his breath.

"I was wondering how much longer you were going to take." Matthew smirked.

"I wasn't sure you'd want to see me." His eyes shifted from his face to the forearm of the arm holding the door open, taking in the tattoo there. Dark red ink created waves of hair around a soft, round face. Strawberry colored lips curled into a brilliant smile and that brilliant light sparked from the deep forest green eyes. Eyes that were bracketed by lines that symbolized just how often that face laughed and smiled.

The time and care put into the lifelike piece of Clarissa, Matthew's mother, Lucius's late wife, was remarkable.

"She truly was the most beautiful woman." Lucius nodded to the tattoo before bringing his attention back to Matthew's face. A face so much like Clarissa's. "That is excellently done."

"It should be for what it cost and how long it took for it to be complete so that it would stay." He finally stepped back, motioning for Lucius to come in.

"I haven't come to drag you back to Alleyette like a dog on a leash."

"Good. Because I have a job to finish and you'll have to excuse my lack of desire to be back in Alleyette. Ever."

"I don't know how I can assist with 'ever.'" He turned to face him. Slowly, like a child that recognized he wasn't about to be scolded for being naughty, the rigidness that had held Matthew's body straight, melted. His shoulders dropped and he slipped his hands into his pockets. "I can help cause a delay."

Matthew leaned back against the island counter and pulled his hands from his pockets, then crossed his arms over his chest. "What exactly is going on right now? There's never been, in my near century and a quarter, an all hands on deck call."

"It's Madigan."

Matthew straightened, face tinted with shadows, the essence of his magic filling the room. "Where?"

"A small town in Maine. He's been there for several months, but after seeing the pattern there, we've been able to track the locations he's used since he disappeared from Alleyette."

"Who confirmed?"

"Róisín."

Matthew sucked in a sharp breath.

"That's why I'm here. I know you two have..." He turned to Matthew and raised an eyebrow. "A history. I also know you two have moved beyond that. She needs us, Matthew."

Matthew moved to the refrigerator and took out a beer. He held up a second to Lucius, who shook his head. "What of the council?"

Lucius pinched his lips together, nostrils flaring wide with his frustrated exhale. "I tried. Knowing the more she has behind her, the better. For all of us. The only votes with me are Nanette and Shasta."

"Shasta?" He blinked. "Hasn't she been one of the most vocal against Róisín since Brenna died?"

"Shasta has..." He sighed. "She appears to have come around and is ready to try to break through the wall again. She hopes with Aoife gone now that whatever she placed around Róisín weakened and she can break through." He slipped his hands into the pockets of his slacks and rocked back onto his heels. "You two are all I have left."

Matthew cracked his knuckles. "What would I do?"

"She absolutely cannot be alone with him. Róisín is powerful, but she is young. They forget that because she has accomplished so much in her short time. She has cloaked herself, her power, but..."

"It's only a matter of time. He's been dark for so long, and he wants power. From all of us, but if he comes to realize the power she has. He'll —" Matthew paced. He drained his beer, then crushed the aluminum.

Lucius lifted a brow before shifting his eyes from the decimated can to where canvases lined a wall. Scenes of bright, colorful mermaids lounging along rocks at the ocean's edge. Bold splashes across landscapes from around the realms. He knew the deft strokes of a brush anywhere. "You're painting again."

"She came to me a few months ago. Said she missed seeing me create." Matthew came to stand next to him.

"She comes to me often." His voice was quiet, soft. "Asks me to check in on you. I know she can do it on her own, but I think she's worried our relationship will fade without her here."

"You're my father." Matthew's tone was firm. "That relationship is forever."

"But really." Lucius let out a heavy sigh. "I'm not your father."

"You are in every way that counts or matters," Matthew whispered.

With that, the two men finally embraced. Holding one another for a long while, before pulling apart.

"I'll reach out to Róisín. Find some excuse to at least drop in and visit, see what I can learn. Make sure she's okay. Pick on her a bit, lighten her mood. Remind her that we've got her."

Lucius nodded. "Thank you, son."

"Come on, there's an Italian place a few blocks away I know you'll love. My treat."

CHAPTER 12

Róisín knew he was there before he had even crossed the town line into Greens Glen. Despite his cloaked magic, after over a century of friendship, she and Matthew had grown to be connected in a different way.

Her best friend. A constant presence in her life, before her mother passed, after Aoife stepped in. She fell down, he picked her up. And when he fell down, she was there with her arms around him, pulling him to his feet. They had grown up together, trained together. Even without having a tethered connection, they always could sense one another wherever they were.

She tucked a bookmark into her mother's book before placing it under a stack of others on the coffee table. She wasn't sure why she'd hidden it. Matthew wouldn't question it, and neither Caid, nor Wyatt, who'd helped Caid with the work on the house the past few days, would have any idea what it was.

She opened the front door then leaned against the jamb, waiting. The air turned warm, campfire woodsmoke wafting closer and closer the nearer he came.

There was no stopping the grin that split her face seeing the sleek, black

Audi nearing the end of her cul-de-sac. She stood rooted, the vice that had clutched her heart since arriving in Greens Glen twisted tighter suddenly. For several weeks, she had been there alone, disconnected from her people. She had Lina, perhaps Caid, and even Wyatt there, but there was so much she had to hold close to her pained chest from them. It was different when she could be open, be free, be herself as much as she knew of herself.

When Matthew pulled to a stop at the curb near the walkway, calm wrapped around her like a hug the way it always did when he was around. It was then that she raced down the steps and pathway, launching herself at him the moment he had unfolded himself from the car.

They wrapped one another tightly, both taking in long breaths and sighing. Róisín did her best to keep her tears at bay.

Wyatt let out a not-so-subtle cough behind them. Róisín slipped back to the ground and turned.

"The lumberyard said the door would be in around noon tomorrow. We'll get that old one out first thing, so the kitchen won't be wide open for long," Wyatt said.

"Okay. Do I need to do anything tonight?" She looked between him and Caid, but Caid's eyes were hard on Matthew. When she slid a quick glance up to Matthew's face, he was returning Caid's look. She glanced between the two men, like a child at the zoo for the first time watching peacocks strut around their enclosure, feathers out.

"Nah. We did all the prep, but it's still sealed up tight. You'll be fine." Wyatt glanced over his shoulder to where Caid was standing like stone, hands shoved in his pockets. Wyatt cleared his throat. "Right, Caid?"

Caid remained silent. So opposite of when he'd stuck around after they picked up for the day. They'd sit on the steps out front and chat for nearly an hour. Talking about nothing and everything. When he opened up, the tenseness he always carried relaxed a little and his face softened, his eyes brightened. Every evening, the words creeped up her throat, trying to dance over her tongue, wanting to confide in him. And every evening, she bit down on her tongue and swallowed those words, her past haunting her.

Being open about who she was with a human wasn't an option for her.

Not anymore, not after Alexandria.

Pulling her attention from Caid, she turned to Wyatt and said, "Okay. Thank you for all the work you've both done so far."

Wyatt beamed at her. Róisín had taken a quick liking to the childhood friend and employee of Caid's. He was always smiling and laughing, and she had quickly learned that food was something he cherished. Every time she cooked, he always appeared either with his head through the door, or face at her kitchen window, asking if he could have a taste.

It had spawned the idea of making him and Caid lunch on occasion or baking them cookies. Amid the chaos rising in her life, she'd found a sense of normalcy in having them there working on her house.

"Oh! Where are my manners?" She turned to Matthew. "Matthew, this is Kincaid and Wyatt. They're taking care of some water damage to the back of the house from a leaky door."

Matthew's eyes narrowed on Caid, his nostrils flaring as if he scented him for a moment. It happened so quickly, Róisín was sure she imagined it.

"Nice to meet you." Wyatt extended his hand, oblivious to the tension.

"Same." Matthew shook his hand, placing his other at the small of Róisín's back before accepting and shaking Caid's reluctantly offered hand.

Once both of their trucks had disappeared down the road, she spun to Matthew with a scowl, slapping him hard on one of his shoulders.

"Ow!" He rubbed his shoulder and frowned at her. "What'd you do that for?"

"Um, excuse me?! What was that?!" She motioned in the direction Caid had driven off in. "Don't we have an agreement, Matthew?"

"We do!"

"But..." She motioned for him to go on. There had to be an explanation for whatever that was and why he was in Greens Glen.

"But nothing." His response was muffled by the trunk where he was pulling a bag from.

Hope sprung up inside of her, filling the spaces that had darkened over the past few weeks. "You're staying?"

"For a few days. Pit stop before I continue to Newfoundland."

"You're not going to Alleyette?"

"Lucius said that I wasn't needed there, and here, with family, was of more importance. I get to hang here for a while, then head off to finish my work." He slammed the trunk shut and held out a hand to her.

Róisín pressed her lips together, trying to keep her emotions at bay. She should have known that Lucius would find a way to have someone to help her, and that it would be Matthew that came. Taking his hand, she gave it a light squeeze and led him inside.

He slung the strap of his bag over his shoulder, raising an eyebrow. "You're not mad?"

She could only stare at him, not trusting her voice.

He pulled her against him, hugging her tightly again. "Let's go in and you can fill me in on what the fuck is exactly going on. I'm not talking about here. I can feel that deep inside, it's everywhere."

By the time she had finished filling him in on everything that had happened and all she'd learned, Róisín was nearly curled into a ball on the loveseat, rubbing viciously at her temples where the heavy beat of a headache had begun its concert.

"I feel like I should have seen it." Her anger grew the further her story had progressed. Now, it was a living, breathing thing inside of her. "It's been every day since, a new memory comes rushing to the surface and pulls me under."

"First, you need to relax. I can feel that from over here." He sat on one of her love seats across the room from her, his ankle propped on his knee. "Second, it's not your fault."

"You may not feel that way." She struggled up into a sitting position and shoved the hair from her face. "I can't help but feel otherwise. No one else blocked those memories out. That was me."

He lifted his beer bottle to take a sip, but stopped halfway. "Do you think the council's blaming and punishing you for her because she's not here for it?"

"What else could it be?" Feeling the need to move, she pushed to her feet and paced, twirling a strand of hair around her finger and stalked back and forth. "She always seemed so selfless, so pure. What being a witch truly was. To find out that she wasn't any different from Madigan... I know how I feel learning the truth. I can imagine they feel that same betrayal."

Her neck warmed under his stare, feeling him track her movements as she spun around, charging back across the room, spun again, and stomped back to the other side.

Róisín stopped and wrapped her arms around her middle. "I don't want this, I can't do this. She took it all away from me." Her voice cracked. The strength she had mustered to hold everything together, crumbled.

Matthew caught her and brought her against his chest, woodsmoke soothing her, and he brushed a hand over her hair. He tightened his embrace; the tension coiled in his muscles wrapped around her, the hot metal-like smell of his magic simmering.

Matthew was as close to home as she could get, and with that comfort he gave, she broke, sobs racking her body.

They stayed that way, tightly embraced, on her living room floor, with him rocking her, stroking her hair, until she'd emptied all her tears.

Chapter 13

CAID used his fork as a shovel, bringing his food from plate to mouth like he was a man starved. Or a man in a hurry to get through a family breakfast and somewhere else.

Lina coughed, and he paused, shifting his attention away from the plate of food.

Lina's eyes were wide, eyebrows nearly high enough to disappear into her hairline. She smirked at him, a look she quickly disguised with a napkin, as she dabbed at one corner of her mouth. "How are things going over at Róisín's? I haven't seen her all week."

"Probably because her boyfriend is here and they've been busy," he replied around a mouthful of hash brown and sausage.

Lina's mouth fell open. "Boyfriend?"

"Whose boyfriend?" Thomas returned from the kitchen with Lina's refreshed glass of orange juice. He bent to kiss her cheek, lightly pressing his hand over her stomach as he did.

Caid straightened, catching the quick, innocent gesture. His gaze darted between them, and he lifted a brow in question.

She winked at him. "You're gonna be an uncle."

His fork clattered to his plate, his eyes growing wide.

"I mean, come on, you had to expect that it would happen at some point. We've been together for over twenty years and married for eleven." She rolled her eyes.

"I know, I mean, you haven't talked about it for so long that I..." He stood and reached over the table to shake Thomas's hand, then moved to give Lina a tight hug. "Congratulations... Twins, right?"

Thomas choked on his water. "Jesus." He coughed. "I hope not."

Lina glowered at Caid. "I wouldn't mind. Get it done in one pregnancy."

"But two babies at once?" Thomas gasped out between coughs.

"One for each of us," she replied, her tone sweet and eyelashes fluttering.

Thomas groaned in response.

"Anyway." Lina turned back to Caid. "Tell me about Róisín's boyfriend. She's never mentioned one. I'd actually figured that maybe she was, you know, sort of not into guys."

Caid thought back to the morning after Matthew had shown up at Róisín's house. When he and Wyatt had walked around to the backyard to work the door out of the frame, Matthew sat at her kitchen table in just a pair of sweatpants while she cooked. Or how days after, she and Matthew had emerged from the woods behind the house, her arm around his waist and his around her shoulders.

"Maybe she doesn't have a preference. But she's definitely got a boyfriend." The eggs on his plate suddenly tasted spoiled, bitter almost. He set his fork down and moved the plate back.

An unfamiliar animal instinct kept trying to puncture the surface, urging him to stake a claim to her. He had to remind himself that Róisín wasn't his, that his hackles were up for absolutely no reason.

Just like, despite Lina being his sister, she wasn't his either. She was family, but she had started her own with Thomas. The baby would only further cement that. No, Lina wouldn't leave him behind, but it didn't stop that feeling from snaking around his ankles, anchoring him to that spot in life he was currently at while she moved on.

"Hm." Lina tapped a finger on the table. "Maybe I'll see if she's up for some coffee."

"Don't meddle," Thomas warned her.

Caid snorted loudly. "Oh, she'll meddle. It's her middle name, isn't it, Leen?"

"I will not meddle. I might be nosy, but I won't meddle." She gave a half-shrug, then scooped scrambled eggs onto her fork and pushed them into her mouth to signal the end of the conversation.

CHAPTER 14

T HE pounding started in Róisín's head, dull at first. Like the faint, steady sound that echoed at the base of her skull when she'd first learned to use her magic. Her mother had been so patient and kind with her.

Never command your magic. Those were always Brenna's first words of each practice.

"You and your magic are one, little rose. You work together, in harmony, a beautiful dance of power."

Róisín burrowed deeper into her blankets, trying to shut out the banging and soak in the soothing tone of her mother's voice.

"But how do I make it work, mama?" she asked. Then Róisín pointed at the ground between them and said, "Please, peonies, grow."

Brenna laughed softly. "No, little rose, like this." She moved to Róisín's side and placed a hand on her stomach, just over her navel. "Greet it as you do your father and I every morning. Ask it to work with you today, to create beautiful things."

"Hello, magic. I dreamed I got to ride a unicorn last night, may I have some tea?"

Her mother's laughter filled Róisín, her belly growing warm with the love that filled the space around her.

"Oh, you," Brenna tapped her on the nose. "What will we ever do with you?"

The pounding intensified, and shouting joined, punctuating each thud.

She sat up in her bed, her head spinning. Someone knocked on her door. Her door, because she was a grown adult now, and her mother was gone. A pressure settled on her chest, and a fresh wave of grief passed over her.

Another pound, another shout, garbled from being muffled by the door, had her rubbing at her chest and sighing. The reality of her present beckoned her. It was a Sunday morning, so it couldn't be Caid and Wyatt needing to get in to work on the house. Matthew had popped his head in earlier, just as the sun had pressed through the cracks around the window shades, telling her he was going with David through the wood.

Kicking her legs free of the blankets, she haphazardly tied her hair into a messy bun and darted down the stairs.

She threw open her door and blinked. "Lina."

"Oh, good, you're up!" Lina smiled. "Whose car is that?" She jerked a thumb over her shoulder toward Matthew's car.

She tried to keep her expression neutral and prayed to the Goddess that Matthew and David didn't choose that moment to return from their wooded excursion. "Hm?"

"The shiny black car at your curb." One of Lina's eyebrows rose, her eyes sparkling.

"Why are you here at such a Goddess-awful hour? Is everything okay?"

"I'm taking you on the campaign trail with me this morning."

Her spine loosened, shoulders dropping. "Say what now?"

"I should go door knocking again, and thought it'd be something we could do together. You could meet some more people around town, and we can catch up a bit. I feel like it's been ages since I've seen you."

An idea struck Róisín. This was her unsuspicious way of looking around the town beyond her neighborhood and the downtown village area. She'd seen the gist in passing, but getting closer would only be a benefit.

"Can I get dressed first?" she asked and motioned to her shorts and wrinkled, oversized t-shirt.

Lina's eyes roamed over Róisín, then she shrugged. "I think you look fine like that, but if you want to change, I've got some time."

Before Róisín could ask her in, Lina brushed by her, head swiveling as though she searched for something—or someone. Not wanting to give her a chance to ask about the car's owner again, she dashed upstairs, changing in record time.

They began Lina's campaign trail in a neighborhood furthest from the town's center, both deducing it was easier to work their way in than it was to work their way out. As Lina drove, the house lots became spaced further and further apart. Their yards were large, but sparse. Branches littered lawns, having fallen from dead and dried out trees. The lawns here were not yellow like they were in town, they were dirt. The grass had long been dead and gone.

The moment she pushed open the passenger door of Lina's SUV, she almost crumpled and tumbled to the ground. Her eyes instantly filled, her nose burned, the pungent smell of death and rot around them reaching for her like fingers in the dark. She gripped the door frame, retching at the feel of Madigan's magic simmering in the air. Its thick grime, slick oil-like sensation, seized her throat. She couldn't hold back the loud gasp that escaped.

"I know." Lina rounded the hood of her vehicle. "It's the worst here."

Róisín managed to straighten and release the door. Lina stood at the front of the car with tears in her eyes and a slight frown. "Why is it so bad here?"

"It's where it all started." Lina pointed to a structure atop the hill just behind a house, then surveyed the rest of the neighborhood. "That's Munson's. Here it all looks and feels dead. At least in town, it just feels like it needs Prince Charming to come kiss it and wake it up."

"The smell..." Róisín said around shallow breaths.

"That's taken the longest to get used to, the smell." She shrugged. "Or, the lack of it. No pine, or roses. None of that leaf and dirt smell that makes fall feel like fall. Nothing."

Róisín wished deeply at that moment she was human, so that could smell nothing. The steps she took to join her felt like she walked across broken glass barefoot. The pain shot through her every nerve. Her senses were overwhelmed, and her magic scraped at her insides, begging to be released to remedy what they faced.

Not now. As much as she wanted to, as much as she wanted to use everything she had to end this death of nature, it was too dangerous.

We would be a beacon for him, she told her magic. *We need to stay safe to see this to the end.*

After a moment, the scraping ceased, replaced by a warmth spreading through her. The roiling in her stomach, the burn of her nostrils, the sting in her eyes, all calmed, leaving her able to draw in a deep, relieving breath.

Lina turned to her, face grim. "I need to beat him, Ro. I need to beat Bill so we can get Munson out and save this town, and our residents."

Róisín held her hand out to her. "Then let's go knock on some doors and woo your voters."

CHAPTER 15

———————

THE sun hung low in the late day sky when Caid stepped from the hardware store in town that Monday. Halfway to his truck, he caught sight of Róisín stepping onto the sidewalk of the grocery store. He found himself frozen, unable to move while she smiled at Greens Glen's postmaster, her pretty auburn hair bouncing happily in its ponytail with each of her steps. Like clockwork, the butterflies, birds, anything and everything with wings, released in his belly.

When her ponytail swung into her face as she juggled two bags under one arm so she could unlock her car, his fingers began to itch to move the mane aside and grab the bags for her.

A few feet down the sidewalk, Stewart Munson had zeroed in on her. He quickly moved to approach her, carrying himself with his chin held high and back straight. His steps were long, and sure as he slicked a hand through his inky hair, licking his lips. When Róisín saw him nearing, her body went ramrod straight.

Before Caid could change his mind, he tossed his purchase into his truck and made his way across to her, his steps determined.

"Caid." Róisín exhaled, and her shoulders relaxed.

"Hey." He smiled and hoped his eyes conveyed to her he was there to help, and play along, as reached for one of her bags. "Munson," he nodded his greeting. "Don't you have more people to poison today?"

"McGrath." Stewart gave him a measured look. "I was just going to ask Miss McKenna if she was available for a coffee."

Caid bought his free arm around her waist, hoping she'd understand it as him aiding her, and guided her toward her car. "We've actually got a pretty busy afternoon, don't we, babe?"

Her brows came together as she studied Caid for a moment. "Oh! Lina and Thomas. I can't believe I forgot."

Caid shot Stewart, who stood like a statue, a glare while Róisín popped her trunk open so that he could load her groceries in for her. When he finished, he straightened and made to cross to his truck.

Her hand snagged his wrist.

Caid couldn't pull his attention from where she touched him, it shot electric tingles through him, yet soothed at the same time.

Róisín squeezed his arm, and his gaze snapped to her face. She moved her eyes ever so slightly to gesture to her driver's side door, a signal for him to get in. Then she smoothed back some of the loose strands of her hair, tucking them behind an ear, and glanced back to where Stewart stood watching, waiting.

Carefully, Caid moved his hand so that it held hers, stroking it with his thumb. He took the keys she slipped to him and walked around the car.

"A rain check then, Miss McKenna," Stewart called to her.

Her smile was tight. "Of course."

"You can tell him no," Caid said when they closed the doors.

"Sometimes, telling a man no is the most dangerous thing a woman can do," she replied with a tremor in her voice, her eyes still on Stewart.

Caid reversed out of the spot and onto Main Street, checking the rearview mirror.

Stewart stood still as a statue, his eyes black on her.

Her body visibly shook. "Thank you, by the way. Once I get the groceries put away, I can run you back to your truck."

"We can pull over just up here and I'll walk back. I don't think your boyfriend would appreciate seeing me roll up to your house, driving your car."

"My boyfriend?" She pulled her attention away from the passing buildings to him, her nose wrinkled, lips slightly pursed.

His face warmed under her scrutiny.

"Yeah, the Audi that's staying with you this week. Andrew? I think that was his name." The lie singed his tongue as he spoke it. He didn't think that he could ever forget Matthew's name, or how much like a gut punch it had been every time he saw them together.

"Oh, Matthew." She laughed. *Laughed* to Caid's disbelief. "He's definitely not my boyfriend. He's more like family. Our parents used to work together. I mean, yes, we did have that one time we were dumb, but it was just that time and to be honest, I think we're both more embarrassed than anything about it."

She was rambling, stumbling through her words nervously. To that point of knowing her, whenever they talked, she had always been composed and concise. In a way, perfect, too perfect to have any interest in him. As she chattered on, wiping her hands on the legs of her shorts, she became more human. Almost giving him the confidence that maybe he had a chance for even just one date.

"But yeah," she continued, "he's just visiting before he needs to head to Newfoundland for his job. Heard I was living here now, so on his way over..."

Caid pulled to a stop just on the road that led to her house and put the car in park.

"Either way, I don't want to cause any problems. You're in the clear from Munson, I'm not all that far from town."

"You're sure?" She took her bottom lip between her fingers, worrying it. "I can bring you back, it's really no problem."

"It's okay," he said. He needed to get distance between them. The air had become thick around them and he was fighting to keep his breathing even. Fighting to keep himself together. Time, he needed time to sort through the way he felt for her. And space.

She rounded the hood, stopping in front of him, tipping her head back to look up at him and squinting in the midday light. "Thank you, again."

"Anytime." He shoved his hands into his pockets to keep his fingers from brushing her bare arms. "I'll see you bright and early tomorrow."

He waited until she was in the car before closing the door carefully and stepping back. He stood on the side of the road, watching her car turn into a blue dot, then disappear before making his way back to his truck.

It wasn't until he had driven down Main Street that Stewart drew his attention. He was still standing near the spot where Róisín's car had been, staring in the direction they'd driven off in.

A prickling feeling crawled up his neck and down his arms as he drove home.

Chapter 16

Matthew nursed a beer, petting David's ears on Róisín's porch, when she pulled into her driveway.

"What happened?" he asked as soon as her door shut behind her.

Her insides crawled again just thinking of his name. "Madigan."

"Did he hurt you?" He reached out to her and lifted an arm, turning it to examine for marks.

"He didn't hurt me." She swatted his hand away. "But he probed." A violent shudder rolled through her.

He grabbed her bags before she could, using his other hand to shut the trunk. "Inside."

Rolling her eyes at his authoritative tone, she did her best not to stomp across her pathway and throw her front door open. Once inside, she stooped to pick up David, nuzzling his soft fur and inhaling deeply.

"You need to use Shasta's wards," David said. "He'll keep pushing until you don't have the energy to hold him back."

Matthew's shoulders raised, and he turned to her slowly. His face was stormy, jaw tight. "You're not using the wards? Why not?"

"I..." She shrugged. She had been so used to doing everything on her own, how could she admit that she forgot to set them in place. She had made bracelets and necklaces, but they gathered in the bowl on her kitchen table. The other stones still sat on the shelf in her closet upstairs.

A terse breath escaped through his nose, like a teakettle near ready to burst from its boiling water and steam. "I fucking knew that it wasn't because I warded my magic. It dulls everything, but not that fucking much that I couldn't feel them there."

"Matthew—"

"No. David is right." Matthew threw his arms outward, motioning to the space around them. "Wards, Róisín. If Shasta gave you runes to add power to them, you use that. She doesn't pass those out like candy on Earth's Halloween celebrations. She gives them with thought and care. If the council will not be here or help you, you need to do everything you can to protect yourself."

She dropped heavily onto a chair at her kitchen table. Weariness tugged at her, almost begging for her to root herself and rest. Folding her arms on the table before her, she rested her head on them, waiting for Matthew to put her groceries away. She wanted to ask him to stay, to put his assignment off. Together they could do what they needed here while the other witches did what they needed to do in Alleyette.

The nightmares of losing to Madigan, of not being enough, had crept in two nights before. She tried to trust that the witches did what the council said they would, that they looked through old magic for ways to restore the connection Madigan had with them. To use their power, channeled down that line, together.

With each passing day, she questioned more and more if that were true.

She wasn't completely alone. She had to remember that. Shasta's visit to her room. Lucius asking Matthew to come to her in Maine. The knot in her stomach loosened some knowing she still had them.

"Talk to me." Matthew lowered himself into a chair next to her. "What's going on in there?"

"Clarissa comes to see you?"

"Sometimes." He nodded. "Lucius more often I think."

"My mother..." The tears burned in her eyes. "The Seer told me what happened with my mother. I have always been so mad at her for what she did, and I couldn't ever ask her why because she cannot come to me. Why could she not stay for me? Did she not love me enough? I always dreamed of what I would say if she ever made it to the afterworld and came to visit..."

Silence fell over them. Her heart pounded, dancing its way up into her throat, and she wasn't sure she could find her voice again.

Only witches in the afterworld could visit with living loved ones. When Róisín was younger, she'd imagine all the ways they could spend time together, how her mother would know any children Róisín may someday have.

By taking her own life, Brenna had committed herself to the underworld until she proved worthy of the afterworld. Which meant that she couldn't cross the veil.

"I didn't know that she..." She squeezed her eyes closed, her breath becoming ragged. "That she did it all for me. She loved me, I know she did. I just can't imagine ever having to make that choice, how hard it must've been for her."

He pulled her chair closer to his, their knees interlocking. Having him close, the weight of him, a comfort.

"Keep going," he urged, his voice soft. "Get it out."

"Aoife doesn't come at all either. I don't know where she is. If she is in the afterworld, does she not come because..." Her body shook with her sobs and hiccups. Her muscles grew weak, her body heavy. Each sob came harder, making her gasp, her words incoherent when she tried to continue. She wrapped her arms around herself and turned away from Matthew, feeling the snot begin to run from her nose. The only noise in the room was the pain ripping free of her body in each cry. A napkin from the holder at the center of the table appeared before her. Embarrassed, but grateful, she accepted it, wiping her nose. "She must've known I'd find out." She buried her face in the hem of her shirt, partly to wipe away the wetness that soaked her face, partly to stem the flow of new tears. "What if she doesn't come because she doesn't want my questions?"

"Then she's a coward. If she can't face her granddaughter, she's a coward."

"I feel completely alone here. He's going to figure out who I am. I'm not equipped for this. He's had centuries to hone his skill with his power. Even before he began this journey to consume and feed that power, he was so freaking powerful."

Anger ignited a black powder in her. When it exploded, it propelled her to her feet. She used that fire raging to strengthen her.

"I don't know how to use most of my power, and when I do, I'm instantly drained. I'm exhausted." She clenched her fists, then relaxed them and fiddled with the hem of her shirt. "I cannot count how many times I've wanted to walk into Alleyette and tell them I'm done. Send someone else, and I'll go back to traveling the realms fixing droughts, easing floods, growing gardens to my heart's content."

"Then do it."

"I can't. They put me here for a reason."

He stiffened, clenching his jaw. "That reason wasn't to get killed."

She turned to look at him fully, her voice calm, almost flat and emotionless, when she spoke. "What if that's what the Sisters have seen for me? That I'm the sacrifice to save our people? The Seer even said that I was to fix this. That I'm the one to make it right, which means it's my shoulders. The weight of all this"—she swept her arms out wide—"is on me."

His jaw flexed. "That doesn't mean death."

"It just may, Matthew. It just may."

His eyebrows came down, his eyes darkening. "No."

"We can't stop fate."

"This is crazy." Matthew shoved his chair back and rose. He pushed his hands through his hair, cursing. With a shake of his head, he shouted, causing her to cover her ears and wince.

Moments later, Lucius appeared in her kitchen.

Chest heaving with angry breaths, Matthew pointed to Lucius while looking at Róisín. "Tell him what you just told me."

Lucius's eyebrows drew together, and his eyes shifted as he looked between them. "What's happening here? Is it Madigan?"

"Tell. Him." Matthew's anger seethed in the room, a darkness pulsing around them. "Or I will."

Looking down at her hands, she went through everything again. When she finished, she looked up at Lucius. "Did you know about my grandmother?"

Rubbing a hand over his face, Lucius shook his head. "I had my suspicions, but she was powerful. She could cloak like none of us have ever been able to. Well, except for Madigan," he added. "Clarissa and Shasta knew better of Brenna's relationship with her before she could get away, but I can gather it wasn't good. None of us knew what she did with her Coven, what her intent was with Brenna. But the evidence is there. Exposed now. Unfortunately, too late."

"We have to do something," Matthew pressed.

"There's only so much we can do. We're walking just over the line as it is, if the council finds out... We'll be of no use if we're found guilty of treason."

"Fuck," Matthew grumbled.

"Have you read the book from Brenna?" Lucius asked.

"I finished it this morning." It had been like a spell when she had finished the last page. There was so much more to her magic, their magic, that her mother hadn't been able to show or teach her. A new voice within had risen through the day and it dug in with sharp claws, its voice hot and metallic in her head telling her it was impossible. There was too much to learn and not enough time.

"You'll begin work with Shasta right away then. Nanette as well." He looked at Matthew, who stood with his back to them with his arms crossed over his chest, looking through the new patio door into the backyard. "Matthew is going to finish his assignment, then we'll see what we can learn in Alleyette. Is that all right, Matthew?"

He didn't turn around to face them. "I can leave with you now."

"Are you sure?"

He shifted, looking over his shoulder to where Róisín had sat again, wringing her hands together. "Things have changed."

"All right then. We'll stick to this plan for now. You'll be all right for a few days?"

Slowly, she rose from her chair. "I'll be okay. Madigan keeps up his appearances as this human, Stewart Munson. I don't think he'll risk the use of any blatant display of power."

"You can't rely on that," Matthew said.

"He could grow frustrated and lash out," Lucius rubbed his chin and dipped his head in a slight nod. "You need to be extremely cautious. What is the identity you've assumed here?"

"Well, it was easy enough to stick to my actual work with the auction houses and dealers. With the internet resources, working anywhere is realistic." Her shoulders rose and fell with a slight shrug.

"Are you on a research assignment right now?" Matthew asked.

"No. I've had some requests, but I've put off for a sabbatical because of... Aoife." Her voice fell to a whisper at the mention of her grandmother.

"This is perfect." Lucius straightened his suit jacket, readying to shift back to where he'd been before Matthew had summoned him. "But stay here. Only go into town when you absolutely need to. I'll leave extra protection for you here, so we won't risk your burnout. We need to buy ourselves a few days until we can organize a way for the five of us to meet without raising suspicion, okay?"

The threat of the others being stripped of their magic and exiled battered her senses. She couldn't find herself to be worth that risk. Even with the two men standing in her kitchen that were like kin to her. "If the council finds out?"

"I'll handle the council. Not only will I protect my family, and you are family, sweetheart, I am the chair and oversee this..." He glanced at Matthew. "Shit show. I didn't get the seat because I baked an excellent cake." He winked at her.

Her magic rose inside of her, like arms wrapping her in an embrace, warming her. The declaration of her being his family buoyed her. That she, even in the smallest, darkest corner of her mind, let herself doubt that Lucius, the man that stepped in and helped raise her after her father had passed, that loved her like she was his own, just as Clarissa had done when she was alive, made her want to curl inward with shame.

With the plan settled, Lucius gave her a hug before leaving her with Matthew, who she could still feel stewing.

"Stay close to the carpenter," he said.

"What?" She tipped her head to one side. "Caid? Why?"

"Yeah, if that's the one. The one built like one of those American Football linebackers."

The sudden urge to laugh washed over her, and she found herself unable to contain it, bending over, her arms wrapped around her middle.

"What? What's so funny?"

"Nothing." She snorted and waved a hand in the air. "Nothing at all."

"I'm serious. You can't be alone. Even if it's just human protection you have, it's better than nothing."

Finally, she straightened, trying to control her laughter. "You knew his name." She jabbed a finger hard into his chest. "Just like I know damned well that he knew yours earlier. Why? Why are guys like that?"

"Not just guys. Alexandria looked ready to murder me when she met me the first time, remember?"

At the mention of Alexandria, Róisín's laughter ceased, and the moment became somber.

"Have you talked to her?" he whispered.

"No. She made it very, very clear she was done with me."

Matthew wrapped his arms around her, his embrace warm and soothing. He pressed a kiss to her head, letting his lips linger atop her crown as he wrapped her tighter, creating a cocoon of love and safety. "I'm not kidding, though. About Caid. Or the sister of his you've mentioned. Even Wyatt. Anyone. Anyone is better than no one. Got it?"

Pressing her face against his chest, her voice muffled when she spoke. "Got it."

"Good. I'll leave tomorrow for Alleyette. As much as I'd like to pop off like Lucius, you need to keep the appearance of normal up. You won't do that with me gone and my car sitting out front still."

"He thought you were my boyfriend," she said, her face still against him.

"Who?"

"He called you 'Audi,' the same way you called him the carpenter." She pulled away and looked up at him. "He came to my rescue with Madigan this afternoon." Before she finished explaining to him what had happened in town, Matthew's eyes lit with mischief, and regret splashed over her like a cold bucket of water.

"You like him." He grinned at her. "A lot."

The blush creeped along her neck to her cheeks, warming her skin.

"He's nice, yes, and he's good looking. Very good looking," she murmured.

"You. Like. Him."

She groaned and threw up her hands. "I do. Dammit, I do. Not because he is freaking hot as hell in those t-shirts and flannels he wears. Or the way those muscles flex when he's carrying his tools or wood..." She sighed.

"This is adorable." He chuckled.

"Stop it." She pushed at his shoulder. "Caid is a great guy on top of all that other stuff. If you didn't spend the whole day snarling at him through the door while they worked and actually talked to him, you'd see that."

"Mm, sure. Someday maybe. I'll clear out as early as I can tomorrow. Then you'll have the place all to yourself to pursue the carpenter." He tapped a finger to her nose, laughing when she batted his hand away.

"I could still do that with you here."

"No. No, you couldn't. He already thought we were together. Having me here, even knowing that we're not together, nope." He shook his head. "He won't be down to do anything with me around. Other than stare at you with that 'I want to rip her clothes off and have her on the kitchen counter' look."

"Matthew!" She swatted at him again, but he ducked away just in time.

"What? I get horny just like anyone else, how can I miss that look? He was trying to be covert." He ducked again, erupting in laughter.

Her eyes grew rounder. A small bead of sweat rolled down the side of her face from having grown so hot from his chiding. "Are you serious?"

"Oh, Ro. When was the last time you were with someone?"

She bit her lip and looked at her feet, her cheeks growing warmer by the second.

"Damn." He let out a heavy breath.

"I dumped myself into assignments after what happened. I just haven't had time, and thanks to brilliant minds and technology, I've been able to take care of myself."

He made a gagging noise. "Thanks."

"When you need the release," she shrugged and smiled wickedly. "You've gotta do what you've gotta do." Beneath the layer of joking with Matthew, her mind began churning and a seed of hope sprouted roots somewhere deep inside of her. Had Caid really been interested in something more with her? Could she take that step and explore something deeper with him than their porch conversations?

Chapter 17

FINDING a routine after Matthew had left proved to be difficult. Róisín had grown used to his company and having someone near that she could talk to about her world, magic, the Covens, Madigan. That loneliness she'd felt before Matthew's visit didn't hesitate to creep in stronger, clutching her so tightly it was as if she struggled for air.

She tried to distract herself by re-reading her mother's book while she waited for word from Lucius about another meeting. Time was ticking and reading the same pages over and over again with her mind not taking in the information, was infuriating.

Slamming the book closed, she looked over her shoulder through the patio to where Caid and Wyatt both stood, measuring and marking lengths of sheathing for the backside of the house.

With Matthew gone, and what had happened in town with Madigan, she'd wondered if Caid would start hanging around when he wrapped his day like he had been doing before.

No, she had lied to herself; it had been hope. Hope that it would bring him back to her porch steps with her. She had missed it; she had missed that time they shared.

But he hadn't.

Caid and Wyatt would clean up and Caid would just nod as he passed by, telling her he'd see her the following day.

She was unsure what to make of it, or how to approach it with him, to ask if something was wrong. Lina was an option, asking her if maybe he'd said something, but in Róisín's need to process what she'd learned about Aoife and her mother, she had ducked Lina's text messages the past few days.

Feeling bombarded on all fronts—her witch life, the life she tried to live among the humans—she exhaled a steadying breath and pushed her hair from her face. She needed to get out, to get away even for just a short time. Release her power, scream at the world, shout at the top of her lungs, anything. She couldn't go on in this full-to-bursting way anymore.

She rose from her chair and grabbed her car keys from the table by the front door, then stepped around the piles of tools and wood in the kitchen to where Caid and Wyatt were working.

"Hey!" She lifted her voice over the sound of Wyatt's impact wrench.

Caid lifted his head from where he had been marking a board. "What's up?"

"I need to run an errand and may drop service for a bit. If there's anything you guys need, this is me saying you've got my go ahead."

He tucked the pencil into his ball cap over his ear. "Everything okay?"

"It's good." She forced a smile to her face and cheer to her voice. "I'll be back!"

Before there could be more questions, she turned back into the house and fought the urge to sprint to the door. She climbed into her car, then drove until she couldn't feel Madigan's power tugging at her anymore.

Hours away from Greens Glen, she found a quiet parking lot to a hiking trail she could pull the car into. She sat patiently, waiting for the couple to unload their backpacks into their car, the only other one in the lot. Once they'd left, she cleared her mind, slowed her breathing, and thought of wide open space. Of quiet, of peace, then let herself shift away.

She stood at the top of the Rose Valley in Ely and inhaled, instantly feeling lighter. She had heard Ely suffered a drought during their growing season, and seeing her treasured valley barren tore her heart in half. The valley had been her place of refuge. It had been witness to her pain, her tears, her frustrations. It had swallowed her shouts and screams. Its wind had dried her tears.

She spread her fingers as she moved towards the sparse wheat field, drawing her magic up and letting its power fill her. Earth and life flowed out of her, washing over the valley. Slowly, in waves, the wheat rose. Rose-colored stalks burst up through dried, cracked patches of dirt.

When she reached the middle of the valley, she paused, tipping her head back. The summer sun of Ely warmed her face as if to give her thanks.

Drawing in a deep breath, she let out a shout of rage. Rage for the lies. Rage for the betrayals. A scream of pain, visceral from the grief and pain she'd held onto after losing her father, then her mother. She sank to her knees, tears streaming down her face as she let everything go.

She closed her hands, and brought her arms around herself in a hug, then collapsed onto her back among the wheat. Feeling drained, feeling freed, even if that freedom was temporary, she let herself doze; the stalks sheltering her.

CHAPTER 18

CAID sat on Róisín's front steps when she'd managed the energy she needed to shift home from Ely. Taking advantage of the late afternoon sun illuminating the porch, and him, she studied him through her windshield. His hair was disheveled, and at that moment, he shoved one of his hands through it. The fingers of his other hand drummed against one of his thighs. That small glimmer of hope brightened.

Could he be waiting for her?

It was enough to drag herself from her car when all her body wanted to do was crawl into the house, slip into bed and sleep for days. She was completely drained, her magic quiet, body heavy and bones weary. Reaching for the door handle, her body cried in protest, begging her to stay still.

"Is everything okay?" She closed her door, the sound echoing through the crisp evening air.

"I could ask that of you." His hazel eyes stayed steady on her as she neared him.

"What do you mean?"

He patted the spot on the step next to him. "You've been off for the past week and a half. Quieter, and short when you talk. The way you left today, it had me worried about you."

"No need to waste your time worrying about me." She tried to brush off his concern. The exhaustion that had weighed her stomach down eased, only to be replaced by butterflies fluttering about.

He shifted to face her, one of his knees bumping against hers. "I don't think it's a waste of time."

"Caid..."

"Are you okay?"

She looked out across her yard, taking in the houses around her neighborhood. The warm evening air may have been stale of sounds from nature, but it was filled with the squeals of children playing and the occasional clinking of dishes. Life. The people in their homes, the man sitting next to her, life still moved. Despite Madigan.

"I'm okay," she whispered. "I've just somehow found myself smack dab in the middle of a family thing that's incredibly stressful."

He watched her for a moment, silent. It felt as though she were hanging onto a fraying rope over the edge of a cliff, waiting. Waiting for him to reach out to her. Her body tensed. How long had it been since she'd hoped someone would reach for her, want her, in a way that she had wanted them?

"Can you tell them you don't want a part of it?" he asked, finally breaking the silence.

"I wish I could, but..." She blew out a breath, her shoulders sagging. "There's more than just what's happening within our family that's at stake."

"That's why Matthew came."

"His father asked him to stop by, check in. Lucius was very much a father figure to me when my father passed away. After my mother died, Clarissa, Matthew's mother, stepped in to help me as she could. The distraction of having him here was nice. Now that he's gone back to work..." She rubbed at her temple. "Reality sets in again."

Róisín drew her knees up and wrapped her arms around her legs. She closed her eyes and let out a breath, willing her tears not to break through. As much as she liked Caid, she couldn't show her magic to him—for fear of him running away or rejecting her. Róisín wasn't ready to open herself to that, not yet. Not again.

Alexandria had left before Róisín could draw in a breath after that fateful night. Her ashen face, her brown eyes so wide that Róisín could see the whites around her irises. No words had been spoken, just a shake of her head, and she was gone. Down the sidewalk, tucking herself into the milling crowds without a backwards glance to Róisín.

"Want to go grab a bite to eat?" Caid's leg gently bumped hers. "Change of scenery? You're here all day, every day."

Her bed beckoned to her, her movements sluggish from the energy she'd spent in the Rose Valley.

He shifted to his feet next to her, and his hand reached down.

She slipped her hand into his and let him pull her to her feet.

"You're not alone," he whispered when she stood face to face with him. "You have people here who are friends. Lina may be loud and wild, but she's a good person, and I know she's been worried about you, too. And I..." His Adam's apple bobbed with his slow swallow. "I'd like to think we're becoming friends, too."

"Does that mean you'll talk to me again?"

His eyebrows drew together, and he frowned. "What do you mean?"

"You and I used to talk every day before you left for the day. And now? It's like you can't get out of here quick enough."

His hand that still held hers tensed briefly. "I'm sorry. It started as just not being sure how Matthew would react, because I thought you and he were, and then." He shrugged. "I can't really explain it."

"Try," she whispered.

His head lifted from their joined hands to look at her. "Since the meeting, I can't stop thinking about you. I want to be around you, get to know you. Shit, even if we just sat here every night and talked about nothing, it would feel like everything. That's why I started sticking around. I could disguise it as work related, hope you wouldn't ever notice. Gave me an excuse."

"You didn't need an excuse."

"But I do." He tucked a strand of hair behind her ear. "I didn't want to scare you away."

"I don't scare easily."

His lips tipped up into a half smile as he stepped closer. "Róisín?"

"Hm?"

"Can I kiss you?"

Her lips parted, a giddiness filling her core. She nodded her head. Butterflies took flight in her stomach, surging higher to her chest where their wings pounded as he angled his head down to hers.

A slight brush of his lips over hers at first. What she'd felt when they shook hands that first night was nothing compared to what this light touch of their lips had done. Or what happened when he sealed his lips over hers and a rush of energy charged through her system.

Bringing her free hand up to his chest, she felt the solidness of him, his warmth.

Caid's fingers curled around the back of her neck, his thumb stroking her throat as she opened her mouth for him.

Feeling her legs going weak, she leaned against him, taking their kiss deeper, their tongues caressing.

"Jesus," he breathed out when they came apart, his chest heaving, eyes bright.

She looked up at him with a shy smile.

"As much as I'd like to keep doing that, I asked you to dinner, and we'd never leave this spot because I could kiss you all night."

Her exhaustion had fallen away, her body hyper aware of his nearness, the breeze along her bare arms and in her hair. The way her lips burned when his eyes dropped down to them. Standing, or even sitting on those steps, with his mouth on hers all night sounded better than cake and ice cream at a birthday party.

CHAPTER 19

Róisín's porch door slammed hard against the side of the house. She startled, dropping the book she had been reading. She used her magic to bring the book back to her lap.

"Dammit, Ro, answer your phone, please!" Lina burst through the door.

Róisín grabbed the book from midair and hugged it to her chest.

Lina stopped short when she entered the room. Her cheeks grew red, and she cleared her throat. "Hi."

Róisín pushed her glasses up on her head and blinked at her. "Hi. I'm so sorry, I've been swamped with..." She looked over the piles of books before her. "Work."

"I know, you said it in your text the other day. But sweet Jesus, woman, take a break occasionally."

"You're right." She closed all the books and set them on the table. She stretched her legs out before rising. "Coffee while I apologize profusely and grovel?"

Lina waved a hand in the air. "You're already forgiven. I'm sorry I barged in like an idiot."

"It's okay. I forget about anything and everything when I work on a project."

Lina looked at the worn books. "Doesn't it get boring? Reading about stuff older than creation?"

Trying not to think about how old she was, or how much longer she had left, endless time compared to a human, Róisín pulled her attention away from the books and shrugged. "Not when you love history and old things."

"They say it doesn't feel like work when you're doing what you love," Lina said.

"Shit! Comin' atcha, Caid!" Wyatt's muffled voice came from outside.

"I mean, it could have at least brushed him, dammit," Lina huffed.

"What was that?" Róisín turned from the cabinet she had opened for cups.

"Oh, Wyatt tossing stuff down to my asshole brother." She scowled through the door at Caid before she flipped him the middle finger with both hands.

"Everything good there?" Róisín asked. She knew it was a small town. Lina had surely heard about Róisín and Caid's dinner at the diner two nights before. Róisín didn't know if it would've created an issue between the siblings. Guilt niggled. She should've asked Lina if it were okay first.

"Just be happy you're an only kid," Lina muttered.

"Uh-oh. Here." Róisín handed her a cup of coffee, then sat at the table across from her. "Sounds like we both have had a lot going on."

"Mm." She frowned. "First, let me enjoy the only cup of this I can have today, while I tell you the good stuff." She shot her brother a glare through the door. In response, he threw up his hands in surrender and backed away from the door. "Then I'll divulge why brothers are the worst creatures in the world."

Before Lina could continue, Wyatt's head appeared upside down as he looked down over the staging platform. He smiled and waved at them, the moment relieving some of the tension filling the room. Giggling at him, they returned his greeting.

"Okay, good news." Róisín attempted to distract her from whatever struggle happened between her and her brother.

"I'm pregnant."

Róisín hopped up from the table and squealed in excitement. "Congratulations! Come here." She motioned her close and embraced her tightly. "You've been trying to tell me for almost two weeks, haven't you?"

"Yes." She dabbed at her damp eyes with the sleeve of her shirt. "While you've been off on a wild journey to some super ancient times, judging by the looks of those decrepit books on your coffee table, I've been dying to tell you I'm having a baby."

"I'm sorry." Róisín hugged her again. "Like I said, I get deep in it."

"I wish I had something like that. Something that took my attention so wholly."

"You've had the campaign," she reminded her. "Any idea on how that's going to go when the vote happens?"

"I'd like to say I'm going to win. I heard that scumbag is trying to buy votes around town, though." Her eyebrows scrunched. "I don't know what will happen. Thankfully, I've got this baby and getting ready to be a mom to distract me."

Róisín smiled. "How far?"

"Doctor said seven weeks. Which means, probably a blizzard baby. Hopefully, by then, things here will be better."

She reached across the table and took Lina's hand, giving her a comforting squeeze. "It will be."

Even if Róisín wouldn't be there to see it, she would do everything in her power to make sure it was so for Lina and Thomas, their baby, for Caid...

She looked through the door to where Caid passed a piece of siding up to Wyatt. "Now... What'd your brother do, and do I have to trip him off my back patio into a ceramic planter before the day is out?"

"No. I'd hate to have you aid and abet me in sabotaging my jerk of a brother. It's just..." She sighed heavily. "We don't have the greatest relationship with our parents. Not for the lack of us trying, but both of us, once we were old enough to be out, we were out. He basically wiped his hands of them. Sometimes I get it in my head to try again. Like right now, I want to let them know about the baby. I said something to him about it the other day when he came for our weekly breakfast, but it ended up in an argument."

"Over you telling them?"

"Not telling them, but me still wasting my time on them. If things have changed none of the other times, why would it now? A part of me feels like maybe he's wrong, this might be it, but..."

"The other part worries he's right," Róisín finished.

"Exactly. I've talked to our mother a few times over the years. Cordial, but that's the extent of it. That maybe"—she wiggled her fingers, making quotation marks—"just hangs on. I'm scared though."

"Well, there's time to weigh it out. You're going to be pregnant for a few more months," Róisín said.

"It's just." She frowned. "It gets lonely, you know? I love and adore Caid, he's always been there for me. But I can't stop myself from dreaming of a life where I have parents and not just, well, people who brought me topside." Lina snorted and placed a protective hand over her stomach. "If nothing changes when I do?"

"Then you take the time you need to mourn the relationship that you could've had, and move on with the family you do have," Róisín told her.

"Has anyone ever told you that you're wise far beyond your years?"

If only she knew.

CHAPTER 20

C AID slammed the tailgate of his truck, the latches protesting with loud thunks. When it failed to close and dropped back into his hands, he hissed out a breath.

His day had been utter shit, and a broken truck was the last thing he needed to pile onto it. Taking the top of it in his hands, he put the weight of his body behind the push, forcing it to latch. His chin dropped to his heaving chest, his shoulders rounded.

The chiding from Wyatt throughout the work day had been fine. If he were to be honest, he expected it. Staying at Róisín's house would be noticed. It was a small town, and her house sat at the end of the cul-de-sac where all her neighbors could see. There was nothing to hide, and there wasn't any shame trying to latch onto him over the new shift in his relationship with her.

It had been in the way Lina had looked at him through Róisín's patio door the day before that had been the warning. She was angry with him. Over what, he hadn't known. Until she flagged him down in town on a trip to the hardware store.

Her harsh footsteps had echoed over the linoleum floor of the store as she stomped over to where he was trying to locate a box of nails he needed for Róisín's house. The slap against his bicep stung like a nettle up his arm. They'd exchanged heated words and she had fled the store, tears streaming down her cheeks, leaving him standing there, curious eyes on him.

He wanted to feel regret for the spiteful words that tumbled from his lips, especially when he watched her face fall and her eyes fill. He dug deep, searching for it, but came up empty. The scar he carried from his parents actions had deep roots that had wrapped around his every fiber of being.

He gripped the top of the tailgate, grinding his molars together. He knew he needed to go to Lina, to talk to her. Put his differences aside and let her say whatever she had wanted to say. It was different this time, almost like he couldn't be that brother for her anymore. He was tapped out. Even pretending to care was exhausting. Why couldn't she just give up on them like he had?

"Caid?" Róisín's voice was quiet next to him. "You're going to break a tooth, or your fingers are going to put holes in your truck."

"What?" He blinked and looked down at his bulging knuckles, white from the tension of his grip.

She rested one of her hands over his, the touch breaking him free, grounding him. "Are you—oh."

The word became muffled as he brought her against his chest, his arms wrapping tightly around her.

"You smell amazing. But you're not good, are you?"

"I am right now." He buried his nose in her hair, the scent of honey and lavender filling his senses, stroking along his skin, soothing, calming. "You smell amazing too."

"Do you want to stay for dinner? I worried I would miss you the way you packed up so quickly."

Her words vibrated against his chest, and he didn't want to let her go, but he probably held her too tightly. He let a hand fall to her waist, then used his other to tip her chin up so he could see her.

"Hi."

The wide smile she gave him brought his wildly spinning, wobbling world back to its axis.

"Hi." She smoothed her hands over his chest. "So, dinner? Nothing fancy, just grilled rosemary lemon chicken and some sides."

He stroked his thumb over her chin, reveling in the smooth feel of her skin beneath his rough pad. "Having you as dinner company would make boxed mac and cheese and jarred baby hot dogs feel like a five-star meal."

"Well." Her cheeks reddened, and her pupils dilated. She opened her mouth like she had wanted to say more, but closed it, motioning to her front door.

Slipping a hand in hers, he let her lead the way. She made to let go of his hand once they were in the kitchen, but just before their fingertips lost contact, he maneuvered his hand to grasp hers again. Caid spun her around and held her in his arms, dipping her as though they were in a grand ballroom. Then he pressed his lips against her giggling mouth.

Her lips tipped into a smile, and she let out a hum against his lips.

His tongue stroked along her lip, and he tested to see if she would open for him. When she did, hers was ready and waiting. He sunk into the kiss, feeling her body mold against him.

"Dinner will burn," she murmured.

"We can get takeout." She released a soft sigh when he pressed a kiss to one corner of her mouth. "Or I can take you on another date. Go grab dinner somewhere."

"Three dates in one week? I'm thinking that you like me, Mr. McGrath."

Keeping his hold on her, he pulled back some. For a moment, he lost himself in the whirlpool of blue her eyes were when she looked up at him. His heart banged against his chest so hard and loud, he was certain she could hear it. If she couldn't, she had to see the way it pulsed in his neck. He could feel the flutter-flutter of it there on the left side.

"Hey." Her hands were on either side of his face, her eyes no longer swirling, but a solid, deep, dark Atlantic blue. And she was frowning.

Had he not responded to her? Shit, he was scumbag for taking away that lightness that she'd had on her face only seconds before.

"Róisín..."

"What's wrong, Caid? You're carrying something heavy. I can see it in your eyes, and feel it here." Her hands went from his face to his arms. "You're clenching."

"I'm okay. Just a long day." He didn't even believe his own assurance; he would be surprised if she did.

Rising to her toes, she gave him a light kiss on his cheek. "Don't hold it in. It's not good for this." She pressed a hand to his chest.

His heart kicked up a notch, fearing the exposure of his feelings for her.

"You don't have to let me in yet, but I want to be here for you. Like you were for me the other day. Okay?"

The emotion that clogged his throat left him unable to find his voice, so he nodded.

"Good." Her face lit with a smile. "Now, sit while I check this chicken, and tell me why I looked out back today and witnessed something like a wrestling match between you and Wyatt."

CHAPTER 21

Róisín leapt into the air with a proficient skill that came from decades of training, and spun away from Matthew as he dropped to the ground, sweeping his leg out.

"Something's... different." He dodged one of her incoming blows.

She ignored his probing eyes, shifting away from him, only to duck around to his back and hook an arm around his neck. She leaned their weight backwards, flipping them over, her movement fluid and quick.

Matthew's back hit the ground, his breath whooshing out of him. He grunted.

She followed the momentum of her move and flipped over so that she was atop him, straddling him. The only sounds in the room were their pants and the snick of her blade unsheathing, before she tapped it against his exposed throat.

"I win." She grinned down at him.

"Best three out of four," he said between his clenched teeth.

"You really do hate losing, don't you?" She rose, then offered her hand to help him up.

"I liked it better when you only took this mildly serious." He pushed a hand through his disheveled hair.

"Well, normally when you want to spar, we're not in a doomsday situation."

His lips thinned into a hard line, eyes darkening.

"Best four out of five?" She tucked her blade back into the sheath on her belt.

He tipped his head to one side, the corner of his mouth ticking up in a smirk.

"What?" she asked when the silence stretched, and he didn't move. "You got me first, and I missed the kill mark, didn't I?"

He remained still, silent.

"Matthewww." Róisín stomped her foot. She checked her body over for any sign of his yellow paint that was his kill shot mark. Hers this time was a shade of violet, which now marked his neck, a thigh, chest and stomach. "Stop it."

He chuckled now, a grin spreading wide. "You took the carpenter to bed."

Her eyes grew wide, and she gasped. "I most certainly did not."

"Okay, not yet." He half-shrugged. "What is it then? Sit near one another? A date? Hold hands? Kiss?"

Her face grew hot like the blazing sun on a summer day.

"Oh..." He drew out the word. "You kissed the carpenter! And?"

"And nothing." Róisín waved him off and turned away from him, moving to the weapons wall in the training room. A space they trained in within Lucius's manor in Ely. Madigan was a siphon, and the odds of needing to go into this without their magic had a very high potential. They'd all agreed it was best to spend any extra time they could manage, making sure their physical abilities were just as honed as their magic.

Matthew followed close on her heels. "What do you mean, and nothing?" He picked up a ball flail and swung it around.

"Don't even think about it," She warned and easily hoisted a mean-looking Viking hammer. "I'd hate to club that handsome face of yours in."

"You still think I'm handsome." He smiled, one of his brows tipping up.

"Of course, I do. You're a handsome pain in my butt." Róisín tossed the hammer from one hand to the other.

"Does that mean we've moved beyond..." He waved the ball flail around. "You know."

Róisín shifted her weight to prop her hip on the table, then set the hammer down. Crossing her arms over her chest, she leveled a stare at him. "Beyond what?"

"Uh... that thing we did," he said, his cheeks growing red.

"Are we fourteen?"

"What?" His brow knotted together.

"Just out with it. Have we moved beyond the night we were both heartbroken, got completely shitfaced, then fucked each other?"

Matthew swallowed hard, his throat bobbing. His eyes shifted from her, down to the table. He cleared his throat and thumbed a small jeweled dagger. "Yeah. That."

"You promised it wouldn't make things weird between us. Then you got weird. Then you disappeared, and I was completely alone again." She grabbed the dagger and moved it away from him, trying to make him look at her. "Not only was I shattered about what happened with Alexandria, but then I ended up even more so because my best friend and I fucked up, and he took off without so much as a backwards glance."

Matthew dropped his chin to his chest, his shoulders slumping.

"Why?" she asked quietly. "Goddess, we don't even remember it. We only woke up in my bed. Naked."

"I..." He lifted his hands, palms up, then let them fall back to his sides, slapping them against his thighs. "When I woke up the next morning, I felt like an asshole. Partly because of all that." He cleared his throat. "But because somewhere in the night, I let the lines blur. I don't know when it happened, but it did. I should have been a better friend."

"It's not like it doesn't take two to tango," she snapped, her voice bouncing off the stone walls. "I just as much let the lines blur as you."

He shook his head and sighed. "Then I thought leaving you, letting you have space alone, would be better than me staying. I was supposed to be that friend that helped you get your feet back on the ground. Not do these idiotic things like take you drinking or sleeping with you."

"You were hurting too. We could have figured it out together. Like friends do."

He covered his face with his hands, then spun around, letting out a frustrated groan. "This is a shitty time to hash out something that happened over forty years ago."

"That's because we never talked about it. We only had that moment before. I don't know about you, but I know I was not in the best decision-making position."

"I was far less than you, trust me," he said.

"Look." She moved away from the table and crossed to him. "Did I, at one time, have a little bit of a crush on you? Absolutely. When I was *nine.* You were older, cooler, and you had this insane ability to control your magic like it was second nature to you. The more you started coming to the cottage with Clarissa, the more I got to know you, and it shifted. I stopped crushing and—"

"Stopped crushing? You make it sound like I sprouted horns."

She laughed, placing a hand on his forearm. "No, you have always been handsome in my eyes. But the more I got to know your mind, your heart, the more I not only understood we were never meant for, well, that, but I knew our bond was different. Like fate had intended us to be together in life a different way." She cringed. "This is also now the Let's Be Friends talk. I'm so sorry."

"I felt it too," he said. "Right in my gut. This grabbing need to be the one that looked out for you, picked you up when you were down, showed you how to do shit. Give The Talk to anyone who may take your heart and hurt it."

"Be family."

"Thank the Goddess we really aren't," he muttered.

"That aside, just think about it, though. My figurative brother came to be that person who tugged me to the light, but instead of getting me there, he left. Not only left but disappeared for ten damn years."

"I didn't mean for that. Really." He frowned, falling quiet for a moment. "When reality hit that leaving was a mistake, I felt like a pile of shit. I didn't think you'd want to see me or to talk it out and move on."

"Why were you really in Shianshani that day?"

"Sh-I—" He kicked his foot at the ground. "Mum sort of knew about it, about us, and—"

"Matthew!" she shrieked, her voice pitching higher than she meant. She slapped his shoulder.

"What the Hells was I supposed to do? Deny it? She was a descendant of the Seer on her mother's side, for the Goddess's sake!"

Róisín squeezed her eyes shut and pinched the bridge of her nose with her thumb and forefinger. She held her breath, waving her other hand at him, motioning to continue.

"Anyway, she said you were there, working to restore the northwest rainforest after that fire. I almost lost the nerve to go, but I somehow managed."

"I'm happy you did." She opened her eyes now.

"Me too."

Silence fell over and around them. With a curt nod, Róisín grabbed the hammer again and stepped into the center of the room. She tossed the hammer from hand to hand before she spun it in her right then shifted into her fighting stance.

Matthew set the ball flail down and grabbed the mace that had sat next to it, instead. "Best four out of five you promised?"

"Something like that." She smirked and beckoned him closer.

Chapter 22

CAID leaned against the kitchen door frame with his hands in the front pockets of his jeans.

Róisín moved from her stovetop, to the sink and back. When he had walked in moments before, it had been just after she had finished cleaning up a pot of cooked pasta. Her knuckles had been white as they gripped the pot when she rose from the floor, lips pressed together so tightly they were just as white. She dropped the pot into the sink then tied her hair into a hasty bun, her sigh shaking her shoulders.

He had greeted her and asked if she had needed any help, but all she offered him was a smile before turning back to her cupboards, pulling out a new box of pasta and a pot, her movements jerky as she went.

"Want to talk about it?" he finally asked once he couldn't handle the silence any longer.

Her shoulders stiffened, and she stopped stirring the sauce she made.

Caid waited, patient.

She set the spoon down and placed her hands on the countertop, pausing a moment, her shoulders rising and falling, before turning to him. "Will you tell me about your parents? After?"

His face hardened, his teeth grinding. He couldn't escape it. He couldn't escape them.

"Please?" she asked softly.

Could he? He had spent his entire life surrounded by people who knew his parents, knew what they were like. He had never had to dig inside and find that voice that could be strong enough to talk about them. But there was something bothering her, deeply. If he had to give a piece of himself in order to get a piece of her, he would try. He gave her a small nod.

Róisín wrapped her arms around herself, hands rubbing against her bare arms. "Some of my research I'm doing for work, it's..." Her mouth moved soundlessly as if she struggled to find the words. "I've discovered some of my family's history in it. And I... I learned something very unexpected today. Something about my grandfather that changes everything I thought I knew."

Clasping her hands in front of her, her knuckles turned white as she wrung her hands together. She exhaled.

"It's harder because I don't have anyone to process it with. No one to ask the questions I want, no, that I need the answers to. Because they're gone. My grandfather, my grandmother, my parents. They're gone."

It had bothered him then that she had been alone, and now, his chest burned anew with his heart's hurt for her.

"My parents never wanted to have kids." Caid pulled his hands from his pockets and as he straightened, he crossed his arms over his chest. He swallowed, the softness of Róisín's features giving him the strength to continue.

"My father, he just sort of took it in stride when I came along. He was more about appearances, playing the role. Which meant he was at least physically there. Came to the school stuff and was on the sidelines at sports. That was where his support ended. My mother?" He shoved a hand into his hair, pushing it back until he reached the base of his skull. The tips of his fingers dug in, pressing hard against the skin. "There was always inconvenience there. I had ruined her life. Now she had to have less because they had me. I still don't understand why they never just put me up for adoption."

Her eyes stayed steady on his. She opened her mouth to speak, but instead closed it, offering him a small smile before turning back to the stove and turning the cooktop off.

"Then they had Lina. That's when I started getting angry at them. She didn't deserve that. If they didn't want me, and they wouldn't let a family who wanted me raise me, they should've been more careful." He struggled to keep his voice down, but his heart beat furiously, his lungs constricted, and his heart tightened as it always did when he thought about his parents. "I think it was worse for Lina, because while dad did his public duty by me, he couldn't be bothered with her at all. I did whatever I could for her. She wanted to do dance, so I talked to Marie Finnegan, who used to run the dance studio in town, and convinced her to let me clean the studio weekly for Lina's tuition."

"How old were you?"

"Ten. Lina was five. That's how it was from the start. I made sure she had the love and support our parents didn't want to give her."

She nodded. "You're a good brother."

"Maybe," he muttered. Lina didn't think he was good at anything at that moment. He couldn't muster the courage to face her and apologize. "She wants to tell them about the baby, thinking it will make them snap out of whatever it is and suddenly want to be a part of her life."

"I think even you can admit, it's at least better to try, and to know, right?"

When he looked up from where he had stared at the floor, she had moved around the table toward him and now stood an arms-length away. "If they shut her down again, she'll be devastated. I don't want her to go through that. To feel that."

"It's a risk," Róisín agreed. "She has you, she has Thomas, his family, their friends. You can try to protect her from the hurt, but it'll only hurt her more. Just be there to help her when the times do hurt."

He huffed and brought his eyes back to her. "I don't know what's going on with the research you're doing, what you found, but I'm here for you, too. You shouldn't have to shoulder it alone, okay?"

She nodded. "Do you want to stay again for dinner?"

"On one condition." He moved toward her.

"What's that?" She kept her eyes on his as he backed her against the table.

Instead of offering her an answer, he scooped her up, sitting her on the table, and his mouth crashed against hers. Her legs came around his waist, pulling him closer, and he released a groan at the contact.

Caid ran his hands down her arms, bringing them to her waist, then to her ass, cupping it. When he ground his hips against her, she pulled his bottom lip into her mouth, biting gently.

"I was going to suggest that you let me have a taste for dessert," he said against her mouth when he pulled back. "But an appetizer sounds good too."

"Why not both?" Her voice was thick and her eyes hooded.

He went completely still.

Unlacing her fingers from behind his neck, she brought them to the small buttons of the shirt she wore. His skin tightened and his cock pressed against the fabric of his jeans as she slowly undid each button, stopping halfway so that the shirt fell open exposing her breasts.

With effort, Caid dragged his eyes away from where her fingers had paused, his heartbeat pounding in his ears. He drew an index finger down the column of her neck. The work roughened pad tracing a line over her chest, then to her breasts. She released a soft sigh when he stroked a thumb over one of her nipples. She lowered her elbows to the table, moving in a way that made her shirt open completely.

His eyes traced along the slight tan lines around her neck, down to her smooth, milky-white colored breasts. Her pink nipples were taut, beckoning his mouth closer.

"You're so fucking beautiful," he said roughly, his eyes back on hers.

Pressing a kiss to the base of her throat, he stroked a hand over one of her breasts and she released a soft whimper, tipping her hips to press harder against him, and his control slowly weakened.

Moving his hand down Róisín's stomach, he undid the button of her shorts and skimmed his fingers down below her panties, drawing along the line of her entrance, feeling the heat and wetness there.

Her breaths became pants, quiet whimpers, and moans as Caid explored and stroked her body with his hands and tasted with his mouth. His name was a soft, breathy moan from her lips when he pressed a finger in.

He added a second finger, stroking deeper, while murmuring against her neck, "You're so wet."

Róisín responded by rocking her hips against his hand and whimpering.

Dropping to his knees on the kitchen floor, he gripped her shorts, pulling them, and her panties down in a deft movement. Having her in his hands, exposed like this, his lungs worked overtime to draw in air and his heart thudded heavily in his chest. The anticipation of this moment had begun to build that moment in the gym and he couldn't deny it. It had built to a pressure point and now it took every bit of control to not let it burst.

With his hands on her hips, he scooted her to the table's edge so that her entrance was level with his mouth. He lifted his gaze to her as he drew his thumb lightly down along her folds, then brought the pad to his mouth, licking it. He let out a rumbling sound of pleasure.

Her chest rose and fell rapidly with her quickened breaths, eyes hooded as she watched his every move. Caid brought his tongue back to her, stroking with it. Her soft cries of pleasure filled the kitchen around them.

She fell back to the table, gripped his hair with her hands and began writhing and rocking against his face. He used one arm to hold her closer, then lifted his other hand to spread her further apart, giving him the opportunity to press and stroke deeper into her heat.

He wanted to watch her come apart before him. To hear her shout out his name as her orgasm took her.

She clenched around him, her body tightened. Her hips bucked when he pressed his thumb against her, and she cried out his name as the orgasm rocked through her. Her body shuddering, hips rolling as he continued to taste and explore while she came back down from the orgasm's high.

He grinned and pressed a kiss to the inside of one of her thighs, then rose over her.

Her cheeks were flushed pink, her blue eyes half-opened from the bliss of her orgasm, and her chest heaved with pants

"I've never..." She gasped and reached for him, bringing him close. "Never had an appetizer like that."

"Oh, the appetizer isn't done yet." He brought her closer, licking the taste of her from his lips. "I think it's just getting started."

She wrapped her legs around him, then took his mouth with hers and rocked hard against him. The smell of her, the taste of her, awaking something animalistic in him. He couldn't stop the growling sound from vibrating in his throat. When she tipped her head back, eyebrow raised, he asked, "Skip the dinner?"

"Maybe we should make this a three course meal," she replied devilishly, scooting back some. She reached between them, her fingers skimming the top of his jeans.

He lay his forehead against hers, closing his eyes when she undid the top button, then slid the zipper down. "Table seems pretty sturdy," he murmured.

"Mm..." She nudged his jeans down over his hips. "The woman at the flea market said that her great-great-grandfather built it as a wedding gift to her great-great-grandmother."

She took his cock in her hands.

"Oh?" he said through clenched teeth.

"Had thirteen kids," Róisín went on. She stroked him once, twice. The heat built at his core again. "I think it can take, um, quite a bit."

"I hope like hell it can."

CHAPTER 23

Róisín inhaled a slow breath, stretching her limbs. In those first waking moments, she let herself burrow deeper into her bed and enjoy the quiet of the space. The late morning sun filtered in through the curtains that danced slowly in the breeze that came through the slightly opened windows. As much as her body wanted to stay, her limbs aching in a gloriously used way after her night with Caid, her mind urged her to finish waking.

Her thoughts raced, and no matter how hard she tried to close her eyes and tune them out, they were a hammer against her skull. She needed to get to Alleyette to talk to Shasta about her recent discovery. The sooner she could get there, the better. It weighed heavily on her and Róisín didn't doubt it changed their situation. And not only did it reveal more of the mystery behind Aoife, but it also brought more questions.

Could she be strong enough to handle the secrets that her family had kept? If she wasn't, how was she going to be strong enough to face Madigan?

Frustrated with herself and the self-doubt that clung to her stronger than her own shadow, she rolled over, finding herself against a wall of warm muscle.

"Morning." Caid's sleep roughened voice greeted her.

She hummed, and a slow smile curved her lips. She pressed a kiss to his bare chest, smoothing her hands over the light spray of sand colored hair there. "Very good morning. You're built like a Lumberjack, Kincaid McGrath," she murmured against his side.

His body shook with laughter. "More like a trade worker who lifts sheetrock and plywood all day long."

"Whatever it is." She shifted closer. Her skin lit with tingles of excitement, her heart picking up a galloping pace. "It's perfect."

Her hands drifted over his shoulders to his arms feeling the solidness of his muscle beneath. The air grew warm around them despite the cool air drifting from the window, over their bodies. He had the bulk of muscle his hard work had created, but he didn't have the hard, sharply defined planes of it. It suited him through and through, the fierce protector of those he cared for, but the gentleness that lay within that only those he cared for were privy to.

Her body urged her to move closer. Her mind hammered at her, a reminder of her need to go to Shasta. Go, go, go. Now...

If she thought the kiss they'd shared earlier that week had changed things between them, she had been wrong. She had also been incredibly wrong about her resolve.

"You good?" Caid asked.

She nodded, not trusting her voice to help her lie.

He brought the large hand that had rested at her hip to her arm, brushing his fingertips over her bare skin. Goosebumps rose, chasing his touch. Then he cupped her chin, tipping her head up to look at him.

"Talk to me," he whispered.

She searched his face for a moment, the intimidating man from the first night they met was nothing like the man on the inside. The man who cared for those around him—for Lina, for Wyatt, and now, for her.

She cleared her throat, trying to shake out the lump building there. "Is this, is it just a one-shot thing?"

His brows drew down and together, his eyes darkening and narrowing on hers.

"I only ask because it's just been a really, really long time since I've been with someone," she added.

Caid's expression softened, and he stroked his thumb along her jaw, then his knuckles over her cheek. "I think I knew from that moment in the gym, this wasn't going to just be a thing between us, Róisín." His fingers cupped the side of her neck and he used his thumb to nudge her chin up to look at him. "Something tells me you knew, too."

She swallowed her own vulnerable admission.

"No, it's definitely not just a one-shot thing." His tone was firm, his words bearing a sureness to them.

Oh, this is going to hurt when it ends. I'm not even going to crawl away from it.

"Have you ever been in love?"

"Once." He nodded and continued rubbing her arm.

Jealousy crept up the back of her neck, surprising her, and she pushed it down. "What happened?"

"I'm a small-town guy, content with living the small-town life. She wasn't okay with that, so she left. Moved to Boston, then later to Los Angeles." His hand had settled back on her hip and squeezed. "What about you?"

"Once." Those familiar, overwhelming emotions rose within. Her heartbeat quickened, dulling the noises around her and squeezing her chest. It hurt more that this response was in reaction to heartache, when decades before, she'd felt them the morning she awoke next to Alexandria realizing she never wanted to live another day without her. That for all her relationships with others before, it was nothing compared to the power she gave Alexandria when she whispered those three words in her ear, and Alexandria said them back, firm and clear.

"And?" He tipped an eyebrow up.

"She couldn't accept who I was. Didn't even try. The moment she found out, she walked away. Left me on a sidewalk when we were out one night. She didn't even come to get her things. That's how badly she felt about me."

"It sounds like she didn't deserve you then," he whispered, his breath warm against her.

Her heart fluttered and then her chest tightened further. Róisín had never shaken the feeling that maybe she hadn't been the one who deserved Alexandria. Just as now, she didn't feel that she deserved his touch, his kisses, or the way his eyes told her at that moment he wanted to be the one to take her hurts away, fill her life with love and happiness.

"Róisín," he said on a breath before he drew her closer, taking her mouth with his. He kissed her so tenderly that her emotions shifted, tears threatening. More than that, her heart steadied in her chest, the tightness loosening its grip on her. The noise in her mind quieted. Never had anyone in her lifetime given her the peace she felt at that moment.

It wasn't long before the peace moved aside to make room for more. The throb started at the inside of her thighs, and spread upward through her center, settling in her belly.

Róisín moved closer, then hooked a leg over his under the blankets, leaning against him and pushing him onto his back.

"I'm going to be late for work," he said, but the laughter in his eyes belied his concern.

"Wyatt will get started without you." She nipped at his chin and started trailing kisses and soft bites down his neck and over his chest.

A low sound of concession rumbled through him.

She traced the midline of his abdominal muscles, then took his length in her hands, and he hissed. She stroked him from root to tip, letting her nails scrape lightly before she moved her body down so that she could take him in her mouth.

"Fuck," he rasped, his hips bucking.

Róisín took him to the back of her throat, and then dragged her tongue and stroked with her hand, moving in a repetitive motion that had him groaning.

The rustle of him fumbling for his wallet on the stand at his side of the bed was followed by the rip of the condom package, and she lifted her head, finding his eyes, heavy lidded from his lust, watching her hungrily.

"Get up here," he demanded.

"Hold on." She took the condom from him before he could roll it on. After she had it in place, she took him in her hands again, lifting herself and slowly lowering over him until she was fully seated on him.

Feeling him fill her, she let out a long, deep moan of pleasure. He swore, saying her name, and pushed deeper into her.

Taking his hands in hers, she brought them to her chest and covered her breasts with them. Róisín rocked her body, the fire within quickly turning into an inferno.

His hands moved over her chest, his thumbs grazing her nipples, then he gripped her hips, driving himself hard into her.

She cried out his name, her moan becoming heavy pants as he thrust again before sitting up and wrapping her in his arms for better leverage.

"Caid," she gasped, slanting her mouth over his, hungry to taste him.

Her orgasm rocked through her, and he swallowed her cries, her nails digging into his shoulders, clinging to him as she rode the crashing waves of bliss. His own followed only moments after.

Caid brushed her hair from her face, trying to catch his breath. After a moment, he pressed a gentle kiss to her forehead.

"If I ask you over for dinner later, will you actually eat what I make?"

His laughter vibrated through her chest as he held her close. "I promise."

"Good. Because you'll need the fuel for later."

"Shit, Róisín." He laughed again.

After a moment, she leveraged herself off him and climbed off the bed. "There's a towel in the closet through there." She pointed to the adjoining bathroom. "I'm pretty sure I've got something that doesn't smell super girly in there, too. I'm going to make us some coffee."

While Caid showered, she stood in the middle of the living room, taking slow, steadying breaths, centering herself. She drew up her magic, moving it through the house, up the stairs and let it quietly wrap around him, protecting him. After his words, their reality had sunken in. He didn't know what she was, he didn't know about Madigan, or the dangers that lurked everywhere that Madigan could reach.

The ward settled over Caid, and her power wavered slightly in its over-extended effort to hold the magic in place. The protection she kept around the house, and herself, rippled, struggling to hold. She pushed too hard, stretching herself thin.

Closing her eyes to gather herself, she quietly prayed to the Goddess that they would receive the help they needed. Soon. She felt as though their quintet against Madigan wouldn't be enough.

CHAPTER 24

Róisín's gut churned as though rocks settled within it, and with each step through Alleyette's castle halls, they knocked together. Her time with Caid only a brief reprieve from the bombshell discovery she'd made the morning they had come together.

"We can't talk here," Róisín said the moment Shasta opened the door to her room.

She reached out and grasped Róisín's hands. "Come with me."

Moments later, they were in Shasta's home on Molennius. Like the burst of flame at the end of a freshly lit match, the heavy pull of grief halted her. She brought a shaking hand to her chest.

Shasta rested a hand on her shoulder, rubbing in soothing circles. "We can go somewhere else if this is too painful?"

"No." Róisín shook her head, digging for her resolve. She had unearthed an officially recorded document with the Council of Covens that shifted everything. The ghosts of her past would have to move on. "I need to face this. It's been forty years. I need to move on. She certainly did."

Shasta studied her for a moment, then embraced her. "Our hearts break a hundred times in our lifetime. Most of us are far older when we experience our first."

She dabbed at her eyes and straightened her shirt, then blew out her breath. What she was about to say next was a catalyst. A fuel to the fire already burning. A gnawing sensation returned in the pit of her stomach. Those gnashing teeth turned her guts around, making her nauseous. Would she lose what little support she had once she uttered those four words?

Madigan was Róisín's uncle. Bernard, her grandfather, was his brother.

The caress of a dark voice in the back of her mind stroked over her heart, urging her to keep the secret. To bury it deep and forget what she had learned.

It warned her that the others would abandon her once they knew the truth. Warned her they'd see her as rot like Aoife, like Madigan. She would be yet another enemy in their eyes.

No. She couldn't hold on to it. She had already clutched it too tightly for too long. It needed to be released. She needed to be free of the burden it weighed her down with.

"Madigan is Bernard's brother."

Shasta sucked in a sharp breath so quickly, she sent herself into a coughing fit. Thumping a hand on her chest, eyes wide. "Excuse me? Did you just say..."

"I've carried around one of my mother's trunks with me for decades, but never once went through it. Figuring it was just clothes, some photos, things like that. The other night, I went through it. At the bottom, there were books and journals of research about my family, about my Coven. My mother connected Bernard to Madigan." Róisín took a settling breath. "Not just by Coven, Shasta, but by lineage. Records note that they have the same father."

"Holy mother of —" She spun around and threw her hands up, waving them wildly. She let out a growl that turned into a shout, then a scream. "This is... What the fuck?! Not just that Aoife was married to that monster's brother, but that somehow they'd been able to keep it secret."

Shasta paced around the spacious living room. The wall of windows that faced Molennius's grand snow-capped mountain range adorned with pale pink satin curtains, sheer enough to let the winter sunlight filter in. A memory of sitting at the same windows as both a child and a grown woman struck Róisín—watching the snow fall with Shasta, drinking hot cocoa.

The gnawing eased, and the voice inside quieted. With her eyes still focused on the mountains, there was a shift inside. Spaces once dark, now light. A dawn rising and revealing what lived inside the dark crevices of her mind. "I used to come here. A lot."

Shasta stopped and turned to her, brows pinched. "Every few months, you two would come and stay for a week. Your favorite was our winters."

Róisín moved toward the window. Pushing aside one of the curtain panels, the light inside her grew brighter. "I remember making snow-people with you both." She glanced over her shoulder at Shasta. "I could never lift the bellies or heads when I was small, so you would help."

Shasta closed her eyes, smiling—radiant and bright. "You told me I made the best hot chocolate in all the realms."

"You did. It was so rich in chocolate, and creamy, too. I think I've been chasing finding it in all the cafes around the realms over these years." She just hadn't known why every taste she'd sampled had never filled that void. What had happened to her? What had caused her to forget?

"Have you ever found a match?"

"Never," she answered wistfully, but then sobered. "Why? Why did she do what she did? She sacrificed herself to set the course that the Sisters saw for our future. I lost my mother because of what Aoife was." She lowered herself to the cushioned bench at the window, looking up to Shasta. "Was it Bernard's fault? Was he like Madigan? Did she used to be full of love and peace before she met my grandfather?"

Shasta shrugged, a frown tugging at her mouth. "It seems like our path keeps leading us to more questions than answers."

"I just wish I had someone I could ask."

"The Seer?"

"They told me all they could the day I went to Roidon. What they could tell me, I'm still trying to work it all out. Not that life was easy, but at least I had some grasp on it. Now, I don't know anything and to be honest, I never really did. Part of it is my fault. Of course, the simplicity of it all was comfortable, they don't kid when they say ignorance is bliss. Now that the veil is off, and I can see..." She sniffed. "I'm so alone."

"Sweetheart, you're not alone." Shasta took her in her arms and led her to the mahogany edged sofa, lowering them both to the soft suede cushion. "You have me. You have Nanette, Lucius. That pain in the neck, Matthew."

Róisín groaned, then chuckled.

"You may not be close with our Covens, but you have them as well. They go where we go. And." She stroked a hand over Róisín's hair, tucking the strands that had fallen over her face behind her ears. "You have the woman you have made friends with in Greens Glen."

"I can't tell her any of this. I may move on from what happened with Alexandria, but I will never, ever forget that look of terror on her face when she saw what I did, what I am." That familiar ache speared her chest. She lifted a hand, pressing her palm against the pain.

"Not all humans are like that," Shasta whispered. "There are those out there that will accept you for who you are, love you regardless and unconditionally."

"Maybe once this is done. Once we put the balance back in place."

"You're no longer going into this like a ball of fire to be extinguished, never to return?"

"I just..." She rubbed a hand over her face. "I know what the Seer said, I'm to right the wrongs of Aoife, I'm the one that can fix this. They never said if that meant giving myself completely, or if I would get to come back from it." Wringing her hands in her lap, she chewed on her bottom lip. "I just want to be prepared. I want to make sure that if I'm not making it, I'm at whatever peace I can find."

Placing her hands on her shoulders, Shasta turned her so that she looked at her squarely. "This isn't a suicide mission, Róisín." She squeezed her shoulders before giving her a light shake. "Not only will I not allow it, I know what the Seer told me the day I went to Roidon just after your mother died. You need to trust us. Can you do that?"

Róisín pressed her lips together and drew in a slow breath through her nose. "I trust you. I trust you all."

"Good. Now." She rose. "We got some really shitty news today."

Róisín coughed, surprised at her use of her second curse of the day.

She rolled her eyes at her. "It's a far better word than crappy at this moment. Anyway, while we're here, away from the prying eyes of magic from the Covens. I'll make some hot cocoa and then we can get to work on Brenna's magic. Once you get that, the rest will follow."

"I don't know if I can," Róisín said slowly.

"You need to learn to control all the magic within you. That night, you moved aside all your other power and let Brenna's have that space alone. That is why you were powerless after."

"How did she do it?"

"You may be the only witch among us with the true power of life magic, but we all have a drop." Shasta lifted a hand, her index finger and thumb held an inch apart. "Just enough to create a balance within and keep our life force strong as we use the power our gifted magic has. It replenishes us. It's also why we live so long."

"This isn't going to be easy, isn't it?"

"Sweetheart, even if we weren't under pressure, there is nothing easy about any of this. Magic is hard. That's why so few of us carry it."

Róisín gathered her strength, pushed aside the rest, and followed Shasta into the atrium of the far side of the house.

Chapter 25

R óisín dove headfirst into her training with Shasta and Nanette. She'd always been confident in her skills in hand to hand, and weapons combat, but she did her best to dig deep and dial it in more.

Lucius and Róisín met after each of her training sessions with Matthew, when her body and brain were worn and battered. Lucius had said that would be the best time for her to learn how to protect her mind and use her magic to create false directives should she need them if Madigan made his way through her wards.

In the weeks that had passed, Róisín had grown stronger, not just physically, or mentally, but magically as well. There was less effort for her to hold the wards around herself, Caid, and Lina.

Despite her worry of David being out longer and longer, sometimes days at a time before returning to her, when she was in Greens Glen, a cautious hope was building within her. Not only that they could find victory against Madigan, but that she could also have a chance at a future with someone. She held on tightly to that hope.

In Greens Glen, Róisín let her friendship with Lina continue to blossom. There was something unexplainable there in their growing bond. How relaxed and at ease Róisín felt when they were together, like they had always been friends.

She sat at her kitchen table turning the pages of a wall paint book, trying not to cringe at some of the colors Lina had marked as possibilities for the baby's nursery. Lina sat across from her with a similar book. She had just finished telling Róisín a story of when she and Caid were small when she reached for a bracelet that sat inside a glass bowl at the table's center.

"This is such a neat bracelet." Lina turned over the rune bracelet Róisín had made from the collection Shasta had given her.

"Try it on," Róisín offered. She had been trying to find a way to present one of the runes to Lina and saw her opportunity. "I found it in one of the last boxes I unpacked this morning, and it made me think of you."

"Really? Have I ever told you—ouch!" she yelped. "It shocked me."

The catalog thumped to the table when it slipped from her hands. "Shocked you?"

"Yeah." Lina took it off and turned it over. "Maybe it's just static electricity from me having socks on and walking across your living room carpet today."

Róisín's stomach told her otherwise. Alarm bells clamored in her head.

"Maybe, try again," she suggested.

"Shit, it did it again!" Lina cried.

Róisín's stomach dropped. "Lina." She took the bracelet in her hands. "Have you, by chance, seen Mr. Munson lately?"

"He's such a skeeze." Lina cringed, making a disgusted face. "He must be worried I'm going to beat Bill because he's kissed my ass all week. Bought me a coffee this morning, actually."

"Crap." Róisín clenched her jaw. "Shoot!"

Lina's eyes went wide, her mouth dropping open. "Are you all right?"

"Did you hear him say anything, maybe whispered or maybe under his breath?"

Lina wrinkled her nose. "Like sweet nothings in my ear?"

"Do you trust me?"

"We've only known one another for a few months, but it feels like—"

"Lina." She held her hands up. "Do you trust me?"

"Of course, I do."

"Sit down, don't move." And with that, Róisín sprinted for her bedroom.

She knew she risked exposure to remove the start of his thrall on Lina, but she would figure out her next steps later. At that moment, all she could think of was protecting Lina and the baby.

Róisín returned and dropped one of the books from Nanette on the table.

"Holy cow, that book is old," Lina said.

"It's only a few hundred years old," Róisín said offhand.

"What?! And you...have it? Why isn't it in a museum or something?"

"Family heirloom." She flipped through the pages, muttering curses when they either folded or stuck together.

"Róisín, what's going on?" Lina asked, her words coming out shaky.

Landing on the page she was searching for, she turned back to Lina.

"I'm going to show you something, and you have to swear to me this stays between us, okay?"

"While I'm incredibly freaked out right now, I can say that I'm probably a better secret holder than Fort Knox. Ask Caid. I've got nearly a thousand of his I've been holding on to," she replied.

"A thousand?" Róisín gave her a sideways glance.

"He was very far from a well-behaved child, then a very non-behaved teen. Don't even get me started on college..." She lifted a shoulder. "My lips are sealed."

"Good." Róisín motioned for Lina to give her one of her hands. "Now give me the hand he touched."

"Who touched? Oh! Munson, that douchebag." Lina held out both hands. When Róisín lifted an eyebrow, she shrugged. "I tried to keep my other hand from him, but he was too quick. I scrubbed them twice in the restroom before I left the coffee shop. I hope it doesn't ruin this, this, whatever it is you're doing."

"Remember to breathe, and don't move." Róisín's tone was firm, but her hold gentle.

"You—you're glowing." Lina sucked a breath in with a squeak. "Oh... oh my god."

The whispered words from the book flowed from Róisín's lips, spreading the magic through her and into Lina. It danced in her veins, unused to be wrapped around the words of spells. Then, the warmth came. Sliding over her, through her, to Lina. Róisín let her eyes sink closed as she herself sunk into the feeling, taking hold of her magic and dancing with it.

"It tingles." Lina wiggled her fingers.

"It's healing," Róisín explained. "Sit still."

"Healing?"

"Sh," Róisín said, finishing the last words. Then, she layered new protections over Lina. Finally, she released Lina's hand and let out a steadying breath.

"What. Was. That?!" Lina blinked rapidly, turning her hands over and back, studying them with wide-eyed curiosity. "That was magic! You know magic!"

"A little." Róisín's voice was small. She tried to appear embarrassed.

"Oh, stop." Lina waved a hand at her. "I'm not going to run out into the street shouting about a pyre or stoning you. This is—damn." She blew out an excited breath and grinned. "Amazing!"

"You're not scared? I'll understand if you don't want to be friends." Róisín bit her lip, waiting for the inevitable.

"What?" She looked up from her hands and frowned at Róisín. "No, oh, no, Róisín, Ro. Did someone? Do I have to go hunt someone down and smack them?"

Róisín carefully closed the book and kept her gaze down at her hands. She tried to keep her body still when Lina reached over the table, took her hands, and squeezed them lightly.

"What happened?"

"Someone I cared for, deeply, found out I knew a little bit of magic, something passed down through my mother's family. They didn't like it. It scared them and made them uncomfortable."

"Well, I guess look at our history, what fear of difference does to people. Not all of us are like that though," she said. "I'm not going anywhere. Cross my heart."

Róisín squeezed her hands back and smiled at her.

"But I will say, be prepared for questions. I have lots of them. For starters, what the hell did that creep do to me? Is he like you?"

"No, he's not like me," Róisín lied. "But when I met him, I felt something inside of him. Like a disease. The same one I feel a bit of in Mr. Smithfield."

"That's rather alarming. Can he pass it on?" Lina made a face and cringed.

"I don't think he knows he's unwell, just as I don't think he can very easily pass it on. I've met so many people in town, and it's only been one other person, which makes it possible it's just a coincidence."

Lina slid the bracelet on again, then held her arm out to admire it. "Is it some kind of sickness detection stone?"

"Sort of..." Róisín sorted out in her head a way not to reveal too much. Guilt needled her over the lies before they'd even been spoken.

"Does Caid know?"

"Caid?" Róisín arched a brow.

She tsked. "Ro, I don't know if you've noticed yet or not, but my brother is over the moon about you. All goo-goo eyes. I get the feeling, given what I've heard in the town rumor mill about his truck being here overnight a few times, and you two being spotted at the diner that you've maybe got a crush on my brother, too. So?"

"No, he doesn't know." She shook her head.

"It'd blow his mind." Lina grinned and chuckled at Róisín's widened eyes. "Don't worry, I won't say a word. That's for you to decide when and how you tell him. If you even want to tell him."

"Thank you."

"I should probably get out of your hair. Thomas comes home today so I need to pester him to help me narrow down the list we made today. Which, I'm sure he'll want me to pass along a thanks for sparing him the full ordeal of it all."

She rose as Lina did, gathering their coffee cups.

"And Ro? I'm dead serious about what I said earlier." When Lina looked at her square on, determination shone in her eyes. "This changes absolutely nothing in our friendship."

Lina neared. She froze when Lina wrapped her arms around her. Then, as relief settled into her bones, she set the cups back onto the table and hugged her back.

"I want you to come over this weekend, for dinner, lunch, something. Then we can paint splotches all over the baby's room walls while I become the most annoying person in the world because I'm indecisive as hell and am currently being faced with too many choices to make."

Róisín laughed, releasing her. "Coin tosses always work when I can't make a decision."

"Oh! Now that's an idea! Perfect." She clapped and did a small dance in celebration. "Just let me know what day works best for you."

When Lina was gone, she moved to the sink to wash the cups, noticing David bounding across the back lawn towards the door. She walked over to the new door, nudging it open for him.

"Where on Earth have you been?"

His ears drooped. "I'm sorry. I know I've been away for a time, but they needed me."

"Who?" She drew her eyes up to the forest edge.

"The spirits of what's left in our wood," David said. "He's getting stronger."

Chapter 26

Lucius's magic reached out across the room. Like a spider, it inched along the arm of the chair she sat in before stopping to watch the beat of the silent tune her fingers tapped out. With opportunity to advance between the taps, he slipped along her thumb, up her arm, then tucked neatly inside her mind.

He took his time, exploring, prodding. He didn't knock on any of the walls he discovered, he pushed or shoved the full force of his power against them. Only polite witches knocked to be let in.

A flicker caught his attention to the right, so Lucius redirected, moving towards it. Before him unfolded a playground scene of a small, red-haired girl. She looked very much like Róisín as the child he remembered all those years ago.

Her unruly curls, the color of a warm mid-autumn day, had been tamed by someone and were braided into pigtails that bounced along as she darted around the slides and swings. Her peals of laughter filled the memory.

"Róisín, your mother is here to pick you up!" A cheery voice called out to her.

Róisín stopped in her tracks, turning to the fence of the playground. A dark-haired, olive-skinned woman stood with one of the teachers at the gated entrance, watching her. A reed thin woman, with hair the color of flame waited on the other side of the gate.

"Come on sweetheart, we need to go get your sister so we can get on the road to Disney!" The red-haired woman waved her over. It was Brenna, but different. Róisín's memory had shifted Brenna's features just enough to make her unrecognizable to anyone who may have known her in life.

"Vacation!" Róisín squealed in delight and raced for the fence.

"Have a wonderful time, Róisín. We'll be excited to hear of your adventure when you come back." The teacher smiled at her before swinging open the gate.

Lucius pulled his magic from her mind, and his lips curled into a proud smile. Smoothing the front of his sweater, he said, "Disneyland and a sister."

Róisín looked up from the book she'd read in front of the fireplace in his study.

"You have done amazing with your practice." The pride he felt toward her warmed him like a hug, making his heart sing. "Not one wall flinched as I pounded along them, and your created false memory was flawless. Were you able to feel any of it?"

She shook her head. "It wasn't until you were close to that memory that I felt your prodding there. So far, every time Madigan has reached for my mind, there's been a brushing sensation, sort of like fingers stroking before he makes contact." She shivered and wrapped her arms around herself.

"He most likely hasn't needed to be secretive in the years since he received Bernard's magic. Didn't need to hone it because humans can't sense that invasion as we can. However..." He rose from the desk to sit in the chair on the other side of the fireplace. "This does not mean we have the affordability of growing lax."

"I have no desire in doing that," she said.

"I know you don't. You've made it very clear through all your training with us that you're not giving even an inch of space. You've always been steadfast and dedicated. I see something new in you. A light and a strength that hadn't been there before."

She closed the book and set it on the table between them, then looked from him to the fire. "David has returned. He said that Madigan gained more power. We spent the day yesterday in the forest, but it hasn't changed much. Still that slow leeching of life. There is no one sick in town, no recent deaths. Where could it be coming from?"

"What about the nearby towns?"

"They're still untouched. Could he be—" She swallowed audibly. "Is there spell work that can make him stronger?"

"The only place it truly has a stronghold over our magic is in warding, which is why we use it for such a thing. We only gain more power when we inherit that power. Or"—his features hardened—"when that power is taken."

"If he's focusing on getting stronger quicker…" She wiped her palms on her leggings. "Our time… it's running out, isn't it?"

He rested his elbows on the armrests of the chair, then steepled his hands before him. He tapped his index fingers against his chin. "We need to come together to get things into place. I think you're right."

"Does he still have any access to Aunellion?"

"Once he severed the connection with all of us, he disowned his Coven's realm. The Goddess immediately set a lock into place, and there is absolutely nothing and no one that can get to Aunellion. If by some miracle of the Goddess they can, they're unable to leave."

"Even Madigan?"

"Are you thinking that he found a way? That this may be where he is gaining his power from?"

Róisín nodded. "All that power can't all be from Greens Glen. It must be coming from other places too."

"This may risk my life in the afterworld should the Goddess or the Sisters overhear what I am about to say." He leaned forward, voice dropping low. "It is possible. I'd like to hold faith that what they did is enough, but we also believed that our connection to our own Coven members was un-severable. And here we are. And with all our recent discoveries, I'm liable to believe that anything is possible."

Róisín shifted in her chair, pressing her lips together. If he had been able to shield her from Aoife, able to shield her from this ordeal, he would without hesitation. They were all caught in this line of precariously stacked dominoes. Their steps needed to move in a certain direction, or they would all be damned to the deepest of their Hells. Where the true monsters were.

Lucius studied her. She twisted a lock of hair around her index finger, her eyes downcast while she chewed on her bottom lip. "Clarissa once told me that you would be a force to reckon with. That you would forge a new path for all of us. I can't help but wonder if she knew what was to come, if she knew why Brenna left us, or the secrets, the burdens we all carry, handed to us from the Sisters."

Róisín rose and moved toward the fire, holding her hands out for the heat of the flames to warm them. "I'm going to do my best to make sure these burdens of ours, of mine, are only entries in our history books for the witches of our future and not the end of us."

Lucius stood and joined her. "The Goddess and Sisters chose wisely. I can think of no better witch to lead us through this." He lifted an arm around her shoulders and brought her against his side, pressing a kiss to the top of her head.

"I wouldn't be here without you, or Matthew, or Clarissa," she said. "You've always been there for me. After my mother... It was what grounded me. Knowing I had you."

His hand rubbed her upper arm, then squeezed her shoulder lightly. "You've always been loved like you were one of our own."

Lifting her arms, she wound them around his waist. "I love you, Lucius."

"I love you, too, sweetheart." He rested his chin atop her head and closed his eyes, soaking in the moment, pushing away those dark edges of worry that pressed in. They'd be okay. They had to be.

CHAPTER 27

MATTHEW stalked down the halls of Lucius's spacious home atop the Cascade Mountain range in Ely. He paused only a moment at the doors to the study before pushing in.

"How much longer is this shit show going to go on?" he demanded of Lucius.

Looking up from his notes, Lucius nudged his glasses back up the bridge of his nose, then slowly lifted his eyebrows.

"It's only a matter of time before the other Covens figure out that we're working directly to help her. Then what?" He threw his arms out wide. "A war between the Covens while we're trying to deal with that jackass?"

Lucius motioned to the chair across his desk, and Matthew dropped heavily into it. "As long as we each stay in our separate realms, we're fine, Matthew."

"How can you be so sure?" His palms slapped against the wooden armrests with a loud crack.

"To the Covens, Nanette, Shasta and I remaining apart in our realms gives the appearance that we're doing as the other Covens are, researching. Perhaps passing information along to be noted about Madigan that may help Róisín." He waved a dismissive hand. "They don't know, and will not know that we are doing far more than that. There will be no trials for treason, no will there be a war between the Covens. Our tracks are more than covered."

Matthew shifted in his seat, rubbing a hand over his face. "It's bullshit."

"And I agree." He nodded. "I've had a growing suspicion of the line within the council, and the discord among the Covens, but many, many investigations uncovered no burden of proof to bring to a judgment."

"You've certainly got it now," he muttered.

"I will certainly handle it," Lucius said. "However, the most important thing for us to focus on is that we have Madigan's location right now. Despite her growing power, he still doesn't suspect Róisín of being more than a hedgewitch, and he thinks nothing of it if he isn't leaving. We act now against the Covens and the leaders of those Covens, we can tip our hand in their favor, then what? Madigan obviously had connections, look at what we discovered about Aoife. It is absolutely no secret about her closeness with Mildred."

"Do you think Mildred?"

"I'm not sure," Lucius replied with a sigh. "I have a few from our Coven, and a few from Nanette's looking into it. So far, it has all been dead ends."

"We've only got so much time," Matthew bit out. "We need to get our shit together so we're ready and can actually do something. What have we accomplished? You've got me sitting in a library with Nanette's granddaughter, reading dead language books that are as helpful as a child's coloring book right now. There's got to be something more."

He hadn't minded the time spent with Lily Wallingsford. Something simmered there just under the surface when he was near her. But, there had been too much wasted time, idle time. The last time helplessness had gripped his body and mind in the way it had at that moment was when his mother was sick. Róisín wasn't sick, but she was in danger. She was in the center of the ring, and they were all watching from the stands. He couldn't lose Róisín. She and Lucius were all he had left. Time pressed desperately at him, and anger had begun to build below his skin's surface at the lack of action on their parts.

"I know, son, I know. At the same time, we must tread carefully because what good are we to her if we get found out?"

Matthew sat back in the chair, looking around the study. Their Coven's entire history lined three of the walls, floor-to-ceiling in books. They'd spent hours upon hours thumbing through them, taking notes, desperate for any guidance from their ancestors. "The friend knows about her magic."

Lucius stopped his writing and looked up.

"She's passed it off as, what'd you call it? A *hedgewitch*," he said with a smirk.

"And?"

"She said that the friend didn't bat a lash." He shrugged. He brought his gaze from the windows that overlooked the sprawling city of Cascadia before them to Lucius. "It's hard to put my finger on it, but it's changed something in her. I think another human knowing and not dismissing her has helped her heal. At least some, anyway."

"Is she and this friend?"

"No. It's a platonic thing, nothing more."

"She's carrying herself with more surety and confidence. I venture to say more than she ever has before. Shasta has concerns about her mental wellbeing with the burdens each new door unlocks to her Coven's past."

"I think we should encourage her to tell the carpenter. And by tell, I mean everything. Not just what she's told Lina," Matthew said.

"Is that wise?"

He lifted his hands, palms up and shrugged. "Fuck if I know, to be honest. She needs support there though. If we can't all be there physically without tipping Madigan off because he would recognize you, Shasta, or Nanette... She needs someone in her corner. And I know she won't risk her friend by telling her everything because she's pregnant. That's too much to ask Róisín to consider."

"Tell me about this carpenter." He rose and moved around the desk to sit in the empty chair next to Matthew.

"His name is Kincaid McGrath, he's the brother of the friend."

"Is this information you're going to divulge coming as that of a brother or that of a jealous ex-lover?"

Matthew's gaze darkened. "We slept together once. We were drunk as hell, and it was a moment of weakness for both of us, right after Alexandria had left her and Heather decided she wanted to be with other people. You forget that neither of us spoke to each other or came near each other for a decade after because we were both embarrassed by what happened."

"It doesn't cloud your judgment?"

"If I'd known this would lead to you grilling me about the biggest regret of my life because I lost my best friend in the process, I'd have gone to Nanette or Shasta."

"You didn't lose her, son."

"I did. We've made our way back to being friends after it, but it'll never be the bond we had before."

Lucius was quiet, his head tilted slightly, studying Matthew. "All right. I trust your judgment about this, do you feel this young man would harm Róisín?"

"No, I don't believe so." He wanted to squirm under the way Lucius stared at him, like he'd caught him slipping the good bourbon from the back of the cabinet when he knew it was forbidden. "I didn't pry. I never do that without consent because I'm shit at it, and I want people to know I'll be in there stumbling around so they're not alarmed. His mind remains untouched."

"Okay then. I'll send word to Nanette and Shasta, and then we'll discuss it with Róisín."

Matthew stood. "I'll go stalk around the Alleyette Library, make it look like our Coven's lacked any progress on this."

Lucius gripped his hand, shaking it, then pulled him into a one-armed hug. "Keep an ear open, see if you can pick anything up that might help us."

Matthew let out a grunt, then crossed the room to the massive oak doors. He reached for the doorknob and turned back to Lucius. "We'll be ready for him, dad. We'll beat him."

"Keep a tight hold on that hope, son. Don't let it go."

He wouldn't. For Róisín. For their Covens. For all of witchkind.

Chapter 28

R ÓISÍN carefully stepped over a root along the pathway, her elemental magic guiding her, allowing her to keep her gaze on the canopy the firs and pines created overhead as they stretched toward the sky. Their deep greens mixed with the lighter greens of the birch and oak leaves.

"It's so luscious and green," she said. So different from what'd she come to see in town.

"Because it hasn't been spoiled by that shit coming out of Munson's factory," Caid said from where he trailed behind her.

That morning, as they'd laid in his bed, he told her there was somewhere he wanted to take her, somewhere he wanted her to see. He wouldn't divulge any specific details, but by the way his face had shifted, more open and soft, as he gave her small nuggets of information, she could sense it was special. Then he had packed a hiking backpack and her curiosity piqued.

When he'd driven them two hours out of town, and she'd dropped most of her shield, she could feel his excited energy pulsating from him. The one thing she hated most about the need to ward her power was how it dulled her senses, making it harder for her to sense the energy that people carried with them.

Nearly an hour into their hike, she didn't care if it was just an out and back loop of nature. She relished the vibration of life around her, the trees, the birds, the animals that skittered to safety as they carefully traversed the narrow path upward. The trees, the flowers, the rich scent of earth. The further they went she could hear water trickling from various streams around them.

Her soul was full in a way it hadn't been in months.

"It's just up ahead here, on your left," Caid said.

A few minutes later, they came to a clearing with a pond. Wildflowers bloomed in an array of colors around the edges, a beach of small pebbles at one end. Stepping closer to the water's edge, she closed her eyes and inhaled.

"This is amazing." She whispered it, afraid to disturb the birds and critters she felt around them. She opened her eyes and glanced at Caid.

"Isn't it?" He grinned at her like a child showing her their new, shiny toy.

Understanding dawned on her. "You come here a lot."

"I try to," he said. "Especially as of late. The fresh air, that clean smell. It's like plugging me into a charger if that makes any sense."

If you only knew how much it did. "Can we swim?"

"Why do you think I told you to put on a suit when we stopped by your place?" He unclasped the chest buckle of the backpack. It dropped from his shoulders with a thud, then he pulled off his t-shirt.

For a moment, her mind blanked. The muscles of his arms, chest, and back flexed, and he shucked off his boots, then socks, followed by his pants. Gathering herself, she scrambled to catch up, stripping off her shorts and tank top.

"Last one in buys lunch," he called over his shoulder, darting toward the water.

She chased after him, trying to strip off her own clothing quickly. "But you packed one!"

The icy chill of the water sent her yelping when her body collided with it. Unfazed, Caid jumped in, head disappearing beneath the surface.

When his head popped back up, she said, "You've lost your mind." Hands clasped together, she inched into the water. Every muscle in her body clenched as she tried not to shiver. "It's f-f-freezing."

"Once you're in for a bit, it'll be fine." He beckoned her closer with a wave of his hand. "The slower you go, the worse it feels."

"I'm building up to it," she mumbled. Then she remembered her latest lesson with Shasta and tapped into some of her great-grandmother's elemental magic, feeling a warmth spread from head to toe inside. On a sigh, she dipped under the water.

"See? Not so bad," he said when she came back up.

She let herself become buoyant, and floated on her back, staring up at the blue sky framed by the tops of the trees surrounding the clearing.

"It's something else, isn't it?" he asked quietly.

"It's perfect," she whispered.

"I've seen how much you wander out to the woods behind your house." His voice was at her ear now, so she pulled her feet under her body and kicked her legs to keep her afloat, using her arms to maneuver herself to face him. "You look so upset when you go out, but you're always sort of glowing when you come back. I've wanted to bring you out here for a while now." His cheeks darkened with a blush.

She felt her own cheeks warm. "Thank you. I really needed this."

His arms came around her waist, drawing her closer. "How about this?" He kissed her lightly.

"Mm, not sure." Her lips slid into a smirk. Tipping her head back, she watched as a Bald Eagle flew over them.

Caid trailed his tongue up the column of her exposed neck, then kissed down to where it met her shoulder, giving her a gentle bite there.

She couldn't hold back the soft sigh that escaped her lips.

"Or this." He dipped his head to where the top of her breasts peeked over the water, licking there.

She wrapped her legs around his waist and arched back.

"Maybe this." He took one of her nipples into his mouth, sucking gently.

She let out a small whimper of pleasure, her hands digging into his hair. "Still not sure." The breathlessness of her voice exposed her lie.

Caid brought a hand between them, knuckles grazing over her stomach, making the muscles there ripple and quiver in anticipation.

Nudging her bathing suit bottoms aside, he then stroked a finger along her seam, and she rolled her hips into him.

"Maybe..." She brought her head forward to look at him.

"Oh? Just maybe?" Mischief glinted in his eyes.

"Mmhmm." She bit her bottom lip. "Maybe."

When he took her mouth with his, he pressed a finger into her, pushing deep and swallowing her moan of pleasure. He slid a second in and began a steady pace of stroking his fingers in and out, while his tongue sought out hers.

The pace was leisurely until she tightened her legs around his waist, and her mouth filled his with her little mewling noises and pants as her ecstasy rose. She rocked against his hand, desperate for release to fill her. Her skin grew tighter, her breasts heavy. When the orgasm shook through her, she broke away from the kiss, crying out wildly, sending birds scattering as though a shot had fired.

She murmured his name over and over as he pressed kisses along her throat, shoulders, then her chest, before he slipped his fingers out and wrapped his arms around her.

"Are you hungry?"

"Let's just float here a bit." She turned in his arms so that her back pressed against his chest. "Let the feeling come back to my body."

His laugh rumbled through her as he tightened his arms around her and let the water hold them.

She had never been so full of that warmth one could only feel on a cloudless summer day. It radiated through her, setting her every fiber alight. As she dropped her head back against his shoulder, she could only think of one word that could describe it. *Glorious.*

Chapter 29

THE sun slowly dipped down behind the hilly terrain when Róisín and Caid had finally begun their descent.

Róisín would've stayed for days, letting the life around them charge her, fill her. She didn't lie to him when she'd said she wanted to lay down for a bit on the blanket he'd brought. However, she also just wanted to sit with the peace, the quiet, the life. Feel the creatures' heartbeats race as they moved through the forest. Hear the trees whisper to one another in the gentle breeze. Things that were so silenced in Greens Glen, it smothered her.

She was grateful for the time they had to prepare, to take all the steps they would need when the time came to face Madigan. They needed every second they were given. The expanse of time had her on edge though, and it didn't feel right.

They neared the narrowing midway of the path down, and Róisín edged closer to the hilly side, giving herself space from the drop off several feet on the other side.

"How did you find this place?"

"A school field trip, believe it or not," he replied. "Our gym teacher bet us all lunch and ten bucks that we couldn't make it to the clearing at the top."

She knew that tone well. She'd first heard it in Matthew when they were much younger and had heard it in several others over her years. The tone of someone just itching to prove a naysayer wrong.

"Something tells me." She paused so she could focus on her steps down a steeper section. "That just making it to the top wasn't enough for you."

"Oh, hell no." He chuckled deeply. "Not even close. Wyatt, and our friend Max, we made a bet among ourselves on who would be the first. Winner got a thirty rack."

"Thirty rack?" she asked.

"Thirty pack of beer."

She stopped and turned to him. "How old were you?"

His immediate response had been to lift a brow. "Oh, you're completely serious," he said. "Let me guess, you were one of the good kids in school, never partied or drank underage, all that jazz?"

These were the conversations with humans that were the hardest for her. Even her mother was smooth and quick with the lies to keep their identities hidden. Brenna, the most kindhearted person Róisín had ever known, could throw lies out like candy at a parade when she needed to keep them safe.

"I, uh, was more focused on my studies. I knew we didn't have the money for a good university, so I had to rely on my grades." She turned and started moving again, hoping he would follow and not ask her more questions.

"I guess that makes sense."

She let the silence fall over them again, soaking in the last steps of this haven before they had to return to their reality of the dying woods and poisoned waters.

Finally, curiosity got the best of her. "Who won?"

"No one had a chance in hell against me." His response was quick, and proud. "Between being on the soccer and basketball teams, and a sprinter for track, I had the legs for it."

"But you shared your thirty rack," she said.

"Of course, I did," he replied as though there were no other options to consider. "That's what best friends do."

The ground by her left foot shifted, sending rocks spraying down the steep drop off. She slapped her right hand against the large boulder, grasping for purchase. Her feet slipping on the skittering gravel.

Caid lurched forward to catch her.

More gravel fell away, the ground sweeping out from under them.

"Caid!"

"Hold onto me!"

They tumbled, and one of his arms banded around her waist, the other reached for something to grab hold of and his heels tried to dig into the ground for purchase.

You can save each other, her magic seemed to speak to her.

She fought the urge to shake her head. Her magic was not meant for human or witch life.

The rocks tumbling with them dug into her side and one of her legs, making her grit her teeth to bite back another scream.

They slammed onto the ground, coming to a bone jarring stop. Nearly twenty feet from where they'd stood, just off the pathway they'd been looping around to.

Caid moved to stand them up and hissed out a sharp breath.

"Are you okay?" She wasn't sure if her voice shook on its own, or if the way her body felt as though it were violently shaking caused her voice to be unsteady.

"I'm less worried about me, and more worried about you." He turned to face her, but he took a step and gingerly set his right foot down, his face contorted with pain.

"Sit down." She pointed the indent their bodies had left in the soft dirt of the slope. "Let me look."

"I'm fine, I just twisted it funny," he ground out.

"Caid." She huffed out a breath. "Please? We made it down here in one piece because of you, let me just look. Then we can hobble you back to your truck, get it up and put some ice on it."

He carefully took his boot off and rubbed his ankle, wincing as he did so.

She put her hands on her hips, chewing on the inside of her cheek to keep from snapping at him. It was then that she noticed the river of blood running down the back of her own right leg and the deep gash that ran the length of her thigh. Closing her eyes, she drew in a steadying breath. It was not the ideal time to pass out.

"All right," he said. "But I'm telling you, it's just rolled. I need to walk it off."

Róisín kneeled before he caught sight of her leg and gently placed her hands on his calf, then moved them downward to his ankle and his foot. Her life magic traced along his skin, diving deeper through the tendons and ligaments down to the bone. Through it, she could feel the jagged edges of fractures. The biggest being at his ankle; it was shattered.

When she looked up at him, his eyes were closed and face twisted from the pain he was trying to hide where he leaned against the dirt.

There was no way she could get them both the rest of the way, and with the state of his ankle, it'd cause him more harm. Her choice was easy to make despite the consequences. Even if her feelings for him hadn't grown deeper over their time together, there was no question what she should do. She let her magic rise, let the power fill her hands, and she worked to heal the broken places. It took effort to keep the heat from her hands so that he wouldn't question it.

"I guess you're right." She stood when she finished. "Just feels a bit swollen."

He opened his eyes, first blinking up at the sky, then shifting his attention to her. His eyes narrowed. "Holy shit, Róisín, your leg."

"It's fine," she mirrored his defensive tone. "It looks worse than it is. Just needs to be washed."

He went to his knees so that he was eye level with her thigh. "It needs more than that, Róisín. It needs stitches. We need to get you down the hill and to a hospital."

"I'll be fi—" She swayed. The loss of blood and use of her magic caused her energy to wane. "Fine."

He rose to his feet, testing the weight on his ankle. Before he could scoop her into his arms, she blinked her eyes rapidly, her body swaying again, almost causing her to collapse, but he managed to catch her.

"Put me down, you'll hurt your ankle more," she said hoarsely.

"I'm not quite sure I like this game of who can be more stubborn." His tone was sharp.

"I'm not being stubborn, you are." Her voice grew faint, and her eyes fluttered closed.

"Róisín." He squeezed her. "Stay with me."

She mumbled something incoherently, then passed out.

CHAPTER 30

T HE world around Caid tipped, blurring out of focus. The air felt heavy and his heart squeezed so tightly he had to fight to stay upright. He held Róisín's limp body in his shaking arms against his aching chest. He wanted to sprint the rest of the way to his truck, but between his ankle and not wanting to jar her because of her own injury, he had to settle for walking as briskly as he could. The sun was still just at the top of the mountain range to his left, indicating that he still had day left.

He wished now he hadn't left his phone in his truck and instead had placed it in his pocket like he did when he came out alone. But he was selfish, wanting the day with her, uninterrupted. He wanted to soak in every reaction from her the further they hiked, when she came to the clearing. Now, he cursed himself for being selfish.

"Róisín." He fought to keep his voice calm.

Her head lolled to the side, her lips as colorless as her face.

How much blood had she lost already?

He struggled to recall from the moment they'd fallen to the moment they stopped. The way she was up quickly, moving to the side. Moving like she'd known she was hurt, but didn't want him to know.

A quiet, dark anger built inside of him, and he wanted to shake her awake so that he could ask her why. He should be the one taking care of her, his own injury be damned.

Instead, he ground his teeth together and focused on getting her down to the parking lot where he could call for help.

"Oh my goodness." Another hiker gasped when Caid had stepped off the trail, which felt like an eternity later, and into the parking lot. He was sure they made quite a sight, feeling the way her blood was sticky on his arms, and at the edge of his sight, seeing the stains of it on his shirt from carrying her. "Is she okay?"

"Call 9-1-1, please." He struggled to get the words out, dropping to his knees still clutching Róisín to his chest.

The hiker pulled their phone from a vest pocket and dialed. A moment later, they appeared at his side, kneeling next to him.

"They're on their way," they said, moments later, reaching out to put a reassuring hand on his shoulder.

"Thank you," he managed. The edges of his vision were blurred. His lungs squeezed tightly as though they were being crushed in his chest. Carefully, he laid her on the grass, and tried to gather himself as he dug through his pack, pulling out the blanket. He paused for a moment, thinking about how just moments ago her eyes were alight with mischief as she trailed kisses over his bare chest. Shaking it away, he balled it up and leaned forward to press it against her leg.

"May I?" the hiker motioned to her leg. "I used to be a guide, so I have some basic first aid experience."

He nodded, not trusting his voice anymore.

"The name's Tim," the hiker said. He placed steady hands on the one spot on Róisín's leg that was bare of blood, and gently shifted it to reveal the gash. Then he took the blanket from Caid. "May I?"

It took Caid a moment to bring himself back to awareness, panic having given way to fear. Clearing his throat, he brought his eyes from her leg to Tim. "Pardon?"

Tim lifted the blanket and made a tearing motion with his hands. "For strips, may I?"

Caid nodded. "I'm Caid, and this is Róisín."

Tim smiled at Caid. "My late wife was a Rose as well." He took a strip of blanket and tied it tightly around Róisín's leg just above the wound.

Caid's brow furrowed.

"Róisín, it's Gaelic, means rose," he offered.

Caid could only blink in response.

"Was it an animal?" Tim asked.

"No, we um, we slid off the edge about halfway down the pass. Near Eagle's Rock," he added.

The wailing sound of sirens grew in the distance. The weight of worry fell from him, and he took a breath, the air filling his lungs to capacity.

Tim sat back on his heels and exhaled. "I'm going to give it to you straight, kiddo, this is more than a bandaid, or even stitches. But this," he nodded at the tied blanket, "will slow the bleeding."

Before Caid could give his thanks to him, he saw the Emergency Medical technicians rushing toward them.

For the next twenty minutes, Caid felt like he was stuck in quicksand, helpless and being swallowed deeper with every breath he managed. He struggled to explain to the techs what had happened.

A vibration, almost like a shaking, began to build inside as two techs slipped on medical gloves to look at her leg, then bandaged it tightly. One checked her vitals, while the other made sure her body was secured on a board to move her to the waiting stretcher.

"Sir?" One of them waved a hand in his face. "Sir?"

Caid snapped back into himself, blinking some of the fog away.

"We need you to come with us so we can get an x-ray on your ankle," she said, pointing to the swollen joint. "You're her partner?"

He nodded.

"Okay." She offered a smile. "Let's get you loaded. If there's anyone that you need to reach, we can help you get that taken care of when we get to the hospital."

He nodded again, letting her lead him to the back of the ambulance where the other technician frantically worked to connect Róisín to a heart monitor and get fluids into her. When he lowered himself onto the hard bench inside, he kept his focus on Róisín's face, willing her to be okay, to wake up, and let the sounds around him fade.

If she woke up. He shook his head. She would wake up. When she did, he wouldn't waste a minute with her. It had only been a few weeks, but there was no denying how he felt, and he needed her to know too.

Chapter 31

THE disinfectant clean drowned Róisín's senses, and she opened her eyes. She blinked and her focus cleared on the stark white room, the machines beeping and chirping to the right of her, the rolling tray table to her left. The more her body and mind awoke, so did a burning feeling inside her body.

Then she remembered everything. The fall, healing Caid, collapsing after from using her magic, and how much blood she'd lost. Things became spotty after that. Echoes of new voices, the peal of a siren from somewhere overhead, hurried conversation.

Blood.

They'd given her a transfusion. She remembered trying to stop them. Her body wouldn't cooperate. Her mouth had refused to work for her, as did her limbs which remained limp at her sides as they had moved around her in the operating room.

My shield! There was no way she could draw it around herself. Not when her magic burned and scoured the new blood that greeted it. Working like a safety checkpoint, removing any threat, and it wouldn't quiet until it knew that the blood from the transfusion was safe for her.

The act would make her a beacon, the power it expelled was potent. If there was ever a way to tip off Madigan of her power, it would be this moment. She wished she could call for Shasta, or Matthew, but there was nothing she could do until it was done.

Now she was stuck in a hospital somewhere, powerless, vulnerable. Tears built and she lifted a shaking hand to press her eyes closed before they could spill over.

The soft rustle punctuated by a creak and groan drew her attention toward the corner of the room. As Caid's large frame shifted, the chair he was asleep in groaned again. His arms were crossed over his chest, lines bracketing his mouth from the pinched way he held his lips in sleep.

He was still in the t-shirt and shorts he'd worn on their hike down the trail, only now, both were stained a deep red-brown from blood. Her blood.

"Caid." Her voice was hoarse and rough from disuse.

He snapped upright, eyes wide on her. "You're awake."

"How..." She looked to the window, then the door. "How long have I been here?"

"Just a day. They had to repair the artery in your leg and give you blood."

Despite how far away from her bed that he sat, she could see every hour that passed etched on his face, the worry, the fear.

"How's your ankle?"

"Just a light sprain." He leaned forward in the seat, placing his elbows on his knees.

She chewed on her bottom lip, studying him still. "I'm okay," she said finally.

That was all it took to break him from the fog that held him. He shoved to his feet and pushed a hand through his hair, shaking his head. "You very easily could not have been, Róisín. Shit. They said just in time, *just in time*," he stressed, his voice strained. "Between how much blood you'd lost and the artery in your leg getting cut open. Why? Why didn't you say anything?"

At that moment she could've opened up to him and been honest. She would have healed fast on her own. She'd hoped her wound wasn't that deep so that she could get home and quietly heal. It was her chance.

"Your ankle," she said instead.

"Fuck my ankle!" He nearly shouted the words, making her flinch.

The burning of her magic moving through the blood quieted at the shock of his outburst. He'd always been so even tempered, even the day they'd posted Lina's signs and she had made the joke about lefts. She ran her hands through her hair, before bringing them to her lap, twisting them together.

"Even if I broke it, I would've lived." He spoke the words through clenched teeth. His body was stiff, but his chest heaved with his harsh breaths. "Could it have been worse getting to my truck? Sure"—he slapped one of his hands against his chest—"it's a risk I would've gladly taken at that moment. I'd risk never being able to use my damned foot again if it meant saving you."

"Um, I'll come back," Lina said from the doorway, glancing nervously between them.

"No, you stay. I need air." He didn't look at either of them as he pushed past Lina.

"Is everything okay? Is he okay? Are you going to be okay?" Lina slowly came into the room, letting the door close behind her.

"I don't know, I don't know, and I think so," Róisín answered.

Lina studied her from the foot of her bed. "Are you sure you're good?"

"Depends on which part of me it is that you're asking about," she replied honestly.

"Let's start with your leg." She rounded the bed to sit on the edge of the mattress.

"It hurts like heck, and it's stiff. I don't know if it's from being bandaged so tightly, or from cutting it open."

"You can feel everything?"

"Screaming at me like an alarm clock on a morning that I'd rather stay in bed."

"Can you?" She wiggled her fingers. "You know?"

"I can't, no." She shook her head. "I can only do small things like paper cuts if I really tried."

"No magic herbs or anything?"

Róisín's brows rose. It was still foreign to her to have someone in her life that wasn't a witch know who she was and accept it. Lina may not know just how much magic Róisín had, but she knew she had it, and it didn't bother her.

"What about"—Lina nodded her head toward the door—"your heart?"

"I don't really know. He's so angry at me." Her chin trembled and she pulled her bottom lip between her teeth trying to stop it. Her heart thundered in her chest and a tightness began to squeeze around her middle. What would her decision do, what would this moment do to change things between her and Caid?

"He's a stubborn ass, but he'll be fine. Trust me. I've known him for thirty-five years. He just needs to blow off some of that steam. He'll be back to that quiet, broody Caid we all know and love."

Róisín looked down at her hands, wringing them together. She had tried to convince herself that she had used her magic only to help him because it was the only way for them to get off the mountain. Which was a lie.

She loved him, and it terrified her. In her life, love had never meant sunshine, or rainbows. With Aoife, love had been weaponized. Her mother's love had been full of secrets. Alexandria's love had been fear. Fear of Róisín.

That was the one that left Róisín on edge. Caid was human. She had been here before and knew how it ended. Would loving Caid be different? She didn't know how much longer she could hold onto her heart before he had it completely in his hands and held that power over her as others had before.

"Is there anyone you need here for you?" Lina asked.

"It's just me." Her shoulders rounded as she brought herself inward. The fire inside of her was burning stronger. Sweat gathered along her back and neck.

"No friends? That guy that was here visiting for a bit?"

"I can't bug Matthew. He's on a big work project right now in a different country."

The soft rustle of the bedding indicated Lina had moved closer. "Ro."

When Róisín lifted her head, Lina's eyes widened. "What's wrong? Do you need the nurse?"

"No." She clenched her jaw to fight the grimace of pain. "I'm okay."

"Are you sure?" She leaned toward the button to the nurses' station at the side of the bed.

"It's just that the—oh, Goddess that hurts now." She gasped, eyes widening before she squeezed them shut. Tears spilled over her cheeks. She blinked quickly, over and over, trying desperately to clear them. "They gave me a blood transfusion, and it's not—" Her breath grew ragged with each word. "It's not like mine."

Lina gasped, covering her mouth too late to stifle the sound. "This is bad, this is so, so bad. What can I do?"

"There's nothing anyone can do. I just need to—" She let out a sorrowful moan and doubled over. "I need to let my body adapt to it."

"Jesus, Róisín, you're soaked." Lina rose and pulled back the sheets. "Let me get you a cool cloth, see if it will help any."

Róisín thrashed and rolled onto her side, drawing her knees into her chest the best she could given the bandage secured tightly to her right leg.

"Here." Lina carefully sat behind her. "Roll back over if you can."

With her teeth still clenched, she panted, her eyes screwed shut, and tried to roll to her back as smoothly as possible. The cold cloth Lina pat across her face, neck, and chest was a balm against the heat inside.

"Caid," Róisín struggled. "He can't, he doesn't know."

"I'll lock the door in just a second. We need to get you breathing through it." Lina's voice and touch soothed her. She put the cloth in the pitcher of water she had filled from the bathroom, wrung it out, then patted it over Róisín's exposed skin again.

Róisín moaned, bracing her body against the pain, then bit out a chain of curses.

Lina paused her movements.

"What?" Róisín asked.

"I think that—" She blinked. "I think that's the first time I have ever heard you swear."

"My mother, she never said a curse in her entire life. Her best friend was the same way. I guess I just—" Róisín gasped, rolling back onto her side, clutching her middle. "Subconsciously picked up the habit."

"Caid told me once that swearing makes it hurt less," Lina said. "He wasn't wrong. I say either fuck or shit anytime I stub my toe, whack my elbow against something, bump my knee. The hurt never stays long."

"I don't think there's enough swears for this," Róisín panted.

"How much longer?"

"If it hurts like this right now..." The wave of fire burned through her. She caught her breath and finished. "I hope that it means not much."

"Okay." Lina picked up the cloth. "I'm right here. You don't have to do this alone."

CHAPTER 32

Caid's hand hovered over the handle at Róisín's door. Once his anger and fear had receded back into the depths, guilt had replaced it. His harsh words and shouting at her, that wasn't what she needed right now. He moved to grip the handle, stopping when he heard Lina laugh loudly.

"Oh, no, no, it gets better," Lina exclaimed. "He didn't go forward, somehow the truck got stuck in reverse and he backed right through Mrs. Daily's fence, through her rose bushes."

He nudged open the door and leaned against the frame, looking from his sister to Róisín. She wore a different hospital gown than when he left, and he quirked a brow.

Lina followed his line of sight and flicked her gaze to Róisín. "The nurse came while you were out for *air* and helped with a shower."

Róisín smiled at Lina and squeezed her hand.

Caid had no one to blame but himself. He'd deserved her shutting him out when he snapped at her and stormed out.

"Do you feel better?" Lina asked, pinning him in the doorway with a look only a sibling would dare. When he didn't respond, she stood, nodding. "Good. Now, I'm going to make myself useful by grabbing good food, while Caid here grovels and begs forgiveness for being a jerk."

Róisín's eyes widened. "It's okay. He has a right to his feelings."

"He is also standing right here," Caid said.

"He"—Lina stopped in front of him and narrowed her eyes—"is a jerk and doesn't deserve the recognition of standing right here. But!" she exclaimed. "That's just my opinion after decades of being at the receiving end of that very, very stubborn brotherly love."

He narrowed his eyes at the hidden intention behind her statement.

"I need to make a few phone calls, see if I can persuade a few voting holdouts to actually vote for a change. Bill and the sleazeball have taken a business trip to California, so hopefully I can get that to swing in my favor. It's weird they left at such an important time." She turned to Róisín and waved. "I'll be back with a loaded ham sammy, Ro!" She drifted out of the room and down the hall.

"I'm sorry," he said from where he stood in the doorway

"Caid." Róisín shook her head.

"Róisín." He dropped his chin to his chest, shoulders slumping. "Don't, please don't."

He heard the rustle of the bed and looked up, seeing she'd moved to the edge, her legs dangling over the side. The hospital gown was short enough to reveal the bandage on her thigh, stark white against her tanned legs. His throat worked as he swallowed the lump lodged there.

"I can't be sorry about getting angry when I realized you hid your injury," he confessed. "I can be sorry about how I handled it. I shouldn't have snapped at you. There's no excuse for it. Even being stubborn, as my sister has so graciously pointed out, it's not an excuse. I just, shit, there was so much blood. Then you just..." His hands fell to his sides. "Dropped. There was a hiker at the trailhead when I got there. He was a guide once I guess. He helped until the ambulance came. Thank God because I just froze and couldn't manage fuck all."

"Caid," she said, her voice faint. "I'm sorry. I froze, then I panicked. You were hurt, and I knew I wouldn't be able to get you down myself. When I saw the cuts on my leg, they just looked like scratches from the rocks. I said I was fine because I thought I was fine."

His gaze trailed over her, noting that the color had returned to her cheeks and her eyes were clearer.

"Come here, please." She pat the bed next to her.

He hesitated for a moment before crossing to her. He had to fight down the urge to pick her up, take her in his arms, and hold her tight. Instead, he slowly lowered himself next to her, careful not to cause the thin mattress to shift and jostle her.

Róisín brought a hand to cup his cheek. She turned his head to face her. "Let's never do that again, okay? Any of it."

Closing his eyes, he let himself lean into her touch for a moment. He pressed a kiss to her palm first before he brushed his lips over hers. "I'd be more than okay with that." He laid his forehead against hers.

"Will you bring me home?"

"Can you go yet?"

"The nurse said the doctor would be in this afternoon. If everything looks okay, I can leave."

He laced their fingers together, his thumb brushing hers. "Is there anything you need for home to help?"

"They showed me how to clean, prep, and re-bandage it just before you got back. That's all that I need to do until it's time for the staples to come out. I'll need to come back here for that."

He braced himself in time to hide the cringe from the image of her lying on a table in the operating room, being stapled back together the same way that he stapled water barriers in place on the outside of houses he built.

"I can do that," he said. "Anything else?"

She gave him a small smile. "Another kiss wouldn't hurt."

CHAPTER 33

S HASTA paused at the road, taking in the old farmhouse with an amused smile. Róisín had always held an affinity for old things. She'd told Shasta once that it was because they were already there, established and sure.

She crossed the yard to the front door, and despite the light touches of plants and shrubs in Róisín's yard, her lawn was pale green, nearly yellow. Shasta paused and looked over her shoulder.

The other homes in the neighborhood had trees that bore no leaves, and the cedars either had browning foliage or it'd dropped, leaving the trees bare. The lawns were all the same color as Róisín's. There were no flowers. And gray. So much gray for a time when things were supposed to be thriving in full bloom, and colorful. A chill rushed through her to see Madigan's magic at work.

Some of the amusement left Shasta when she took in what they were all facing with Madigan. Unknown, unsure. Certainly not steady. Róisín had put on a face of strength and confidence for them all, but Shasta had a growing feeling that it had been an act. Despite their decades apart, they had just as many together. She still recognized Róisín's tells.

She lifted her hand to knock when the sight of other cars parked with Róisín's caused her to pause. A black pickup truck and a larger red sport utility vehicle were tucked behind Róisín's convertible. Turning back to the door, she worked out how she could play out her arrival. She knew Róisín wasn't expecting her, so she didn't want to cause alarm.

Despite that, Shasta was only there because she herself was alarmed. She'd not seen nor heard from Róisín for a week. Since the day when Róisín had told her of Madigan's connection to Bernard and being on Molennius had jarred something loose within Róisín, the memories beginning to return, things between them had shifted.

Not to mention the missed training with all of them. She decided in that moment to explore the possibility of Róisín becoming a part of her Coven, so they'd at least have a line to one another that ran deeper than the tether that ran between Coven leaders. Shasta could reach through her Coven line and know where her people were, if there was trouble, or need. The leaders didn't have that ability. Róisín had been alone long enough. She needed people, a Coven.

Shasta straightened her shirt, squared her shoulders, then pushed into the house.

"Hello! Ro-Ro?!" she called out, pushing extra cheer to her tone. "Where are you, sweetheart? It's Auntie Shass! You go a whole week without returning my calls or texts, you—Oh." She came to an abrupt halt, eyes alight. "I didn't know I was interrupting." She smiled broadly at a wide-eyed Róisín and the two who were clearly the brother and sister Matthew had mentioned.

"Hi," Róisín said flatly, despite the look of suspicion she gave her.

"That's the greeting you give your aunt?" Shasta drew a single eyebrow up, a corner of her mouth following.

"Aunt?" the young woman asked.

"Shasta and my mother were very close," Róisín explained to her.

"Oh," she said, drawing the word out and swinging her attention back to Shasta, face bright with excitement.

Ah, the friend that knows. Shasta sent her a wink of understanding, and the woman flashed her a toothy grin.

"*Auntie Shass,*" Róisín said. "This is Caid and Lina. Lina is going to potentially be our new town's select board chair when Bill Smithfield, the current chair, returns from California with Stewart Munson, and we can hold our re-vote."

Shasta let the veiled information about Madigan sink in before nodding. "Pleasure to meet you, Lina. I've heard quite a bit about you."

"I hope all good things." Lina rose from her spot to shake Shasta's hand.

Shasta patted her hand, smiling. She could feel the excited energy and the waiting questions vibrating off her.

"And Caid." Róisín motioned to the young man. "Lina's older brother. He so kindly replaced my back door and fixed all the damage caused by the old one."

Like his sister had done, Caid rose, unfolding his tall frame from the chair he'd been in.

Shasta tipped her head up, studying him carefully.

"Pleasure," she purred, shaking his hand. That was when she felt it. Róisín had been casual in the introduction, but Shasta felt the ties coming together to bind him with her like a jolt up her arm. Grief tugged at her as she wished she could call on Brenna. Tell her friend that they hadn't been too late, as they had feared all those years ago.

Róisín attempted to rise, and Caid and Lina quickly moved to her side to help her, causing Shasta's brows to draw together. The blanket on Róisín's lap fell to the floor, revealing the wide bandage that stretched from her knee to almost her hip.

Unable to hold in her gasp, Shasta was immediately in front of her. "What happened?"

"It was just a fall, nothing to be concerned about. Caid got me down the mountain. The hospital got me patched up. I'm good." She kept her eyes on Shasta's. There was a tickle along her mind, and she opened to Róisín.

"Did you catch that? He's not here," Róisín asked in her mind.

"Thank goodness for that." Shasta gave a slight dip of her head.

Róisín looked from one sibling to the other. "Um, if you two could just excuse us for a moment, I just want to check in with my aunt."

"I need to get home to check in with Thomas. He is supposed to land in Portland around four so he can make it home for tomorrow's baby appointment. I'll drop by in the morning?"

"Of course," Róisín replied. "You still have to show me that trick with the bread starter and update me where we're at with those last voters on the call list."

They exchanged a hug.

"I hope we get to connect while you're visiting," Lina said, turning to her.

"I look forward to it." She smiled. Lowering her voice so that only Lina could hear, she added, "I'm sure you have many questions for me."

"This is so awesome," Lina said under her breath. She turned, giving her brother a casual wave, and ducked out the front door.

"I'll run to the store and grab some stuff for dinner," Caid said.

"Nothing too heavy, the painkillers make my stomach feel like I'm on a boat in the middle of the ocean." Róisín brought a hand to her stomach.

"Okay. Need anything else? More Tylenol? Maybe something fizzy to drink to help with the stomach?"

She placed a hand on his forearm to quiet him. "I still haven't gone through everything you brought over yesterday."

"If you change your mind, just call me, okay?"

Shasta bit her bottom lip to hide her smile. If Róisín could move on her own accord, Shasta would've given them privacy by ducking into the kitchen. Instead, she waited quietly off to the side.

After Caid brushed a quick kiss over Róisín's cheek and left, Shasta whipped her head around giving Róisín a pointed stare. "Why haven't you let the magic heal you?"

"I," Róisín began, then stopped, letting out a sigh. "Everything happened so fast. One second, we were standing on the trail, the next we were falling. His ankle was broken, my leg was gushing blood like a broken pipe. Next thing I know, I'm waking up in a hospital with three dozen staples in my thigh, and my magic fighting through a human blood transfusion. It may have looked a little suspicious if I let my body do its thing where so many eyes had witnessed the apparently very thin line from death I was walking."

Shasta clicked her tongue, processing the details. "I hate it." She gritted her teeth. "I agree, but I hate it. This is why you've been missing for a week." She frowned. "We really need to talk about you joining one of our Covens. You cannot be alone anymore. If you were with one of us, we would have felt it, we could have been there for you. Especially with human blood."

Róisín dropped with a heavy thud back onto the couch. "I'd heard stories about it. Nothing, nothing can prepare you for how it really feels."

Shasta sat next to her and slid an arm around her shoulder, tucking her close against her side. Pressing a kiss to the top of her head, she said, "I am so sorry you had to experience that. Even if we hadn't been able to stop it, having one of us there with you..."

"Lina was there. I don't think I could've gotten through without her there with me."

"I like her," Shasta said. "She's not like the others you've spent time with. She's a walking ray of sunshine and a bundle of *good* curiosity."

"Maybe that was the problem," Róisín muttered.

"Not every human is like Alexandria, sweetheart." She stroked a hand over her hair, soothing. "Some people fear what they don't understand. Our magic, that power, is something that we don't even understand sometimes, and it's a part of us."

"She didn't even flinch, Lina, I mean. When she found out, and when we were in the hospital. She was just there. Unwaveringly, there."

"That's a good friend," she said. "She has a pure heart, a pure soul. Something tells me it takes a lot to rattle that young woman's cage."

"Once you get to see how she and her brother interact, you'll see why."

"About the young man." Shasta straightened, causing Róisín to groan. "Now, now. I missed so much because of Aoife. I promised Brenna I would keep an eye on you, look in on you, be there for you whenever you needed someone. It's been a promise I haven't been able to fulfill for many decades. If you want to keep things at an arm's-length with us, I'll accept that. I will not push for something you don't want. However, I think we both deserve it."

Silence filled the room as the weight of Shasta's words settled over them.

"I remember a little more as time passes." Róisín sank back into the sofa, her voice quiet. "It's almost like being at your house opened that door. Even things about my mother I'd somehow forgotten. Signs were there, that strained relationship she had with Aoife. The conversations I would hear between her and my father. The memories that have come back about him, about all of us. So much was lost for so long. To know that some of it was my doing, closing them away into rooms in my head, and never looking back because it hurt…"

Shasta took her face in her hands, using her thumbs to wipe the tears that had fallen away. "No one can ever truly know why someone gives into the darkness. No one is immune to it. When they succumb to it, it consumes them. Their every waking thought, their every action. We forget in order to protect ourselves. It's how we keep our hearts from shattering. How we go on living."

Róisín lifted her hands to cover Shasta's. She gave them a light squeeze, then stroked her thumbs over her wrists.

"Will you at least think about my offer to come into my Coven?" Shasta asked.

She twisted the end of her braid around her finger. "Do I have a time limit?"

"I'd prefer to know before I go back to Molennius, but no. Take your time because I understand how important leaving a Coven to join another is. What it means to the witch who makes the choice. In the meantime." She smiled now. "Tell me about the boy. Don't you dare tell me it's nothing because I know better. I'm your *Auntie*."

Róisín busted into laughter, wiping the fresh tears from her face. "I guess I can spill my guts, Auntie Shass. You'll have to get the summarized version, because I can guarantee he's literally sprinting through the store, throwing things in the cart to get back as soon as possible."

Shasta brought a hand to her chest and closed her eyes. "Ah, he's already won my heart."

CHAPTER 34

"YOU have questions."

Shasta and Lina stood in the potting shed of Lina and Thomas's backyard. Shasta filled the clay pots lined before her with soil. The muskiness of human curiosity filled the room, overpowering the smell of the potting soil and fertilizers. It had been a long time since she had felt her magic sing as though it were calling to the sun and warmth.

If only I were a full elemental and could really put on a show.

"I'm sorry," Lina cleared her throat, "I was staring. That's rude. You're just—it's that—you hear it all the time, don't you? That you're gorgeous?"

Shasta chuckled and started to gently press seeds into the soil. "You'll want to use the roots from this one." She wrote on the small piece of tape on the plant pot.

"Is this one for cooties?" Lina leaned closer.

Shasta turned her head and lifted a brow. "Cooties?"

"Like colds, the flu. Things like that."

"And that libido," she winked.

"Oh, I-I," Lina's neck grew red, then her cheeks. "I didn't realize there was a plant that could actually help with that."

Shasta laughed softly and moved the pot to a shelf near the window.

"Modern science is a marvel, but much of it can be handled with simple herbs. You won't want to touch this until after you're done nursing the baby."

"Ro is a knockout too." Lina cleared her throat. "Those bright eyes with her dark hair. Is it magic? Is that what the secret is?"

"Oh, honey." Shasta faced her. She had come with Lina to her house to show her how to grow and blend herbs, berries, and plants together to create her own kind of magic. To ease pregnancy woes, stay healthy, and per Lina's specific request, keep her sex drive up. "Have you looked in the mirror lately?"

Lina's cheeks grew pink.

Shasta twisted a lock of Lina's hair around her finger, growing thoughtful as she studied her. She had been in love only two times in her life. That deep, heart squeezing, soul grasping love she had for her wife, Evelyn. And that light, buzzing, happy love she felt for Brenna. Lina's energy was buzzing, loudly. "You love her, don't you?"

Lina's mouth trembled. She pressed her lips together and nodded. "I feel like I've been waiting for her, you know? I've never had a friend like her. Ever. And when she got here, this connection... I don't know how to explain it, but it just clicked into place."

Ah, there it was. "You're wondering if it's her magic."

"I'm a horrible person." Lina bit her lip and squeezed her eyes closed.

"No, sweetheart, you're not. I know, because Róisín told you about her magic, about us, her people. She let you in, because you're a good person, and she trusts you." She moved closer to Lina, bringing an arm around her shoulder. "Not only that, but you stayed with her and helped her when she was in the hospital."

Lina dabbed at her damp eyes with the back of her wrists. She sniffled and leaned against Shasta, accepting her embrace.

"Thank you." Shasta pressed a kiss to the side of Lina's head. "For being there for her."

"I wish I could've done more for her. She was in so much pain. Caid would've been there if I called for him, but he... She hasn't told him."

"Do you believe in fate, Lina?" Shasta pulled the gloves from her fingers and placed them on the bench. She brushed a finger along the clay of one of the pots and green shoots stretched through the soil, her magic waking the seeds from their slumber.

"That's amazing," Lina whispered. "I don't know if it's fate. I believe things are given or taken from people for a reason, just as certain people cross our paths."

Shasta smiled. "That's fate, honey. I believe that fate brought my girl here to meet you, to meet your brother. It's been a very long time since I've heard happiness in her voice on the phone or have seen that light in her eyes."

"We'll take good care of her, I promise." Lina took one of Shasta's hands, giving it a light squeeze. When Shasta squeezed back, Lina's face brightened. "Oh! I think the baby moved! Oh my gosh, that tickles." She brought her hands to her mouth as she giggled.

"Creating life is a beautiful thing." Shasta pressed a hand to Lina's belly, feeling the strong heartbeat, the life within. "A very beautiful thing. Now, let's get these next few potted and I'll show you how to cleanse the water without needing to boil it."

"Just for plants, or can we drink it too?" Shasta heard the hope in her voice.

"You can do whatever you want, sweetheart. Even throw a glass of it in your brother's face the next time he teases you about there being twins growing in your womb."

Lina burst into laughter and moved closer to watch Shasta's movements.

It took effort to ready the dirt for the next pots. The memories flooded her of the work she and Brenna had done all of those centuries before. The spells they used to urge things into place more surely, not trusting fate to work in their favor and be on time. Her hands shook and her heart broke anew. She understood why Brenna had to go, but she would do anything to have Brenna here at her side witnessing the bond not just between Róisín and the boy, but his sister as well.

CHAPTER 35

R óisín waited at the door when the sound of Caid's footsteps thundered up the front steps and he burst through the door.

"I got here as soon as—"

She fisted his t-shirt in her hands and maneuvered him against the wall next to the door. Then she sealed her mouth over his, hungry for his taste.

He opened for her immediately, his hands first on her hips, fingertips gripping. Their tongues slid together, twisting, stroking, and his arms banded around her, pulling her tight.

"Where's Shasta?" he said once they had broken apart, both gasping for air.

"She left ten minutes ago with your sister, which is why I said to come now." She nipped at his chin, pressing her body harder against his. The feel of their bodies together ignited her, like a spark to a kindling. The heat they created, addicting. "I've been dying to do this for days."

He rumbled with laughter, stroking his hands along her back. "I can't deny that I've been feeling the same way."

Caid spun them so that she was against the wall, a stability her body relished—he weakened her knees. Resting an arm on the wall next to her head, he brushed his knuckles over her cheek before cupping the back of her head and kissing her softly.

"Can we? Can you?" he breathed against her mouth.

"Are you okay with that?"

He pulled back, a look of puzzlement crossed his face.

"It's just that you've been handling me like I'm breakable. Like I might crumble if you touch me."

His eyes shuttered. "Róisín..."

"Even your demeanor has changed. I miss the lighthearted, funny Caid. You've been so hard, so serious. I want..." She smoothed her hands over his chest, the solidness of him grounding her. "No, I need that Caid to come back."

"I'm right here."

"Are you?" she asked. "I can feel you holding back. Hovering just close enough, but still far enough away."

He dropped his forehead to hers and closed his eyes.

"Talk to me," she pleaded.

"I can't shake it." He drew in a deep, unsteady breath. "I know you're okay, I know you're going to be okay. I just... I can't shake that feeling of you limp in my arms." He shook his head as if trying to rattle the memory loose from his mind. "That feeling of helplessness. Not knowing if you'd make it. I try like hell, I do, because it's haunting me... I can't."

She reached up, tracing his jaw first, then the harsh line his eyebrows had set in. "How do we move forward?"

"I wish I knew."

"Caid..." Her magic finally stirred. "Come with me."

She slid her hand into his and tugged him toward the stairs. While her nerves were frayed with Madigan gone, whether to California or another realm, she was grateful for the reprieve. Even if she didn't know for how long.

She could take a breath, let her magic rest from guarding and use it in ways that charged her. As she pulled Caid into her bedroom, her magic rose and filled her. She couldn't stop thinking about how those moments in the water with him had felt. So different from any other experience she'd ever had with any of her partners. Every inch of her had been more alive than ever before.

"Sit." She pointed to the bed.

When he hesitated, she moved closer and gently pushed him down. His lips were slightly parted and his pupils were dilated, the black nearly swallowing the irises. After he lowered to the edge of the bed, she moved between his legs and settled her hands on his shoulders. Róisín released her magic, then let her energy entwine with his. She smoothed her hands over his shoulders, following her magic, and his body relaxed degree by degree.

"We go slow," he said hoarsely. "If it hurts at all, let me know. Promise?"

"Promise," she whispered. She pulled off her shirt, then unsnapped her bra. The straps slid from her shoulders.

On an inhale, Caid wrapped an arm around her waist and pulled her against him. His mouth closed over one of her nipples, tongue stroking, teasing. She arched, pressing harder, digging her hands into his hair to bring him closer.

He gently tugged the nipple between his teeth, then stroked his tongue over it. Caid's hand replaced his mouth, cupping her breast, while his thumb and forefinger rolled her nipple. His mouth nipped and pressed kisses over her chest, up her neck. Her skin grew tight, her wetness coating her, slicking the insides of her thighs.

Her voice was like air. "I need you."

His teeth grazed her chin, and his other hand moved to the back of her head, gripping her hair to tip her head back more, exposing her throat. "You have me. You'll always have me."

It wasn't the way he sucked on that sensitive spot below her ear after he said it. It was the words that sent a wave of pleasure rolling through her body, making her tremble.

"You're mine," he said against her shoulder before rising. Careful of her leg, he picked her up and laid her on the bed.

Keeping her eyes on his as he rose over her, she adjusted her legs so that he could settle between them. "You're mine."

Wrapping her hands around the hem of his shirt, she pulled it over his head and tossed it on the floor. Then she explored the muscles of his back, stroking along, tracing with her fingers, while he kissed and licked his way down her body, stopping only long enough to untie the strings of her shorts, to tug them off before continuing along his exploration.

Caid's mouth closed over her, his teeth gently nipping at her entrance through her panties, and she bucked and cried out from the jolt of ecstasy that shot through her. He eased the soft cotton down, taking extra care around her bandage. The cool air coming from her opened window replacing the warmth of his body in its absence only stoked the fire the storm inside of her created.

Lifting her uninjured leg, he made his trek upward again. Stroking hands and tongue over every inch. Róisín tried to still her body, but she couldn't stop. Writhing atop the bedspread, she dug a hand back into his hair, her other hand coming up to cup and squeeze one of her breasts.

His tongue teased along her folds. Her hips rocked, and she choked out a sob. She was so close, had been so close from the moment he touched her body downstairs. It took every shred of control she had to hold on—to savor, to prolong. She wanted to let go. To drown in the bliss of the moment.

Caid's fingers pressed into her while he used his lips and tongue on her clitoris. She moved closer and closer to the edge, her release coiling low in her belly, ready to let go. He paused for a moment, and Róisín growled and glared at him. He huffed a laugh, and then used his tongue again.

Her heart stuttered in her chest. The sight of him between her thighs was enough to undo her. She knew then she wouldn't be able to drown. He wouldn't let her. Caid would keep pulling her above water, just enough to catch her breath.

The orgasm exploded in her and her hips moved, riding his fingers and tongue while she cried his name in gasps and pants, over and over. It wasn't until her body had slowed, then stilled, that he stopped, kissing the top of the bandage softly.

Caid stood and rid himself of his pants before he moved back up and over her.

"You're fucking amazing," he said, voice low. He gently lowered himself between Róisín's legs. "How much longer do we have?"

"Enough." She brought his mouth to hers.

He lowered his hips, pressing against her. The feel of his length there, the taste of her in his kiss. The storm built again, waves rocking over her head again.

When he shifted, lifting slightly, she reached down between them, letting her fingers trace along the length of him first before wrapping them around him, squeezing lightly as she stroked him. His eyes closed, and he hissed out a breath.

Róisín watched his face as she used her thumb to graze the head of his cock. The way his jaw fluttered, his mouth thinned, the muscles in his neck became corded. His body tensed, his breaths quickening as he came closer to his edge.

Placing her other hand on his chest, she was met with the tattoo his heart beat against her palm. Her words were soft. "I want you inside me."

His eyes flew open, his irises a rainbow of greens, golds, and browns glittered with heat. He reached, with great effort not to move away from her, for his pants at the end of the bed, feeling around and pulling a condom out.

Caid sat back on his heels to open the pack, but Róisín rose and placed her hand over his. She unrolled the condom over him, taking her time and nipping along his shoulder, his groan vibrating from his throat and chest.

When she had finished, he brought an arm around her back and carefully laid her on the bed. He propped himself on an elbow and brought himself level with her, using his fingers first to spread her open.

"You're still so wet." His face and voice filled with awe.

"It's you," she said, her voice rough. "I can't explain it, but when we're together, from that first touch..."

He searched her face, his fingers petting, teasing. Her first wave crested, sending her hips rolling, and she whimpered. Another wave followed, but his fingers stopped. Caid shifted to align with her and stroked himself along her folds before slowly sliding into her.

For a moment, they laid unmoving. Silent but for their heavy breaths. Then, Róisín scraped her nails down his back and dug her fingertips into his backside, urging him deeper with a shift of her legs.

She moved with him, meeting his slow thrusts that built her up over each wave and caught her as she tumbled after.

His mouth slanted over hers, his tongue seeking its entry. She pulled his bottom lip with her teeth, and he thrust into her, her gasp of pleasure making her mouth open. He grinned down at her, then brought his mouth back to hers.

Having him inside of her, his slow, gentle thrusts, his mouth on hers, this drowned her. The waves crashing over her one by one, bigger each time, never giving her time to surface. Her body felt glorious.

"Caid!" she cried out and murmured it over and over again. Her body moved like liquid with his.

He thrust once, twice more before he stilled and joined her, releasing with her name from his lips like he was at worship. His chest heaved as he tried to catch his breath.

Shifting so that his weight was more on his elbow by her head, he lifted his other hand, lazily stroking it over her stomach, brushing her breasts, then trailing her neck to cup her face. His gaze was intense as he looked down at her.

"It's you, too, for me," he said, his voice thick. "Never anything like this before."

"I guess we should thank the Lagree boys for selling their mother's house to me."

His body shook with laughter, and he ducked his head to brush a kiss over her lips. "I'll be thanking them until the day I die. How much longer before your aunt comes back?"

"Um." She twisted so that she could squint at the clock next to the bed. "Probably any minute knowing Shasta."

"You say that like she's walked in on you before." He tucked her against his chest.

"I'll never admit it to her, but the time she did just pop into my mother's house back when I was a teenager, it was perfect timing."

He winced. "Ouch. Bad experience?"

"It would have been with the way he was humping my leg," she answered with a tone she would give a chef who just served her a bland dish.

"And this?"

"I'd bar over all of my doors and windows to keep her from being able to do it again," she said without hesitation.

"Does that mean that we can make a go for another round?"

It was her turn to laugh. "She leaves tomorrow afternoon."

"Well, shit." He blew out a breath.

"We can make it."

"For you, I'll suffer anything."

She fought against the tension that wanted to tighten her body at his statement. The more time they spent together, the more she fell for him, the more risk there was. There was a growing fear that Caid just may suffer with what was coming their way.

CHAPTER 36

S HASTA sat with her legs tucked beneath her, a warm mug of tea clasped in her hands. Her eyes were closed as she took in the complete silence of Róisín's backyard and beyond. She knew of what Madigan had done from Róisín's reports. It was different facing the stark reality of it. Would they be ready for him when he showed his hand?

When Madigan had been a part of the council still, his magic had always burned her senses. The darkness, the dirtiness of it, tainting the air around him wherever he went. It was different there, in the small town of Greens Glen that Róisín temporarily called home. Its potency there was stronger as it burned her nose, reaching inside of her, trying to take hold of her own magic. Almost like it tried to grasp her magic and turn it to ash.

She opened her eyes to the color-drained woods and imagined what it would look like flourishing—the green of the trees, birds singing. She breathed steadily in through her nose and out through her mouth. Counting to five as she did both. Centering herself, reassuring herself that her magic was strong inside of her, and Madigan couldn't take it from her.

It caused a heaviness to settle into her stomach. She itched to be back on Molennius in front of her books, mapping and re-planning. It was time for them to all come together again. To refocus.

"What more can I do?" The sound of Róisín's voice from the chair next to Shasta startled her, her tea sloshing to the lip of her mug.

She took her attention away from the tree line and studied her. Róisín had come out onto the patio with her own steaming cup of tea shortly after she had. Her hair messily piled atop her head; she swam in an oversized hooded sweatshirt that smelled of Caid.

There had been a drastic shift in Róisín's energy when she'd returned from Lina's the day before. Where she had pulsated in muted blues and grays when Shasta had left, she radiated reds, purples, and greens. A clearing of tension, of hurt between Róisín and Caid had clearly taken place in a moment of privacy.

Shasta's mouth tipped into a sad smile. So much pressure for someone still so young. Róisín should be able to live her life how she wants. Hot licks from growing flames began to rise within and she shifted her body, so that she was facing Róisín. "What do you mean?"

"I just feel so..." Her body slumped in her chair. "I feel like I'm not doing enough."

"Sweetheart." She leaned forward. "You were already a very gifted elemental and you've beautifully paired that with your life magic. Lucius knows the Rose Valley was you."

"I–I'm sorry. I know that's forbidden."

"Who told you that?" She sucked her teeth, giving a frustrated nod when Róisín only stared at her. "Well, that's a lie. Unfortunately, like so many other things that woman has told you over the nearly sixty years she had her claws in you. You could go and grow a rainforest in the Sahara or turn the Shianshani jungle into an ocean, it would be fine. Do we suggest it? Definitely not. Something like that would definitely draw attention, and we know what happens with that. Rose Valley is already a place where wheat grows for the people of Ely. Having it come to bloom and be ready for harvest? A miracle from Leilandre."

"Do they really think that?" she asked.

"The Goddess of Harvest has blessed them fruitfully." Shasta's mouth curled into a smile. Lucius had told her of the sudden abundance of rose wheat after a disastrous drought. They had both known immediately it was Róisín. Just as they both had grown worried, knowing that it was only when Róisín felt deep sadness or fear that she visited the valley.

Silence fell over them again. Shasta wanted to convince Róisín she'd already gone above and beyond, far more than any other witch would've in this position.

"You're asking because of the boy, aren't you?"

"I-I didn't mean f-for it to h-happen." She pressed her fingers to her lips as if she tried to keep the rest of the words from spilling out. "It started so small. Just us talking for a little while at the end of the day. There was this tug. It was faint at the very start. That night I saw him at the town vote." She folded her hands together, then pulled them apart. After a moment, she twisted them together again. "Then he waited for me the day I went to the Rose Valley. Sitting right on my steps, hours after they called it a day. Like he knew something was wrong, and he didn't press, he was just there for me."

"He loves you, Róisín. Do you love him?"

She wrapped her arms around herself in a hug. "I can't."

"Why not?"

"This." She swept a hand out toward the tree line. "I can't put him at risk. I open my heart, and Madigan has someone to use against me."

Shasta reached her hand out, palm up, then motioned for Róisín's. After she placed it in Shasta's, Shasta lightly squeezed. "It is time for you to tell him what you are."

Róisín's body stiffened, and Shasta had to tighten her grip so she couldn't pull her hand back. She would not let her withdraw and hide again.

"He's a part of this. Whether you love him or not. By not telling him, he's being placed in the midst of it all, blind. Telling him gives him time, gives him the eyes and ears he'll need. We don't know how much time we have, so I don't say this lightly" Shasta looked Róisín in the eye, could see the uncertainty in them before she looked away. "Tell him. Not just for your sake, but his. He won't go anywhere. I can hear it in his mind, I can see it in his energy. He has fears, yes, who you are will not be one of them."

Róisín stared down at their joined hands, silent.

"I should gather my things. I need to get back to Molennius so we can confirm if Madigan is in California. If he's also doing this elsewhere. When will you be able to travel with your leg?"

"I, um, sort of, yesterday while you were out." Her cheeks bloomed pink.

She couldn't stop the grin from splitting her face. "The bandage is just to keep up appearances, then?"

"I've been the one that changes them, so I figured if I just kept it on for a believable amount of time..." She shrugged.

"Oh, Róisín," Shasta sighed and waved her up from the chair. "Come here."

"How do I tell him?" she asked, wrapped in Shasta's warm embrace.

"Just start with what you know."

CHAPTER 37

Róisín looked out beyond Nanette's expansive gardens to where the city of Solace lay beyond and tried to pull her thoughts together. Nanette had worded her advice differently—straight to the point and less stern, a gentle urging, a light nudge, as was her way. However, the meaning had been the same as Shasta's. Róisín should tell Caid about her magic.

"Your heart feels the way it does about him for a reason." Nanette drifted away from her, then murmured to a peony bush. It blossomed with wide, white and pink blooms.

"Yeah, well, my heart also has felt that way about others. Look at where it's gotten me." Róisín dropped onto the ground, sending a spray of aster shooting up around her.

Nanette chuckled. "I can't say I'd ever associate my beloved aster as a blossom of rage."

"I'm not angry," Róisín bit out.

"Oh?" She arched a brow high. "I'm just waiting for you to huff out a breath, pout your bottom lip out, and cross your arms."

Róisín let out a sigh. "Ugh. I'm just frustrated with it all. What is Madigan doing? What has been taking him so long? Decades he's been off the radar, impossible to find. And to suddenly find him? There must be a reason. Like he's getting ready to finish his power up, then wipe us all out. Right?"

Nanette lowered herself next to Róisín. "I don't know, I really don't. He's always been a difficult male. I think that most from Aunellion were that way. Very cold, very distant. They certainly never wanted to be a part of the guild and council. I don't think there was one of us surprised when he severed the connection and fled."

"Is it wrong that I'm happy that this happened, though?"

"What do you mean?" She waved a hand over a patch of aster, and small impatiens popped up with them.

"If Aoife didn't die, if I wasn't pushed into this thing with Madigan, I never would've learned all that I have." Róisín shifted to cross her legs and began strumming her fingers on her knees.

The smell of the surrounding blooms filled her with an energy she'd not had in days. The weight of the stress of holding her wards on Earth, the lack of life around her, despite her growing connection with Caid, her friendship with Lina, she felt as though she herself were graying like Greens Glen.

Her fingers brushed along an aster leaf; her voice was quiet as she continued her admission to Nanette. "All of this I carried in my mother's trunk—the one I carried with me for decades. Do I have more questions? Absolutely." She nodded. "I don't know if I'll ever get all the answers, either. What I've learned, though, it helps me here." She tapped a finger on her temple, then moved her hand to cover her heart. "And here."

Róisín's fiddled with the dirt. "There are times I wonder if I can handle another hit," she continued. "Another secret revealed. And they haven't been giving me answers. Just more questions. They've yet to make me feel good, but they open the door a little more to who my family was, what I am."

"Who do you think you are?" Nanette asked.

"I'm the means to end this."

"You may be the key, but you do not stand alone."

"I may have to," she whispered.

"You will only ever need to stand just before us. We will always be there. The Sisters have put the three of us and our Covens with you on this journey for a reason. Fate is fate. Never once think that this is yours alone. It doesn't matter who Aoife was, or what she did." She reached out and took one of Róisín's hands between hers, spreading warmth and assurance through her. "This is what the Sisters wanted for all of us. To change our world, to begin a new future. For you to lead us there."

"You sound so sure."

"Perhaps I am because it comes from the Sisters lips, to mine, to yours." She leaned in and kissed Róisín's cheek gently. "A new sun will rise for us, my love."

RÓISÍN WAS EMPTIED of energy and motivation as she moved through the rest of her day in Roidon, and the next in Ely with Lucius and Matthew. Nanette's words followed her throughout every step she took, sometimes weighing her down, other times carrying her through.

Lucius was silent as he walked next to her through the arching halls of his home. Her body, her mind, her soul were all exhausted. She'd left her leg wound just a scab in her healing, a precaution should someone human see it that knew what had happened. As she became more worn down, the skin around the scab felt tight and throbbed.

"Your mind is quite noisy today." Lucius broke the silence that sat between them.

"I'm sorry. It probably feels like I'm screaming at you."

"Come." He nudged the door open to the study, waving her in. "Let's skip today. You've shown that even in your most exhausted form, you can hold off any probing."

She paused at the threshold. "Are you sure?"

"I'm assuming this is about everyone telling you it's time to tell Kincaid?"

Róisín groaned, fighting the urge to roll her eyes, and Lucius smiled. "Why are you all ganging up on me?"

"We care about you, Róisín." He gestured to the chairs near the fireplace. After she sat, he crossed to where he kept a small bar and filled two glasses with water. Handing her one, he lowered into the chair beside her.

She sipped slowly and looked at him from the corner of her eye. "You won't tell me to, in your own way?"

"Not at all." He tapped a finger against his glass, the reflection of the orange and yellow flames danced in his eyes. "It would be redundant at most. Even if I were to put it in my own words, and I see no need to do that."

She drew her legs up into the chair, curling herself on the soft fabric.

"We are all under a great deal of pressure. Not just from the threat Madigan brings to the table. We're conspiring against the vote by coming together to work as a team outside of the council. However, you"—he patted her arm—"sweetheart, are under the most pressure of all. Because of that, and then adding an extra, what is it young people in this century call it? Plot twist."

Róisín's laugh burst from her, and she shook her head. "Dear Goddess, I never thought I'd see the day."

"I can be hip." Lucius inclined his head, giving her an easy smile.

"Oh, no." She gasped, and her laughter embraced her body wholly, causing it to shake. "Please stop. You'll make me snort and that's embarrassing."

"Clarissa used to snort when she laughed hard enough. I used to make it my mission, every day, to make her laugh that hard." He smiled.

Róisín had thought at first that he was joking, but the wistful look that flashed through his eyes proved he was serious. "I miss her."

"Every minute of the day. It's been thirty years, four months, twelve days. I can still smell her scent throughout the house, still hear her laugh." He looked down into the flames before them.

"Hear her snort," Róisín offered.

His smile this time split his face, flashing all his teeth. His eyes glittered when he looked at her. "Every time. Everything, really. I will for decades, for centuries to come, carry her memory in everything I do."

"She was such an amazing being. Even after my mother died, she always made sure I had someone other than Aoife. That I wasn't alone."

"Shasta would've done the same, you know, if Aoife hadn't..."

Róisín straightened. "Lucius."

"Shasta will never talk about the experience, about what happened.

We will probably never know the depth of what she knew or her work with Brenna in those years."

"Lucius," she said again, this time her tone had the edge of a bite to it. "What did Aoife do to Shasta? Is that why I couldn't remember her being my mother's *best friend* until just recently? Why couldn't I remember all the times I spent at her house, even the times I was there as a grown woman?"

"Knowing what I know now about Aoife, who Bernard's true Coven was, I understand how Aoife could accomplish it. We use spell work to enhance the magic we have. However, bring darkness in to hold the hand of spell work, it becomes something else. Something slinking, creeping, gripping. When Brenna died, Shasta suddenly felt an impenetrable wall go around you, she said. She tried to soothe and comfort you at the burial, but she was physically unable."

Something gripped her heart tightly. "Did you? Or Clarissa?"

"No. And I can't express enough gratitude for that. If she'd ripped you away from our lives, it would've felt like losing a child."

She struggled to hold in the sob, and it escaped as a hiccup. "Lucius, do you think Aoife had plans for me? That she fought so hard for me to gain Brenna's power for a reason other than it was rightfully mine to have?"

He patted her leg gently. "I wish I had an answer for you. I have a gut feeling, but that's not truly enough."

"Sometimes gut feelings are enough," she said.

"That is true. Sometimes, our guts are off, and they're telling us filthy little lies. Or trying to misdirect us from what's really important."

She blinked at him, then blew out a sharp breath through her nose. Somehow, she felt Lucius had just, in his way, told her it was time to tell Caid everything.

Chapter 38

A FAMILIAR caress of a thumb stroked along the center of Róisín's neck, and the weight of a body shifted over her. A smile played across her lips, and she sighed, the bliss building inside of her under the coaxing of skilled hands.

Wait, her brain shouted at her, forcing her eyes open.

Blinking, she worked to focus on her surroundings, slow with the thickness of sleep still clinging.

Wind gust through the open balcony window, blowing the sheer green curtains inward to dance just out of reach of the bed.

"No." She struggled to get the word out. "No, this isn't right."

"Where are you racing off to, love? I'm not even near finished yet." Alexandria's deep red hair came into view before her face did.

Róisín sucked in a pained breath, her lungs squeezing, heart hammering against her rib cage.

Alexandria's lush, pink lips frowned, her catlike gold and brown eyes studying her. "What's wrong?"

"This." Róisín shook her head and looked around the room again. The bedroom they'd shared for two years. "This isn't real. This isn't right."

Alexandria pushed up further until she was almost level with

Róisín. She lifted a pale, freckled hand and brushed Róisín's hair from her face. "Another nightmare about your mother?"

"*This* is the nightmare. I need to wake up." Róisín tried pinching herself hard. She bit her lip when the sting of it radiated through her arm.

Alexandria closed a hand over hers. "Talk to me, love. It's never worth hurting yourself over."

Róisín blinked and drew her eyes up to her face. It was just as she remembered it. The splash of freckles over the slender bridge of a nose that tipped up ever so slightly at the end. The lazy arch of her eyebrows, and the freckles that punctuated their ends by her hairline. At that moment, a wall of emotions hit her. How much she missed Alexandria, the time they shared before that fateful night. The ease of being with her.

The realization slammed into her, causing her to gasp. Not loving her. No, she cared for Alexandria, lusted for her. There had been a sense of comfort with her. No, it hadn't been love.

Nothing like what Róisín felt even being in the same realm as Caid. With him, her whole world quieted and stilled. Her heart slowed; her breathing leveled. It felt like her body, soul, and mind could stretch out and rest.

When their bodies came together, she had yet to find words to describe it. Ecstasy, euphoria, an earthquake. Nothing seemed to be quite enough.

"You can't tell him." Alexandria lazily stroked a finger over Róisín's bare chest. She drew a circle around one of Róisín's nipples.

"What?" Her brows came down, and she snapped away from her thoughts.

"He'll run from you." Alexandria licked along her collarbone. "Just like I did when I found out. Because..." She nipped her neck, then laved the spot with the flat of her tongue. "You're the fucking devil, and you'll ruin us all."

Róisín's body jolted, causing her to roll off the bed. She slammed against the floor, knocking an elbow on the bed frame. Blinking, she looked around the now dark room, recognizing it as hers in Shasta's house.

"It was just a dream." She drew her knees to her chest, wrapping her shaking arms around her legs. She could still feel Alexandria's caresses and kisses; hear her words. She shook her head, trying to clear the cobwebs the dream had left. "Just a really bad, messed up dream."

She shoved her hands through her hair and blew out a deep breath. Taking another minute to gather herself, she carefully rose to her feet.

Turning the lights on, she moved about the room while getting dressed. She didn't plan on returning to Greens Glen yet, but she needed to get away. Her nightmare still clinging to her.

Lucius had relayed information to them all from witches he had working discreetly around the realms confirming more areas were being drained of life. Desolate forests, dried lakes, towns and villages that were much like Greens Glen. Animals found dead, but intact, appearing to have had the life sucked from them. Areas with small populations, if any, used to complete his work. If they hadn't searched the realms, hadn't know what to look for, the places could've gone undiscovered for decades, centuries even.

Her reflection in the vanity mirror gave her pause. On the right side of her neck, just above her collarbone, was a light blemish. Right where Alexandria had bitten her in her dream. Her heart stuttered its beat as she moved closer, eyes on the mark.

"He'll run..."

No, Róisín shook her head. Caid was nothing like Alexandria.

Despite how hard she tried to convince herself, worry built. Old habits of withdrawing and hiding itched to surface and take control.

She made her last checks to make sure she had everything, then quickly scrawled a note to Shasta letting her know she'd be back by midday the following day.

Slowly, she'd resolved herself to the chance that Caid may not accept her. If it came to that—no, he wouldn't run. What they had, what they had started, would be over, though. She took a few moments to slow her heart, then draw the wall that had crumbled around her back up.

When her breath had steadied and her hands no longer shook, she went home.

Chapter 39

Lina pressed her fingers to her eyes and blew out a breath. Dropping her hand back to her side in defeat, she glared at the ten steps that led from the pathway to her front door.

"Maybe we should use the back door," she called over her shoulder to Róisín.

"We'll ruin the yard backing around," Róisín said from where she stood in the driveway, at the bottom of two more sets of stairs.

"It's ruined anyway," Lina grumbled under her breath. All of it was ruined. She needed this win on the council. She and Thomas didn't have near enough money to take Stewart Munson and Munson Technologies to court to get him shut down. Someone needed to save Greens Glen and it was a burden she would happily bear to save her home. Because there wasn't anywhere else she wanted to raise her children.

"When you look at what's here, it's not all that much. Two big boxes and the rest can be stacked to make fewer trips," Róisín called up to her.

"I did not plan this very well when I insisted on us buying this house." Lina covered her face with her hands and groaned. "Steps everywhere."

"You can just guide me, and I can carry," Róisín made her way up the stairs to stand next to Lina.

"No." She shook her head firmly, her mouth set in a determined line. "I asked you to help me, not do it for me."

Róisín set the box of baby stuff down she had carried with her. "It's still me helping you."

"Maybe we could just wait until Caid wraps his day, then deal with his grumbling about how he could have just kept his truck instead of letting me use it..." She turned to Róisín and squinted her eyes, studying her. The shadows under her eyes and the way she appeared dull, having lost the glow she had been carrying for the past few weeks. "Something's going on there. Between you two, I mean. You clearly need some space from it all."

Róisín bit her bottom lip. "I—it's..."

"We don't have to talk about it." Lina waved her off. "You can tell me if you want, when you want. It's between you and my brother and not you, my brother, and I."

Róisín released a sigh and Lina left her standing at the first landing to sit on the steps in the shaded spot, closer to the house. After she settled, she patted the spot next to her with one hand, beckoning Róisín to join her with the wave of her other hand.

Róisín tipped her head back, her throat flexing with the movement of her swallow. Then she hung her head, her shoulders slumped, and she trudged toward Lina. She let out a grunt when her bottom hit the step next to her. "I've started the conversation in my head so many times. What to say to him, but then I freeze. What's the explanation, fight, flight, freeze? I'm a fantastic freezer. It's a switch, and I just shut off. It's always been easier for me to withdraw and hide, to shut people out when they get close."

"Oh." Lina drew out the word, her eyes growing round. "Shit. You're worried he'll freak out, aren't you?"

"Massively. Only one other person knew before you, and they couldn't run away fast enough."

Lina reached over and rested a hand on Róisín's knee, giving her a light squeeze. "Caid is a very stubborn man, as you know. He's also super rational, with his head square on his shoulders. But that doesn't mean that he's not open-minded. I feel like that's the requirement of being my sibling." When Róisín's expression didn't lighten, she added,

"I'm serious. I'm a little flighty. A daydreamer, ask Thomas. He's got stories, trust me. Caid, he always unquestionably supported me growing up. With anything, even if he didn't exactly like what I wanted to do or was doing."

"I don't know. This other person... they seemed to be open-minded, welcoming. But fear of the unexplained and unknown, that does something different to people." Róisín folded her hands together in her lap.

"Do you want to practice with me? Find the right approach? The right words?" Lina knew her brother better than anyone. Deep in her heart, she knew he wouldn't flinch if the time came where Róisín found the courage to open up to him. However, she also couldn't imagine what it was like to carry something as big as Róisín did. Knowing history was riddled with witch hunts, the deaths, the prisons. "Ro?"

"It's easier with you because you know. He... I can't even look at him right now. Like if he sees my eyes, he'll know without me even telling him."

"He's a good reader of people, but trust me, he's not that good," Lina said softly. "Maybe just grow him a big ass palm tree in his back-yard and be like"—she threw her arms up in the air, wiggled her fingers, grinning—"'surprise! I'm a witch! Now come kiss me, you big fool, and tell me you love me.'"

Róisín blinked, then burst into laughter.

"Oh, but I'm dead serious. It's a good idea. Then maybe he'll also finally admit openly he's in love with you."

"He is not in love with me," Róisín replied.

"Sweetie." She patted her leg. "I've known the man my entire life, he is wildly in love with you. He has been for a bit now. Probably before the big lug even realized it himself."

"Mm, maybe. Until he finds out I can grow him a big ass palm tree in Maine."

"With a wiggle of your pinky," Lina added, bumping Róisín's shoulder with hers.

"With a wiggle of my pinky," she murmured with a nod.

"I wouldn't mind a few small-ish palms out back, you know. I mean, my birthday is coming up, so it'd be a perfect present idea," Lina said. "Put them in a square sort of shape though, so I can hang something like chili pepper lights running between them. Oh! And a fire pit with chairs in the middle!"

Róisín turned away from where she had been staring at Caid's truck loaded with nursery furniture, facing Lina. "You are one hundred percent serious, aren't you?"

"Absolutely," she beamed. "Would you? I mean, we can get those big tree container things, so it looks like I bought them. No one would ever know except you and I."

"And your brother."

"Eh." She shrugged. "Only if we want him to. Best friends can have secrets, you know. Even if one of them is dating the other's brother."

Róisín lifted a brow.

"I swear it." She held up a pinky. "If it wasn't already clear before, I mean. Anything you tell me stays with me unless you ask or tell me otherwise."

Róisín's mouth curved up into a small smile, the silver shimmer of the tears gathered along the bottoms of her lids. When Róisín hooked her pinky around Lina's, Lina drew her in, wrapping her arms tightly around her. She'd had a feeling early on that Róisín didn't have many people in her life she could trust, and now she understood why.

Lina glanced down at the loaded truck, thinking of her brother, and cringed. They'd already had it for over an hour. Only one box, a small box at that, had made it to the front door of her house. She let out a heavy sigh, tears gathering behind her eyes. She hadn't planned this well at all.

The deep maroon sedan parked across the street, and up a few houses from hers drew her attention. It couldn't be the same one that had been there when they had first gotten to the house. She didn't know the car, and no one came to visit Greens Glen anymore. She blinked her eyes, trying to focus, clearing away her building tears. Stewart Munson sat in the driver's seat focused on her house.

Róisín rose and brushed her rear off, but Lina kept her eyes on Stewart, clearly watching Róisín's every movement. A chill ran over her skin, and she fought back the shiver.

"I'll take the big stuff, you take the small?" Róisín offered. "This way you're not regretting buying this adorable house on the hill, and your brother can't say crap about us stealing his truck earlier?"

She turned her head away from the road, looking up at Róisín. "You're an absolute genius."

If anything, Lina would've been happy abandoning the idea of getting anything into the house, except for the two of them. Lina tried to stare daggers at Steward and made her way down the path to the driveway. It didn't deter him, he was so focused on Róisín, he probably didn't see Lina watching him.

"I'll tell you what." Lina pulled the smaller boxes forward. "We get this all inside in the next fifteen minutes, I'll make us that egg roll in a bowl you loved the last time you were over."

"Oh my gosh." Róisín's face brightened. She shoved the crib box forward, then hopped out of the truck bed. "You have a deal."

Relief surged through her body, and she stacked two smaller boxes and followed her.

Chapter 40

C AID wanted to wait. He wanted to wait so badly that he paced his living room to kill time. His hair stood on end from how many times he'd run his hands through it, and if he rubbed the back of his neck one more time, he could rub a layer of skin off.

Róisín had returned from her work trip. She'd at least sent him a text to let him know. Aside from one more text that declined to make plans to get together, that had been it.

She was swamped with work, she'd said. She would let him know when she'd be surfacing for air. Something about the way she'd worded her response, there had to be more going on.

When he saw her that afternoon in town with Lina, he couldn't deny what his gut told him. The distance she placed between them was palpable. He could almost see her racing to stack the bricks to the wall between them.

Something had shifted her feelings about their growing relationship while she was gone, and now, what had felt solid and sure for once in his life found itself drifting downstream, away from him. Caid stalked across his kitchen, jingling the keys to Lina's SUV in his hand, waiting. Waiting long enough that he hoped when he went to retrieve his truck, Róisín had gone home.

He wasn't avoiding her. No, he tried to avoid dealing with the emotions that all of this had created within him.

At one point, he'd reasoned that he could have the lumber yard deliver the plywood the following day to his job site in the next town over and keep Lina's car until she came for it.

He glanced at the clock on his stove. It was nearly six in the evening. That would have given them almost seven hours to unload and gave them the added time to put anything together. Róisín would have to be gone by the time he got over there.

Deciding, he strode to his front door and climbed into Lina's SUV.

"Shit," he grumbled when he swung into Lina's driveway. His truck was backed up to the pathway, with the tailgate still down. Róisín's car was tucked up by the garage.

He looked from the car to his truck, drumming his fingers on the steering wheel. It'd be easy enough to pull his out to the road, park Lina's next to Róisín's, then take off without either of them knowing he was there.

He could deal with Lina getting pissed about it later.

Backing out of the driveway, he parked Lina's with the hazards on, then made his way up the driveway to his truck.

"Jesus." He knocked his right knee on his dash. Tapping a button on the side of the seat, it shifted into its saved position to accommodate his long legs.

He'd just parked in front of Lina's when he caught sight in his rearview of the maroon sedan parked just beyond the house on the side of the road. Rubbing his knee, he moved the mirror so he could see better.

"What the fuck is Munson doing parked outside of Lina's house?" His shoulders automatically rose, straightening his spine. It had been awhile since he had hit someone with his fists, and a part of him had been waiting for the perfect moment that called for raising just one and swinging it at Stewart's well manicured face. Would it be worth the jail time?

Caid leaned closer to the mirror, immediately noting Stewart's line of sight was clearly on the house. Despite the distance, he was sure he didn't see the man blink once in the five minutes he let pass as he watched him.

His concern mixed with anger, making that blackness building inside of him potent. It unfurled, stretching its toxic, grimy limbs and wrapped around his veins driving his adrenaline up a notch. His hands gripped the steering wheel in front of him, his muscles growing taut.

The town vote was just days away. Stewart had to be worried about losing his champion in the chair. Was he trying to intimidate Lina? What would happen once he left? Once Róisín left, and Lina was alone for the night? Thomas was out of town for two more days.

Climbing out of his truck and locking it, he moved Lina's to the spot next to Róisín's, and without a second thought, went to the pathway to the front door.

He didn't know how he would do it, he just needed to convince his sister to have a sleepover with her big brother.

"Oh, this is freaking perfect," Lina greeted him, almost breathless, as she came down the stairs at the same time he pushed the front door open. "Kitchen, now."

He stood frozen in the doorway.

"Now, Kincaid James McGrath." She gave him a pointed stare.

"Practicing for when the miniature versions of you are born and give you a taste of your own medicine?" He lifted a brow.

She huffed a breath and closed her eyes. "Can you just, I don't know, not be you right now? I need to talk to you about something. I'd rather Róisín not hear, because it has to do with her."

Caid went on alert, muscles tensing. "What's up?" He tried to play it cool, leaning a hip against the countertop.

"You need to figure out how to convince her to let you take her home and crash at her place tonight. Even if it means you are sleeping on her sofa."

"Why?" His body went rigid. "What's going on?"

"That dirtbag Munson has sat in front of my house since around noon, watching her every damn move when we were out there. I don't like it. At all. I don't know what he's doing, and I know she's had issues with him in the past. I don't trust him. She wants to go home, she's clearly exhausted from work, but she came to help me today anyway because that's just who she is. I'm running out of excuses to keep her here because I don't want her to be alone. I know she'd catch on if I said I wanted to come chill at her place."

Caid let silence fall over them. His legs urged him to move, to throw open Lina's door and go to Stewart. He flexed his hands at his side, trying to work out the itch that was growing to hit. One fist, straight to Stewart's face. "She doesn't know he's out there?"

She shook her head. "No. I saw him earlier, not long after we got here. I thought maybe he would talk to me about dropping out of the race now that I'm pregnant. I noticed he was watching Ro. Her hand moved, he was watching it. Shit, if she scratched a shoulder, he was watching. It's creepy as hell."

Caid's jaw tensed. If it wouldn't cause a bigger issue, he'd try to talk some sense into Stewart, but even he could admit the way he stared—not blinking—was creepy. He'd have to figure something out. "She hasn't talked to me since she got back. How am I going to get this to work?"

Lina chewed her bottom lip and shrugged. He narrowed his eyes at her, she must know more than she let on. Róisín would've confided in her, and it grated on his nerves a little. She was Róisín's friend first, before they became whatever it was they became, he had to remember that.

"You can come home with me," Róisín said quietly from the doorway.

They both jumped.

"Are you sure?" they asked in unison.

She nodded, then turned to Lina. "You're still coming for lunch tomorrow?"

"I promised." Lina drew an x over her heart. "I'll be there around eleven."

"Okay." She crossed the kitchen to hug her.

Caid stayed planted by the island, silent, waiting. When she turned back to him, he felt his breath hitch in his chest. There was such a heavy sadness in her eyes when she looked up at him. He desperately hoped that if he'd been the cause, she would let him fix it.

Then, he would make sure that whatever he did to make her so upset, he'd never do it again.

Chapter 41

Róisín unlocked her front door and braced herself. Caid's questions simmered just under the surface of the tension between them. In that moment, as the door swung open, she wanted to open the door of her life to him, show it all to him.

"Is everything okay?" Caid asked from behind her, his voice strained, but soft.

She conceded to let Caid take her home to avoid the inevitable fight and awkwardness that would only keep her away from the house longer. Longer meant more risk. Risk they couldn't take.

If Madigan had stayed near Lina's house, watching and waiting, he wasn't doing so without reason.

"You, you don't have to sleep on the sofa." She rubbed her temples, trying not to turn around to see him.

Everything suddenly crashed down around her. Madigan's potential discovery of her before they knew what his intentions truly were. The weakness of her power that had crept in since returning from Molennius this latest time. Facing Caid but running from him and the truth instead. Her chest was tight, and she fought, trying to push herself to keep going.

"Where am I supposed to sleep then? With you when you couldn't even look at me in town earlier? When you haven't said anything to me in four days? I can crash on the sofa, it's fine."

She needed more time. Not just with Caid, but with everything. The walls closed in, and her body became heavy, weighed down by it all.

Her chest squeezed tighter. "Caid," was all she managed before her foundation broke.

Shasta's magic wrapped her in a comforting hug, and she let her own wink out. She dropped to her knees, sobs racking her body.

Caid was at her side in an instant, catching and wrapping his arms around her, bringing her close. The smell of him, bergamot, wood and musk, surrounded her. The desire to push him away warred with the desire to curl into him and cling.

Caid rose with her in his arms, and Lucius's magic fortified around them, Matthew's stretching out to the edge where the woods began.

It was the first time she could truly let go since it'd all began. They would keep her safe so that she could take that space. Her tears fell harder. She gave in, gripping Caid's shirt, burying her face in his chest, and he carried her to her room.

When he sat on the edge of the bed, she sensed his hesitation. She pulled back and wiped at her eyes with the heels of her hands. In the light's glow from the bedside clock, she saw the confusion, the worry, the patience on his face.

"I... There's something I need to..." She tried to find her words. Time, she needed time. For everything, but especially this right here.

He lifted a hand, his knuckles brushing along her cheek softly. "Take a minute." He tucked her hair behind her ear, his voice low, deep, comforting. "We can just sit here. If I'm here tonight, it doesn't have to be rushed, whatever it is, okay?"

Maybe Lina would be right, he would stay.

There was still the chance that Alexandria would be right, and he would run.

She could see how much it pained him to wait in the way his brows were drawn tightly together. And she knew he would, for her. Gathering her courage, she found the words that would buy her that time, at least until tomorrow.

A storm was brewing, finally, and she needed to let the others know.

"There's a lot going on right now, with me, and..." She let out a shaky breath. "It's been hard to sort it out because things from my past make certain decisions really hard for me. I just need a little more time to get my feet back under me. I hope... I hope that's okay with you."

"Róisín." Her name was barely a whisper on his lips, and he rested his forehead against hers. "I don't want you to think that I'll ever have an issue with you needing space or time to work things out. If it's me, I need to know, though, so I can make it right."

"It's not you," she replied. "I'm so sorry for making you think that."

His lips were warm on her forehead. Her eyes shuttered closed as the touch spread that warmth through her.

"Will you promise me something?" he asked. "Will you talk to me about it when you're ready? I want to be there to help, okay?"

She brought a hand to his cheek, her thumb tracing his chin. "Okay."

Chapter 42

"I don't think it's a wise idea, the vote," Bill said, exasperated.

Madigan tried to ignore Bill and the anxious energy that radiated from him as he spiraled into a storm of words, his hands frantic.

"It's days, days away! You need to be here. What if she beats me?"

Madigan sighed. "It'll be fine."

He wished Bill would stop his rambling so he could focus on the map that lay on his desk before him.

"You don't understand, it's all at risk. She wins, everything we've worked for is gone."

Madigan knew all too well what was at stake. Róisín McKenna had become a distraction. When he had returned to Earth's realm the week before, he felt that pull to her. What was worse, the day before, he had snapped out of his daze to find himself outside Lina McGrath-Commons' house.

Distractions were dangerous. This distraction could undo all the work he'd put into place, painstakingly, over the past century. He couldn't afford to make any mistakes.

No matter how much that spark inside Róisín had called to him.

He shook his head, trying to shake her out of his head, and drew his finger along the map. Aoife should've been there by now, she had said June. The calendar at the corner of his desk glared at him. The date, July nineteenth. He had reached for her but had come up with nothing.

Then he had fumbled, again, with Róisín.

He couldn't explain it, that draw, that driving, urging need to get inside of her mind. She reeked of humanness, her magic weak, like that of a hedgewitch or a woodswitch. Nothing that would bring him any benefit. Unless... he thralled her to join him.

"I bet she tastes delicious," he mused.

"What?" Bill stopped pacing and faced him. "Who?"

"Nothing." He leaned back in his chair, steepling his fingers before him. "Nothing that concerns you."

"I think it does," Bill snapped. "Whatever it is, you're not focused on what's important. You're telling me you need to go out of town when you have just gotten back. Lina gained significant ground while we were gone this last time. We're going to lose everything."

"I don't need what's here. Not anymore." He shook his head. The only thing here that may entertain him to stay longer would be *her*. However, he had tasks to complete.

"This is ridiculous." Bill threw up his hands.

"Mm, yes it is," Madigan agreed. "Aoife appears to be playing games again."

"Who? You're not making any sense. You've lost your mind, that's what it is. Otherwise, you wouldn't be throwing all our work away like this!"

"I think it's time I pay her a visit." He rose from his desk. "She thinks she has Legianne blocked to me. I think it's time for me to show my hand. It's all going to be mine. Nothing, I mean nothing, is out of reach."

Bill blinked, his brow wrinkling.

Madigan slipped into his suit coat and faced him. "Mrs. McGrath-Commons will win the vote by a landslide." He kept his eyes steady on Bill's while he slipped the gold buttons pressed with the imprint of the head of the Aunellion dire wolf, through their buttonholes. "You will concede. If I have not returned by the time that has happened, you will remain in your home until you hear from me. Do you understand?"

His face blank, eyes clouded, he nodded.

"Good. I'll know if you step out of line. There will be a price to pay," he warned, then pulled his power up, enveloping himself, and vanished before Bill's eyes.

<h1 style="text-align:center">CHAPTER 43</h1>

Exhaustion had clung to Róisín. Despite the urge to sleep for weeks, she needed to send word to the others. It was a priority.

She pooled together her magic and called out to David. He'd spent more and more time in the woods, bounding between realms in search. His form allowed him to quietly access places and information without alerting anyone who may work alongside Madigan.

Róisín had missed him once he had begun to stay away for longer stretches of time. David, like all of them, had a task in this. It didn't mean that she couldn't be lonely when he wasn't there. Or have that urge rise inside to ask him to stay. There had been a comfort in having him close by. Something familiar to embrace.

"What do they want me to do?" She stroked his soft fur. They sat in a chair on her patio, a blanket draped over her legs. A chill had settled into her bones that she could not escape despite the warm Maine summer air.

"Right now, to stay put. They know the shields here will protect you while you rest and gather your strength. That is key. Especially if he can learn more about you. That you're Aoife's granddaughter. That you're his niece."

She traced the outline of his ear, frowning. "They have the same suspicion I do, don't they?"

"They didn't say it outright, no." He nuzzled against her hand in a comforting gesture. "I believe they do, though. The signs all point to that she worked with him."

"I thought I'd be ready. Now that it's on the horizon, I'm not." She shook her head. "I'm not ready at all."

"None of us are," he said. "In all my years, not even the trials. Witches have survived everything, but this, it could very well be the end. For all of us."

"I'm terrified. Not just for us, but the humans, the creatures, everyone... everything. Once he has it all, there is nothing that can stop him. No one stands a chance."

They fell into a comfortable silence, and it was then, faintly in the distance, Róisín heard a bird sing. She straightened in her chair, hugging David closer to her chest, unsure of how to react. It could be Madigan trying a sleight of hand to draw her in. Another bird joined in its song.

"Is that?" she breathed out. Her heart lifted, wanting to soar away.

"It is." David's nose wriggled and bounced in delight. "They're returning. Only a few now, but they're coming back."

She listened to the distant song, leaning back in the chair. "Have you always been a rabbit?"

"In this life, yes. I was a turtle once; I've been various birds. Never a human form, though."

"Would you, if we can beat this, would you stay? Or would you go?"

"That depends. If I was asked to stay, I would consider it. Otherwise, there will be somewhere else the Goddess and Sisters need me. That is where I would go."

"I would like you to stay with me." She closed her eyes to soak in the sounds around them. A homesickness for her childhood home rose inside of her. "Wherever I land after this is over, would you?"

"I would like that." He hopped up to her shoulder to burrow against her neck. "What will your human think of me, though? I surely cannot be expected to be quiet every time he is around."

"My human?" Her mind drifted to Caid, who was still asleep in her bed upstairs. The bed he had returned to, no questions asked, for four nights in a row. Since that day Madigan had watched her.

She had been restless, unable to sleep. Every time she closed her eyes, she could see into the depths of Madigan's night-colored eyes. Once she was sure she could slip out of the bed without disturbing Caid, she crept downstairs and made herself tea, then waited for David's morning visits. "Do you mean Caid?"

"Yes."

"He's not my human," she said flatly.

"You love him."

She let out a sad sigh and shook her head. "Love sometimes is just an emotion. Even if I did, love does not make him mine."

"Why do you fight it so?"

"Because..." she trailed off. *If he leaves, I'll break. If he hates who I am, I'll die.* "There's so many things that can go wrong. He can leave when he finds out what I am. Or I give him my heart. Then Madigan learns of it. He can use him, hurt him, to get to me. It'll never be safe."

"You have decided for him whether he gets to take that risk?"

"I... no. I don't know. I've never been here before." She rubbed aggressively at her temples, a headache was growing with ferocity there. "Even the last time, she—we—it wasn't like this. It was just a person with a knife. That was an everyday risk."

"Perhaps you should think about that last sentence." He bounded down her arm, landing on the deck with a soft thud. "Every day is a risk."

She rose and followed him to the back door, working through what he had said.

"You have pushed him away. You fear he will leave you when he knows. Yet, he has returned every single day, not knowing what is wrong, just that something is. Correct?"

Pushing open the slider, she waited for him to hop inside before she followed.

"Yes." The word burning her tongue from the admission.

"Life, love, any of it, is never without risk. For all of us. There are moments that will be easy, others will be hard. The question you need to find the answer to is, is this life you're living worth the risk of losing love for, over a little bit of fear?"

"I'd hardly say it was a little bit," she muttered.

"It may seem monumental—"

The floors of the old house creaked as footsteps neared the kitchen.

"Good afternoon, Kincaid."

Chapter 44

"Holy shit." Caid stumbled into the refrigerator so hard that the freezer door popped open and released a breath of frigid air over him. "Fuck! Did that rabbit just talk?!"

Róisín looked from him to the rabbit on the floor at her feet, an unspoken conversation passing between them, as though she tried to figure a way to either reveal or conceal a secret.

"Yes, I did, in fact, speak," the rabbit said.

"I'm losing my mind." Caid rubbed a hand over his face. "That's what's happening. I'm almost forty years old and this is it. They say it's the mind that goes first."

"Caid." She took a slow, cautious step closer to him. "Why don't you have a seat?"

He kept his eyes on the rabbit, while feeling behind him for the freezer door, using both hands to close it.

"Róisín? I grabbed the packages on the porch and set them in the living room." Lina stepped into the kitchen and paused, her eyes bouncing between them. "Am I interrupting? I can come back later." She jerked a thumb toward the front door.

Caid opened his mouth to speak, but no words came out, only the sound of a heavy breath of disbelief.

When Róisín offered nothing either, Lina unloaded items from the cloth grocery bag she carried, setting them on the counter.

"Are those raspberries for me?" The rabbit hopped across the floor toward the counter. Its nose wiggled as it drew in the scents of what Lina unpacked. "And strawberries too?"

What the fuck?

She beamed down at it, rubbing a hand over its head. "I couldn't forget my favorite fluffy bunny. The strawberries, though, those are mine and Róisín's to go with the summer salad I'm making for our lunch."

"You..." Caid's eyes narrowed on his sister before they widened. "You know it talks?!"

Róisín nudged the chair from the table toward him. "You really should sit, Caid. Your face has gone white."

He dropped heavily onto the chair, and it groaned. Covering his face with his hands, he drew in a breath, holding it. He shook his head, trying to wake himself up, then shoved his hands into his hair. "I've lost my mind."

"Have you," Lina whispered. "You know... Shown him yet?"

"No," Róisín whispered. "This sort of just, um, happened. I was still working out how to tell him. David here took matters into his own hands." She shot David an annoyed glare. David ignored her, nibbling on a raspberry, the red juices marking his white paws.

"Shown me what?" He couldn't stop himself from rubbing at his face again, pressing the heels of his palms into his eyes as he tried to scrub the scene before him away. This was all a dream, he would wake up any minute. Any minute.

"Maybe you should wait." Lina frowned, studying him carefully. He had covered his mouth with both hands, his eyes watered and his shoulders shook with his laughter. "I think David's shocked him enough today."

"No." The word came out as a strangled sounding chuckle, and he sat up straighter. He lifted and spread out his hands. "Oh, no, no. Whatever it is, might as well get it out right now. While we're here. With talking rabbits."

"Um..." Lina bit her lip, eyes darting to Róisín. "You're sure?"

He sighed loudly, trying to mask another chuckle, making his shoulders shake. "Out with it. Can't be any more bizarre of a dream I'm having than a rabbit, named David, that talks."

Róisín stepped to the table and closed her eyes. Extending her arm, she turned her hand palm up.

Caid shot up from the chair so quickly, it fell backward, clattering to the floor.

Light radiated from her skin, and within her palm, a small rosebud bloomed. When she opened her eyes, they swirled with splashes of yellows, greens, oranges, reds, and hues of purple. Like peering down into a tornado that had consumed a rainbow.

"Shit," Caid breathed out. Emotions, what seemed like all of them, even the ones he wasn't sure he could name, slammed into him all at once. Amazed at the sight before him. And proud. It was a peculiar thing to feel at the moment, but he was filled with so much pride for Róisín. What she had shared of herself with him, to see she held such magnificence within her. How did she not realize how strong she was? It couldn't be easy for her to reveal something like this to anyone.

"Isn't she amazing?" Lina asked him.

"You're not?" He looked between them.

"Oh, I've known for weeks now." She waved him off.

"This is just..."

The rose bloom shrank back into Róisín's hand. When he lifted his gaze, her eyes danced and swirled with vibrant splashes of purple, maroon, and every shade of blue and green he had ever seen. Her mouth was tight, lines bracketing the corners of her lips. Her brows drawn down and together, almost touching just over the bridge of her nose.

His eyes widened and his breath quickened trying to catch up to his racing heart. This was why she'd been so closed off since returning to town. Annoyance tickled the hairs on the back of his neck. Had he given her the impression at any time that he wouldn't want her in his life, even over something like this? He shifted his weight, racking his brain to think of their every interaction.

"I'm gonna..." Lina motioned to the door. "I'll come back later. I think you two need to talk, alone." She bent, reaching for David.

"Don't forget my raspberries," he said.

"Never." She kissed his head and tucked the container under her other arm.

Once the front door clicked closed, Róisín turned to Caid. "You have questions."

"Yes? No? I don't know." He righted the tipped over chair. "My brain, it's pretty much short-circuited, so it's a blank space right now. Shock. That's what it is, shock. I've gone into shock. When I come down from it, I'm going to find out it's some crazy dream."

"Caid." She laid a hand on his forearm. "This isn't a dream."

"Can you, you know? Or is it just plants?" he asked.

"I'm more in tune with nature, so that's easier for me. But yes, I can heal and give life to animals... and humans."

"I really broke my ankle," he said, awareness washing over him. "It wasn't a sprain."

She nodded.

"What about those?" He motioned to the now scabbed over marks on her leg.

"It's never without consequence" She wove her fingers together and her chin dropped to her chest. "My magic is used to heal nature, to help plants grow, to keep the balance there. If I use it for life outside of that, there's a price I must pay."

Every muscle within him tightened at the unspoken implication. "What does that mean?"

"Everything"— she lifted a hand to her chest—"in here, it goes dormant for a time. I can't use my power for anything. I can't even make a blade of grass grow. A temporary exchange of my power each time I use it outside of my purpose."

"You fixed my ankle at the expense of being able to take care of your own injuries." Of course, she had. He knew better than to believe she would've done it differently. She had shown him over and over again that she was always the one who took care of others, and never having someone take care of her. He had hoped he'd been clear enough with his own actions that she could see he wanted to be the one to take care of her. Be her shoulder, be her support.

"It was broken." Her quiet voice pulled him from his circling thoughts. "You wouldn't have made it down the mountain."

He clenched his jaw, swallowing hard, trying to keep his frustration tamped down. "I'd have managed fine. You could have bled to death before we got back down."

"I was fine," she said.

"You were not fine," he said tightly, his nostrils flaring wide with the sharp breath he released. "Carrying you back down when you passed out, then your face, your lips, like the color drained out of you, like your life was draining out of you."

"That was my magic being pulled from me," she whispered. "I was fine. I am fine."

He studied her for a moment, trying not to remember the way she felt, laying limp in his arms. Shaking his head, his voice was hoarse when he spoke. "Don't do it again. Okay?"

"Caid—"

"No. I break my ankle, my arm, shit, even my neck, don't. Okay?"

"I can't do that." Her eyes filled with tears, and she blinked to keep them from falling. "I can't."

"You're not saving me at the expense of yourself," he said. "I can't let you do that."

"I—"

"I can't let you do it." He reached for her, his voice quiet. "I can't," he repeated louder, more firmly. "Somewhere along the way, Róisín, I've fallen in love with you. Wildly in love with you."

"We can't, you can't, it's not—" She shook her head frantically. She laid her hands on his chest, trying not to look at him. "Come with me."

CHAPTER 45

Róisín held one of Caid's hands in hers and led him across her backyard, toward the forest. The way her heart thundered in her ears reminded her of the time when she was small after her father's passing, when her mother had taken her to Baijiola. The shells on the beach there were the size of her head, and when she held one to her ears, the steady droning of the deep sound from within filled her head, vibrating through her.

"I guess it makes sense now why you have the best yard in town," Caid said from behind her. When they stopped at the edge of the woods, he looked down at her feet. "Shouldn't you put shoes on?"

"My great-grandmother Norah, she was theirs." She tipped her head back, closing her eyes and opening her senses. The returning of life, albeit small, reached out to greet her and her magic. "When she left this life, it passed on to my grandmother, Aoife. Now..." She drew in a shaky breath, trying to find the courage she needed to go on. "It is I who belongs to them."

"Who?"

She motioned for him to follow her.

"It's so quiet." His voice was so soft that if she hadn't already had her senses open to the returning life, she wouldn't have heard his words.

"It's dying," she said.

He stopped, turning in a circle to take it in. "It just looks sleepy to me."

She rested a hand on the entwined cedars, reaching her magic deep.

"We remember him," the taller one whispered through her skin. *"He and his friends used to come and climb all of us when they were small."*

She pictured a small, dirt and grass stained Caid, racing through these very woods, crawling up trees, and smiled. "You used to climb the trees here."

He faced her, curiosity wrinkling the space between his brows, causing his nose to scrunch. "Yeah, Max, Wyatt, and I. Mrs. Lagree used to always give us cookies and milk for mowing her lawn or helping with her gardens."

"He kissed a girl by the knotted pine to his left," the trees told her.

"You kissed someone just there." She pointed. A small zing of jealousy rippled through her. How much she had wanted to be his first, last, and only shocked her when she used this moment to show him all of who she was.

He took a step forward, his head tipped slightly to one side as he considered her. "How do you know that?"

"I am theirs." She smoothed her hand over the rough bark.

"You can talk to trees?"

She held out her arms, turning in a slow circle. "I can talk to everything."

He raised an eyebrow. "I want to be weirded out by this. At least, I think I do. I don't know. Maybe a part of me is. But I can't help wanting to know more; as much as you can tell me."

Her next words spilled from her lips before she could stop them. "Stewart Munson isn't human."

"What do you mean? Not human?" His brows slammed down, like angry dashes over his narrowed eyes.

She walked deeper, around the unfurling ferns. She could feel him hesitate to follow her, no doubt watching the ground bloom around her as she moved. The warmth of her magic was a comfort in the confusion of her emotions at the moment. Her heart both sang at the fact that

Caid hadn't left her but hurt as she wondered if it'd only been because it hadn't yet wholly sunk in.

What had it been like when her mother revealed herself to her father? Her home in the few years they'd had with her father had been full of love and laughter. She struggled to recall the quieter moments her parents had. The ones where they thought perhaps she hadn't been watching, when in fact, she had.

Her memories had begun to return after her return to Shasta's home for the first time in decades, but they were still muddled thanks to whatever wards Aoife had built around Róisín when her mother had passed. A faint glimmer of her mother and father dancing in the kitchen. Stephen crooned a song as he spun Brenna around, bringing her close to him.

Love. They had held so much love for one another. A human, and a witch. A human knowing their love was a witch.

She turned her head and caught sight of Caid walking behind her. His steps were clunky, stumbling, his focus more on taking in their surroundings. He said he loved her; he still followed her.

Could she have what her mother and father had?

She stopped at a graying tree, pressing her hand to it, reaching deep within herself, and pulled at what little of her magic she could grasp. Then she tugged it up and pressed it into the trunk's center. "I cannot say he is like me. Like us."

Her mother and father faced wars. Brenna had to shield them from Aoife. Róisín had to face Madigan. She had to carry that burden. Had to carry that heavy pit that'd grown in her stomach with each passing day that whispered to her she would not make it to the other side. That she would not live through it.

"Lina was wrong, amazing doesn't come close to covering it." Caid's voice was filled with wonder and awe behind her.

She had been so worried about him pushing her away when he learned the truth that she failed to realize she could have to be the one to push him away.

It's not safe.

"He's killing them." Róisín's magic wrapped her tighter, soothing her warring emotions, the rising sadness that seeing the damage always brought on. "I come out here every day, find the ones I can still save. There's so many. Time is running out. I fear for many of them." Her shoulders heaved with her heavy breath. "I fear for all of us."

"What does that mean?" he asked.

She bent and waved her hands over a dark pool of water. The red film from the surface rose, reaching for her fingertips. She moved her hand over the water, giving the film space to reach for her. It crept up her fingers, winding around her hand, up her arm. He reached for her, but she stopped him with a slight shake of her head.

"I bring it within, then my magic heals it. That's all evil or darkness is. A bruise, a wound, an illness. Sometimes we need the wounds to bleed out the evil before we heal it. These." She wiped her palms on her shorts. "These have been left to bleed too long, now the balance is off."

"Who is Munson?"

"His name is Madigan. He wants to destroy us. Even though he is one of us." She searched the trees for any new signs of life returning on its own beyond the birds she'd heard that morning. "He wants everything. Power."

Caid stood behind her now. It would've been so easy to lean into his strength. Instead, she took a step away, putting distance between them. Alarms flashed in her to stop, to be quiet. They urged her to shut down, shift away. To flee. She took a moment to center herself. She needed to face this, to tell him everything, for both of them.

"My grandmother, Aoife, was supposed to come. She was supposed to be the one to handle all of this. But she became very ill suddenly. Which is peculiar because witches never become sick. It was when she passed everything began to unravel. Secrets came out, truths revealed." She wrapped her arms around herself, begging her magic to just hold on, to keep her there, in the woods with Caid. It wanted to shift away to where it knew she and it could find comfort. "I learned that my mother tried to protect me from Aoife, but the Sisters handed down my mother's fate, my father's fate. There were choices and sacrifices that needed to be made for all of us. I know that now. I know she missed my father. She didn't want to leave me because of it."

"What happened to them?" he whispered.

"He was human, my father. My mother fell in love with him. They married, then they had me. We had a life. A *good* life, full of love and joy. Then my father was called to the first great world war. My mother took an assignment to go as well. She worked in the hospitals in more modern times, the healer tents before that. She'd help dying soldiers ease through their transition to the afterlife so they wouldn't suffer through a painful death."

"She, she took their lives?" His throat bobbed as he swallowed hard.

Róisín nodded, moving deeper through the trees again. "One day, it was my father's cot she stood at. She knew she couldn't save him, she tried, but she couldn't. She came back so broken. I was young, only a child, but I remember she came back home as a ghost."

She glanced over her shoulder to see if he was still following her, only to see him looking at his fingers, tapping them together as though he tried to count out something. She was about to warn him of a tree when he stumbled on a root. He caught himself and let his hands fall to his sides, keeping his eyes up on her.

Róisín offered him a small smile before continuing on. "Shasta's been teaching me how to balance my mother's powers with my own. How to filter my life force back into me, behind the power I expel when I use another, so I don't drain myself. We don't know what will stop Madigan, and without the full support of the council, the other Covens, I don't know if we'll be strong enough."

She could sense he'd stopped walking, and turned to face him.

His hands were at his hips, the tips of his fingers white from how hard he held there. He opened his mouth to speak, but then closed it, pressing his lips into a thin line. "Does he know you're here, Munson?"

"He knew the moment I walked into your town meeting that evening. I could sense his probing. I also sensed Bill's thrall. I needed him, still need him, to think I'm weaker than I am. He's severed the connection we carry, so he does not know my grandmother has moved on from this life or who I truly am. It's why, as much as I want to, I cannot walk out here and heal all of this or fix the town's poisoned waters."

"Does Lina know all of this?"

"No." She shook her head. "She knows about my magic, yes. That's all. David and I have said nothing about the rest. To everyone here, I'm just a girl trying to work with her new community to stop a mega-rich guy from over-developing the land, killing animal habitat, and poisoning the water with the dredges his factory dumps."

"Meanwhile, you're a magical being, trying to stop a blockbuster movie ranked baddie from killing us all," he supplied.

"It's not just me. I have Lucius, Nanette, Shasta, Matthew, their Covens."

"What about yours?"

"I wasn't lying when I said that I was alone. Aoife took them all. We think she spared me only because of my power, paired with the belief that I would follow her anywhere, do anything when the time came."

He drifted his gaze from her to the surrounding woods.

Róisín's chest squeezed, her lungs burning. She took a slow, unsteady breath and tried to blink the burning sensation away that was building around her eyes.

Finally, he looked back at her. "Still doesn't stop me from loving you."

She threw up her hands.

"What?" he asked. "Did you think taking me out here, showing me what you did, telling me all of that would change a damned thing?"

"We can't, Caid." *It's not safe, you'll die, and I can't bear that. Can't survive that.*

"Give me a really good reason we can't. Just one."

In a sick twist of fate, she realized it would've been easier if he'd run out of her front door the moment she opened her palm. She had finally found someone who loved all of her, and it was dangerous to hold on to it. "One thing? Fine. I'm almost one hundred and twenty years old."

He slowly raised a brow and let out a low whistle. "What, so, you like, live really long?"

"My mother was four hundred-twenty-four years old, my grand-mother almost seven hundred."

He crossed his arms over his chest and tipped his head to one side.

"I can't watch you die." She blinked quickly, trying to contain the tears that blurred her sight.

"We all die someday, Róisín."

"You're human. You have another forty years, at best."

He shrugged and moved closer. "Then we make the best of those forty years. I can see it in your eyes." He pointed at her, still moving closer. "You are digging, searching for something that will scare me off. You're coming up empty every single time, aren't you? There is nothing, Róisín. This is what has been bothering you since you've come back, isn't it? Why? Why try to shut me out? I told you I wanted to help, whatever it is."

"It's not safe," she pressed. "I will admit, I was terrified of you finding out. I was terrified the moment I realized I loved you because love isn't enough to keep people in my life. I didn't want to lose you."

"And I'm still standing here, aren't I?"

He stood almost toe to toe with her now, forcing her to tip her head back to look at his face. "You'll die, Caid. He can destroy you, and I can't keep you safe. I don't even know if I can keep myself safe, let alone you."

"Then let me try to keep you safe," he whispered.

Her heart dropped to her feet. He would try. He would run toward danger, without a second thought, for her. She had been so wrapped up in her history, tying him in with all the others. Lina had even told her, insisted. Yet, Róisín had let her past cloud her mind, filling her with unnecessary worries. The wrong worries, and she found herself unprepared and helpless.

He ran a hand through his hair, his eyes hard on hers. "Róisín... What do you want me to do? Do you want me to turn around, walk back to my truck, and go home? Not look back? Not call you? Think about you? Just forget I ever knew you?"

That wasn't what she wanted, but she couldn't let him know that. Safety, she had to keep him safe. Whatever she had to do to make sure he was, she had to do it.

"Yes," she choked out, fighting that fire that rose inside of her, pushing the pain down.

He looked her over once more before finally nodding. Then,

without a word, he turned and walked away from her. The ferns grew up to block out his retreating form as he made his way back to the house.

She let several minutes pass before letting herself sink to the ground. As her body hit the forest floor, a spray of aster popped up around her.

Chapter 46

CAID stopped at the door of his truck, his hand on the handle, staring at his reflection in the window. His hair a mess, mouth set in a tight, grim line. What was he doing? Was he really letting her push him away?

Yes, yes, I am. He forced himself to open the door.

She couldn't stop him from loving her, but he would not force her to be with him.

A soft wind wrapped around him, and he stopped half in and half out of the truck. It pricked at his senses, feeling as though it tried to pull him back. He turned back to the house, watching, waiting for a moment.

He started to swing his other leg up into the truck when the wind kicked up.

"She needs you," a song-like voice said in his ear.

"What?" He set both of his feet on the driveway, his head jerking around. "Who's there?"

"Go to her," the voice urged, the wind wrapping around him, nudging him back toward the woods.

A wave of urgency washed over him, and then he was running. Around the house, across the yard, to where he had left her.

Róisín sat on the ground, body awash with light. Flowers, brambles, and vines exploding from the earth around her. Her body rocked and shook with jarring, silent sobs. In an instant, he was on the ground in front of her, pulling her into his arms, wrapping her tight.

"What are you doing?" Her cries muffled against his chest.

"I'm not leaving you. There's nothing you can say or do, Róisín. I'm here." He closed his eyes and hugged her tighter, breathing in the smell of her. "I'm here."

"It's not safe for you. You can't..." she choked out between sobs. "What if something happens?"

"Look, I will not even remotely pretend in my head that I can go up against magic. I'm also not going to sit by if something happens to you. Does that mean I have a death wish?" He shrugged. "I have to at least try, Róisín."

When she pulled back to look at him, her eyes still swam with the unfamiliar colors. Slowly, they swirled, fading, until they returned to solid turquoise again.

"I was going to leave," he confessed. "I'd be a lowlife if I tried to press the matter when you so clearly wanted me to go. I was going to go home, lick my wounds, and try to get on with life."

"You came back," she said hoarsely.

"I did." He nodded. "She told me to. Said you needed me, to go to you."

"She?"

"Until a few hours ago, I'd have thought I was crazy and hearing shit, but after all this?" He looked around them. "I'm thinking I need to pay more attention."

She tried to pull free of his hold. "Who told you?"

"The voice in the wind." He said it so matter of fact, he shocked himself.

"What—" She swallowed hard. "What did the voice sound like?"

He thought for a moment, recalling the musical note each word carried. "Pretty. Sort of rolling. A little like singing."

"My mother," she breathed out.

"Your mother?"

"She..." She looked up at the sky, closing her eyes. Then, her whole body sagged and she became something more painful, more shattered before him. Her body shook violently and loud, gasping sobs escaped as new tears streamed down her face.

"Shh." He rubbed a hand over her back, soothing.

"I can feel her. Faintly, but she's here." She buried her face against his chest.

Not knowing what else to do, Caid took her in his arms, then carefully rising to his feet, brought her back to the house. He kicked off his shoes by the back door, then made his way upstairs to her room, laying down on the bed with her.

She finally quieted, her body still, when the sky outside had darkened with night.

"Róisín?" he whispered into the dark room. After a moment of no response, he knew she'd fallen asleep. With her body still tucked tightly against his, he closed his eyes and let himself drift.

CHAPTER 47

Róisín stood at her kitchen sink, lost in the motions of rinsing the soap from the pot she'd used to make the summer marinara sauce they had with dinner earlier that evening.

The surrounding air shifted.

Her heart stuttered. Her breath hitched, and she closed her eyes, letting that familiar lavender scent wrap around her like a hug.

"My sweet rose," Brenna whispered.

Slowly, Róisín turned, taking in the figure of her mother before her. Just as she'd been the last time Róisín had seen her. Her red hair, a wild flame around her porcelain skin, emerald eyes sharp on her, watching her back.

"How?" Róisín finally managed.

"One last act from the Goddess, perhaps." She took a cautious step forward.

When Brenna was near enough, Róisín lifted a hand, reaching out. The solidness of her skin met Róisín's touch, and both women sucked in a pained breath before embracing.

"I miss you," Róisín whispered finally, breaking their silence.

"I miss you, too. We don't have long, and there's much I need to tell you."

"About Aoife."

"You've discovered all about Aoife that I knew. What the Sisters told me."

"How'd she do it? How did she live so on the outside but still on the inside at the same time? What did she want with me?"

Brenna smoothed Róisín's hair from her face, a sad smile lifted the corners of her mouth. "Aoife always believed that the world owed her. She never had love in her heart for anything or anyone other than herself. I did what I could to protect you from that."

Róisín's heart began to beat, front and center, in her throat. She placed a hand there in an attempt to calm it so that she could swallow, try to stop the walls from closing in on her. The words her mother was speaking were the confirmation that Róisín's thoughts of Aoife were right. Aoife wanted Róisín's magic.

"She couldn't have my magic, and she was desperate. I was her prey for centuries until I got away. I was feeling her against that wall. That was when I knew she would find me. I wasn't ready. Then again, I never could have been ready to leave you." She reached her hands out to cup Róisín's face. "I wanted to watch you grow old, find love, start a family, but sixty-three years was all we were to have. You needed my magic. It needed to be *yours*, and she was getting closer. The only way for you to have that life I wanted you to have, was for me to go."

"I was so mad at you for so long. I thought... before I knew what had really happened, I thought you didn't love me enough to want to stay."

She thumbed away the tears on Róisín's cheeks. "I'm sorry for that. I wish there had been a way to prepare you. The less you knew, the better. Especially knowing that Aoife would have her hands on you for a time. The less she knew about what was happening around her, the better." Brenna stepped back, scanning her from head to toe and back. She clasped her hands together, holding them at her chest. Her face brightening. "He's good for you."

"Madigan?!"

Brenna chuckled. "Oh, no, my little rose, not him. Although he is a truly handsome devil. To be frank, I believe that's how he's gotten all that he has. I was, however, talking about the boy currently asleep in your bed. Kincaid James McGrath."

Róisín took a step away from her . "What do you know about Caid?"

"That without knowing where exactly Madigan was going to settle, it was nearly impossible to get the McGrath family to migrate to an area close enough that you two would be put in one another's paths." Brenna spoke it so casually, Róisín had been sure that she had misheard.

"Wh-what are you talking about?" A wide smile bloomed on Brenna's face. Her eyes sparkled. "No."

"Oh, yes." She nodded. "I know you thought it was Alexandria. That was why it felt the way it did during. How much it hurt even decades past what happened that night. It never was her, it's always been him."

"He's human."

"Your father was human."

"You two weren't bound, though."

"There has never been a written rule that binding was meant for witch to witch," Brenna noted.

"That may be true, but there's never been a witch-human bind in our history."

"Mm," Brenna replied absentmindedly.

"Mother," she said.

"I only know what the Sisters dangled before me. Those things were that I would lose your father, that I would lose you, too, if I did not walk away from my life to allow my power to pass to you. I had an idea of what would happen with Aoife, because I knew her well enough to know which choices she would make. I only knew about you and Kincaid because, well, things came into play that caused the need to intervene."

Róisín reached behind herself, feeling for the countertop, then moving back the steps she needed to lean against it before her legs collapsed from underneath her. When she brought her focus back to her mother, she no longer appeared solid.

"What do I do now?"

"You love him, and let him love you," she replied simply.

"That's it? Is he..." Her throat became constricted, afraid to voice her deepest fear. She shifted on her feet, the room growing hot around her, smothering.

"Even if I did know that, I wouldn't tell you. I could never. Not after knowing long before I had even met your father that I was going to lose him. It taints everything." She reached a fading hand out toward Róisín. "Trust yourself. Trust him. The others will be by your side. Trust them. I love you, my little rose."

"What comes next? Don't go, please!"

Róisín thrashed awake in her dark bedroom. The bed shifted next to her before Caid's arms came tightly around her.

"It was just a dream." He pressed a kiss to her head. "Just a dream."

Gasping for air, she clung to him like he was a lifeline. Her mother said that they were bound. Instinct told her to fight it, to protect him. A bind snapping into place would put a beacon over him for all witches, good and bad. However, the conversation with her mother, the message she brought her, had her pulling back to look at him.

His sandy hair was still mussed from sleep, but his hazel eyes were alert, watching her.

"I love you," she said. "I'm sorry for trying to push you away earlier. I had been so worried that you would leave me when you found out the truth, that I never thought to consider what would happen if you stayed." Her chest rose and fell with her gasping breaths. "When you did, I tried to push you away again. I panicked. I'm still panicking. I'm sorry now for the things that will come, what can, what may, what probably will happen to you. I love you."

He cupped her jaw. The feel of his thumb as it stroked her cheek soothed her. "I get why you did it. Don't apologize. For that, or anything else. Okay?"

She nodded, covering the hand on her face with hers.

"I'm here for it all, for as long as I've got." He brought her closer, laying his lips on hers.

Chapter 48

Róisín laid curled against his chest, her breaths soft against his skin as she slept. The past twenty-four hours of his life had shifted him off course into uncharted territory.

Magic was real.

And it wasn't books, potions, and words. It was something utterly different from what his childhood imagination had conjured up all of those years ago.

She had simply opened her hand, then grew a flower in her palm. She had spoken with the trees in the forest. There had been no other way she would've known about the time he had snuck out there with Stacy Freeman, who had, in those days, lived next to Kitty Lagree. Max, nor Wyatt hadn't even known about it. That moment had not been one of his proudest. Driven by his hormones, he had been all teeth and hands, nearly coming in his pants two seconds after his tongue had touched hers.

Magic.

Something else from her confessions had hung with him like a black cloud. That one thing out of all of it had set him seething. Stewart Munson.

"Does he—" He cleared away the thickness that had risen in his throat with the rage that burned like an inferno inside. "Does he know who you are?"

Róisín stirred, the flutter of her lashes kissing his skin as she opened her eyes. "No."

Relief should have come at her simple, firm statement, but it didn't.

"I've shielded the full strength of my powers while I've been here. Plus, my father was a human," she explained.

He pulled back slightly to look down at her, unsure of how to ask the question that formed.

"I, um." A finger tapped lightly on his stomach as she thought. "I think the easiest way to explain it is, I smell different as a child of a witch and a human. With that, the wards around me, for Madigan, I'm just a witch whose Coven lines have been diluted. I'm weak, and not a threat."

"So... all witches don't know one another?"

Her laughter was light, and she shook her head. "It's true that there's few of us left. But no, we don't all know one another. All the Coven leaders who sit upon our council know one another, that's it. Even for every member of the different Covens, that's too many."

"And you lead your Coven?"

"If you want to call it that."

He heard the sadness in her voice, and his chest tightened. He drew her closer to him, pressing a kiss to her forehead. "If, as you say, you're all searching for a way to do what you need to with Munson, Madigan, why are you the only one here?"

"Aoife was the one who was originally going to come, she was so powerful, she could not only conceal just how strong of a witch she was, but she had cloaking abilities. She could become anyone, anything. It needed to be someone with power that Madigan wouldn't sense or recognize and after she was gone, I was the only one left. Should he act on me, I could hold my ground."

"You're powerful."

"Even before Aoife died. Once she..."

"You're more."

She slipped from his arms and sat on the edge of the bed, back to him. He felt her pull away more than physically at that moment.

"Róisín." He shifted across the bed so that he was behind her.

"It's a lot." She sighed. "A lot to take in. I'm a witch, and next to Madigan, probably the most powerful one alive. My grandmother was, by lack of any better definition, evil. She was also either working with him or looking to take his power for herself. Not only did my grandmother kill my Coven, but my mother also sacrificed herself so that I could inherit her power because she had that much faith that when I did learn the truth, I would do the right thing. That's a lot for even myself to process."

He lifted a hand to sweep the hair that had fallen over her shoulder, shielding her face, back, but paused. Sitting up, he moved so that their thighs touched. "She found out, didn't she? The one you mentioned before when you said she couldn't accept who you were."

Her eyes shuttered, and a lone tear rolled down her cheek.

Taking her chin between his thumb and fingers, he turned her head to face him. "I'm not going anywhere. I'm not leaving you alone to deal with this. I don't know what I'm going to do if something happens, but I will do my damndest to keep you safe. Got it? I don't care if when all of this is done, you let the shields around you fall, horns of fire suddenly sprout from your head. It will not change any of this."

"You've seen me without my shields."

His heart stopped. "Why would you risk that?"

"We weren't here. It was when we were hiking. His magic stopped prodding because I was out of reach, so I let all the wards and shields fall away so that I could breathe."

"Well shit, I just thought that glow was because I'd just rocked your world."

"I mean, you did." Her eyes sparkled at him like an ocean under a summer sun.

He couldn't help the smirk tugging at his mouth. "Got plans this morning? I'd like to take a moment, or fifty, to rock it again."

Hesitation flashed in her face, like she was waiting for him to rise from the bed and walk out. Taking one of her hands in his, he linked their fingers. Her gaze dropped to where his thumb stroked over her hand.

"When this is all over." She cleared her throat. She brought her shoulders up, and her attention fully on him. A show of her confidence returning. "I can't wait to show you what it's like when I'm completely open and free from any wards and shields."

"Oh?" He dragged the word out, blinking slowly. "If I like, maybe decide I want to go on vacation to Florida tomorrow and bring you with me, would you need to be, you know?"

She let the laughter rumble out of her before launching herself at him, knocking him onto his back on the bed.

CHAPTER 49

S ECONDS after Róisín turned the shower off and stepped into her steam-filled bathroom, she heard Caid's shout, followed by the clatter of a pan hitting the floor. Panic rocked her to her feet, and she tightened a towel around herself, then raced downstairs.

"Matthew," she gasped.

He stood near the table, wearing an amused expression, while Caid stared at him with eyes as wide as saucers, unblinking.

"He's in Legianne," Matthew blurted.

Air didn't just leave her lungs, it was like it had been pulled from the room. The weight of the feeling, of Matthew's words, crushing her. Bringing a hand to her mouth to stifle a cry, she said, "He's looking for her."

"Who? What's going on?" Caid asked.

"If he's looking for her, Róisín, he's going to find out she's gone," Matthew said. "He'll figure out who you are."

"He's going to... Wait—" She held up a hand, her mind beginning to move again. "He can't go to Legianne. Aoife made sure it wasn't possible. She said it was to protect us. The last Legiannes."

"Lily got a window..." Matthew tracked Caid's movement toward

Róisín to stand at her back for support. Matthew looked to Róisín, the question in his eyes. She gave him a simple nod in return to convey that she had told Caid everything. "She and Nanette have been working on, shit, I can't remember what they called it. Anyway, Lily could briefly open a window to track some type of line. He felt it and broke it just as he arrived."

"Is she? He didn't?"

"She's fine. Nanette was there with her, supporting her with wards. He won't know it was them."

"Okay." She brought her hands to her stomach to calm the waves thrashing inside. Then she left the two men standing in the kitchen, and she raced back up into her bedroom. Kneeling before her mother's chest, she threw the top back. Pulling out contents, she tossed them on the carpet around her, until she saw the stack of books she was looking for. Throwing on one of Caid's t-shirts and a pair of her shorts, she returned to the kitchen.

"He knows about my mother because of Bernard. There's no way that if my grandfather was alive, he was clueless about her." She set the books on the table. "But, Aoife, it's hard to explain. She had been very particular about making sure we didn't draw attention with my magic. I could always feel in the line that had opened between Aoife and I after my mother died, some sort of wall."

"You think Aoife hid you from Madigan," Matthew said.

"It's a possibility? I'm not sure. She was married to his brother, so she—"

"Hold on." Caid lifted a hand. "This guy who is sucking up all the life around here so he can have more power and take all of you, maybe all of us out... that's your uncle?!"

She pressed her lips together in a tight line. "The thing about my family I learned the day you told me about yours."

He nodded in understanding, then waved for her to go on.

"These books have all my family records, plus the records of the other Coven families from Legianne. If he's there, he's looking for her because he doesn't know she's gone. The question is, why?"

"We need to scour these books." Matthew reached for one.

Caid followed suit, flipping one open. After a moment of blinking down at the pages, he snapped it shut, returning it to the pile. "I'll make us all something to eat."

Róisín dropped into a chair across from Matthew. "This one is the one that I found out about Bernard and Madigan in. This one"—she slipped one from the middle of the stack—"is the Coven history book."

"Give me the family tree one, you take the history." Matthew held his hand out, wiggling his fingers.

The kitchen grew quiet while Róisín and Matthew read through endless pages of the books. The only noise was the occasional scrape of the spatula, or soft thunk of the fridge closing.

"Oh, shit," she breathed out, drawing both males' attention. "I don't think Aoife was coming here to work with him. Definitely not to stop him, this confirms my thoughts on that. But..." She shook her head.

"What do you mean?" Matthew leaned over the table to peer down at the page.

"I wondered if, instead of coming to determine it was him to bring him back for council judgment, she was coming to stop him by taking his power for herself. With what the Seer said, and looking through the books to see that most of the Coven families ended within the same century... that fit and became a more realistic possibility."

"Now?" Caid asked from where he stood at the stove.

"My mother swiped these books after my father was killed. The history book is more of a journal, unwisely kept, by Aoife. This right here." She spun the book so that Matthew could read the section she pointed to.

His eyes followed the scrawling handwritten lines, growing wider as he read. Caid moved closer to them, waiting for someone to fill him in on what was unfolding.

Matthew sat back and rubbed a hand over his face. "They... Bernard... because Aoife wanted to... Jesus fucking Christ. I am so sorry, Róisín."

Róisín looked to Caid, her face pale, eyes glassy. "My grandmother and great-uncle killed my grandfather, because my grandmother was trying to double down her efforts to find my mother. She wanted to take my mother's life to gain her power. My grandfather would not let that happen. That must have been what my mother meant about feeling Aoife against her wall."

"What was Brenna's power?" Caid looked from her to Matthew.

"Death," Róisín whispered.

Caid gripped the back of the chair he stood behind, his knuckles turning white. "That's how she helped the soldiers. Like the Grim Reaper kind of thing."

"She—" Róisín pressed her lips together. Telling him had been one thing, but revealing just what her mother, and now she could do, hit the pit of her stomach differently. "It's hard to explain. No, she wasn't a Grim Reaper. She helped soldiers pass on because that was how she used her magic, its power. There is one death witch born every five-hundred years. Before the council's creation and laws were placed on our magic, yes, those death witches took life however they wanted to. Because her magic was within light, my mother became what was once called a healer, and later a nurse."

"When one of you dies, your magic..."

"Gets passed on to the oldest member of our family if there are no children, and our Coven leader if there isn't any family left to pass it on to. Unfortunately for Aoife, at the time of Brenna's passing, Róisín was already born," Matthew finished, his face set into hard, angry lines.

"Which means." Caid turned his attention fully to her.

"I was already an anomaly to the witches when I was born, as there are only three other recorded witches with the power of true life in our entire history among all our kind. As the last Legianne, I have the magic of every single Coven member to have ever existed. I am both my power of life, and my mother's of death. I am all the elements. I am the mind. I can change my form when I learn how to harness that power. I have the magic within for everything."

She watched as the realization set in. The way his grip grew slack where he had been holding the back of the chair, his chest rising and falling rapidly. He blinked slowly, his shoulders sagging. Her heart raced in her chest, waiting. He had been a solid rock the week before when he'd found out who she really was, but now...

"Madigan?" he asked.

"He's partly elemental, but wholly of mind magicks which gives him access to any magic he desires through enthralling the holder of the power he wants. He's also what is called a siphon. It's how he can make his power so strong." She glanced through the doors to the woods. "It's what he's been doing here. Siphoning life from the Earth, and all of you." She shifted in her chair, trying not to look at him, not wanting to see what may show in his eyes.

"And you?" He asked Matthew.

"Lightweight elemental, I can dabble in most, but my strength is fire. I can also shape-shift," he replied with a casual shrug.

"Shasta?"

"She's mostly earth and water. Like Matthew, she can shift, but nothing large," Róisín answered.

"It sounds like we're talking about Captain Planet." He straightened and shook his head in disbelief. "All right, so your grandmother wanted your mother's power, your grandfather said nope, he wasn't having it. Instead of backing off, she killed him."

Róisín wiped at her face, trying to collect herself. "Aoife was working with Madigan, and he's in Legianne because she hasn't shown up at their meeting place. It is the only thing that makes sense, so we need to assume this is what is happening. It's only a matter of time before he makes the connection from her to me. Before he does, we need to figure out what exactly my role was to be in this for her."

Matthew rose, neatly stacking the books again. "You need to consider Shasta's offer, Róisín. If not hers, Nanette's or my fathers."

She couldn't leave her Coven. Even if it was only her left, something in knowing her mother's sacrifice, in knowing what her parents had lost. Despite that, she had only ever seen the Wurbray city gleaming under the sun, or walked through the fields lit by the Yiananti, small, glowing insects for the first time after she had already lived half of her life. Letting go of Legianne was letting go of her parents. She squeezed her eyes closed, the lie falling from the tip of her tongue with ease. "I'll think about it."

"I'll talk to Lucius about what we've learned here. We'll need to find some way for all of us to come together. Lily and I acting as runners takes too long." Matthew looked to Caid. "Convince her to actually think about it, not just say she will."

Then he was gone.

"Can I ask you just one question?" Caid asked several minutes later.

Steeling herself, she found the strength to say yes.

"Can you do that?" He pointed to the spot where Matthew had stood.

"Yes. We live in different realms, and planes, they don't, uh, make those kinds of trips. We hone the skill early."

He slowly nodded, letting it soak in. "I lied, one more question."

She turned to him and lifted a brow.

"Why the hell don't you travel like that all the time? That's got to be faster than a plane, driving, a train, walking."

"I actually enjoy all of those things. Even when I'm in a different realm. The human modes of transportation open a whole new way to view life. Moving around like that." She waved a hand toward the other side of the table. "You don't get to watch the trees flash by, or the birds fly alongside you. You don't get to see the way the world opens back up when you come through the other side of a dark tunnel."

"When you put it like that..." He smiled. "You make it sound like blinking around is boring."

"Because it is. Especially the more you do it. Are you okay?"

"Why wouldn't I be? I'm fine. I need to know that *you* are okay. That was some heavy shit to learn. On top of all the rest you're shouldering right now. What can I do to help?"

She stepped to him, trying not to melt against him, when his hands came to her waist, his thumbs stroking lazily over her stomach. "Just keep being you. That's all I need."

"I noticed you didn't ask me to help you work out whatever it is Matthew wants me to get you to consider deciding on."

Pressing her face against his chest, she drew in a steadying breath. In her mind, joining another Coven was the easy way out. It also put the others in unnecessary danger. She was not ready to sit down and work through the risks and her feelings. She didn't know if she ever would be.

"It's just a backup plan," she replied. This time, her lie tasted bitter. "I'm not ready to give up on the first plan."

"I'm your sounding board when you're ready." He wrapped his arms around her.

CHAPTER 50

R óisín worked alongside Lily in the gardens around the Wallingsford's home in Roidon. Róisín's lesser powered elemental magic had already been well practiced, but under Nanette's tutelage over the past several weeks, her control of Norah's powerful elemental magic, and her skills while utilizing her other magic to increase her power and capability had grown exponentially.

Lily had needed to learn how to use all her elemental power together, especially as Nanette's heir to the Roidon Coven, and being able to work alongside Róisín had proven to be beneficial. Not only had Lily's own skill vastly improved, but her magic sang when she worked it with Róisín's. It had been a dull hum in Róisín's ears when they had begun working together. Now it sounded like a full choir with a band when they linked.

"Let me get this straight." Róisín looked up from where she and Lily knelt near a cluster of hibiscus. "As long as I'm filtering up all my magic behind whatever direct power I'm using, even if it's with or for a person, I won't become tapped out?"

Nanette sucked in one side of her cheek, expression turning dark before becoming thoughtful. "I'm assuming Shasta covered the bases with you this morning?"

Róisín nodded.

"It stands for any of the magic you wield. We're not defined by any limits to what we can use our power for. It's all in the dance to create the balance you'll need. That's what happened when you did use your power that night on Molennius and to heal Kincaid. You only drew up the one, which is incredibly taxing on our bodies when we're working with people. Aoife took that instance on Molennius, then crafted it to the advantage she needed."

Róisín stilled her hands. "That still doesn't explain after I healed Caid. It happened faster that time. And it was the complete dissolution of my magic. I had absolutely nothing left for days."

"You were also injured that time," Nanette gently reminded her.

"How did my mother do it?"

She made her way through the bushes of peonies to join the pair on the other side of the garden. "Don't think that it wasn't taxing on her. In more ways than one, it was. She always said that she was at peace with what the fates gave her. Although she never liked, or agreed, with war, she knew many would suffer. She never liked to see anyone, good or bad, suffer in the final moments of their life. It's what drove her to use her magic as she did. However, it wore on her soul, her spirit. There was always a war. One would end and another would chase its tail. She never had a reprieve to just live and enjoy life."

"She didn't need to be at every war," Róisín whispered.

"No, she didn't," Nanette agreed.

"Did you know that Aoife killed my grandfather?"

A small gasp escaped from Lily, her hand going to her throat in shock.

Nanette's hand paused on the flower head she had worked to bloom. She slowly brushed her fingers over the petals, lips pressing into a tight line. "Did she tell you this?"

"No, Matthew and I learned about it yesterday in one of the Legianne history books Aoife kept. Somehow, my mother got them from her and stowed them away in a trunk. For me."

Nanette slowly lowered herself onto a bench near where they'd stood. "This must have been what Lucius meant by a new development when we spoke this morning. Tell me everything." She lifted a hand to halt Lily, who had turned to walk back to the house. "Lily, you stay, you should be a part of this going forward."

Lily joined Nanette on the bench, and Róisín detailed the book notes, her new beliefs about Aoife. Their eyes grew wider.

"Your mother, she disappeared for decades. Aoife was furious. She knew she was still alive because the magic never came to her." Nanette turned her hand palm up and small starred blooms, the color of blue grew there. She hummed and then clucked her tongue. "That's interesting."

"What is it?" Lily moved closer.

"I said to my magic that we needed courage, and—" she wiggled her fingers, a smile curling her lips. "It gave me borage."

"I thought borage was for sadness," Róisín said.

"I can be," Nanette said with a nod. "But it's also good for building courage and confidence." She began to twist and braid the stems together. "Aoife tried to have the council take action, but Brenna wasn't breaking any of our laws. The leaders could all still faintly feel her in the line through Aoife's tether, even though she herself could not feel it. That was when things became harder with Aoife. When I think she suspected my motives for keeping her close were... self-serving." With one circlet done, she placed it atop Lily's head. Filling her palm once more, she set to work making a second. "It wasn't until Clarissa got sick the first time that I learned of Brenna, what she had done, what was coming. It was then that I doubled down on my efforts to stay close to Aoife because I knew for us to survive, to make it, it was a sacrifice that I needed to make. Despite my efforts, I knew she didn't wholly trust me anymore, that she kept secrets from me. I didn't know Bernard was one of them, though." She turned to Róisín with the second completed circlet. "That's true for any of what we've learned, to be honest."

Róisín leaned forward, bending slightly so that Nanette could place it upon her head. Then, she placed a hand on Nanette's forearm and gave her a small smile. "We can still fix this. Undo everything she did, stop Madigan, and deal with the other Covens."

Nanette covered her hand and patted it gently. "You're so much like your mother. She'd be so proud of the woman you've become."

A tear spilled onto her cheek, and she managed a small smile. "I'm going to do my damndest to make sure that her sacrifice was for something."

CHAPTER 51

E XHAUSTION pulled at Róisín as she trudged up the stairs to her room at Shasta's. The days of training with everyone. The gathering of them all for hours each day. Letting the door click closed, she sought out a familiar heartbeat. She should rest first, and she also needed to seek out David to find out if there was anything he had found in the woods, found out if the animals still returned slowly.

Looking around her room, she warred with what she should do versus what she wanted. The way her skin grew hot and her heart raced when she thought of Caid, connecting with the sure and steady beat of his heart. Everything could wait. Just for a moment. Then she closed her eyes.

"Holy shit, fuck!" Caid nearly screamed, his body jerked in shock. "Dammit."

Róisín couldn't stop the delighted grin that spread across her face. He stood under the spray of his shower head, gripping a bar of soap in one hand, his other hand on his heaving chest.

"Hi, handsome," she practically sang.

"Fuck, Róisín," he panted, blinking. As he collected himself, he focused on her. His eyebrows slammed down over his eyes when he saw she was naked. "Just what exactly were you doing wherever you were that didn't have a need for clothes?"

"Thinking about you." She bit her lower lip and took a slow step toward him.

"You just, oh, I don't know, magicked yourself here, naked?"

"No, I was clothed when I left Shasta's. I"—she used her index finger to trace along one of his pectoral muscles—"ditched them along the way. Is it a bad time? I can wait for you in the room."

His brows flicked upward when she moved toward the entrance to the walk-in shower. "Oh, no, no, *nooo*. You stay right there, don't even think about it."

Their gazes were heated on one another, locked, and he blindly shoved the soap into a cubby on the wall. He stalked across the walk-in. Placing his hands against the wall on either side of her head, he effectively caged her in. He bent his head down and nipped her ear, then traced his tongue along the line of her throat.

"Are you back, or is this just a—" He grazed his teeth along her shoulder. "Visit because you missed me?"

Her eyes fluttered closed, releasing a soft moan from her throat when his mouth dipped to one of her breasts. "I'm back, and I missed you."

She gasped when he drew one of her nipples into his mouth, gently nipping it before licking it with his tongue.

"Perfect, because I've been thinking about taking you against this wall for longer than I care to admit. I missed you, too." He straightened, looking down at her. "But first, was it okay? As good as it can be given everything else?"

Placing a hand on his cheek, letting her thumb stroke his chin, then his bottom lip, she wanted to tell him everything right then. Her need for him was stronger. "Later," she said when she found her voice. "I'll fill you in later. Right now, I just want to forget it. Right now, it's you and I, bringing that shower fantasy of yours to life."

He didn't blink, his jaw flexing once, twice. It was in the set lines around his mouth and eyes that he could see she carried heavy discoveries. Instead of pressing her for more, he grabbed her beneath her rear, lifting her, pressing her against the cool tiles. She wrapped her legs around his waist and let the abyss swallow them both.

240

Chapter 52

Róisín sat in an Adirondack chair in Lina's backyard, surveying Thomas's handiwork that shaped Lina's select board win bar-b-cue celebration.

Lights were strung from the deck posts, and plastic palm trees dotted the yard, making Róisín smile. A long table was covered with finger sandwiches, fruit dishes, vegetable platters, chips, dips, and sweets galore. Thomas and Caid stood steps away from where she sat, both sipping from their beers, talking over the cooking burgers and hot dogs on the grill.

She turned to where Lina sat next to her. "So, what happens now?"

"Right now, I bask in the glow of the win." Lina beamed at her. "Then, Monday, I'll get sworn in as chair. That's when I need to figure out the best, sound way to approach this."

"You're sticking to your plan?"

"Of course, I am." Lina's brows furrowed. "I mean, yeah, I'm pregnant now and I wasn't when I decided to run. It changes nothing, though. This town deserves to be growing and thriving again."

"I didn't mean—I wasn't—" Róisín sighed. "Sorry. I don't want you to think that because you're pregnant I think you should have let Bill keep his seat."

"I know." Lina reached over and set a hand on Róisín's knee. "If anything, I want Stewart Munson gone more now than ever."

Róisín didn't fail to see how quickly Caid's head had snapped up, hearing her words. His eyes found hers, and she signaled to him with a slight shake of her head.

Lina shuddered. "He's always given me the heebie-jeebies. Even more lately."

"Bill seemed unsurprised that he lost." Róisín tried to steer the conversation away from Madigan. She saw the way Caid still stood, his body tight with tension, half-turned away from Thomas, and his eyes cold. It was a look, a reaction, she had not yet witnessed in him, and it caught her off guard that he was so coiled with that anger.

"I know. It was weird. It really makes this all so much easier. I had been prepared for him to fight, to challenge and demand a recount if I won, so it was nice for him to shake my hand, give me a congratulatory shoulder pat, then move on."

"Congratulations, Lina," Mary Wallace, the town's postmaster, said by way of greeting as she approached where the pair were sitting. "We knew you could do it!"

"Thank you, Mary." Lina rose to hug the woman.

Róisín rose as well. "I'm going to, uh, duck into the bathroom."

Weaving around the celebrating crowd in the McGrath-Commons backyard, Róisín picked her way across the yard to the house. Once in the bathroom, she leaned against the closed door and let out a breath.

From the crawling feeling beneath Róisín's skin that had started days earlier, her gut told her their time was truly running out. Madigan was ready. In an hourglass, it'd be a pinch of sand they were left with.

The pain had started that morning as a dull ache at the base of her sternum. She tried to push it off the same as she had tried to do with the sensation of being underwater all day. She couldn't break, not now, not when they had made it this far.

"Róisín?" Caid's muffled voice came through the door. "Lina said you'd come inside. Are you okay?"

"I'm good." She forced cheerfulness into her reply. "Just too much water today, I guess." She reached over from where she stood at the sink, flushing the toilet for good measure. The ache burned now. She pressed the palm of her left hand against it, focusing on slow, steady breaths. It looked like she would take these past few weeks of practice with Nanette and Shasta and put them to use soothing her current disordered state. She had just pulled her magic up when she heard the soft thump against the door.

"Róisín.... Let me in."

"I'll be out in just a second." No, this isn't right. She brought her magic through her hand, pressing it back into herself, suddenly feeling as though the air had been pushed from her lungs. It shouldn't feel like this. Something was wrong. She looked up into the mirror at her reflection, watching as her summer sun kissed skin turned ashen. The burn inside became a raging inferno. She grit her teeth and her vision blurred, her body shaking.

"Róisín." His voice was less calm as he tried the handle. The jiggle of the knob sounding like thunder in her ears.

She tried to speak, to tell him she was coming out. Instead, her words were a choking gasp. Her hand fell from her chest, moving to clutch the sink counter. She gripped the edge so tightly, one of her nails broke free from its bed.

Caid's voice sounded like it was coming to her through mud, calling to her, distantly. A roaring built around her. She had to fight the urge to cover her ears, knowing the moment she let go of the counter, she would fall.

Her lungs seized in her chest, sending her into a gasping, coughing fit. Doubling over, she positioned herself completely over the sink in time to cough out a mouthful of blood. She was struggling to remain upright while her body convulsed.

The black edged her vision, her knees buckling, just as Caid broke the door in and wrapped his solid arms around her.

"He's found me," she gasped out. "He knows who I am."

Chapter 53

C AID managed to get her into his truck unnoticed. Once she was in, he circled back to the cookout, letting Lina know he was leaving, taking Róisín, who felt unwell, home.

Lina, naturally, had been worried, wanting to talk to her. He still hadn't been sure how he'd convinced her that everything was okay, that they'd talk the next day.

Madigan had found her.

His heart raced in his chest. Raced faster than he could drive across the small town to her house. The place he assumed would be safest, remembering her mention of the wards, aided by the others' powers that were in place.

What he would do once they got there, he didn't know. He still tried to wrap his head around what else may exist out there if magic was real, let alone what his place in all of this was. What could he do to protect her? Could he protect her?

"I need—" Róisín stirred in the passenger seat, trying to sit up. She licked her lips. A guttural moan escaped instead of more words. She wrapped her arms around her middle tightly, her breath coming in harsh gasps.

"We can figure it out when we get home." He jarred both of their bodies when he jumped the truck over a sidewalk when he took the turn onto her road tightly.

"Shasta," she said hoarsely.

"We're almost there." He pressed the gas pedal harder, like he didn't already have it against the floorboard. When he pulled into her driveway, he jammed the shifter into park, then sprinted around the truck, flinging open her door. With the dome light on, he could see the blood running from her nose, over her mouth, to her chest. It took every ounce of control he had to keep himself calm as he pulled her into his arms and quickly got them inside.

As he crossed the threshold, she went taut in his arms, before her limbs loosened and her breath steadied.

"Let's get you cleaned up, then you need to tell me what to do," he said. "Up or down?"

"Up. I need the tub. Water. The burning," she answered, her voice raspy.

Taking the stairs two at a time, he used his foot to first nudge open her bedroom door, then to open the bathroom door. He started to take her tank top off, but she waved him away.

"Just put me in, start the water, please," she begged. "I'm so hot. So hot in here." She motioned to her head first, then her middle. "Like I'm on fire."

He scooped her back up and stepped into the tub. Holding her with one arm, he reached with his other for the knobs.

"You—"

"We do this together," he said. "We do this together," he repeated, his tone firm. "Got it?"

For the first time since he'd pushed in his sister's bathroom door, Róisín's eyes opened. They were a swarm of colors, but unlike the vibrance that shone in them when she showed him her magic, they were clouded, as though they were unseeing.

"Not right now," he told her. "First this. Then tell me what happened, what we need to do next. Okay?"

She nodded, blinking.

"You're safe here?"

She nodded again.

"Okay." He let out a relieved breath. "Okay. Good."

She let him use a wet cloth to clean the blood from her face. After, she laid against his chest as he examined her ruined finger. When exhaustion pulled her down, she curled against him, tucking her shaking body tightly against his. Silence filled the space between them.

When she finally stirred, she cleared her throat. "I need to tell the others."

"What happened?"

"There must have been something in Legianne that led him to my mother's home in Ireland. It was the only way he could have found it. Her books, my mother's books, she spoke of how she found magic to hide herself away from Aoife and the home she created inside of that safety in Northern Ireland. Aoife had to have found it after my mother died. He found it, and by finding it, he found me."

"If he knew Aoife, wouldn't he have known about you before?"

"That's what I thought, but—" She shivered. "I know now that he didn't. He knew of my mother, but nothing about me. It doesn't make sense," she said. "Just like everything else in this."

When shivers racked her body again, he stood them up in one fluid movement. As she stood on the mat, teeth chattering, he carefully stripped her down, then wrapped her in a warm towel. She stopped him when he began to pick her up again.

"You'll get sick if you don't get out of those wet clothes."

"I'll be fine."

"You'll get sick," she whispered.

He stepped back, running a hand through his hair before he conceded and stripped as well. Carrying her to the bed, he tucked her under her blankets, then gathered their wet clothes, bringing them to the washing machine.

Outside her bedroom door, he paused. His head swam, fear and rage fighting a battle within him. Once he had settled himself enough, he stepped into the room. She had propped herself up with her pillows against her headboard. Although her color had not yet fully returned, her cheeks were lightly dusted with pink and her eyes were beginning to clear. He hoped it was a sign that the worst had passed. Her bottom lip was pinched between her forefinger and thumb, her eyes unblinking as she stared straight ahead.

"What do we do now?" he asked.

"I need to tell the others." She turned to look at him, face filled with sadness, her eyes sorrowful. "I'm sorry."

Before he could ask what she was sorry for, she was gone.

CHAPTER 54

SHASTA leaned over her desk, squinting at the coded words Matthew had scratched across the small slip of paper he had sent her. His handwriting was atrocious, and she had even tried crossing her eyes to see if it would make it easier to decipher.

She blinked a few times to clear the blurring in her eyes away, then moved closer to decipher the last few words.

A whimper drew her attention, bringing her head up.

Róisín's naked body appeared before her and immediately crumpled to the floor.

"Holy Goddess, Róisín!" She shoved her chair back. She leapt over the desk, her fingers frantic as they pushed Róisín's hair from her face. "Are you okay? What happened?"

Róisín's mouth moved, but no words came out.

"What happened?" Shasta repeated, a tremor in her voice.

"He... he found—" The words were faint, thin, through Róisín's shaking lips

"Who? Madigan? Where's Caid?" Róisín's lids fluttered, her eyes rolling back. "Róisín!" She lightly slapped her cheeks. "Where's Caid?"

"So—" She gasped. "So hot. I can't..."

Shasta looked around her office, debating reaching down her line to let her Coven know they needed to rally, to have them send word to the others. She gathered Róisín in her arms and felt the tremors roll through her. In that moment, she decided she needed answers before setting the alarm off, and took them back to Greens Glen.

At the sight of them, Caid nearly lunged onto the bed, but a shake of Shasta's head halted him.

"Madigan found her," he said. He took in Róisín's prone body, and his face hardened. "I don't know what happened, but whatever it is, it's hurt her. Her nose was bleeding, and she kept saying she was burning inside."

Shasta pulled the blankets over Róisín, then she gestured toward the door. "She needs rest. And you need to tell me everything you know."

SHASTA SETTLED INTO the sofa and listened to him carefully. This was the night that changed everything. They were now tipped over that edge they'd hovered on for months, and were about to fall into the awaiting darkness.

After Caid had done his best to tell her everything from the bathroom at Lina's to Róisín leaving for Molennius, Shasta blew out a breath.

"Shit," she muttered. "We knew we would not be in this holding pattern forever. We knew if we could find him, that time was close, but..."

"Whatever is happening, it's here now, isn't it?" Caid asked.

She nodded.

"She's not safe here. She needs to be with you, or one of you. I can't—" His voice broke, and he shook his head. "I can't do anything."

Shasta tipped her head to the side. "You'd be surprised how much power a human can hold over us."

He let out a nervous chuckle, then rubbed a hand over his face, scoffing. "What am I gonna do? Shoot the guy? He'll probably laugh at me and heal up like The Terminator. Then I'm done for."

Shasta's response was just a click of her tongue. There was something different about the young man sitting before her tonight, yet she couldn't quite put her finger on it.

"Is it possible that he didn't know she existed?" His eyes darted toward the stairs.

"Brenna, she found a way to conceal herself from Aoife. She had always known her mother had a darkness within her and was willing to risk anything for her freedom from Aoife."

"She was still hidden when she had Róisín?"

"She was." Shasta nodded. "Róisín didn't appear in Aoife's line until Brenna died. I know Brenna had hoped it would stay in place to keep Róisín protected." She knew Brenna had worked and worked with spell work and wards, trying to create ones that would outlast her life on this side of the veil. Including the ones she'd wrapped around the young man sitting across from Shasta that looked like he was barely holding all of his pieces together.

"Wouldn't Madigan have known then?"

"By that time, Madigan had been gone for several decades. Judging by the timeline of the books Róisín brought us, he set to work severing the connection after they killed Bernard and Brenna had disappeared. Without the connection, he would have no idea of births or deaths among us."

"The day Matthew came and they searched the books." Caid rubbed at his temples, eyes downcast. "Róisín said she suspected Aoife worked with Madigan when they learned about what happened with her grandfather, what they wanted to do to her mother."

"There's a lot of this that's confusing and makes little sense," Shasta replied, following his line of thought. "For argument's sake, if they worked together, but she kept Róisín hidden somehow, trust me when I say Aoife wouldn't have done it with good intentions. I knew the woman for my entire life. She never did anything that wouldn't serve her own needs and desires."

"If that were the case, why would she not fight to get Brenna's power for herself after her death if they weren't going to let Róisín have them?"

"That's simple, she didn't want him to know that she was coming to take his power," Róisín answered roughly from where she stood, muscles in her forearm taught from gripping the banister to keep herself upright. Her face still pale, eyes large and glassy.

Shasta and Caid were both on their feet. Shasta wanted to go to her, wrap her arms around her, to soothe her as a mother would do. However, from the look on Caid's face, and the way Róisín looked at him, she knew they needed their moment first.

"I'll go make some tea," Shasta said, excusing herself.

Chapter 55

Less than an hour later, Róisín was on the sofa, tucked against Caid, struggling for focus as the room buzzed around her. Shasta had beckoned everyone to the house, insisting that Róisín was not fit for travel. Caid's agreement with Shasta was clear in the way he refused to let go of her.

It hadn't taken long for the group to have deduced that Madigan going to Legianne had been the catalyst in his discovery of Róisín's existence. Yet, her mother's wards, and whatever Aoife had cast over Róisín to keep her presence shielded from him, had been too strong for him to locate her specifically. It had been when he'd found their home in Ireland, when he had burned it, nullifying all of her mother's work, that he could locate Róisín.

Shasta and Nanette associated the burning within Róisín to be the wards burning away with those walls of their home. With the quiet inside of her now, she knew there was nothing left to her childhood home. The home her parents had built, that had held so many memories of love, laughter, and tears.

Róisín could only sit in awe at how powerful her mother had truly been. There had been much she had learned in the recent months, but to use magic and spell work the way her mother had, weaving it into a structure that would stand in place far longer than she would be on the living side of the veil, to keep Róisín safe when she was gone... Tears gathered in her eyes, regret, guilt, and grief warring with one another inside of her.

"This has most likely pushed his hand," Lucius said from across the room where he sat next to Matthew. "He's sure to act now, rather than later."

"I'd rather that than waiting," Róisín mumbled.

"While I agree, this on-edge waiting has certainly frayed our edges." Shasta paused, her attention solely on Róisín. "It has given us the time we need not only to prepare you, but to prepare ourselves. Going into this blind would have led to disaster."

Nanette hummed in agreement. "Each unearthing has changed our course drastically. Where we were months ago is far different from where we are now. Time has allowed us to be better prepared. As anxious as it makes us all—it's been incredibly beneficial rather than harmful."

"It's all my fault," Róisín whispered.

"How?" Caid looked down at her, his hand rubbing up and down her arm..

"Think about it." She straightened, pointedly looking at each face around her. "I've been hauling that damned trunk around for decades, refusing to look at it because I was angry at her. Turns out, oops, my anger was misdirected. I thought she hid Aoife from me. That gave Aoife an opportunity to dig in and fuel that anger. Feed me the lies about my mother. I let myself be vulnerable enough to believe it all." She pushed her hands into her hair, tugging, trying to free the frustration that was trying to break free of her skin. "To believe my mother wasn't a good person. To believe her selfishness and that she had this vendetta against her parents, which is why she left. Why she hid." Her voice rose as the pounding in her ears grew louder.

"I let Aoife basically control me. I lived in fear of using my power, for all things. Exactly as she wanted me to be. Why would she want that? Well, so that when she convinced me to use my mother's power to kill Madigan, I would be weak. Weak enough for her to kill me. Then, all of you with the magic she gained from me."

"Róisín." Shasta moved to sit on the other side of her. She took

Róisín's hands in hers, setting their joined hands in her lap. "There are things I knew in the beginning, after Brenna left us. Even what I knew, what my gut told me about Aoife, I could have never, ever imagined it went this deep. None of us could."

"I was one of her friends," Nanette pointed out. "Granted, I only stayed close out of my distrust of her, and I suspected she cursed your Coven. She was always so good at her magic tricks. That sleight of hand."

"She used your grief to her benefit. You didn't know any better. You do now, and what you do now, what we all do now with the knowledge we have"—Shasta squeezed her hand—"that's what is most important."

"What do we do now? If Lucius is right, this discovery may be the catalyst," Róisín said.

"I could gain access to the lower level in the Alleyette Library," Lily said, looking around the room at all of them from where she sat next to Nanette. "Matthew helped me copy down some pages that I think may be the missing piece we need in all of this."

Róisín didn't miss the way Lily's cheeks turned pink when her eyes lingered on Matthew. Or the wink he gave her, his mouth tipping into a lopsided grin.

She caught Matthew's attention, lifting one of her brows in question.

He shrugged in response.

That's interesting.

"There is a way we can reestablish his connection to all of us." Nanette shifted forward, her expression lightened. "Just us in this room, no one else."

"If we can successfully do it, then we can channel our power through you as a conductor," Lucius said. "If the literature holds true, you will then be able to gather all of that power with yours, and send a, what did you call it, Matthew?"

"Blast of epic proportion." Matthew mimed an explosion with his hands.

"That," Lucius said, nodding his head toward Matthew, "down the line to Madigan."

"Which will?" Róisín asked.

"Basically, the power surge will be so intense, it will essentially cook him from the inside out," Lily answered.

"Despite the wards, he'll know we've come tonight after what happened. Having this much energy in one place is a beacon. We'll have a day, possibly two. Beyond that, I don't know," Shasta said. "Which means you rest here. Thursday, we'll gather to finalize this plan."

"Don't we need to make sure this is even possible?" Róisín asked. She tried to stop the butterflies that began excitedly flapping around in her stomach, but her body betrayed her, her heart joining the dance. Could this work?

"We do." Nanette rose, motioning to Lily, who stood, joining her. "Which is where Lily and I will start tomorrow. Assuring we can connect the five of us exclusively, away from the other Covens. If we can do that, then we can tether him."

Róisín chewed her bottom lip for a moment, trying to work out what they'd laid before her. "So, to yours Thursday, then?"

"Yes." Nanette nodded. "Come when you're rested enough that your power will be ready."

Róisín moved around the room to hug each one before they went back to their realms. She lingered with Shasta, who stood last. "My mother could come somehow."

"She told you," Shasta said, her eyes shimmering with the tears she held there. "I've had to carry it all for a long time or risk the Goddess. Even when I wanted to step in, knowing it wasn't just myself I risked, but you as well, held me back. It had to happen this way, Róisín. We all hate it, even Brenna, but it had to be."

Róisín wrapped her arms around Shasta, gripping her. "Do you know how this ends?"

"No," she answered. "She only knew until Aoife's death, and you coming here. The Sisters only gave her that."

Róisín let out a defeated breath.

"It's easy to blame yourself. It's also pointless. If the fates demanded the road be littered with all of this... shit, for this to not be the end of us, then the road littered with shit is the one we travel. What?"

"You said shit. Twice," Róisín emphasized.

"I've heard you say your own fair share of cusses lately too, sweetheart," she said, pointedly. "I won't lie, you humans." She looked at Caid. "And your studies about how it helps with stress. You're not wrong."

"I don't know, I swear a lot and my stress level is through the roof right now," Caid said.

"It is for all of us." Shasta rubbed his shoulder. "Go rest, the both of you."

And then she was gone.

"I'm never going to get used to that." Caid blinked at the spot where Shasta had just stood. "Can you take people with you?"

"Is there somewhere you want to go?"

"Florida?" he suggested, clearly trying to lighten the mood that pulled them down like quicksand. He kept his eyes on her as she moved closer to him, relief and exhaustion tugging when she wrapped her arms around his middle, pressing her face against his chest. He bent his head, pressing a kiss to the top of her head. "We should go to bed."

"Can we just stand here like this? Just for a minute. I don't know if..." Her voice turned breathy with her last words. "I don't know what will happen after tomorrow. I need to soak this up, soak you in while I can."

"We can stand here as long as you need." He held her tighter.

Chapter 56

Tʜᴇʏ were back to waiting. Caid tried to keep his frustration down. Instead, it simmered just under the surface of his skin, waiting for its moment to break free. He'd never done well with idle time and empty hands, and that was exactly how he felt now as he and Róisín lay in her bed, darkness blanketing them. He blinked up at the ceiling, trying to calm his mind.

Two days of waiting. Two days of doing nothing. Two days to let his fear of something happening to Róisín grow. Two days for him to sit with the realization that there was absolutely nothing he could do to protect her. Or anyone. Despite what Shasta had said, he was helpless. If Madigan were to appear in the house that night, would Shasta's wards and Róisín be enough to stop him, to protect them?

"Who takes care of you?" Róisín's quiet question broke through the silence of the room.

"Hm?"

"I can hear your thoughts shouting all over the place, Caid. Who takes care of you? When things go to hell, I mean?"

"When things go to hell, I put them back to rights," he said, as though it were the simplest answer to any problem he faced.

"Is it because you never ask for help, or is it because if someone offers, you close them out?" She placed one of her hands on his chest, then lifted her head to look at him in the dim glow of her bedside clock. "You can't do it all alone."

"You have," he pointed out.

"You had to grow up fast, too fast. There were responsibilities you had early, while everyone else was off getting to do things you should have been able to do, too."

He studied her for a moment, then closed his eyes.

"I'm sorry," she whispered.

"Don't be. It's not your fault. I chose my path. I was the one that wanted Lina to have better than I had."

"You deserve to have what Lina has."

The words hit him in his chest in a way that he hadn't expected. His heart beat loudly in his ears. His throat grew tight with emotions building.

She sat up, tucking her legs beneath her. "I can hear it here." She brushed a finger over his brow. "It's so loud. That constant noise of you weighing out the options of how you can give yourself to not just Lina, but everyone around you. You'll give until you've got nothing left to give, then what?"

Slowly, he pulled himself up against the headboard, but he still couldn't find the words to speak. He fought the urge to rub at the ache that grew in the center of his chest. The emotion that rose inside of him was foreign, unfamiliar.

"I love you. One reason I love you is because you are that type of person who rarely exists anymore. That one who is so easily able to give themselves to others to help, to care about them. Those people would be there, in a heartbeat, to repay in kind. But only if you let them. You've closed yourself off so much, no one dares to even think of offering. Except me. I dare. Let me take care of you. Take care of you, worry about you, worry for you, the way you do me. Please?"

"Róisín..." He heaved a sigh, trying to push away some of the heaviness. Maybe then, the stinging behind his eyes would cease.

"One of these days, your cup will be empty, Caid. What happens then? What happens when you've run dry?"

He heard the tears in her voice, and his heart tore. He took one of her hands, let the warmth of them ground him, to bring him back from the edges of the room he had scattered to when she uncovered him, stripped him bare with her words.

"We don't have forever." Her voice was barely audible as she struggled to keep herself together. "I don't want to spend the time we do have watching you give away every last piece of yourself."

Still holding her hand, he laced their fingers together, then pulled her into his arms. The moment he wrapped them tightly around her, she broke, the first sob ripping free, followed by the rest held back by the dam she'd tried to hold.

After several minutes, she quieted in his arms. Still feeling the small shudders from the quiet sobs, he tightened his hold on her. Finally able to pull himself out of his own emotions that had threatened to swallow him, he said, "I draw the line at being tucked into bed every night."

She pulled back to look at him, her eyes wide. She blinked slowly, then burst into laughter.

"What? I'm serious." He scoffed. "I would take some milk and cookies next to the bed every night, though."

"Oh, my Goddess," she wheezed, squeezing her eyes shut.

Hearing her laughter was a balm for the ache within him. His heart started to return to its steady, slow beat. His lungs loosened so that he could breathe again.

"Any other requests?"

"Sponge baths wouldn't be too bad," he offered, sending her into another fit of laughter. He waited until she calmed, wiping the tears from her eyes. "On a more serious note, it's not going to be easy. I'm pretty sure I've proven on more than one occasion how stubborn I am."

She lifted a brow.

"For you, I'll do anything." He pressed a kiss to her forehead first, then the tip of her nose, followed by brushing his lips over hers.

"Thank you." She curled against him.

"So..." He tipped his head toward the bathroom door. "How about that sponge bath? You do me, I do you?"

"Why do I feel like that was a double entendre?"

"Mm." He gave her a mischievous grin. "Maybe you should come find out."

She chewed on her bottom lip for a moment, the weariness she wore on her face earlier when everyone was there, now gone, her eyes bright again.

Slowly, she unfolded herself from his lap, then scooted off the edge of the bed. Pausing at the bathroom door, she pulled off her shirt and slid her cotton shorts down her legs. When she stood, she looked over her shoulder. "Are you coming?"

His voice was deep and rough, full of love and desire, when he answered, "Oh, I'm coming all right."

CHAPTER 57

"Is she going to be okay?" Lily asked, causing Matthew to lift his attention from his book. Just like falling from a cliff, his efforts at pretending she wasn't within arms reach of him so that he could focus on his book, tumbled over the edge.

Lily tipped her head toward the end of the table, her strawberry blond hair slipping over her shoulders, beckoning his hands. When she turned back to him, her pupils flared and cheeks reddened, and suddenly, his breath caught in his chest.

He ripped his eyes from hers and glanced toward where Róisín was bent over an ancient tome with torn pages, chewing on her thumbnail, eyebrows set in a scowl. They had been in the Molennius Archives all morning, reading through the extensive Coven history books.

He wasn't sure just how he could honestly answer the question. Despite Róisín's charge forward attitude she had carried when this task fell into her hands that no, she was not okay right now. It was still questionable if she would be okay at the end with all she'd learned about her family.

"She's been through so much," Lily whispered. "She's... amazing."

Matthew blinked slowly.

"I'm serious. Even when we were all younger, I've always thought that." Lily's eyes glossed with her shining admiration for Róisín.

Amused, Matthew would've wondered if Lily would attempt to muscle Caid out of the picture with Róisín. But he wasn't the only one that had felt that faint tug of a bond trying to snap into place the last time he and Lily had been in the Alleyette Library.

"Are you?" He wiggled his eyebrows at her, then inclined his head toward Róisín, making his implication clear.

"What? Oh!" Her cheeks darkened more. "I mean, I've thought about other women in that way, sure," she admitted. "Beyond that, though, I... no." She turned serious, spinning quickly to face him. "Are you—" She cleared her throat and moved her chair closer. "Are you going to, um, ask me on a date?" she whispered.

Matthew coughed in surprise, then thumped a hand hard against his chest, hoping his voice didn't croak when he answered. "Do you *want* to go on a date?"

Her eyes flit to where Nanette and Shasta stood, hands clasped, mouths moving to the words that lay on the page before them. They'd tested new spelled wards all morning. "When we were at the manor, in the library, and we... did you... feel anything?"

He tried to remember how to breathe, nearly failing, another cough scratching at his throat. Count, he needed to count, distract his brain so his body would remember what it needed to do to live.

"In the room. A." She paused as though she were trying to choose her words carefully. "Tugging of sorts."

"Tugging?" He managed hoarsely.

"Maybe it was nothing." She shrugged. "I've been super paranoid about the council finding out what we're doing despite my grandmother, Lucius, and Shasta's protections. I've heard and felt things for weeks now."

Her shoulders came up, her spine straightening, her mouth dropping open as the realization hit her.

He grinned, barely managing to hold back his chuckle of delight. "Surprise?"

"You? It's you? I thought—" She glanced back at Róisín. "Wait, you two aren't?"

"Nope." His grin grew wider. "Pretty sure it's her and the human."

"But…" She brought her hands to her face, placing them on her cheeks. "I need to step outside. It's boiling in here all of a sudden."

The scraping of their chairs on the floor made Róisín lift her head, blinking at him.

"Is she okay?" Róisín asked as the door practically slammed shut.

"Uh, she will be?" He shrugged. "I don't know why she's embarrassed."

"Embarrassed?"

"I think I'm quite a catch."

Róisín's mouth dropped open, then quickly snapped shut, and her eyes grew wide in excitement. "I knew it. The other day at my house on the couch! Oh! And the power around you two was different today. Oh, oh," she drew out the word. "She just figured it out, didn't she?"

Matthew rose, gathering up the book he'd been looking through, then made his way closer so they weren't shouting to one another.

Róisín studied him after he settled into the chair next to her. "What makes you think she's embarrassed?"

"Her face got redder than a tomato, then she said it was hot in here."

"That's not necessarily embarrassment, Matthew. She could be…"

"Well, shit." He looked at the door. "No. We need to talk about it all before anything moves forward. It also wouldn't hurt for us to spend more time together outside of all"—he waved his hands over the table—"this shit. Get to know each other, really fall in love, not just lean on the bond and what feelings come with that. She deserves that."

"Isn't this a cozy little distraction?" She beamed at him, her face bright. "The heirs of their Covens being bound together."

"Is that weird? Has that ever happened?"

She shrugged and reached for her hair tie on the table. "I mean, there must be a reason. I guess we won't know until you two…" One hand held her hair in a ponytail, the other waving the elastic to the door, then at him. "You know."

He tapped a finger on his chin. "What if she doesn't want it? I mean, she is an heir, too."

"You two could try to fight it," she suggested. "If you're bound, fate will just keep bringing you back to one another until you commit."

"Kind of like us." He gestured between them.

"You're just a pain in the ass brother that won't go away. That's different."

He hummed in agreement. "It's fun. Ah, fuck."

"What?" She closed her book with a thud. Shifting in her chair, he waited, watching, as she looked him over. He saw the very moment it hit her, what he had meant, in the way she winced ever so slightly. "Oh. That."

"Did you tell Caid?"

"Caid knows everything."

"Everything, everything, or just everything?"

"All of it, Matthew," she said firmly.

He slumped in his chair, sighing. "I'm going to have to tell her."

"You are," she agreed. "It's not that hard. Trust me."

"Not that hard." He barked a laugh.

"Hey, at least she already knows you're a witch. I mean, Caid knew about you and me the day he rescued me from Madigan, and had thought you and I were together. That spilled out in one of my rare, I-can't-shut-my-mouth moments. I had to tell my boyfriend that I'm also a super powerful witch, who also has a very rare magic. Ah, but wait, I also had to tell him I am probably going to die saving my people."

Matthew quickly sobered. "You will not die."

"We don't know that," she whispered.

"You will not die," he repeated with such ferociousness and finality that it made her flinch. She wasn't used to the more serious side of Matthew, and he knew it. He felt bad for snapping, but he needed her to see, to understand. "You're going to kick the shit out of that pile of shit. Then you and the carpenter are going to get married. I'll be there throwing rice at your face, I promise you that."

She stared at him for a moment. In her eyes, he saw past the weight of all the realms on her shoulders. The terror that lay deeper. He grabbed her hands, gripping them. "You will not die, Ro. We'll find a way. This isn't over, for any of us. Okay?"

She nodded.

"I'm serious," he pressed. "We'll find a way."

"I hope we do, because I don't want to die." Her voice cracked as she answered him. "I'm not ready."

CHAPTER 58

Caid moved to step over a stack of recently delivered lumber at his current job site, tripping and stumbling into the rear quarter of his truck when he didn't quite clear the wood pile.

"Ya good, man?" Wyatt called over, slinging his tool belt over his shoulder. "You've been wicked out of it all day."

Caid waved him off, then stalked to his truck, dropping the tailgate to load his tools. Róisín had been gone for three days. The first day had been fine. By the morning of the second day, the inability to reach out to her set in.

Was she okay?

Had Madigan found her? The others?

The not knowing ate at his sanity. As the third day ended, he wasn't sure he had any sanity left, or even remembered what it was.

David had come in the evenings. Caid felt awkward talking to the rabbit and was convinced that David's frequent presence was just to check up on him for Róisín.

Did David have a way to reach her?

As Caid shoved the rest of his tools into the truck bed, he hoped he saw the rabbit again to ask.

He mumbled his goodbyes to Wyatt, climbed into the truck and

265

closed the door with a slam. Róisín had asked him to stay at her house while she had been gone, insisting it would be safer for him. He heard the desperation in her plea when he had stubbornly tried to push away her concern.

Now, as he fought the urge to duck his head as he passed Lina on the road, there was a relief to know that he headed there instead of his place, which felt empty, almost desolate, in their time together.

His phone rang, pulling him from his spiraling thoughts. He hesitated to answer when he saw Lina's number on his truck's dash screen. He hadn't talked to her since Róisín left on a 'business trip' for a few days. Since then, he'd avoided her calls and texts because he hadn't trusted his own poker face.

The longer Róisín was gone, the harder he fought to keep his emotions down. There would only be one person who could see through the mask he wore, and that person was Lina.

"It's about damned time." Lina's loud, exasperated voice filled the truck's interior when the call connected. "Are we fighting? Did I say something snide again and piss you off?"

"I've been busy working, which, shouldn't you have almost no free time between the impending arrival of the twins and running this town?"

"STOP saying it's twins," she groaned. "The more times you say it, the more it'll come true."

"Twins, twins, twinsitty-twins."

"You're an asshole," she muttered.

"Just fulfilling my duties as a brother. Is there a reason you've been harassing me, Leen?"

"Maybe I'm just fulfilling my role as a sister."

"Touché."

"Anyway... Do you know when Ro will be back? Thomas's sister has been chomping at the bit to plan my shower and I've told her she can't do it without Ro. I called her this morning but got the 'out of service area' message."

"You'd have a better idea than I. Thomas does business trips, how long is he usually gone for?"

"At least two or three days at a time, but always different," she answered casually.

"And there's your answer. She'll be home when she's home." He was grateful to be pulling into the drive as he made that statement, because the words hit him right in his guts with a hard punch.

Lina's heavy sigh burst through the speakers, causing the sound to crackle around him. "Okay. I'll tell Ashley I'm working on my registrations, and then when I'm done, we'll plan. Should be plenty of time for Ro to get back so we can all come together and plan."

Swallowing suddenly seemed impossible. Shaking his head, clearing his worries away, to cheer her up he said, "I can help plan if Ashley's that gung-ho."

"Oh, hell no. Love you, but hell to the n-o-p-e."

"Can't say I didn't offer."

"Mm, thanks for that much. You're an asshole, but you're my favorite asshole."

"I do my best," he replied, scanning the tree line for a dot of white.

"Answer next time I call you but, I need to get going. The town lawyer wants to meet about my proposal to get Stewart Munson out of town."

That snapped Caid back to the moment. "Do me a favor, be careful with Munson, okay?"

There was a long pause, as though she wanted to ask him questions. "I will. I promise," she replied, instead.

"Love you, knucklehead."

"Love you too, asshole."

He waited until static from the disconnected call filled his speakers before he shut his truck off, then went inside. After grabbing a beer from the fridge, he settled himself into a chair on the patio, waiting for the rabbit to come.

Chapter 59

Róisín came to Caid in the night. The feeling within her chest at the sight of him in her bed hit her like a wall, leaving her wishing that she could be selfish with her time, her magic, with him. Quietly, she curled against his chest, taking in his warmth, his smell, the feel of him.

A different urgency had chased her home from Molennius this time. The edges had closed in, nipping at her heels.

They were out of time. Madigan was coming for her.

Instead of telling the others first, she went to Caid. She went to be with him, to love him for just a moment longer; to say goodbye.

Caid brought his arm around her tightly, pulling her against him, then rolling so that she was over him and he could bring his other arm around her.

Wordlessly, she brought her mouth to his. When he opened to welcome and taste her in return, she prayed to the Goddess he couldn't feel her sorrow, her desperation, as she sunk deeper into their kiss, frenzied to consume as much of him as she could.

His mouth froze on hers the second one of her tears splashed against his cheek. "Hey," his voice was soft, and he cradled her face in his hands, thumbs stroking away her tears.

"I'm okay, I've just missed you." She struggled with the lie.

He kept his thumbs stroking her cheeks. The moonlight streaming in through her windows illuminated his face, and his features shifted as if working out whether he wanted to press her, or let it go. Using his hands, he brought her back to him, sealing their mouths together. This time, his desperation mirrored her own. Like he knew.

When she rocked her hips against him, he rolled her onto her back and rose over her. He skimmed a hand over her chest, stopping to take one of her nipples between his thumb and forefinger. She moaned into his mouth, and he swallowed it down, cupping her breast, moving his hand down along her stomach to her hip. His fingers pressed against her skin as his palm cupped her hip, drawing her closer to him.

The feel of his length against her had her arching against him, breaking their kiss as she pressed harder against him.

"I need you," she breathed out. "I need you, now."

With his mouth on her neck, nipping, and kissing down to her shoulder and back, he shifted them both so that they aligned. When he stroked the head of his cock along her entrance, she reached for him, fingers digging into his hips.

"Jesus Christ," he murmured against her skin, pushing in deeper.

He fisted her hair, tugging, tipping her head back to give him access to her neck. He sucked the skin there, causing her to cry out his name when a white, hot heat slammed into her core. She rocked against his thrusts, then, needing to feel him deeper, she wrapped her legs around his waist.

As the edge came closer, something came together, tightening. Something unfamiliar. A wall coming down inside of her. Something rising in the space left behind.

The sensation grew inside of her. It was light, airy, like a balloon floating in the air. A thin thread stretching from the balloon, to her, tethering them together.

No, no, no. Not him, not Caid. Energy, like she had never experienced, hummed down the tether, surging through her body, setting everything alight and lifting the hairs along her skin.

Stars exploded behind her eyes, and she cried out again as the orgasm moved through her, its ecstasy crashing into and filling all the empty spaces inside of her. Her hips moving frantically against his as she exploded into pieces.

She couldn't be bound to Caid.

"There has never been a written rule that binding was meant to be witch to witch." Brenna's voice flooded her.

She wanted to stop, wanted to flee. A small hope to save him. Her body and heart propelled her forward. Ignoring the pleas from her mind, it reached forward for the bond, accepting it.

When she rose over him, his hands bracketed her waist. Pressing up into her, he moved her hips to seat her on himself fully, cursing as his hips bucked. She saw it on his face then, what she was feeling, their bond snapping into place as he accepted it, unknowingly. The magic visibly pulsing around them in flashes of red, blue, and purple.

Sitting up, he brought his arms around her, holding them still for a moment, his chest heaving.

"I love you," she whispered.

"I love you," he said and took her mouth with his again.

The tears threatened to spill over. There wasn't anything she could do. Fate had this planned for them.

Their orgasms crashed into one another, her screams, his shouts, filled the room as their release came. After, she sat with her legs around his waist, head against one of his shoulders, when she realized that there was something she could do. That she could save him. She had to send him away.

She had sensed Madigan's nearness the moment she'd returned. Like fingers dancing along her skin, trying to find a way in, stronger than before. The acrid air his magic left behind smelled stronger. It had drifted in through the open bedroom windows. He was creeping toward the house. He had been all while they were making love, sealing their future as bound. Swallowing, she tried to tamp down her rising fear.

"Come, take a shower with me," Caid said, voice rough from their lovemaking.

Wordlessly, she let him take her hand and lead her off the bed and into her bathroom. She stood in the walk-in, eye level with his chest, tracing the outlines of his muscles with her fingers. Trying to work out a way to get him away from Greens Glen without raising suspicion.

She was damning him to a life without her. She had to be okay with that because she would not damn him to death with her.

A hunger still burned hot in his eyes, and he lifted her, pressed her against the shower wall. When she fell over the edge this time, she felt herself shatter completely, knowing this was their end.

CHAPTER 60

MADIGAN edged into the woods behind the house. Lifting his arms, he sent his magic out in search of her.

Oh, how Aoife had been cunning. Nearing the edge of the wooded area, he felt Róisín's magic reaching for his, blocking it from passing.

So much power. His wickedness gleeful at the thought of wrapping itself in the magnitude of it.

Come, sweetheart.

A hesitation in the shield before it came back stronger, forcing him to take a staggered step back. He would've expected nothing less of her.

Would she have Aoife's black heart, or was she more like Brenna? Too soft, too kind, which would be of no use to him. Although, he supposed as he waited in the dark of the woods for Róisín, that assumption of Brenna was false. In his recent journeys through the realms in search of Aoife, he'd learned just how much like Aoife Brenna had truly been.

"Come," he called. He heaved the magic upward, pushing it outward from deep within, shattering the shield. Streams of thick, black smoke crept across the yard, searching.

It had been most peculiar. How he hadn't even realized that he could no longer feel Aoife's essence of life within him. Their Coven connection had long been severed when he ripped himself free of all the witches. But he and Aoife, they had been different. There had been something, a current, just beneath the surface.

He had known he couldn't trust her. What he didn't consider was just how deep her cunning ran. His searches in Legianne and Ireland changed everything.

All his waiting, his planning. All the work he had done spanning the decades to amass as much power as he could before he acted, knowing only a fool would take such an important leap too soon. And he was no fool.

He pressed the coils further. Wait he would no more. There was the rarest, finest gem in history, ready for his taking.

"Ah." He grinned, his magic wrapping around her, crawling into her body. "Now, let's try this again, my sweet. Come."

He waited a beat, perhaps she had pushed him out. Then she appeared on the back patio, her movements stiff as she crossed the yard to him.

"Yes," he hissed. Without another word, he led her deeper. And as he moved, he took with him every drop of life she'd brought back to the wood. If she could break her thrall, he would need every bit. Her power hummed, vibrating from her. It was like nothing he'd ever seen or heard of before.

When they neared the ravine, he lifted from the ground, maneuvering so that he faced her. He would use the edge as a failsafe. Should she be able to break free, a quick blow with his power could send her plummeting to her death before she could react.

"Stop," he said, just as she came to the edge of the drop.

From his place before her, he took in her features. He couldn't stop himself from reaching out to smooth a hand over her milky-white cheeks splashed with freckles. Stunning. It'd be a pity to ruin her.

She could be mine. He stroked along her skin, examining. There'd be so many benefits to keeping her alive. He'd have to thrall her, for certain.

Madigan shifted closer to her, trailing a finger along her neck. "You really are quite beautiful," he murmured. "These fingers are just itching to play with you, my love."

Róisín's turquoise eyes had gone creamy and blank. They stared back at him, unblinking, waiting.

"Mm." His hand cupped her chin, licking his lips. "Your skin feels amazing. I bet—" His fingers danced over her chest. "Inside feels just as amazing." His voice shocked him, how thick with want it had become. He swept the line of her shirt, then dipped his fingers to trace along the crest of her breasts.

"Quite amazing." He moved closer, drawing in a long breath through his nose, marking her scent.

"You could be my pet," he mused. "We could create. Much like Aoife and I had done. And..." He leaned in, using his tongue to taste along her jawline, his teeth to bite just below her ear. "I can smell it so clearly, that power you hold. So much more than she could dream of having. I would no longer need to risk my exposure before I've amassed the power I need for my magic. All of this could end." He lifted his eyes to the surrounding woods. "Create my own power source."

He cupped a breast, his thumb brushing roughly across the nipple. There was a primal urge to take her. He took her mouth with his, commanding her to kiss him back. His body throbbing at the taste of her when she opened for him. He could taste the power of her magic on her tongue, a hot, delicious liquid filling him, trailing down his throat to his core.

In a swift movement, he tore her shirt front, exposing her. Pulling back, his eyes were greedy, and he took her in. Yes, he would keep her. He would siphon her. He would plant his seed in her, over and over. His new plan made him harder, and his cock strained, throbbing almost painfully against the fabric of his pants.

Her body swayed, eyes becoming wholly white as they stayed steady on him, his thrall sinking deeper. Her nipples puckered in the breeze, and he groaned.

So precious. Absolutely precious.

Madigan moved to her again, his feet settling on the ground in front of her. He nudged her a few steps back to safety, then sealed his mouth over hers again. His hand went to one of her breasts, squeezing one of those puckered nipples hard. She expelled a gasp when her body responded, her breath hot, and his cock pressed harder against her stomach through his pants, begging to be inside of her. Instead of freeing it, he ground himself against her harder.

He groped, he squeezed, claiming and marking as he brought her closer. He pushed his tongue deeper, delighted at how far he could reach, imagining what it would be like to have his throbbing cock in there, milking her throat.

"Yes," he snarled as he took more of her. He slipped his hand up through a leg opening of her shorts, pressing his fingers into her pliant body. Her warmth enveloped him, warmed his palm.

"Such a good little witch," he crooned. "So wet and ready for me."

Oh yes, his free hand moved to the belt of his pants, he would keep her.

CHAPTER 61

THE moment Caid opened the door to his truck, he sensed something was wrong. The air was heavy, smelling of something hot and metallic.

"Hurry!" The deafening silence that surrounded him was broken by David's shouts from the backyard of the house.

Quickly pushing his body into motion, Caid rounded the house. David bounded toward him, ears pinned back.

"Hurry!" David called again. "He has her. He got through her shields and took her."

Caid's heart slammed down into his stomach, and he willed his legs to move faster. He dug deep, pushing himself past every limit that he could, leaping over logs, darting around bushes and stumps. His eyes stayed trained on David, who had become a white dot ahead of him.

Too long.

Panic gripped his chest tight. It's taking too long to get to her.

"Róisín!" He roared her name.

He moved so fast, he almost raced past David, who had stopped and sat on his haunches just before the tree line ended at the ravine.

"No." He shook his head. "No, no, no," he repeated frantically, moving toward the edge. "Róisín!"

Suddenly, a scream pierced the air. Everything around him seemed to stop, including his heart.

"She's alive," David panted.

That was all Caid needed to shake himself free of that feeling of falling into quicksand and get moving again. They raced down the path that traced the ravine edge toward where Róisín's scream had come from.

Something red and hot exploded in him at the sight of Róisín's ripped shirt, its new, tattered seam fluttering in the wind as she stood at the edge.

Stewart—no, Madigan stood just inches from her, eyes as black as the ink-like coils shifting and swirling around his face and arms.

Caid's knuckles popped from the tightness in which he squeezed his hands into fists. His mind warred with thinking first, acting second, and the way the rage at the scene before him seared him from the inside out, demanding he act now.

Before he could move closer, her magic erupted from her body, sending a shockwave out. Madigan plummeted into the ravine.

Caid barely had time to scramble and grab David before they pushed back into the brush at the woods' edge.

Madigan rose into the air. His face was dark, shadowed by the smoking coils dancing around him, but Caid could see that for the first time since Madigan had strolled into Greens Glen – he was unkempt. His suit was wrinkled, its shirt mis-buttoned. His hair was a riot of waves around his face.

"We could have had it all," Madigan said.

"Never," Róisín said in a voice so raw, so dark, it sounded like she'd dredged it from the depths of hell. Caid set David down, then pushed to his feet.

Róisín lifted her hands at her sides. Looking down at them, her lips pursed, her head slightly tipped off to the side. She rotated them so that her palms faced up, then wiggled her fingers, a smile briefly touching the corners of her mouth. As she rose from the ground, Caid halted in his path to get to her.

She lifted higher into the air, one of her hands rising as she went. Vines erupted up from the ground below Madigan. They quickly twisted around his legs, his waist, stopping only when his arms were pinned at his sides.

Caid looked down at the ground at his feet, searching for something that he could use as a weapon. He needed to do what he could to get them the hell away from there.

"It's a pity." Madigan shook his head. The vines binding him turned to dust, freeing him. "That we could not come to some type of... agreement."

"It is a pity," she crooned. "Especially now to know if something happens to me, my power goes to the stone, and not you."

Madigan's eyes darkened, narrowing on her.

"Your thrall didn't quite have the hold on me you thought." She moved closer to Madigan. "To have the power that you have, it's a pity that you couldn't feel that."

Shadows crossed over her face, confirming Caid's worry and a burst of rage that had risen inside when he'd seen her shirt.

"You may have tricked me, just as Aoife did. I *will* have you and your power. However, you forget, I'm a siphon," he said darkly.

"As am I, but—" Her body glowed brighter while a dark smoke seeped from her pores. "Unlike you, I am both life and death."

"You're not ready to wield that power against me." He lifted his hand, fisting it. Quiet fell over them all, and he looked her over. When he opened his hand, his magic blasted into her, sending her spiraling to the ground.

Caid didn't hesitate, he threw himself from the ravine edge at her tumbling body. After their bodies collided midair, he braced for impact.

Slamming against the ravine wall, he reached up with one arm, trying to dig in a hand to find purchase on something to slow their descent. His other arm gripped Róisín around her middle so tightly his muscles burned. Their free-fall jerked to a halt, the impact of the abrupt stop rattling his bones.

"Caid," Róisín gasped, looking up at him with a pale face. "You need to get out of here."

"I can't." He sucked in a pained breath. Every muscle in his body was on fire. "I can't leave you behind."

She tipped her head back, looking overhead. When her eyes

widened, Caid followed her line of sight. A cluster of tree roots had burst through the ground at the top of the ravine, snagging his arm and snaking down around his body, wrapping around her. Her mouth fell open.

"Thanks for saving us," Caid grit out, and he began pulling them up.

"It... it wasn't." She shook her head.

"Róisín! Kincaid!" Nanette's head appeared just over them. "Give me your hand."

Lucius and Shasta were behind her, leaping over them toward Madigan. Matthew wasn't far behind, fire already blazing around his clenched fists.

It took Caid a moment to collect himself. In the heat of the moment, he'd succumbed to being dazzled by the open display of their magic.

"Kincaid, your hand," Nanette said.

He felt Róisín's legs and arms wrap around his middle and he shook his head free of the distraction, bringing his now free hand upward toward where Nanette waited.

With surprising strength, Nanette grasped Caid's hand, pulling both him and Róisín up with ease.

"We need to reestablish the connection," she said quickly to Róisín. "We need to do it now."

Róisín brought her lips between her teeth and shook her head. "We don't even know it will work. We've only read about it, never actually proved that it was possible."

"Then we're just going to have to pray it works." When Nanette turned to Caid, her golden eyes glowed. "We also appear to have a new development." She eyed him curiously. "We'll talk about that after we handle this. We must be quick."

Matthew's angry bellow rang out around them as he launched himself into the air at Madigan, pressing the fire out as he went. Lucius moved to attack Madigan from the opposite side.

"I—"

"No." Nanette took both of Róisín's hands. "You can do this, Róisín. You can. We're all here with you. The Goddess and Sisters sent you here. The Seer gave you what you needed to do, what had to be done. You can do this."

Róisín pushed her hands through her hair, then looked at Caid.

Doing his best to bury the feeling of doom and dread he felt sitting heavy in his gut, he nodded before giving her the words he knew she needed. That he needed. "I love you."

Releasing her breath, she closed her eyes and lifted away from them on a gust of wind.

CHAPTER 62

Róisín opened her mind, reaching out with her magic—feeling, searching. While the others distracted Madigan with their own magic, she searched first for Matthew's string.

She knew she grasped it when he looked over at her, relief washing over his face when he saw her. Next, she searched for Nanette's. When she tied that with Matthew's, she tied them both to hers. Knowing time moved quickly, that they had none to spare, she fumbled through the surrounding energy to find Lucius's and Shasta's strings, securing them.

As she worked, her magic had lifted her up and away from everyone. When she opened her eyes, she nearly shrieked in alarm at the height she had risen. Trying to calm herself, she watched the battle below her. Her friends, no, her family, expertly throwing blasts of magic, wind, rocks, Matthew's body-sized fireballs, while dodging everything Madigan pressed back against them.

Careful to not take too much from the others, or to send her own down the lines to them, she flowed outward, around all of them. The healing light fought to explode from her as she reached further and further, seeking the frayed end of Madigan's string.

When she found it, her magic and all its power almost guttered out from recoiling so sharply at the stench of his darkness.

She had nearly tied them all to the tattered bit when he felt her there, then he pressed that darkness toward her without ever taking his attention off the others. She grit her teeth, fighting to keep control, focusing on tying the knot.

There. With a quiet satisfaction, she yanked it tight.

Madigan's body went as taut as a bow, making him shout a curse.

"Now!" Nanette shouted from somewhere below her.

Together, they all pushed their magic down the line. A piercing pain shot through her, stealing her breath away.

"No," she gasped, reaching for her throat. Madigan and Aoife had come together, creating life. The act had created a tether deep within herself to him. Everything they all channeled into him also came back into her, burning her power and herself out.

She clutched at her side, doubling over from the pain as it grew within.

"Róisín!" Caid called out to her.

Her vision blurred. A deafening roar grew in her ears. She could see Caid running along the pathway toward her; his lips moving, but she heard nothing beyond the roar.

Overcome, she let her magic go.

CHAPTER 63

Róisín was dead. Unable to move. Unable to draw in a breath to fill her lungs. Everything felt heavy and empty at the same time. Despite her efforts, her eyes wouldn't open. Silence surrounded her.

Not even her own heartbeat echoed within.

Róisín prayed to the Goddess that with her death, it meant Madigan was gone as well.

She knew the others would pick up the pieces, handle the council and move the future forward for witchkind. This was her sacrifice so that they could all have that. She knew. She had told the others; they hadn't believed her.

Caid.

Caid.

Where she should have felt that shattering break of her heart, she felt nothing.

No pain, no sadness, not even worry.

She never got to tell him she was sorry.

Never got to tell him she would have chosen life if she could have.

She would have chosen him over anything.

A coldness settled over her, but she didn't shiver.

Instead, the darkness swallowed her motionless body.

Chapter 64

Caid's only focus was Róisín. The surrounding noises had faded away until he heard nothing except the beat of his own pounding heart and harsh breaths.

"Breathe," he pleaded. He tipped Róisín's head back, pinching her nose, and he blew into her mouth as they'd shown him to do in the CPR class Lina dragged him to that one time. He'd thought it was stupid then, but now he couldn't be grateful enough for it.

"Breathe," he said more desperately, pressing on her chest.

He had torn his left leg open sliding along the edge of the path, trying to get there to catch her before she'd hit the ground. The warm blood soaked his jeans, dripping onto the ground through the tears in the fabric. He wasn't sure if it was broken or not, only caring he'd somehow gotten to her fast enough. Their bodies had crashed hard. His taking the brunt of the impact.

She had already gone. Her face ashen, lips tinged blue. The others scrambled in different directions. Lucius and Matthew had gone after Madigan while Shasta and Nanette had worked overtime to throw up a shield around Caid and Róisín.

No one knew what had happened.

Róisín had screamed in such an agonizing, broken way before she crumpled, then fell.

Madigan's face had twisted in delight. Thankfully, he could not take action, out powered by the quartet of witches. He quickly fled, leaving behind a scene of chaos.

Now, Caid bent over Róisín's lifeless body, trying with everything he had to bring her back to him. He pressed on her chest, counting out the compressions, while his own chest felt as though it had been flayed, his flesh left hanging from his body.

Before she had screamed, something grew there, a tightness, something straining at its limit. As he willed his legs to go faster, racing to her, that strain suddenly began fraying, fiber by fiber. When the last snapped, a pain like never before erupted inside. Time slowed, it seemed, as he struggled to move, to breathe. His heart in his throat, his lungs spasming.

Was it fear? Was it knowing the moment she fell, he was possibly too late? The acid-like burn spread through him, clouding his vision, and for a moment, it was as though he only imagined the feel of Róisín's body crashing into him. Disoriented, he felt as though he still ran, still shouting to her to hold on, he was coming.

The coldness of her body snapped him back. His heart found a jagged beat, and his lungs began a slow, but stuttered in and out. The tearing pain inside was forgotten, and he bargained quietly with every God he could think of. Even if it meant his life for hers, he would gladly accept that fate.

He breathed into her mouth again, tears burning his eyes, and he worked to keep his movements steady. He sensed motion behind him, but his focus stayed on Róisín.

"Come back to me, baby, come back." His voice cracked with thickness from his emotions, the scream that wanted to tear free from him. His throat had grown so tight, it was like he was being strangled. As he counted out thirty more compressions, his entire body shook. When he moved back to her mouth, he was almost knocked backward by an invisible force slamming into his chest.

Róisín gasped, her arms reaching up, her body thrashing around. Then her screams pierced the air.

"Róisín," he breathed out and scrambled closer. "Róisín, you're okay, you're all right." Caid took her in his arms, pulling her against his chest.

Her body stiffened for a moment. He could feel her slow breath as it rattled through her chest. Her eyes fluttered open, and the tension that bound his body fled. His breaths that had been painful to draw in only seconds before soothed his aching lungs.

"Caid." Her voice was strained, as if her vocal cords had been squeezed tightly. She brought her arms around him, clinging so hard, her nails broke the skin on his triceps. "Caid."

"Shh." He stroked her hair, raining kisses over her face. "You're here, you're okay."

"Oh, thank the Goddess." Shasta dropped to her knees, her eyes damp with unshed tears.

Nanette placed a comforting hand on Shasta's shoulder and looked at each of them. "We need to get her out of here."

Shasta lifted her eyes from Róisín's face to Caid. "Take her to Molennius."

"Where?" His brows drew together. He struggled to keep his focus. His head turning light, his vision hazing as new pain washed over him. He worked to keep himself composed, to listen to their words around him, while his chest squeezed, and needle like pricks, trailed by a pulling, dragging sensation. His heart raced, sweat beading along his spine.

"My realm. The house will let you in. You'll be safest there. We don't know if Lucius and Matthew will be successful, and if not..." Shasta's mouth pressed into a tight line. "He's coming for her."

Careful of Róisín in his arms, he stood, trying to balance on his ruined leg. "How do we get there?"

Nanette gave him a slow smile. "Ah, yes, it happened so quickly in the nth hour, I'd almost forgotten. Our surprise elemental."

Shasta's head jerked in her direction.

"When we fell," Róisín's voice was small and muffled where she had it buried against his chest. "That wasn't me."

"It certainly was not I," Nanette assured them. "We were still in the woods when you fell."

Caid's brow knit in confusion. Had he missed a part of their conversation? Something was happening inside of him, he wasn't sure what, and it was happening quickly.

He wanted nothing more than to vomit.

"Well, then." Shasta huffed with a grin. "How about we get back to the house where I can show you how we travel, Kincaid. You're going to have to get her there because she's not strong enough to take you both."

He wanted to argue that he couldn't, that he didn't know what they were talking about. Instead, his legs carried him and Róisín, his damaged leg causing him to limp, trailing after Nanette and Shasta.

CHAPTER 65

THE chilly winter air of Molennius greeted them when they arrived on the wrap around porch of Shasta's home. Shasta's power and energy wrapped lovingly around Róisín. She couldn't stop herself from leaning into it.

Caid carefully set her on her feet, eyes so wide in bewilderment, she couldn't help the smile that spread across her face.

"I guess it's different when you grow up with it." She tried to sound casual as she took in the mountain view before them, but inside, she was just as shocked as the rest of them to learn that Caid had elemental magic.

When they'd cleared the woods, returning to Róisín's house, Nanette had explained that it was rare. Something that had only happened once humans began their witch hunts across all the realms. More damningly in Earth's realm. The slaughtering of humans and witches alike over centuries. Witches struggled to live more in secret, to protect their families and their Covens. Many gave up practicing magic in a way a child stops playing sports in favor of spending time with friends or taking up a new hobby.

The witches who had stopped never spoke of it to their children. Over generations, the knowledge of magic and power had disappeared

288

within their families. The result over the passing centuries were the lines becoming diluted. The magic often stayed in a state of slumber from that ignorance paired with a lack of use.

"Under the duress of the earlier day, it must have felt called to, and rose," Nanette had reasoned. "It would explain many of the things from the roots to your speed when you moved, Kincaid."

Róisín had to give him credit where credit was due. He didn't argue it, didn't get angry, or demand answers. He took it in stride. She was sure that was because he knew the only way they would get out of Earth's realm was if he was on board completely. As he'd held her in his arms, energy radiated from him in waves. That fierce, driving need to get them away from Madigan's reach.

She shook her head and pushed open the front door of Shasta's home, trying not to jump at the fire that roared to life in the massive stone hearth in the living room. She glanced over her shoulder to sneak a peek at Caid.

Shasta had repaired his leg enough for the journey, but it would still need to be healed. Sleep tugged at Róisín, her body depleted of more than magic. But she was the only one who could fix the tattered flesh properly.

"Sit," she demanded.

He jerked to a stop, whirling to her, a questioning look on his face.

"On the sofa." She pointed.

"Róisín, you need to rest. Everything else can wait."

She fought the urge to grind her teeth. Instead, she took a moment to calm her growing frustration. Her frustration stemmed from everything but Caid. To take it out on him would only make how she felt worse.

She had let herself become thralled. The result had been the violation of her mind and body by Madigan. She hadn't been able to shake him. He was everything around her. What was worse, she still felt him inside of her.

"I can rest in a minute," she said to Caid. "I can fix your leg for you."

"I told you not again." He shook his head. "You're already drained."

"Sit on the fucking couch, Kincaid," she growled at him.

"Róisín…"

She moved closer, her eyes on the tattered material of his jeans. She scanned the wound, working out the best way to repair it in her mind. With a nod, she said, "That's fine, I can do it from here."

"No." He hastened toward her, reaching out to grab her hand.

Before he could hold her, she placed her hands firmly on his chest, shaking her head. Her body glowed with her healing light. "Just trust me, Caid. Please. It's bad and can get infected."

"You said you can't heal humans without consequence, Róisín. I saw what happened, and that was when you hadn't just died."

The glow brightened in response. She closed her eyes, visualizing the muscles of his calf and quadricep on his left leg knitting together, the ruined tissue and ligaments smoothing, the ripped skin coming together. When she heard him hiss out a breath, she went further inside, soothing the pain he battled from the injury. The pain from the remnants of their broken bond, and the disjointed way it had repaired itself when he'd brought her back.

When she came to the pain within his heart, she opened her eyes to find his hazel ones on hers, wet with tears.

"I thought I'd lost you," he choked out.

She hesitated, wanting to choose her words carefully, still feeling raw over the moments before. "Just before I fell, everything just went dark. Then it stopped…" Her voice thickened. "I knew I was gone. I knew…" Her breath hitched. "This morning we…"

He was at her in two steps, taking her face in his hands, his mouth over hers, their teeth crashing as they both pushed their tongues into each other's mouths as fervent desperation and need overtook them.

She pulled back with a gasp when she tasted his tears on her lips.

"I wish you had listened to me." He rested his forehead against hers, eyes closed.

"What do you mean?"

"My leg. It doesn't matter how bad it is, you can't take that risk. Not now, not ever."

She lifted a hand to his face, stroking a thumb along his bottom lip. She reached for their bond, Caid's love, using it to shove away the memories of earlier. The feel of Madigan. His smell.

"Shasta has shown me how to work with all my magic to balance the use of one with another. It was never that I couldn't use my magic for humans or other witches. No one had ever taught me how. Aoife had been the one to tell me I couldn't heal people, that my magic served only nature. She told me if I tried to do more, I would be punished by the Goddess. I think she was scared that I would learn the truth about her, then use my magic to stop her."

"You'll be okay?"

She nodded. "I'll be fine."

"About this morning." He tucked a strand of hair behind her ear, then pressed a kiss to her forehead. "You felt that? What was it?"

"We're tied together now, for eternity." She offered him a small smile through her own tears. "Which, given that you have awoken the magic within you, means you've got way more than forty years left."

"Holy shit." He pushed a hand through his hair. "Okay." He nodded and shrugged. "Okay. I'd ask now what, but my brain is fried from information overload, and you really need to rest."

"No." She moved to him, placing her hands on his chest. "I need a favor from you first."

"Anything, I'll do anything you need me to," he answered without hesitation. He took his fingers under her chin, tipping her face up to his. He frowned at the pained expression she couldn't hide.

"Just... I can still feel his hands on me. I've tried, I can't..." Her voice shook. "I need it gone. I need that feeling gone." She squeezed her eyes shut, a tear escaping down her cheek.

"You told him that his control over you hadn't worked," he said, his voice rough from his barely restrained emotion.

"He'd gotten through my shields enough to have some control. I was partly thralled. I don't know what happened. I couldn't stop myself from going to him. Then I couldn't move. I was like a bystander in my life for those moments, screaming at myself to do something. Then you shouted my name. At that moment, it was enough of a distraction I could get myself back. He didn't know at first, and my magic, it was so slow to come back to me."

She shuddered, wrapping her arms around herself, trying to shake off the feeling of Madigan's hands on her breasts, the way he pressed against her, into her. The way he looked at her like a hunter on his prey. *He bit me.*

Caid brushed her hair over her shoulder. His eyes grew dark when he saw the bruise that formed there, along the side of her neck and on her chest.

"Shasta kept my room upstairs for me all of these years," she whispered.

"What do you need me to do?" His eyes searched hers.

"Erase the feeling of him from my body."

Chapter 66

Róisín fell into a fitful sleep after Caid's lips and hands had covered every inch of her body. When they'd moved to join themselves, panic had risen inside of her, and all she could feel was Madigan pressing his fingers into her again. Caid immediately stopped, despite her protests. He pulled her into his arms, holding her until she finally gave in to her exhaustion.

Madigan tried to seep in through the edges of her dreams. She felt his phantom touch across her chest, along her neck. She had dreamt of sitting with her mother alongside a stream near their home in Ireland when his smell overpowered her again.

She always came back to her mother. Regardless of how many times Madigan tried to steer her off-track in any of her dreams, Brenna and Róisín always came back to one another. Brenna like a shield from him, protecting Róisín, driving the dark away like a mother does for a child at night.

Róisín sat with her beneath a hawthorn tree at the edge of the property of her childhood home. The trickle of the creek soothed Róisín as she braided wildflowers with her.

Brenna finished the flower circlet she had been creating, setting it upon Róisín's head, giving her a loving smile when their eyes connected.

"He's human," Róisín said.

"There has never been a written rule that binding was meant for witch to witch," she said.

"That may be so, but there's never been a witch-human bind in our history."

"Mm," Brenna replied absentmindedly.

Róisín's eyes flew open as she shot up in bed; Caid was next to her instantly.

"She knew," Róisín breathed out. "She knew." She turned to him.

He stayed silent.

"My mother came to me that night after I told you everything. In the middle of the things she had said—she told me that you and I were bound."

Caid pulled back, straightening. His brows came down over his eyes as they narrowed on her. "You knew?"

Sensing the anger rising through his tone, she reached out, placing a hand on his forearm. "She had said we were, but never, ever in our history has there been a human bound to a witch. My father and mother were just in love. There wasn't a bind, a tether between them. I didn't trust it, I didn't want to. Not with what it could mean for you in this. I knew I loved you, and that if I made it out of this, if we made it out of this, then I wanted all the time with you, the life with you I could have."

"You knew," he said again. He pushed the blankets off his body and rose from the bed.

"I did." She let out a breath that was trying to sear her lungs. She could only watch him as he silently paced the room, occasionally running a hand over his face or through his hair.

Finally, he stopped, turning to face her.

"I didn't say anything because it was all very new. Not just that you knew who I was, what I was. You knew *everything,*" she stressed. "No one has ever known that. Alexandria, she ran away at just a glimmer. Being in love with you, that was something huge, something important. Being bound? It changes everything. Only half of the witches in their lifespan find theirs."

"What happens when you're bound to someone?"

"It's..." She searched for the words. "For a lack of better explanation, you know those books Lina reads? The ones about fae, monsters, and whatever?"

Slowly, one of his brows rose, and he pressed his lips together. His eyes quickly changed to something mischievous.

Sitting straighter, bringing her shoulders up, she shot him a glare. "This is serious, Caid."

"I, nope, hold on." He shook his head, quickly looking away. She saw his shoulders shake slightly, then heard his quiet snort.

"Caid," she groaned.

"Hold on." He lifted a hand, waving it at her. "I just—" A chuckle escaped him. "Are we really going to compare real life to a fantasy book?" He laughed again, tears filling his eyes. "This is it." He bent, placing his hands on his knees, body shaking as he laughed harder. "This is a sign." He gasped. "A sign I've lost my damned mind. I'm laughing when my girlfriend just died, and I found out I'm some magical being. Then, my girlfriend, who was just dead, but thank fucking Christ is alive again, just compared our relationship to..." He stood to look directly at her, suddenly serious. "Books about faeries."

"Well, I mean..." She extended her palm, letting a small forest rise from the center.

His head dipped slightly. "All right. Point taken."

"As I was saying," she said, her tone clipped. "I guess it's like that. We're... mates of a sort."

"Like pack dogs." He giggled like a child again. He covered his mouth, but his eyes glittered with mirth.

She threw herself back onto the bed, reached for his pillow, then held it over her face, screaming into it.

"Okay, okay, okay. I'm sorry." He came back to the bed. He pulled the pillow away from her face, then smoothed her hair back. "On a serious note, we're tied together for life, right? Is that what you mean?"

"Pretty much." She pushed herself back up into a sitting position.

"If you die, do I die? As morbid as it sounds, I'd prefer it that way."

"I know if I need you, there's this line between you and me. I can tug it and you'll know. I know we can channel our power together when we need to. Otherwise, I don't really know much else. Nanette could explain better, she was bound."

"Yet she lives long after her significant other has passed," he noted with sorrow.

"My mother knew. About you, your magic. I didn't realize it that night. In the dreams I've been having here, I keep coming back to that conversation. The way she reacted when I pointed out you were human. That it's never happened before."

One of his fingers traced along her jaw to her chin, hooking under it to tip her head up to look at him. "Would it have changed anything if you knew then?"

"About you? No, but"—her cheeks flushed—"I have a confession."

"Uh-oh," he replied.

"I'm pretty ecstatic you are like me. A witch, I mean."

"Why? So, I can grow and water all the plants while you can watch instead of work?"

"Only if you do it with your shirt off." She bit her lip. "Or maybe everything off." She laughed when he scowled, then she playfully pushed his shoulder. "Although it's quite appealing now that I picture it, no, I'm ecstatic because, while I accepted we had little time to make a life together, we now have longer. A lot longer. Not only do I want longer with you, I need it. Nothing quantifies as long enough with you."

His eyes darkened, and he moved so that he was almost over her. "You said witches live pretty long, right?"

She nodded as he moved even closer, causing her to lie back on the bed.

"You also mentioned something about..." He nipped her chin, then kissed down her neck, giving extra care to where her fading bruises were. When his mouth closed over one of her breasts through her shirt, she sucked in a breath, arching up to him.

"I said something about?" She urged him to finish.

"This with no barriers around your power." He settled over her, nestling himself between her legs. "How's it work when we both have it? When we are connected the way we are?"

"Oh," she said, surprised, her eyebrows rising. "I... I don't know. This is a first for me."

"A first?" She heard the possessiveness in his reply. "Are you good? Is this okay?"

She opened her mouth to respond. Instead, unable to find her voice, she could only give a nod, feeling the fire build in her core.

"If you need me to stop, you need to tell me, and I will. Don't be brave about this, Róisín, okay? If you're not—"

"Caid." She brought an index finger to his lips. "Shh."

He gently stroked a finger along her folds, and the next sounds she made weren't coherent words.

Her skin lit with desire when his thumb circled her clitoris, then he pressed his index and middle finger into her slowly, while he watched her. She gripped his arms, nails digging when he slowly drew his fingers out, thumb still stroking.

Madigan tried to creep in through the edges, her chest growing tight, her pulse quickening with fear. Gritting her teeth, she closed her eyes, working to wall him and the memories of him in a place where he couldn't touch her. A weightless feeling overtook her when he was sealed away, then she soared.

"You." She put a hand behind his head, pulling him closer. "Now." Her breath hot against his mouth. "Please."

Slowly, carefully, he lifted away from her, repositioning himself. Once he was seated inside of her, he laid his forehead against hers. His eyes were closed, his breaths a soft pant over her face. "Jesus Christ. I don't dare to move. This is..."

"More than love," she whispered, her fingers brushing over his back. "This is forever."

He opened his eyes, revealing to her the inferno burning there. She knew her own eyes mirrored them. She slid his hands over his back, gripping his ass. Her nails bit into his skin.

"This is everything," she nearly moaned, feeling him shift deeper inside of her. She tipped her hips, reveling in the feel of her fullness. "You're mine."

Slowly, he drew out, his eyes remaining on hers. "You're mine." He drove back into her, making her cry out.

Holding on to what felt like a thin shred, that release already there, demanding she let go, she tipped up again, clenching possessively around him. "Forever."

"Forever," he said and claimed her mouth.

Chapter 67

CAID was an oarless boat, drifting downriver, moving further away from the life that he'd always known. That surety, that routine, that steadiness, the expected. All of it watched him from shore as his boat became smaller and smaller.

He had sat vigil next to Róisín. Her lids fluttered, her hands clenching so tightly, even the small freckles on the backs of them stretched white. When his eyes grew tired, they tried to fool him, her body fading away, leaving him staring at an empty bed. The way his heart would stall, the air would leave his lungs. She could be gone. If he didn't save her, the bed would be empty.

What happened when they faced Madigan again?

Shasta had given him two days before she prodded him. He was useless sitting there staring at her, she had told him in a firm, motherly voice. She'd nudged him first to the third-floor library, where he sat for hours during the day, his eyes hungrily consuming every word he could find written in English. Accounts of the two originating witch Covens, how they grew as other witches sought them for protection, safety in numbers. The creation of new Covens and migrations to the realms.

After a week, Caid's worry had grown teeth and gnawed at any part of him it could find and latch onto.

"She'll be okay." Shasta's hand rested on his forearm, bringing his attention away from Róisín's prone form. "You need to learn the magic."

He looked back to the bed, eyes lingering for a moment, before finally looking up at Shasta.

Her lips tipped upward at the corners, a soft smile belying the concern that etched the lines between her brows and around her eyes. "Your instinctual magic is good. The roots catching you both, the way you used the wind for speed when you needed to run…"

Had it been the wind? He only remembered moving faster than he'd ever done before, needing to get to Róisín before she crashed to the rock and root covered earth. "I don't—" He cleared the roughness away from his voice. "I don't know how I did it."

"Come to the atrium with me." She stepped back and nodded toward the bedroom door. "You won't be far. It does no good to sit here and stare at her all day long. I'll start your training with you here, and then we can have Nanette, or even Lily help you more." She paused, briefly turning to Róisín, before reaching for the doorknob. "He'll be back, hon, and we need to be ready."

Shasta slipped from the room without another word, clearly expecting him to follow.

He took a step forward before an unseen thread tugged at him. Caid hesitated.

If he had commanded roots and wind just from desperate instinct, what would he be able to accomplish when he had knowledge and intent? That skin of helplessness that had grown when Róisín told him who she was, about Madigan, what her kind were facing, cracked.

This was his chance. This was his way. He not only needed to shed that sense of helplessness, but he needed to shed that quiet life he lived. If he couldn't leave it all behind, embrace and live this new life, there was a chance that the next time, the bed would be empty when he faced it again.

He dug his heels into training, letting them take root, crawling, reaching further and further out. Quickly collecting and excelling at the most basic skills, learning how to reach within for the power of his magic, letting it filter through his body so that when he chose the element he wanted, it was right at his fingertips. Literally.

"My thumb is on fire."

Nanette, who had joined them later in that second week of Róisín's sleep, stood next to Shasta in the atrium with a smile on her face, her eyes dancing with laughter. "Were you thinking of fire?"

"Kind of?" He blinked rapidly, goosebumps rising along the back of his neck as he thought of the fire extinguishing, the flame fluttering out immediately. "More about how awesome it'd have been to have this in my back pocket for those bonfire parties in fields back in high school."

"So, your hand, like a lighter?" Shasta asked.

"Yeah." He nodded, and his thumb ignited again. "It's easy, but hard too. Does that make sense? I mean..." He spread his fingers out, each fingertip lighting like candles. "In here, without distraction, it's easy, sort of automatic now that I've got the hang of it. But what about when, you know?"

A weight settled in his core, wrapping around his spine.

"Caid." His name was a harsh syllable from Shasta's lips.

Shaking his head, he blinked rapidly at his hand fully engulfed. It only confirmed his biggest fear.

"This is all new to you. You've already done exceptionally well after just a week of training. We need to shift your training to accommodate for any distraction, be it physical and mental." Nanette moved across the atrium to a bench at the far end. When she picked up the small, maroon suede pouch, she rolled it between her hands, thumb smoothing over the material. Before she returned to where he and Shasta stood, she took the leather-bound book that had been beneath the pouch from the bench. "You're a true and pure elemental."

When she gestured for his hand, he offered it, palm up. The weight of the two objects surprised him, and he used his other hand to help balance them. "I don't know what that means."

"We don't have time to dig for familial lines right now to determine your Coven origination, but now that the magic within you has released, I can feel it. It's an old line that ties that power. A nearly undiluted, old line."

Out of his depth. It echoed through his mind hundreds of times a day, even more than when David greeted him the day the curtain came down, revealing all of this. Yet, that constant thought kept chasing at his heels like a small dog.

"My familial lines travel back centuries and are also pure and true. This is a family book, it doesn't have much in it by way of magic, but how we've found the mental fortitude we need to wield that power."

Removing the pouch from the top of the book, a title-less cover greeted him. "A self-help for witches."

Nanette tipped her head to one side, pursing her lips. "More or less. There are chapters on meditation, habit creation, and, well, yes. You're right. It will help us with your training."

"The pouch has more ward runes," Shasta added. "Your bond with Róisín was shielded, but with it being in place now, it's possible that it is no longer that way. Bonds can be like beacons."

Caid heard the unspoken words. He was a lighthouse, flashing out into the dark, ominous storm waters, beckoning anyone to the shore where Róisín was. For all that skin he had shed after just a week of learning to work with his magic, he could feel some of the bare places pulling the old skin back on.

"We need to work on that too." Nanette looked to Shasta, seeking a confirmation of something.

"This," Shasta said with a tap to the side of her head.

Fuck, I am so out of my depth.

CHAPTER 68

WHILE Róisín slept, and Caid prowled and paced, Shasta cooked. A comfort, a distraction. She needed to keep her hands and mind occupied. Something about the act of creating meals, or baking, centered her and quieted her mind in a way that nothing else had.

Róisín was okay, she knew that deep in her bones. Yet, the image of her colorless face and bluing lips, still slithered along next to her, just within her peripheral. That haunting image held her in her kitchen baking pile after pile of cookies, bread and cooking extravagant dinners with more food than anyone in her house could eat.

When she reached across her island counter for the bag of chocolate chips, her hands shook and she drew them back to her sides. Fisting them, she shoved them into the pockets of the sweatpants she wore, as if the act would mean the emotions she felt didn't exist.

Tipping her head back to look up to the ceiling, she counted backward from twenty, breathing in deeply through her nose, expelling through her mouth.

"Oh, Brenna, I need you so much right now." Her whispered words drowned out by the low hum of her oven heating.

There was so much that her friend hadn't disclosed all those years ago. She had told Shasta of the bond within the McGrath family lines, and they had searched for years for them. She'd held onto that secret for Brenna, just as she'd held on to so many others.

Yet, it was now clear that Brenna had held on to secrets still, right until her end.

Kincaid McGrath was not only an elemental, but a whole and pure elemental. It meant that he was possibly the descendant of one of the lost, once extremely powerful, Covens. When she had arrived on Molennius to help with training, Nanette had suspected he may be a descendant of the original elementals from Earth whose Coven disappeared after the witch trials of the late 1500s.

Although Shasta understood Brenna's urgency in finding the McGrath bloodline, upon learning of Caid's magic, Shasta had more questions. Ones that only the Goddess could answer.

She lifted her head from the dough she kneaded on her counter, pausing as she heard the soft murmur of Caid's voice just overhead, Róisín's response to him muffled.

It had been a relief when she had finally awoken. Shasta had taken Caid under her wing, drawing him into the library to learn their history, teaching him how to use the magic that now hummed within him. The way he had warred with leaving Róisín's side each day, but he quickly shed that worry and concern, and replaced it with drive and determination to learn, harness, and master his magic.

"Oh, Bren, your son-in-law." She sighed and chuckled lightly. "You've got a good one. He's handsome as hell. He's steady, and he's good. To the bone, he's good."

Now that she was awake, but her strength hadn't wholly returned, he doted and fussed over Róisín every minute that he didn't train. Bringing her food, shuttling books back and forth for her.

She let them have some time together, alone, before she made her way up to the room. Since, she took a few hours each day to sit on the bed with her, just as she had so many times before... before.

Before it all changed and Aoife put the wall up, keeping Shasta from even being able to talk to Róisín about their past. Took the ability for Shasta to say aloud that she loved Róisín.

They couldn't make up for their lost time, Shasta had accepted that.

Instead, each time she nestled next to Róisín on the bed, wrapping them both in one of the many throws that Brenna had made while Róisín grew within her womb, she worked on forgetting the years in-between, and focused on what she had now.

Her niece, in her arms, while they talked about memories from before.

Lucius and Matthew still hadn't returned from their search, and with the wait for Róisín to wake, they still hadn't a grasp on what exactly had happened that day.

Since waking, Róisín still hadn't spoken to anyone about what had happened before they had all arrived. She had tried with Caid and with Shasta, only to become overwhelmed, her body trembling. For Róisín's wellbeing, Shasta pressed her to rest and give it time.

Róisín had been successful in tying him to all of them, that much they knew. It was also how they knew he was still alive. Once he figured that the connection only tethered them, that it couldn't be used to locate them, there was a steady, violent tugging from his end as he tried to break himself free.

Her front door banged open, Lucius and Nanette trailing in wearing matching looks of defeat.

"Shit," Shasta said, earning a raised brow from Lucius.

"How is she?" Nanette asked softly.

"As good as anyone's guess, still. She seems to be okay. I think she's been able to tell Kincaid more than she's been able to tell me."

"The last few times I helped him with training, he's been particularly determined." Nanette lowered herself onto a stool at the island bar top.

Lucius sniffed the air, turning his attention to the fresh cookies sitting on a cooling rack. "Has she come down at all?"

"Not yet." Shasta frowned, drawing her brows together. "He's been bringing her food. I've been up a few times to talk about things we used to do. Something to help keep her comfortable because whatever happened, it not only changed her, but I have a feeling it's going to change everything."

He picked up a cookie. "May I? He's said nothing about what she told him?"

"He said it was for her to tell us."

Lucius's face turned childish with enjoyment over the cookie, and Shasta smiled.

"We need to remove her connection specifically," Nanette said. "I can feel him using his magic to search for her. It's only a matter of time before he uses that connection to do it. I know the spell work we used to create it doesn't allow it, we also know there's a possibility when the will is strong enough."

Shasta's expression turned grim and she turned back to Lucius. "What about you?"

"I've come up empty handed," he said around his third cookie. "Matthew should be here shortly. It would be best if we could get Róisín to join us. Unlike before, I don't feel as though we have the luxury of time."

"Do you think he knows about Kincaid?" Nanette asked.

"The magic? I don't know if, in the heat of the moment, he would have sensed the extra source of power there in the ravine with us. The bond?" Shasta questioned with a casualness that brought their attention to her. "He won't."

"Won't?" Nanette and Lucius asked in unison.

"Mm," Shasta hummed with a slight nod. She set the last glob of cookie dough on the pan before moving to the oven. Pulling open the door, she bent down to slide the pan in. With a smile, she added, "Brenna made sure of it."

CHAPTER 69

DAUGHTER of the Goddess, Past, lowered her willowy frame next to Future at the loom. Studying the ever-moving threads, she frowned.

They knew Róisín had returned Madigan to the Covens as much as she could with her connection to him. The act had snapped back together the frayed ends of fate's threads that had broken when Madigan severed them the century before. Since then, the loom worked fervently.

"What does this mean?" Past asked.

Future lifted a hand the color of moonlight, her fingers tipping toward the threads. An uneven breath escaped from her pale lips. "Things have changed. Something in the human world as well, but I cannot see it."

Present joined them on the other side, her lips stained a dark purple from the intensity in which she'd chewed on them, trying to piece together this quickly altering future they raced toward and how what happened now would impact not just the witches, but the humans.

"Mother warned us," Present said finally to her Sisters, speaking of the Goddess, their creator. The creator of witchkind. "She told us this day would come."

"No." Past straightened, pulling her deep red eyes from the loom to look at her Sisters. "Not this day in the way you think of."

Future could only nod, her attention focused sharply on the threads as they danced around the longer timeline threads, creating a design of random splashes and color. The design was nothing in the eyes of anyone but hers. She saw everything in an intricate, infinite pattern.

What was most alarming to Future, was watching Madigan's future shift and change. She finally broke the silence that had settled over them. "Sister is right."

"Which?" Present and Past asked in unison.

"Róisín will still accomplish her task, but something has changed, something is different." Her fingers struck a finished line.

"In the human world," Past finished.

Future nodded again. "And ours. Something I cannot see. Something that has been hidden from us all. Something is coming," she said in an ominous tone.

"There has to be a way we can find out," Present said. "Find out if it harms us."

Future gasped, her hands going to her throat. Her fingers grasping and clawing frantically as though she fought to pull something away. The black of her pupils grew, swallowing her violet irises. Her face reddened, and she struggled for breath.

Present and Past leapt to their feet, eyes searching for what had crept beyond the forbidden barrier, into their home.

"Call upon the Mother," Future gasped out through clenched teeth.

Their voices ruing strong and clear, Present and Past chanted the verses to call for the Goddess.

Ad astra, ad oculos, bono malum superate, Mata dea...

The fire guttered out in the fireplace, plunging them into darkness. The only sounds that filled the house were the quiet swishes of fate's threads and Future's gasping breaths.

"My daughters." The Goddess pulled back her cloak hood to survey them from where she stood in the doorway.

Future tried to speak, but only a choke sounded.

The Goddess' eyes darkened, and she lifted a hand, closing her fingers into a fist. "Vade!"

Future slipped from her seat at the loom, crumpling on the floor. Her hands still at her neck, but her chest heaved with the lungful of air she drank down.

Present and Past rushed to her side, soothing and stroking her white hair.

The Goddess moved to them and knelt next to Future. She took her daughter's face in her hands, examining.

"It is not just he that we face," the Goddess said.

Present's head snapped up.

"Our Róisín has a much larger battle ahead of her, for the sake of all beings, not just witchkind." She took Future in her arms, helping her rise. With the back of her hand, she brushed a stroke over Future's cheek, restoring her and healing the bruises at her throat.

"There was a shift in the human world through the loom, that's when—" Future touched a finger to her neck, her body shuddering at the memory.

"I only felt it barely a moment before." The Goddess nodded. "It is powerful."

"Why can't we see it? Why can't we see what will happen with the witches?" Past asked desperately.

The Goddess' eyes shifted from emerald to amethyst, then settled as garnet while her magic reached through the realms.

"Because it is cloaked. From even myself," she replied coldly.

"This… this changes everything." Present wrapped her arms around herself, hands stroking over her bare arms. "How? What we've seen for centuries, it has never changed."

The Goddess turned to the loom, her mouth set in a grim line.

"It appears we severely underestimated just what Aoife has accomplished beyond the veil."

CHAPTER 70

R ÓISÍN sat on a loveseat in the atrium. Her head tipped back, her eyes focused on the glass roof, taking in the stars that dotted the sky overhead. She heard the chatter from the others in the main house but struggled to find her strength to rise and go to them.

She had told Shasta she was ready to tell everyone what had happened. Yet, that was a lie. However, she had no choice in the matter. Madigan was still out there, and he wouldn't wait for her to be ready. That day, she'd learned a valuable piece of information, and lived to tell the others.

Which was why she needed to dig deep within, gather her strength, and go to them.

"I can tell Shasta you're not ready." Caid appeared and lowered himself in front of her. He closed his big, calloused hands over hers, giving them a light squeeze.

"No." Róisín shook her head, an attempt to clear the fog that still settled there. "They need to know."

"I could tell them," he said.

She freed a hand and lifted it to cup his cheek, giving him a small smile. "I love you."

His eyes danced in a swirl of browns, golds, and greens as his magic rose inside of him. Now that it had awoken, she noticed when his emotions were strongest. Despite a lack of outward reflection, they were revealed within his eyes.

"You'll always see it all." Caid squeezed her hand. "I'll never have secrets from you."

She stroked her thumb over his cheek, the hair from the beard that'd grown since they arrived tickled the pad. "You're the first person I've never been able to hide from. You've always been able to see right through me."

"That's how I know you're not ready to go out there. That once you tell them what happened, it makes it real." He pulled her from the loveseat into his lap. "They will not look at you differently, Róisín. Madigan and Aoife having children will change nothing about how they love and care about you. Aoife's choices and secrets are not yours. I know you're carrying them around like they're your burdens. They're not."

"What if..." Her throat worked, swallowing down her fear. "What if I'm like her?"

"You're not," he replied firmly.

"You can't know what choices I'll make in the future."

"No," he agreed. "I know you, I know this." He swept a thumb over her forehead. "And this." He moved his hand down to place his warm palm over her heart. "There isn't a choice you would make under purely selfish intentions."

The atrium door creaked opened, and Shasta appeared, concern etched on her face. "Do you want me to postpone?"

"Madigan certainly won't postpone." Róisín's tone was flat. "Regardless of how I feel right now, it's already been too long."

CHAPTER 71

Echoes of Róisín's power thrummed through Madigan's veins. He stretched out his long frame in the copper tub, giving room to stroke himself. The feeling of her power had brought him to a state of euphoria like he'd never experienced before. Just as the feel of her beneath his hands, of her breath on his skin, the taste on his lips and tongue had sparked something far more primal in him than he'd ever felt.

With the sensation that moved through him when he siphoned life, it had been electric, much like the way it did when he came to release. It was heady and full. He craved that feeling as much as he craved the power that came with it. With Róisín however, it had been something else. Far more. Even more than when he'd felt that snap and tug that came with accepting fate's bond with another. It was dangerous.

Every time he'd made himself come in the weeks that had passed, he reached down after, into his depths to pull his anger back up into its rightful place. It helped him bring his focus back. He couldn't lose sight of his plan, not after all the work he'd done to make sure he wouldn't fail. He would have his justice, and he would reign over them all.

He'd just have to adjust his plans to include her. Because not having her was not an option. Not now. Not after what it was to have her beneath his touch. What she tasted like. What her power tasted like.

Madigan groaned at the memory, desire pulsing through him, and he gripped his cock tighter with each stroke, his climax building. His hips jerked once, twice, then his body shuddered as release moved through him and he came. He let go of his cock and shifted in the tub again, his arms resting at its sides.

He had wanted to snatch her away when she had plummeted from the sky that day, but they were all there, and the feeling of her true power had overwhelmed him. Aoife had held high power in her magic, but even that had paled compared to this.

When Lucius and Matthew had come for him, he knew in his state he needed to leave. They could have easily overpowered him, an admission that infuriated him. He needed to gather himself, quiet the noise inside that had turned back on with Róisín reestablishing his connection to the witchkind. The noise she alone rose inside of him.

He couldn't remain in Earth's realm, or go to Legianne, they would have looked for him there.

A bitter taste rose in his mouth at the thought of his home. How he had been banished from Aunellion. How the Goddess had sealed it from everyone. He had tried before; the magic that held the shield in place was too powerful for even him.

Filled with a rage darker than that which he had carried for most of his life, he pushed out of the water. He stalked to the main room of the suite, leaving a trail of water in his wake, and shoved open the wardrobe doors.

He would need to sever the connection again with the witches. It was not as it had been before. Before, it had been clear. He could know immediately where any witch he desired to reach was. Could feel their power as though it were a solid mass in his hands.

Now, it was like trying to catch the fog that persisted in the Aunellion fields behind his family seat. He could reach for it all he wanted, but never grasp enough of it to gain purchase.

Not with her, though. Róisín's power tethered to him in a way that frustrated him. He could reach out, grab hold of it, yet he couldn't budge it. He couldn't give that tug to set off the beacon that would help him locate her.

A growl emanated from him, as just a glimmer of the thought of her had him hard again.

"This is going to create a problem," he snarled, looking down to where his cock jutted out.

Quickly, he dressed in a black business suit. He adjusted his cufflinks, studying himself in a large mirror that stood next to the wardrobe.

His tailor settled into place bringing deep, time weathered lines around his mouth and etching out from the corners of his eyes. The appearance of a man who laughed and smiled a lot amused him, given he couldn't recall ever having done either in his long centuries. Gray streaked from his temples. Aged freckles dotted his hands.

His eyes dropped to where he pressed against the seam of his pants, and he sighed. Thinking of Aoife's betrayal, her secrets, his cock became flaccid as quickly as it had hardened.

"Only a problem until I have her," he assured his reflection before turning away.

Then he made his way from the suite to the streets of Ely.

Chapter 72

MATTHEW would have his molars ground down to his gum line if he couldn't ease the throbbing in his head. It had started as a dull ache at the base of his skull the moment Róisín had snapped the tethers in place, but adrenaline, then the search for Madigan, had worked like a natural painkiller of sorts.

In the quiet of the library in Alleyette with Lily, he couldn't push it away.

Being connected to other witches was far from new to Matthew. By council laws, he needed to be tied to his Coven members. Through Lucius, once he accepted Matthew into the Ely Coven, he was connected with the council. Having been born with that instantaneous connection, it had been just another piece of his life, learning early on how to manage it.

Not only were these tethers to Shasta, Nanette, and Róisín new, but these were connections he shared with Coven leaders. Which meant feeling every Molennius and Roidon witch, every moment of every day.

The sigh from across the table drew him from his misery. He studied Lily, a finger twisting a strand of her hair around it. She chewed on a corner of her mouth, amber and gold eyes scanning sentence after sentence in the book before her.

He hadn't acted on his feelings since the last time they'd found themselves in this room, when he had felt the tug of their bond. Not that he didn't want to. Goddess knew how badly he wanted to tangle his own hands in her strands, to nibble on those soft, lush lips. How much he wanted to be around her, just to soak in her presence. Not only had she made it clear she wasn't ready, but Madigan had also shown his first card on the table, changing everything.

Several cards.

They had to proceed carefully. Róisín was ready to go all in again, but he'd seen the dark, murderous look on Caid's face as she told everyone what she'd learned, what had happened. He also remembered the way his own heart dropped into his stomach when she fell from the sky. The way Lucius had been eerily silent for most of the days they'd spent searching for Madigan, clearly as affected by the moment as Matthew.

Matthew shook the memory from his whole body. He needed a distraction. "How does it feel, being the heir of Roidon?"

Lily dropped her hand to her lap, releasing her hair. The coil she had created with her twisting bounced. She looked up at him, blinking a few times. Clearing her throat, she straightened. "Well, how does it feel to be the heir of Ely?"

He only stared at her for a moment, unmoving, then finally shook his head. "I asked you first."

"It's, um…" She pressed her lips together, eyes darting around the room as she visibly warred with her answer. The truth lingered just under the surface, knowing the chance the room could've been spelled with prying ears, she wanted to choose her words carefully.

"Daunting," he finished for her.

"So much," she agreed, letting out a deep breath. "My mother was supposed to have this role. It was never meant to be mine so soon."

He nodded. Lucius had named Matthew as heir a century earlier. He had at least known it was coming, as Lucius had no children of his own. He could've named his brother or one of his nephews heir if it had not been for Demitri's challenge against their father when Lucius had been named.

"Grandmother has had me in training for two decades now, so I'm far more understanding of what will be expected of me. How to execute my duties," she continued. "It doesn't make it any less intimidating to be responsible for every being in our realm."

"Do you." He paused, unsure how to phrase his question. How to ask why.

"Wonder why we were chosen?"

Relief lightened the weight upon his shoulders.

She closed her book and folded her hands atop the cover. "They have seen something. It doesn't feel like they chose us on a whim. We can only trust them to reveal those reasons at some point."

He was at a loss for words, unable to look away from her.

"Matthew—"

"You need to live, Lily," he said. "You need to make it through this, okay?"

"You too," she whispered.

"Can I?" He motioned to the chair next to her. When she nodded, he rose quickly. "I'd like to kiss you."

Her mouth curved into a smile, her eyes lighting. "I'd very much like that. I promise I won't run away this time."

"Thank the Goddess," he breathed out then took her mouth with his. She tasted of honey and smelled like the grass after a summer rain. There wasn't any way he would ever get enough of it.

"We shouldn't take too long," she said against his mouth. "We don't want to, you know."

"Draw attention?" He arched a brow.

"That," she agreed. "But, I meant being overly friendly."

Matthew froze, her bottom lip still between his teeth. In an instant, he opened his mouth, releasing her. "Shit. You have a point."

"Not one that I can admit to enjoying having." She frowned. With an index finger, she traced the line of his bottom lip, her eyes trailing the movement.

"That's not helping anything," he warned.

"I'll find the rest of the books we need." Her bottom lip quivered as she drew in a breath. "I'll check them out so we can... go."

His body became unbearably hot, his pulse racing as she stroked her finger over his lip again. "It's probably wise to grab those books right now, Lily."

"Mmhmm," she practically moaned.

"Lily," he said more sternly.

"I'm going." She stroked again, biting her lip this time.

He caught her wrist in his hand before she could make another pass with her finger. "Books, Lily. I'll clean up what we have out here, then I'll meet you down at Ember Cafe in twenty."

Her eyebrow drew together, the cutest divot in her forehead.

"I think it's best we step out of here solo," he explained.

"Okay. Ember in twenty." She nodded, rising.

He stood, facing the table, moving his leg just enough to adjust himself within his jeans. He had just started to stack their books when he heard her cursing from within the book stacks.

"They're gone," she said when he approached.

"What are gone?" He glanced around at the rows of books surrounding them.

"The books we need." She waved a hand at the empty space before her.

"We've read a lot of dead-ends today, are you sure these wouldn't have just been more?"

She put her hands on her hips, rolling her eyes then pinching the bridge of her nose in frustration. "Before you interrupted me, I was making headway on something. When I finished that book, I needed these books." She motioned aggressively at the empty space again.

"And all of them are gone." He dropped his chin to his chest in defeat.

CHAPTER 73

C AID dropped his head under the spray of the shower head, the heat pelting his skin. It was moments like this that he wished he could go back. Not all the way to the start of it; to before his power enveloped him. Feeling helpless without it made sense to him. Now, with magic, it woke a new sensation inside of him, one he didn't understand.

A darkness had gnawed at him from the inside. A black rage, an anger like he'd never felt before. It drove him to Shasta and Nanette, day after day, learning all that he could. He was greedy for it.

Could he face Madigan himself?

He wasn't foolish enough to believe so, before or now. But he couldn't lose Róisín again. He wouldn't.

There had been a burning sensation growing within him for days now. He'd equated it to heartburn when he tried to describe it to Róisín and Shasta the day after everyone had met for Róisín's briefing. From the look the pair shared, he could sense it wasn't good.

"Madigan has probed the connections he has with all of us," Shasta had explained. "Because he's an outlier, no longer a council recognized witch, our power flares up and rebels against him when he reaches out. It feels like a fire in our veins."

"Is it like our connection?" He turned to Róisín. He had been learning the workings of his connection with her. The way he could sit across the room from her and a gentle tug of that line that bound them brought a soft smile to her face when she looked up at him. There was a way for them to use that line to know where the other was, but Róisín had yet to teach him how to do so.

"No. He's more with me than the rest of us." She looked to Shasta.

Shasta nodded. "Because of what he and Aoife had, shared creation of life, it creates a sort of loosely tied bond with Ro through half-relations. While we all feel that faint, just out of reach one with him, theirs is much closer to what Coven members share with one another."

"Which means he can find you." Caid clenched his hands into fists.

"No," Shasta said. "If she was a member of his Coven, or he was a Coven leader and the tie was our born one, then yes. That full tether is impossible to restore once severed."

"Then she's safe?"

"She is right here." Róisín crossed her arms over her chest. "I'm as safe as safe can be, given the situation."

He sighed, closing his eyes to gather himself. "What I meant was, he can't yank the line, find you, then show up. He has to look the old-fashioned way. How we're doing with him."

"Depends on what you mean by old-fashioned." She smirked.

"You know what I mean," he shot back in annoyance. This was not a moment he was going to argue with her about how opening doors for her whenever they went somewhere was not old-fashioned. It was polite.

"Kids." Shasta sighed. "Don't let him do this to you, to us. Okay?"

"Yes, Auntie Shass," Róisín crooned.

"Dammit." She threw up her hands, then let them fall, slapping against her thighs.

"You did it to yourself." Róisín laughed.

"While I enjoy seeing you back in fighting form"—Shasta gave her a motherly look—"we all need rest. It's been a long day, with a lot happening. Hopefully tomorrow Matthew and Lily will have something to report from their findings in Alleyette."

Róisín's jaw dropped, a mischievous glint flashing in her eyes. "Are you sending us to bed?"

Shasta looked from her to Caid and back. "Just... behave, all right? Don't break anything." She crossed the living room toward her bedroom door. "And for the love of the Goddess, sound spell the room, please!"

The hands on his chest brought him back to the present moment. Lifting his head through the shower's steam, he looked into the dancing colors of autumn on a stormy day. He had known she wouldn't sleep. That her curling on the bed, closing her eyes, was an act. The growing bruises under her eyes from her exhaustion revealed the truth.

"I... I couldn't... he." She looked down.

Wordlessly, he brought his arms around her, holding her close.

"Every time—" A shudder rocked her body hard. "I can't sleep. He's there. I've tried to block it, close it away, but it creeps in more and more."

He pressed a kiss to the top of her head, then took a steady breath. He closed his eyes, trying to steel himself from his own rising emotions. "Can you tell me?"

Her body tensed against his. "I..." Her shoulders slumped. "No. Not yet."

Stepping back, he took her face in his hands. "What do you need from me? What can I do?"

"Can I..." She swallowed and her throat bobbed. He covered her hands with his. "Can I show you?"

Not trusting his voice, he nodded. She had yet to open up to him about what had happened. He only knew it haunted her, clung to her. Instead, she battled it alone, only coming to him when she hoped that their coming together would erase whatever it was chasing her. Every time, he gave himself to her, hoping that it would pull her free.

He staggered back a step as he was temporarily blinded by sunlight, the shower spray soaking over his head. Then he stood frozen. That anger, that rage he'd felt inside, growing, clawing at him as he saw and felt everything Róisín had that day.

CHAPTER 74

"I'M going to kill him."

The darkness and venom in Caid's voice was so guttural, so unexpected, Róisín pulled back, severing their shared vision.

"I'm going to find him. I'm going to make him regret the day he was ever brought into whatever realm it was he was born to."

"Caid." She rested her shaking hands against his chest. His heart thundered under them; his chest heaved. "Caid, you need to breathe. Look at me, please."

When he looked down at her, the black of his pupils had consumed the hazel, and crept into the whites of his eyes. It was a sign that his magic controlled him.

She swallowed hard. Gathering her own, she wrapped it around them. "Don't give into it. Please."

A deep growl rumbled from his chest in response.

"Caid," she whispered. "It will feed off your anger if you don't push it down. Look at me."

His jaw fluttered as he clenched it.

She moved her hands to either side of his head, pulling him down closer to her. Almost nose to nose with him now, she said, "Don't let it win. Don't let *him* win. Breathe. Look. At. Me."

The pools of black swirled, giving way to the golds, greens, and yellows. Releasing a long breath, he removed her hands, then turned away from her. She brought her magic back in, tucking it away. Then she tried to calm her heart and wait.

"He, Jesus Christ, Róisín." The muscles in his back tensed. "And I—"

"No." She reached out to touch him, hesitating a moment before pulling her hand back. "I came to you. I asked. I asked, knowing that you would give me or do anything that I needed or wanted. I thought... I hoped it would be enough."

He turned to her now, lips pressed into such a tight line they were colorless. His nostrils flared wide from his heavy breaths. "If I had known, I would have found a different way. I wouldn't have done *that*. Because after what he did, it makes me no different from him."

She took a step toward him, opened her mouth to speak but closed it, there was nothing she could say to make him feel differently.

"I felt your heart stop," he said hoarsely. "I—" The breath he took sent tremors through his body. "I felt you die, Róisín. Being on the other side of it, seeing you not moving, so pale. The entire world had ripped itself apart and set itself on fire around me at that moment. But to feel you die? Feel that last breath leave your body as I had you in my arms? That last beat?"

He closed his eyes, the tears that had built, splashing over, rolling down his cheeks.

A pain that she hadn't known before bloomed in her chest. Reaching out, she took one of his hands. "May I?"

Caid's eyes searched her face. He took one of her hands, bringing it to his chest, he swallowed hard, his chin trembled slightly. Drawing in a deep breath, she lifted her free hand and placed it at his cheek.

It felt as though her legs were immediately swept from underneath her, and she began to collapse, entering his memory in the moment her magic's power had surged outside of her. As she struggled to her feet in the memory, the steel of Caid's arms banded around her, supporting her in the present.

She felt when his magic had awoken when they both fell into the ravine. Hers had risen to greet it, bringing her fully out of the thrall

Madigan had placed her under. Before she could question how she had missed that, she was sprinting along the path, shouting.

Then it struck her. She had thought her heart, her soul had hurt only moments before, but as she curled into herself, a scream ripping through her body, she knew that it had been nothing compared to what he had felt when he took her limp body in his arms. Their freshly tied bond severing, shredding Caid apart inside. The burn, the tearing. Her chest was wide open, her heart, lungs, everything completely raw and exposed.

When her eyes opened and that first rattling breath struggled free, Róisín released the memory. She was on the shower floor, still in Caid's arms, sobs racking her body.

"Now, do you see why I want to kill him?" His voice vibrated against her ear resting on his chest.

"I can't let you go after him, he'll kill you." She turned in his arms, burying her face against his neck.

"Then we'll go together."

She pulled away quickly, a coldness blooming in her stomach, her eyes wide.

"What?" he asked. "I'm just supposed to let you go alone? I know the others are doing all they can, hoping to come up with a way to beat him without you dying. If they can't? I'm not doing it again, Róisín. I'm not losing you again. It's together, or I find some way to lock you in a room somewhere, then go solo."

"Together?" The word, the risk that just one word carried, weighed heavy. Their magic reached out to one another through their bond. "Okay, together."

She moved to step from the shower, but his hand grabbing hold of hers, stopping her.

"What does it mean if he's not your uncle?" His voice was so low, she had to strain to hear his words over the sound of the water coming from the shower head.

"I don't know." Of course, he'd felt her reaction to that discovery when she had slipped past Madigan's thrall. The shock had rattled her right down to her feet. "Don't tell the others. We don't have time for my family's shit anymore. He's made his move, and he won't wait so long the next time."

"Róisín—"

She shook her head, slipping her hand free. She turned her back to him, slipping from the shower, back into the bedroom before he could reach for her again.

Chapter 75

Caid's body and mind were exhausted. He felt as though he could build one hundred homes from the dirt up to the completion, on his own, and never feel the tiredness that pulled him down that morning. That he had done no sort of physical labor in the little over a month since they'd come to Molennius, the exhaustion both humbled and frustrated him.

He carefully shifted his aching body on the stool at Shasta's kitchen island, regretting scoffing at her that first day she had worked with him and his power. In the days that had passed since Róisín and he shared their moments from the ravine with one another, they'd worked on bringing their powers together, testing their capabilities when their bond had opened fully. Then he was shipped off to Roidon to work with Nanette and Lily.

Nights, he spent laying awake worrying about Lina. Róisín had shown him how to use his phone to call from the realms, but lying to her about where they were and being so far away had begun to rub his heart raw. He knew it had to be done, the less she knew the better, the safer. It still hurt just the same.

Matthew and Lily had returned from Alleyette with news of books that had been stolen from the Alleyette Library. Books they had needed; the information they contained had been what they searched for.

The pit that sat at the bottom of Caid's stomach grew larger with each passing day. He and Róisín hadn't discussed what had happened in the shower that night, and that only added to the weight he carried.

"What's on the agenda today?" he asked no one in particular.

Róisín looked up from her scone, giving him a weary look.

"Weapons training," Matthew answered.

"Weapons training?" Caid pulled his attention from Róisín to look at Matthew, seeing the broad grin stretched across his face. "Like knives and shit?"

"Knives, maces, swords, throwing stars. Whatever your heart's content." He downed his coffee and offered Caid a half-shrug. "Róisín has one mean-looking katana."

Caid jerked his attention back to Róisín, eyes wide.

"You ever use any?" Matthew asked, oblivious to the tension radiating from Róisín at her end of the island. Lucius and Shasta remained silent, glancing between the trio.

"I've, uh..." Caid blinked, then swallowed. "A twelve gauge. I've shot a twelve gauge hunting with friends and their dads when we were growing up."

"You'll be training with Brent," Lucius said. "These two." He nodded his head toward Róisín and Matthew. "Will spar first. Then Brent, our weapons master and trainer in Ely, will get you situated with a weapon that best fits you. Then you will start learning how to use it."

Róisín slowly set down her cup and turned to Lucius. "Wait... You're saying..."

"I am." The expression he wore was grim. Lines etched his face around his eyes and mouth. "When you two spar, choose your regular weapons as they'll be staying with you from here on out."

"When was this decided?" She looked at Shasta.

"Last night," Shasta replied. "We can all feel him through your connection. It's not like before, when we just waited on edge. Yesterday, he started trying to sever all our connections to you. It's an effort to stop us from knowing he's coming. He's getting ready to move again, to come for you."

Róisín's hand reached for his under the island top, and he gripped it.

"Which means we need to be ready," Lucius said.

"And we shouldn't dally around." Matthew popped the last of his muffin into his mouth, rising from his stool.

"After you three are done with training, Róisín, Caid, and I will go to Legianne," Shasta said.

"What?" Róisín and Matthew replied in unison. Matthew coughed, then thumped a fist against his chest.

"Why?" Róisín added.

"There are things there we will need for what comes next. Helen and Lily could finally track them down earlier this morning. Brenna had far more tricks up her sleeve to ready us for this than we knew."

Róisín blew out a breath, her hand trembling in Caid's. Outwardly, she sat with her shoulders up, back straight, but the intense heat that surged through their tether from her in shockwaves told him she was crumbling inside. He squeezed her hand and stroked his thumb over her skin. His legs urged him up, to take her in his arms and run. Go back to Maine, wrap her in his arms and do all that he could to protect her from the hurt that her home realm held.

Róisín cleared her throat and gave Shasta a slight nod. "Okay, we go to Legianne."

From the way Matthew had talked about training, Caid imagined training hall to be a replica of a movie set. Something straight out of the Hugh Jackman movie, Van Helsing, or some other medieval setting, would maybe be too far-fetched. However, as he surveyed the massive stone room with its high vaulted ceilings and walls dotted with sconces, he wanted to laugh at himself.

"Of course, it'd be just like a damned movie," he muttered.

Brent stood next to him with his hands clasped behind his back. His hair, the color of a starless, moonless night, was tied into a neat bun. His gray shirt buttoned almost to his chin. He stood just slightly taller than Caid, yet it wasn't the size of him that had intimidated Caid as he shook his hand upon introductions. Brent's sharp eyes, the color of spring grass, held such a ferociousness, despite the kind smile and melodic voice. Caid was certain this man could kill without even a hair moving out of place.

Róisín and Matthew moved toward the weapons collection. Matthew hefted a battle axe, spinning it like a baton, a wide grin on his face. Róisín shook her head, her hands brushing over a table full of swords, hammers, axes, before stopping at the daggers, her eyes lighting with mischief when she looked to Matthew.

"You cheat when you use those," Matthew said. "No. Use your weapons."

"Only if you use yours, oh honorable warrior." Her tone was light, joking, as she pointed a jeweled dagger at Matthew's battle axe.

Would any of this ever feel normal to him?

How would turning a century old feel? Or five hundred?

What would happen if Lina didn't have magic like he had, and her mortal life ended? He had always figured he'd be the first to pass on, that he wouldn't have to discover what life would be like without the only family he had. Without his sister, his best friend.

His mind tried to wrap around his new reality and the walls closed in on him. His chest grew tight, and he could never get enough air into his lungs. As it always did, the pressure built, the alarms inside would ring, demanding he slow down, that he breathe.

Panic. He tried not to, but it slipped into him, trying to control him.

"You went to Solene to drink, Matthew." The annoyance in Róisín's voice was clear as it rose enough so that they could hear from their side of the room. "*I* took care of the Krogor." She stuck her tongue out at Matthew, making him laugh in return. Pulling a hairband from her wrist, she readied it like a slingshot in her hands.

"It was my birthday. I had vacation time slotted," Matthew returned casually, holding his hands up in surrender.

"Not even ten minutes," Brent said, fondness in his tone. "They began training with me when they were eight. Their joint training started when she was ten and he was fifteen. It was only two minutes before the bickering began back then. Seems time may wear them down after all."

"We don't get vacation time, you nitwit." Róisín scowled at Matthew. Once she pulled her hair into a tight ponytail, she shoved two small blades into holsters she had strapped to her thighs.

"What is your profession in Earth's realm?" Brent asked.

"I'm a..." Róisín's movements distracted him. The ease in which she tucked two more blades into sheaths at her lower back, her conversation with Matthew uninterrupted as though this were an everyday occurrence to the both of them. "I build things." He cleared his throat, dragging his attention away from Róisín and the heat that curiously stirred inside of him, raising a particular body part inside of his Carhartt's. It was far from the ideal place to discover something new to turn him on. "Houses. I build houses."

Brent motioned towards a table where an array of weapons were scattered atop, with several more on the wall above. "Anything you may be familiar with?"

"Depends on what you mean by familiar. Have I seen these in movies, or read about them in books? Yes. Have I ever actually touched any? Nope."

"What are the tools of your trade?"

"Hammer, pneumatic tools, battery powered tools. My brain."

Brent inclined his head. "We can work with that."

"Best six out of seven?" Matthew called over to Róisín who now stood across the room from him readying herself. He rolled his shoulders while he bounced on the balls of his feet.

A wicked grin tipped up the corners of her mouth. "You only say that because you can never beat me."

"Ever think that maybe I'm letting you win?"

"Oh, Goddess." Brent's heavy, resigned sigh sounded almost like a parent's at the end of a road-trip vacation. "This will be ugly."

"That." Róisín pulled the blades from her thighs. They glinted in the light as she effortlessly spun them in her hands. "Was probably the dumbest thing you could have ever said."

Then she charged him. As she neared, she dipped low to dodge an incoming blow, her laughter echoing around the room as she spun around, launching to her feet so that she and Matthew had traded places. She tapped a blade on his chest before he could completely turn to her.

"One," she declared.

"Dammit," Matthew growled.

Caid stood silently as they moved into a blur of movement again, taunting one another and bickering back and forth as they did.

"You said that they've been training with you since they were young." Caid tracked their movements, trying to memorize the steps. "Do you... Is this really something that you all need to do? Train like this?"

"Not everything can be handled with our powers," Brent explained. "Sometimes a witch's power will wake, just as yours did, away from the help of a Coven. Sometimes it is discovered by the council early enough. Other times," his voice dropped, taking an ominous tone. "In an untrained witch, that power is like a disease. The power feeds, becoming hungrier. It is especially dangerous for all, human and witch alike, when there is no Coven."

It settled into the pit of his stomach like a brick. It was what could have happened to him.

"As the power grows, things come into being. Even the most powerful of us." Brent tipped his head slightly toward where Róisín was a whirlwind of autumn and glinting silver as she spun, ducked, dodged, and parried with Matthew. Their own conversation was muted by the sounds of their blades clanging together. "Can't always stop it."

"So, you train with weapons and hand to hand," Caid said.

"Yes, we train." Brent nodded.

"If Madigan takes..." Caid didn't want to finish his thought aloud, to speak it into existence on the chance it came to fruition. "If he takes her power, will she still be able to fight like this? Save herself this way?"

"Sometimes a witch has been so drained of power they have needed to rely on their training. However, none that any of us have gone against has held the strength that Madigan has. Perhaps if it were before. Now that he's had nearly a century of building his power? I cannot say. I can only hope."

"Oh, come on," Matthew shouted, drawing their attention back to the center of the room.

Róisín knelt over him, her short blade lightly tapping at his throat. "Five. You can call it now, you know."

"Fuck that." He rolled to his side, then leapt to his feet. "Again." He took the ready position, his weapons gripped tightly in his hands, then nodded to her.

"You're such a glutton for punishment," she replied giddily and lunged at him.

Caid couldn't help but note the levelness of her voice. That she wasn't yet winded despite how intensely she and Matthew had fought for the last several minutes. Not just fighting, they'd dueled and talked to one another while doing so. Yet, neither she nor Matthew appeared phased by the physical demand.

Once again, Caid found himself extremely out of his element and wondering if he could grasp any level of skill with his own power, let alone physical fighting, in time to be of any use to them, and protection for Róisín.

Chapter 76

Róisín had kept a cautious eye on Caid for the rest of the day. The silence that had settled between them after leaving their training had become deafening. She tried to keep her focus on their task at hand, Legianne.

Shasta carried an adamant air with her, and with Madigan ready to come for her again, as shown by his efforts to sever her ties with the others, she needed to trust them.

Given what she had learned about Aoife and her mother in the past year, Róisín's ability to trust those closest to her proved harder than it had been to keep herself together when she was literally face to face with Madigan.

"You two go to the cottage." Shasta motioned toward where a small two-bedroom cottage nestled in a copse of the thick trunked, red leafed Noce trees native to the Legianne capital, Wurbray.

Róisín hadn't set foot near Wurbray in decades. The cottage had been a home for her mother, and seeing its peak over the trees from her room at Aoife's had been too difficult.

She had thought that her mother had kept her from Aoife for selfish reasons, buying every morsel of a lie that Aoife had handed to her. So as

333

she opened the door, facing the gates that would lead to the small home, the crack that had grown in her chest with each new truth she learned, nearly cleaved her wide open.

"What am I to retrieve?" Róisín linked her hands together in front of her, trying to hide the shake of them.

"Oh, just a second..." Shasta reached into her pocket and pulled out a sheet of paper. When Róisín made no move to take it, she passed it on to Caid.

There were whispered words exchanged between them, too low for Róisín to hear over the thumping of her heart drowning out all sounds around her. Caid's hand settled at her lower back. His touch, the first since they had left her room that morning, startled her back to the moment.

"Are you okay?" he asked, his eyes steady on hers.

She nodded. "It's just been a bit since I've been here."

"Do you want to stay with Shasta? I can go and grab these things?"

She looked over her shoulder to where Shasta had stood. She caught the glimpse of Shasta's violet cloak swishing through the doors of Aoife's study at the far end of the hall.

When the doors slid closed, it was as though clouds had parted, revealing the sun to her. Closing her eyes, she drew in a long, steadying breath, the understanding that Shasta had brought her there for something else settling over her. What it was, she did not know. The list in Caid's hand was a falsity.

She straightened, her senses suddenly wide open. Turning her attention back to Caid, she mustered up a smile. "I'm good. I just need to get my bearings again."

He took her hand in his, squeezing once. "How about a distraction?"

"Oh?" She glanced from the heavy wooden doors of the study, back to him.

He chuckled, grinning down at her. "As much as I am incredibly hot over watching the way you handled those blades earlier, that's not what I meant. That part will come later when we're back in your room."

"I didn't scare you away?"

"Say what?" His brows shot up, eyes grew wide. "Róisín, if I was going to be scared, it would have been the moment your rabbit said good morning to me. Hey." He tugged her closer. "Even without the bond, I was all in, no matter what."

"You've just been so quiet since we left Ely."

"I..." He snapped his mouth closed, shaking his head.

"What?" she pressed.

"I've partly been so quiet because, well—" He caught his bottom lip between his teeth. "You moved like you were made of fluid, Róisín. Like you didn't have a spine. The way you twisted?"

His cheeks grew a dark shade of red.

"I never realized just how active that part of my imagination was until..." He rubbed a hand over the back of his neck, waving his other in the air in front of him. "Until, um, this morning."

Slowly, it settled in what was on his mind. Her eyes widened, then she grinned up at him.

"You follow me now?"

"Oh, I do." She stepped closer, pressing herself to him. She dropped her voice low, so the words came out throaty. "I definitely follow."

His throat bobbed with his hard swallow, and he clenched his teeth, his eyes fluttering. "This really isn't helping. We've got to go get the things on Shasta's list."

"Well." She ran her hands over his chest. "It's a good thing that I am here for a different reason than whatever is on that nonsense list."

"How do you know?"

"Call it intuition. There's something else," she said, noting the tense lines bracketing his mouth now.

"Remember the night you asked me to let you take care of me?"

"Caid—"

He lifted his hand to silence her. "That doesn't mean I don't still want to take care of you or won't. The problem is, the more into this we get, the less I know how. The more I wonder if I even can."

"This is uncharted waters for all of us. We've had to fight for our lives against humans our entire existence. There's even been things my people have faced at the hands of other witches. This? This is something far more than we could've ever thought we would have to be up against. Not only does he want every drop of our power so that he can rule all, he's also so Goddess damned powerful that this could very well be it for us all."

"Róisín," he whispered hoarsely.

"I don't know what the end holds. I do know I'm the key to this. I can't do it without the others. There's no way that I can do this without you. The only thing keeping me going is knowing that if I can beat this, beat him, you and I have forever. Dammit, that's all I want. After all of this... this shit, that's all I want."

He combed his fingers through her hair, moving it behind her shoulder. Then he cupped her chin, tipping her head back. "That's all I want, too. Yeah, having some kids running around wherever it is we land when this is over will be nice. I hope we get to have our own family, but if we don't, as long as I've got you, the rest doesn't matter."

She blinked back the tears that stung her eyes. "You've got me."

"Anything can happen, though," he replied sadly.

"Then we're just going to do whatever it is we can to make sure we both make it to the other side, because I can't lose you either. Okay?"

He searched her eyes for a moment, finally nodding before he rested his forehead against hers.

She framed his face with her hands, rising to her toes to brush a kiss over his lips. "I guess we should go see about this wild goose chase Shasta is sending me on."

"You really think that's what this is?"

"She's up to something. What, I have no idea, but it's definitely something." She glanced over her shoulder one last time before leading him to the front door. She paused, expression turning thoughtful. "What was it you were going to do to distract me?"

"Ask what the fuck a Krogor was. All I heard from that argument with Matthew earlier was lots of hands, and a rattling tongue." He shivered.

Stepping into the courtyard, she fought back a laugh. "A Krogor is a creation of a child witch. It feeds off their fear when their powers awaken."

"Like the witch version of the boogie man, but with magic. And lots of hands. Is the tongue like a baby rattle?"

Now she did laugh, taking his hand, then leading him toward her mother's cottage.

Chapter 77

Róisín felt the air change around her before she heard the voice speak. A warmth paired with the smell of vetiver and lavender. Brenna.

"You're far taller than I had expected." The sound of something hitting the floor with a thump punctuated her mother's statement.

"Your father wasn't much younger than you are now the last I saw him," she continued, unbothered.

Róisín dumped the armload of things she held onto the table in the kitchen, then rushed into the other room.

Caid stood near one of the living room windows, mouth open, palms up, eyes so wide, she could see the whites around his pupils. The books he'd held lay at his feet. If his eyes hadn't darted between her and her mother, she would have believed that her mother had frozen him.

"She's... she's your..."

"Caid, my mother, Brenna." Róisín stepped to her mother's side. She studied her carefully before continuing. "Mother, this is Caid. Something tells me you already knew that though."

Brenna's eyes sparkled, her face lit with her broad smile. "You two do not know how long it's been that I've waited for this moment."

"Why didn't you tell me that night you came? How are you here now?"

"Ah, but I did tell you. You just didn't hear my words." Brenna turned to her, placing a solid hand on her cheek. "Someday, my little rose, you'll be a parent. Then, everything I've done here, all that I've risked, will make sense."

Brenna gestured for them to sit. Caid was instantly at Róisín's side, bringing her closer as they sat on the small sofa.

"After the Sisters came to me, I knew my fate was sealed. At first, I resigned myself to it. I would meet someone incredible, I would have my family, know what love and joy truly were. It would never be mine for long, but it would be mine. You..." She lifted her eyes to Róisín, her voice solemn. "You're not only meant for more, you deserved more."

"I don't—" Róisín shook her head, her voice thick. "I don't understand. What you said that night..."

"You were not meant to walk away from this." Impatience flickered over Brenna's features.

Every muscle in her body tensed. Caid's hand flexed on her thigh.

"Once I met Stephen, reality settled in. Things were in motion, so much so that they moved quick. I had learned a way to hide away from Aoife and keep my connection with the others there. It was muddy, no one could quite grasp it, but it was still there so that I wouldn't be breaking any council laws."

This was the part that confused Róisín the most. They had lost track of Madigan when he had completely severed his connection with the council. There had been no other Aunellion witches left for him to be tied to when he completed the act. "But, even that way, couldn't they tell where you were? Find you?"

"Can you feel Madigan now?" Brenna looked from her to Caid.

Róisín bit her bottom lip. She had felt Madigan. More than just the echoes of his touch, his invasion of her body. More than the ghost of him in her dreams every night. There was something lingering inside of her, but she had yet to grab hold of it. She only knew from the grimy feel of it when it brushed her senses that it was him. She realized she hadn't answered her mother's question when Caid shifted to face her, his expression dark, almost as though he knew what she held back, still, from him.

Brenna lifted an expectant brow at her.

"Some," Róisín finally admitted. The room grew hot, and she felt lightheaded. "When we forced the connection with the five of us that day, it's been there. A sort of misty, fog-like way."

Brenna inclined her head. "And you can't track him that way, can you?"

Róisín shook her head.

"It was very much like that. Even fainter with my tie with Aoife. I needed to be very careful, especially not to draw attention from the Sisters and the Goddess. Especially them because I technically interfered with fate." Her eyes shuttered closed, and she grew still. The floor-to-ceiling clock in the corner near the fireplace ticked away the passing seconds loudly in the quiet room. Róisín held her body as still as her mother, watching, waiting. Hovering at the precipice, waiting for the fall.

When Brenna's eyes sprung open, the whites had swallowed all color. Caid's body jerked in surprise next to her. "Aoife had burned our Coven down to just she and I," Brenna finally continued. "They knew the choice she would make, and the one I would make. Both left you the sole possessor of a millennium of power. Despite my pleading, despite your power coming from the light, they insisted it would change you. To keep the balance once Madigan was gone, you would need to—" Her voice hitched. Her chin dropped to her chest; her shoulders heaved with her breath as she wrung her hands together in her lap.

"But Madigan is defeated." Róisín moved forward to the edge of the sofa, that fall now facing her, she just needed to take that last step. "That's what the Sisters said. Once Madigan was gone."

Caid's tone was sharp next to her. "You can't be serious."

A sad smile shifted up the corners of Brenna's mouth. "She would, Kincaid. She was set to do it when this started, and she would now. Despite Shasta, despite Matthew, despite even you, she would if it meant you all got to live."

Caid pushed to his feet, stalking from the room. The front door to the cottage slammed in his wake.

"He'll be back," Brenna assured her.

Róisín fought the shiver that threatened as a chill wrapped around her with Caid's departure. She knew what she had told him at the main house earlier, but that was before her mother arrived. It wasn't a promise, but the guilt tried to creep in.

She wanted to go to him, to get him to understand, to see that she didn't want to leave him, that she wanted to be selfish. But there was a cost to her selfishness. Her people would die. *He* would die. Instead, she took a slow, steadying breath and focused on her mother. "How are you here again? I thought we only had that one time."

"Sometimes, you just need to break the rules." She winked at her. "There's nothing the Goddess can do to me now that isn't any worse than an eternity in solitude. Your father is in the afterworld, I'm forever in the underworld. I can see and feel you both in your worlds, but I can never be with either of you. I held on as long as I could, waiting for this moment. Shasta thinks I'm crazy, but then again, she thought I was mad when I told her what I had to do. It killed her, you know, letting you go."

"Then why did she?"

"Because I asked her to. I had to. Otherwise, she could've been punished. Or her Coven. You know Lucius and Nanette wouldn't have let her go alone. Then we'd be looking at a very different future for witches."

"You're risking darkness, forever darkness, worse than the underworld, to tell me we defeat Madigan, and I'll die?"

Brenna's gaze drifted to the window. Róisín followed, turning her head. Caid stood in the middle of the garden, hands in his hair, head tipped up to the sky. They both could hear the curses he shouted.

"I'm here to tell you everything. If I'm going into the darkness, I need to know that everything I did before I died wasn't for naught."

Chapter 78

━━━━━━━━━━

Brenna and Róisín looked around the room they sat in, the silence that enveloped the space after her mother's statement suffocated her. Did she had ever spend any time in the cottage, or if had she left before she was to take it over as her own home?

"No," Brenna answered. "I was still in the big house, which made planning that much harder. Thankfully, it was a time of war. They were lapsing together, never leaving time for the realms to recover. I could be gone more than here. I used that time wisely when I wasn't on the fields or in the tents. There were plenty of witches out there that worked in spell work along with their powers that were not fans of Aoife, making that part shockingly the easiest."

She paused when Caid appeared in the doorway. Both women watched as he surveyed them, then the room. Time stretched for what seemed like an eternity before he finally stepped over the threshold.

Once he sat, Brenna continued. "I needed to skirt the Coven laws. For myself, for any future partner or children I may have. I was determined to live and live my life. I wasn't going to let her win."

"The Sisters had a different idea for us, though." From the corner of her eye, Róisín saw Caid press his lips into a thin line and his nostrils flare slightly. His posture was tight, rigid, like he was trying to hold himself down. Worried he would leave again, she reached between them, finding his hand. He looked down at their joined hands, then to her. Please stay, she tried to wordlessly convey to him. I need you.

He gave her a slight nod before bringing her hand into his lap, closing his other over it.

Brenna folded her hands in her lap, her shoulders moving with what appeared as more of an afterthought of a shrug. "The Sisters came to me not long after I moved away from Legianne and began working on severing spells. Things never felt right with Aoife. After years of planning, I had finally been able to safely leave."

Lifting her free hand, Róisín pressed her fingers against her chest. Something inside had turned over when her mother had begun her story. The feeling of grains of sand, time ticking by, pressed against her chest. The grains nearest their exit trickled away from her heart, burning on their journey to the pit of her stomach, beginning to build weight there. The tug of the weight at opposite ends threatened to pull her apart. "What'd the Sisters tell you? What, exactly?"

"I often wonder if the Sisters waited for me to get everything figured out and in place before they came to me." Brenna grimaced, her eyes squeezing shut, nostrils flaring on her sharp exhale. "Once all my spells snapped into place, Sister Future was there, telling me what she had seen. It was then that everything started. She told me about Stephen. I would have him, love him fiercely, we would make you." She pressed a hand to her mouth, covering the shake of her bottom lip.

The first tear rolled down her cheek, and Róisín wanted to go to her, to hold her. Yet, when she shifted to move, she found she was rooted. She darted a look at Caid in question, but his face was stone, expression blank as he stared out of the window facing the garden. The only movement came from the flutter of his heartbeat pulsing in a vein at his neck and the steady rise and fall of his chest with each breath he took.

"Mother." Róisín tried to move again. Her desperation grew fingers, reaching, trying to grab hold of something, anything, to move her forward.

Brenna dabbed at her cheek with the sleeve of the shirt she wore. It was then that Róisín realized somehow her mother held her at a distance, physically.

"I knew I would lose him," Brenna's voice cracked. "Before I had even laid eyes on him to know he truly existed, I knew. I would have time to be a part of your life, to love you and teach you. I had a choice to make when they came to me again a few years after you were born. Stay and damn us all, or go. Either way, I died. Either way, you would die. It wasn't just that your life would end. The Goddess feared you using your power against the witches, she had your fate sealed to the darkness."

Róisín's body jerked as though she'd been hit, and she sucked in a sharp breath. "What?"

"The moment Sister Future said you would not live after defeating Madigan, once she said where the Goddess would place you after, I knew I had to do something quickly and I couldn't do it alone."

"That's when you told Shasta."

"Oh, Shasta knew all along." She waved a dismissive hand, making a scoffing noise. "I told her the day after I was visited the first time, by all of the Sisters. She was prepared when I went to her when Sister Future came again. She discovered a way to locate bloodlines of bonded before that connection even snapped into place. That's where we started." The clouds had parted from Brenna's face as she watched Caid. The relief that was painted there now spread, shifting the air of the room. "The problem with that method is, we only knew the bloodline. We didn't know if the bonded had already been born, lived, then passed, if they had not yet been born or when they would be. Worse than that, we didn't know if the bonded would be with the light or the dark. It was a huge risk we were taking." She glowed, her cheeks lifting as she beamed at them both. "I can't even say how grateful I am that you had not yet been born," she said to Caid. "That we hadn't missed you."

Róisín turned to him. With her focus on him, she spoke to her mother, "How does this make what the Sisters said change?"

"Oh, it changes everything." Her tone was conspiratorial. "You are no longer a Coven of one. Even if Lina never shows magic, she and her children, her husband, their parents, they're all a part of our Legianne Coven now."

Róisín chewed on her lip, thoughts racing to connect the pieces her mother was giving her. "But how? Wouldn't they remain a part of their ancestors' Coven?"

"When their ancestors made the active choice to no longer practice, to let their magic grow dormant, it was considered a dissolution of their Coven. I could not find where the last active generation was in his line, so I didn't even know which of the old Covens they were a part of. What do humans call it in sports on Earth?" She spread her arms outward. "A free agent."

"I'm still not following, though." Róisín swam in her growing frustration. Why couldn't her mother just tell her. Why was she taking her on this dance around the bushes? "How does having a Coven again change anything? I still hold all my powers. Nothing changes about that."

"It's more the bonded pair part of this." When Róisín only stared back at her, she sighed. "You two are a bonded pair now. That bond has been tied neatly in place within the light. It's a counterbalance to the bonded pair that brought us all to this time and place of darkness."

"Counterbalance to..." Róisín's hands went to her mouth. She gasped, shaking her head as understanding set in. "When I connected to him, I felt the lives they created. It wasn't just that they had had children, they were... Oh my fucking Goddess!"

Caid lifted a hand, coughing lightly. "Odd person out here, can someone explain?"

"Aoife and Madigan were bonded, two very dark powers among our kind. The Goddess, taking myself as a product of Aoife, basically said I wasn't an asset beyond taking out my great-uncle. I was more of a risk to keep alive. Not just that, but..." Róisín looked to her mother for confirmation before continuing.

Brenna gave her a confident nod in return.

"She was so worried about me being in the afterworld, or passing any test in the underworld, then moving on to the afterworld, basically having my abilities to contact any living witches, that she had me damned straight to the darkness, despite me never having done anything to warrant that judgment."

"That changes how?" Outwardly, he seemed aloof, scratching his chin. The tension coiled in his muscles vibrated next to her, humming like a swarm of bees down their tether. "With me?"

"Our power lives either in light." Brenna lifted one hand. "Or, in dark." She lifted her other. "My father's power was in light, that passed on to me, and again on to Róisín. Even with Aoife's power being dark, Róisín's light is far stronger than any darkness Aoife could pass on. Bonded with your power, Kincaid, which is also in light, it balances out. It shifts Aoife's power away from the dark. You." She pointed at him. "Are pure, Kincaid. Both of you are. Being bonded, it has sealed and tied the hands of the Goddess and the Sisters."

"You changed the threads woven." A chill swept over her.

Brenna's back straightened, her chin lifted defiantly. "I did."

"But the risk—"

Brenna waved her hand as though she were sweeping the idea away. "It's all worth it. I'm never going to be released from where I am. I'll never see your father again. I'll never be able to see you again. If they're able to find out I could come to you from there, I'm damned anyway. I had to come. I had to see you, to tell you."

She wrinkled her nose, feeling the press of a new urgency rise at the base of her skull. "Why didn't you come before?"

"What needs to be done to appear before the living when you're in the middle, it's not..." She licked her lips, her face flushing of color. "It's not easy, Róisín. I had tried many times but failed. It took decades to get it right. By then..." She looked to Caid. "Things were well into motion."

The urgency ebbed with her loud exhale. Blinking back the tears that had stung her eyes, she asked, "What do I do now?"

"You live, Róisín." Brenna pressed her palms together, bringing them to her mouth, and she pressed her lips together. Her own eyes glittering with tears. "You live."

Róisín startled when Brenna's frame began to flicker and fade out. "Wait!" she cried out, lurching to her feet.

"I would do it all over again," Brenna told her lovingly. "I love you, my little rose."

"Mom!" Róisín sobbed, reaching for her.

Brenna's ethereal eyes turned to Caid. "You take care of her, Kincaid. Love her with everything you have."

"I will." His voice was rough with emotion when he responded.

"Be good, my love, you were meant for so many more great things than just saving us." She gave Róisín a sad smile. "I love you."

"I love you." Her voice was thick, hot tears streamed down her face as Brenna faded away.

"Róisín." Caid's voice was behind her. His magic reached for her to come closer.

She turned, falling against him, her body trembling. He took her in his arms, bringing them back to the sofa, holding her tightly with one hand, making soothing circles over her back with his other.

As Róisín emptied her tears, guilt, grief, pain, and anger rose within her. Learning the truth would never have been easy, learning it when the future of her kind was at stake, when her future with Caid was at stake, crushed her.

She had said they would defeat Madigan, but at what cost?

CHAPTER 79

WITH staggering steps, Caid stretched an arm out, reaching out and latching onto Shasta's island top to hold himself up. Not only did Róisín's pained screams echo through the house, they echoed through him like razor blades, slicing, ripping.

Shasta looped an arm around his waist, guiding him closer. "It's the bond."

"I can't—" He put a hand to his chest, patting it, unable to say more.

"You're going to feel everything she feels."

"Is there anything I can do to help her?" he asked, desperate. He had wanted to follow her into the atrium, but she had used her magic to block him, then to bar the door from anyone entering. Everything Brenna had just told them had not only changed everything, but it had also ripped Róisín's mind wide open and she had been inconsolable since Brenna had left them.

Shasta shook her head, then helped him sit on a stool. She crossed to the refrigerator, leaving Caid struck by the normalcy of the act. Róisín had magically sealed herself into a room, yet Shasta pulled food from the refrigerator to make dinner.

"Can't you just, you know." He waved a hand at the vegetables she'd taken out.

"What? Oh." She looked down at her peppers and laughed. "We can and do sometimes. But really, we're not all that different from humans."

Another scream shot through the house, bouncing off the surrounding walls. Caid clutched the countertop with one hand and his chest again with the other. He winced at the pain from her heartbreak and grief.

"Not that different, yet you've got magic and live for a really long fucking time," he grit out.

"You have magic too," she reminded him.

"Does Lina?" They had all been so busy since Madigan's first attempt, that they had yet to broach the subject of the possibility Lina also carried power.

"There's always a possibility, sure. However, even if she has it, it may never rise in her as it did you. With long dormant power, it rarely does."

Caid folded himself so that he could lay his head and chest on the cool surface of the stone counter top. He closed his eyes, clenching and unclenching his jaw, warring with trying to use his own power to knock down the barrier Róisín had created to go to her. "Wouldn't giving birth be a reason it could, you know, rise?"

Shasta paused in the middle of chopping the peppers. "It could be. Her body can process it as a trauma, which could trigger it." She winced at the next scream, that became a growl, before becoming a long howl. "She'll be okay," she said as much for him, as for herself.

"Her mother told her everything."

"I know, Brenna and I talked last night. She felt it was time."

"Róisín knew we weren't there for supplies."

Shasta only hummed in response.

"What is the darkness that Róisín and Brenna talked about?"

She paused her movements. He saw the slight shake in her hands as she sent things on the counter before her. "Once we leave life behind, there are different places we go depending on how we live or how we die."

"Róisín seemed shocked to see her again—" He gripped his middle, pain rippled through him again.

"In the underworld, we can no longer communicate with the living or the dead. We're alone in that world either forever, or until redemption, and we are released to the afterworld." She set the knife aside she had been using on her vegetables. Her features became tight, lines revealing her age around her eyes and mouth that he hadn't noticed before, appeared. "The darkness is the pit. People like Aoife go there automatically. There is no chance of redemption. That's it, you're done."

"Like the underworld, but forever."

Her face drained of color. "No. It's worse, far worse. It's the place that we all fear because we're not there alone. We are also there without our power."

"What's there?"

"Beasts? Demons? Everyone has a different word for it."

"And without power..."

"Exactly."

His stomach churned at the thought of the Goddess determining where Róisín would go when they set the plan into motion to rid the world of Madigan. Róisín who had, even under Aoife's lies, been good, would not be extended the same resting place as other witches who had led the same life. Shasta's warm hand settled on one of his and slowly, he lifted his head.

"Brenna took care of it," she whispered.

"But she risked that for it."

"She would have risked anything for Róisín. Just as I did from the moment Brenna came to me, telling me everything. Stephen hadn't even become a part of the picture yet, but I knew."

Without hesitation, Caid would do the same. He didn't want to spend an eternity apart from her. However, he knew that if his going to the darkness meant she was given the afterworld, he would do it in a heartbeat.

"Fuck." He ground his teeth together, pressing his forehead against the counter again. "If she won't let me in physically, is there anything I can do otherwise?"

"I don't know if it'll work, but you could try," she said. "Just let her feel your love."

He closed his eyes, focusing on breathing in, breathing out, steadying himself. He thought of the first time he had seen her in the Greens Glen High School gym, his instant draw to her. That electric energy that surged between them when they had first shaken hands. He let his mind move to the first time they sat on her front steps that first Friday evening at the end of his first week working at her house. The relief he had when she came back after leaving her house so abruptly that day. How their first kiss had lit him up inside after.

Slowly, some of the crushing pain, the fire within calmed. He pulled up the memory of the moment he realized she was all he wanted or needed. When he had grasped that the feeling he had for her was love.

Shasta slid the crockery with the dinner she had prepped into the oven, slowly closing the door, listening to the now quiet house. She held herself still, ear tipped in the direction of the atrium. When they didn't hear the door open, she leaned over the countertop and patted his hand. "Small steps," she whispered. "She still hurts, but she knows you're here."

Feeling as though he had just been hit by a train, then swept up into a tornado, Caid slid his battered body off the stool. "I'm gonna go." He motioned toward the atrium. "Sit by the door."

"I'll bring you some of this when it's finished. Maybe by then we can get her to open and eat something. We all need to stay as strong as we can."

Caid could only nod before shuffling away toward the atrium.

CHAPTER 80

MATTHEW drummed his fingers against the armrests of the chair he sat in, his knee bouncing. To stop the nervous twitch, he pressed through his heels, rocking the chair back onto just its rear legs.

Nanette stood on the other side of the table in Lucius's kitchen, rubbing at her temples. Finally, with the last tap against the foot of the table, she snapped.

"Would you stop with that incessant tapping?!"

Matthew coughed. The front legs of the chair crashed back to the floor. His body rocked forward with the abrupt movement.

"Thank you," Nanette bit out. "Now, can we focus on the topic at hand?"

"Which"—he glanced from her to Lucius—"neither of you have said what that topic is that I'm to hold in these hands." He lifted his palm up, causing Lucius and Nanette to share a groan. "What?"

"Could you just, for one moment." Lucius took in a calming breath. "Act your age?"

Matthew's eyes narrowed, brows coming down over them. "I do. Quite often. I'm sorry if a moment where I'm trying to keep that gnawing feeling of existential dread down and not puke up my guts with

352

breakfast is making you uncomfortable. Give me a solid five. I'm sure the gallon of coffee and four muffins I had this morning will make us all much more uncomfortable all over this table."

Lucius sighed, flopping into a chair across from him. "Apologies son, we're just trying to figure out what is happening here, that's all. Plus, we're all on edge with Madigan growing near."

"So," he drew out the word, waiting.

"Are you planning to step back from your duties as heir to the Ely Coven?"

Matthew sucked in a quick breath, and burst into a coughing fit. "What?"

Nanette crossed her arms over her chest. "There has never been heirs or leaders bonded before. Most likely for good reason. And with Lily—"

"Wait." Matthew shot to his feet. "Are you telling me that if Lily and I accept the bond, that's it? Only one of us can take our place as leader to our respective Coven?"

They nodded in unison.

"Why me?" Matthew asked Nanette.

"It would be the proper thing to do. You can't ask her to upend her life, all that she's been working for," she answered.

"But it can be demanded of me to do that?" His voice rose in disbelief. "No. There's a compromise; we'll find it."

"You're accepting the bond, then?" Lucius asked.

"Of course, I am," he shot back in response. There was something there with Lily, for them, together, and he wanted the opportunity to explore it. To fall in love. He wanted that fiery love that he saw between his mother and Lucius. That electric sensation that shot excited shivers along his nervous system when Lily was near was all the proof he needed that they could have that.

"Then I strip you of your duties as heir," Lucius stated.

"Excuse me?! You can't be serious," he shouted. "This can't be real. You're fucking with me, right?"

Nanette and Lucius stared back at him.

Something niggled at the base of his skull, a quiet alarm.

"This isn't real." He tried to slow his breathing. "This isn't real."

Looking between the pair again, he lifted a hand, slapping his own face, feeling nothing.

"Shit. Shit, shit, shit," he cursed. He spun around the room, taking the space in, looking for any rips in the false reality built around him. The large bay window to his left caught his attention. Without hesitation, he ran for it, throwing his arms over his face just before bursting free.

He hit with a rolling landing, then sprung to his feet. Glancing over the shoulder, the house was gone. Only the desolate space of the Dead Forest that surrounded the Seer's house looked back at him.

"What the fuck is going on?"

He checked himself for shards of glass and splintered wood. He had taken two steps towards the Seer's home when a dark figure moving through the shadows toward the house caught his attention. As the figure stepped on the bottom step of the house, it turned to face Matthew. Recognition was a gut punch hard enough to send him falling to his knees,

"Madigan."

Matthew shot up in his bed, hollering for Lucius before his feet even hit the ground.

Lucius's head appeared through the library doors.

"We need to get to Roidon!" Matthew called, running past him.

"What? Why? What's happening?" Lucius raced to catch up with him. "Nanette?"

"Madigan."

"What do you mean?" Lucius nodded to Brent, a silent command, as they approached the front doors.

"I just saw Madigan walk into the Seer's."

Lucius came to an abrupt halt. "It begins."

Chapter 81

BATTERED until she had cracked. That was how Róisín had felt. Each time she had remembered a part of her past, or learned more about her family, it had been another swing of the hammer against her entire being. The hits rattled her to her core, over and over. Bang, bang, banging, until the cracks slowly began to form. Her mother's visit in Legianne had been the biggest hit, sending cracks sprawling across her body and soul.

When she felt as though she were strong enough to face her life again, she clawed her way back to Caid.

When she rolled over in bed that morning after waking, she found him staring at her. "How long have you been staring at me?" She asked.

He lifted a brow. "Since sometime in April? Or was it May?"

Her heart fluttered against her chest and a warmth spread through her.

"How are you feeling?"

"Loved," she whispered.

One of his arms slid over her hips, his hand palming her lower back before he pulled her closer. "Because you are," he said, his voice raspy.

"Caid, I—" She closed her eyes, then drew in a steadying breath. "Thank you."

He pressed a soft kiss to her forehead. "For?"

"I felt you. Yesterday. Those memories and feelings," she nestled against his chest, letting his scent surround her. "They anchored me. Thank you for picking me up every time I've fallen down."

"I'll always be there to take care of you, too. I love you, Róisín."

She shifted so that she could sit up. "Will you come with me this morning?"

"I'll go anywhere with you."

Róisín had wanted the morning trip to the cafe to be the start of moving forward. She knew the truth, and she understood why her mother had done what she had and wouldn't pretend to understand Aoife's motives, or seek those answers anymore. There was nothing left but for her to heal, and face Madigan.

It had been on the sidewalk outside of a cafe she had often frequented with her mother when they were on Molennius that her progress forward would be tested. A place that she had avoided, even in passing, in the years since her death.

Caid tucked her scarf around her, pressing a light kiss to her nose. But she had been distracted. It had been the long, deep red, almost mahogany colored hair across the street from where they stood that had caught her attention. All of the times she had twined her fingers in the soft locks, all of the times she had gripped them tightly in the moment of passion.

Alexandria. Or at least Alexandria as she had remembered her. The younger version stood next to an older, beautifully aged version of Alexandria. Her daughter.

Róisín's breath caught in her throat.

She waited for her heart to pound, for her hands to sweat. She waited for the overwhelming sadness that always crushed her heart when she thought of her as she looked across the way at her. Only, nothing came. There was only the calm and warmth that had settled inside of her that morning when she'd wrapped her arms around Caid, buried her face in his chest, the feel and smell of him grounding her.

Alexandria's eyes darted to Caid, then back to Róisín. It was then that she let her magic rise inside, knowing that her skin would glow, that her eyes would change with it. When Caid's responded in kind, it seemed to give Alexandria the answer she'd wordlessly asked.

The moment only lasted seconds.

"Are you all right?" Caid asked against her ear. "Is that?"

"I'm okay, and yes." She turned, looking up at him.

"You sure?"

"Very." She nodded. "Thank you."

"For?"

"Loving me, accepting me as I am."

He had frowned at her words. "Róisín, don't let one person's actions make you think you're not worthy of love or happiness because of who you are."

She pressed her face into his chest, inhaling deeply the smell of him. It had been weeks since he'd worked, yet he still smelled of freshly cut wood. "Never again, because you've shown me I am."

THE STILL SMOLDERING remains of her childhood home spread out before them.

When she'd planned to take him there earlier that morning, she didn't know what to expect. Guilt or regret, perhaps. She closed the house after her mother's death, walking away, never looking back. Her anger outweighing any feeling of grief she would've had.

The moment they had arrived, her heart became a heavy stone in her chest, beating a staccato song. Grief from the loss of her father, of her mother. Moments in time she lost believing Aoife, following her blindly.

A small bloom grew, understanding. Slowly the pieces came together, the lost memories of times with her mother, her father. The trauma their deaths had caused. Her attempts at surviving by clinging to whatever she could. Even Aoife.

"I met Alexandria after my mother died." Róisín kept her eyes on the rubble, feeling everything that came to her at the moment. Since her mind had opened, it had been like a dam flowing freely. That morning had been the first where the crashing memories let up enough so that she could breathe.

Caid, who walked around the remains across from her, paused.

"I didn't realize it, but she was a crutch," she explained. "I was still grieving, even after all those years. Truly believing that everything I knew had been a lie."

Remaining silent, Caid pushed his hands into his pockets. His eyes on her were steady, an anchor.

"I thought I was in love with her. She made me feel so much different from any of the other men or women I'd been with before her. Not that she made me feel different, no, I was a different person at that time than I was with the others. Part of me feels ashamed to recognize that now, after so long."

"Róisín," he said.

"I shut it all off, blocked out all the memories." She looked over the debris, tears stinging her eyes. "When my father died, I tried to bring him back. I was only ten, so I had absolutely no clue what I was doing, but I sat over there by the hedge with all my favorite things of his, trying so hard to bring him back. When I couldn't, I went inside of myself, stripping all the memories of him. It happened again with my mother, with Shasta. I let myself close them all out, forget their love, those moments of joy."

Caid carefully made his way around the house to her. "We all grieve differently."

"I erased them, Caid. Shasta—" She turned away, couldn't bear looking at him. "She risked everything for me, and I was so cold to her after my mother died. We used to have snowball fights; bake cookies together. This wasn't just when I was a child. I was a grown woman. I just... I cut her right out of my life."

He reached out and took one of her hands. He didn't pull her close, only stood silently, giving her the space she needed, but letting her know that he was there.

"Aoife came to me, not even an hour after I had found out. Her lies started immediately. She had a tale to spin about everything. I bought it all, every single word. I trusted this woman who came to me out of the blue, that I had never met before, over my mother whom I'd known for sixty years."

"I never met Aoife, but from what I've heard about her from you, from the others, she wasn't a good person. She took advantage of you, latched on in a moment of darkness."

"If she'd never died, I would never have learned the truth. About her, about my Coven. How my mother made sure everything ended with her so that I would have a chance. This." She tapped a finger hard against her forehead. "This would have never let go or opened up. I would still be in that world I let her lead me to."

"You wouldn't be," he said with surety. He surveyed their surroundings. "This was coming whether she lived or died. Brenna would have still come to you. I would have found you."

"How can you be so sure?"

He shrugged. "I can't explain it, so I'm not even going to try. Somehow, some way, we'd have come together. This." He tugged on their line, grinning when she looked up at him. "Proves me right."

She tried to smile, the weight of everything still working to hold her back. Instead, she turned to what was left of her home. "I haven't been here since the day I locked it."

He placed a hand on the small of her back. "You're here now."

"I am. I can't take those moments of anger back, I'll always feel guilty, but..."

The wind that had picked up around them took the rest of her sentence.

"Holy shit," Caid whispered next to her.

The blackened wood changed as Róisín's power reshaped what Madigan had destroyed. Slowly, the house as Róisín remembered it, formed before them. The weathered shingles, the deep pine green double front doors. Windows framed by shutters in the same green. Window boxes, like those that her mother had hand painted with whimsical faeries, mermaids, sprites, spilling over with flowers. To the left of the house, a small shed, similar in style to the house, scaled down, sprouted up before them.

"It might not quite be exactly as it was, but this is what I remember."

"You just... shit, did you just grow a house?" He rubbed a hand along his jaw, his face filled with wonder.

Her smile came easier. "You could say that."

He scanned the yard, and seconds later, a hawthorn tree grew up to the far right of the house. He blinked several times, his face lit up like a child's on Christmas morning. "I can't believe that actually worked."

"A hawthorn?"

"Shasta told me pacing or hovering over you while you slept when we first got to Molennius would serve no one. She wouldn't stop nagging me, so I..." He ran a hand through his hair, shrugging. "Did a lot of reading. Especially about here knowing that this is where you grew up." He gestured. "Maybe it'll prove true about the protection thing."

"And love." She recalled the dreams she'd had when they'd gone to Molennius, sitting with her mother near a hawthorn by the creek. So enmeshed in the moments with her mother, running from Madigan, that she hadn't stopped to think that there hadn't been a hawthorn when she had lived with her mother.

Dammit, Mother. Róisín looked skyward, blinking away the tears stinging her eyes.

"That's already a given." He clucked his tongue. "Isn't it?"

She moved closer to him, tipping her head back. "Very much so. Would you like to come in? I can show you my room."

He drew an eyebrow up, then slipped an arm around her, pulling her tightly against him so quickly, a startled gasp escaped her when their bodies collided. "Your room, huh?"

She hummed, her mouth curving upward against his lips. "I may have taken a few liberties there, made it bigger."

He quickly scooped her into his arms, heading to the front door, and she let out a shriek. Before he could use his booted foot to open it, she moved them to her room.

He looked at her with a raised brow.

"Call me a little impatient to get you out of those clothes."

"Oh, I'm certainly not complaining." He laid back on the bed, taking her with him. "That day you came to my shower..." He flipped them so that he was on top, then trailed kisses over her neck and chest. "That little trick would be really handy right now."

"What trick?" Her laugh shifted into a moan as he circled his tongue around her navel. Her answer came rushed, breathy. "Just, um, picture it."

He lifted his head. "It's really that easy?"

"Mmhm." To prove it, the clothing she wore piled in an armchair near her closet entrance.

"Well, shit." He palmed one of her breasts while taking the other into his mouth, sucking. A moment later, his clothes joined hers. Then he moved down her body, his hands leading, mouth following.

CHAPTER 82

"Ah, my son," the Seer greeted him. "You have returned."

Madigan stepped into the dimly lit sitting room, quietly surveying the frail figure sitting in a maroon wingback, their near skeletal hands gripping a small fine bone china teacup with small wolves dancing along the rim.

"I told you," He crossed to them, kissing the top of their head. "I wouldn't be gone long."

They huffed out a breath, the veil covering their face shifting outward. "I'd hardly consider eighty-three years not long, child."

"That's just semantics, isn't it?" Madigan lowered into a chair next to them. As he undid the cufflinks of his shirt, he looked around the room. "Where's Boris?"

"Hm?" They paused, lips against the cup. "Oh, he got moldy, so I had him disposed of."

"That was from my first hunt." The disappointment was rich in his tone. "If I can recall the words you said as father and I left for that hunt, it was 'make sure it is a Traujus you bring back to me, child.'"

They nodded, swallowing a mouthful of tea. "I had put the particular request in, yes. However, the magic I used to preserve Boris failed due to time and he began to rot."

His eyes were still on the space that the large, horned beast native to Aunellion had been proudly displayed for centuries. "Shall I retrieve you another?"

"Are you to live long enough to accomplish the feat? How will you return to Aunellion?"

"I believe"—he turned to them—"those are questions you have the answer to."

"You're just like those foolish witches out there. Come to me for answers as though I'm a daughter of the Goddess, or even a charlatan from the streets, as though I can look at their palms, tell them their lives. I am a record keeper for the Sisters, that is all."

"Which means." He leaned forward, dropping his voice to almost a whisper. "You know whether I live or die."

"We all die, child." They set the cup on the saucer, then moved the pair to a table on their left. "Even I will die at some point if the Goddess will ever allow it of me."

"I can imagine that is the killer of it all, isn't it? You hold all this power, what could be considered an eternal life, yet you will never know your own end."

"Is that what you've come for? To take the life of the one who birthed you? Who raised you? Gave you all that you needed, ever?"

He reached out, lifting the veil, bringing it over their head. He was quiet, studying their face for a moment. "No. I'm rather hoping that there's been some delicious twist of fate. That not only will my plan come to fruition, but that the delectable granddaughter of Bernard's will be mine as a prize. After all the detestable things I was made to endure when father adopted him, I deserve as much."

The Seer's milky eyes stared back at him, unblinking. "Things have changed."

He straightened, excitement sparking in his veins. "From that tone, I dare say I may bake us a cake to celebrate. Go on." He waved an impatient hand in circles. "Do tell."

"Things have changed in our world, and the humans'. Someone shifted the threads, everything has changed. Everything is at risk. A discovery. A truth." Their eyes darted back and forth, lost to the sight of the future.

"I was to die, wasn't I?"

"You both were. She was to burn your power into non-existence. She would burn herself out."

"And now?"

"Everything's changed," was the only answer they gave him.

CHAPTER 83

CAID buried his nose in Róisín's hair, pulling her tighter against him. He heard her inhale, then her body melted against his. The two days they had spent together, not working on training, or preparing for whatever it was that was coming, had given him a glimpse of what their life could be like.

Would be like. He wasn't accepting that this wasn't what was waiting for them. There was a clarity in Róisín's face, in her eyes that hadn't been there before. Like the clouds that had been hiding her had finally lifted and she could warm herself in the sun. Joy. It was the only word he had for it when he felt those tiny flutters dance through their connection. Slowly, those flutters had been filling him and in turn, he felt lighter, happier, than ever before.

This is what their future would be like.

She idly stroked a hand over his arm, fingers danced along the shape of muscle in his forearm. "If we..." She turned to look at him over her shoulder and lifted her hand toward his cheek, paused, then brought it back to his arm that held her. "If we make it out of this, would you live here with me?"

He tightened his hold and murmured against her neck. "Anywhere with you. That's all I want. Scratch that." He gently nipped at her skin.

"I want two things. For us to get out of this shit alive." His tongue trailed down her neck to her shoulder, where he kissed her. "Then to settle anywhere with you."

"What about Lina, the baby?"

"We can visit her, and she can visit us." He moved downward, kissed along her shoulder, then her arm.

"You're sure?"

He propped himself up with an arm, then nudged her onto her back. "Róisín, do you want to live here?"

Her eyes were a burnt umber that morning, the only visible sign that her magic stirred just beneath her skin. She took in the room, her expression turning wistful. Brenna's magic, the remnants of it, had lifted and softly embraced them both. Trying to blink the tears that filled her eyes away, Róisín nodded.

"Then we live here."

"You make it sound so simple," she whispered.

"Because it is. Do I like Greens Glen?" He half-shrugged. "Sure. It's been... comfortable. The life I was living at that point in time, comfortable was what served it best. Life is different now. Much different. I'm being honest when I say that it needs to close, a new book started. With you, wherever our feet land."

She lifted a hand, her fingertips tracing along his jaw, her gaze heating.

"Okay?"

"Okay." She moved her hand to the back of his head, pulling him down to her, taking his mouth with hers. "Come with me," she breathed against his lips.

"Anywhere." He dove into her kiss, pausing when a gust of wind trailed over his back. He quickly lifted his head, looking around at the change in their surroundings. "What the...?"

Róisín's bedroom had been replaced with open skies, bruised with blacks and purples. Stars glinted among the black, as if saying goodbye to the stars fading out in the early morning purple as the sun rose. They lay amidst tall, rose gold colored wheat stalks that swayed gently in the wind.

"The Rose Valley." She looked at the sky overhead. "I was three the first time I ran away from home. Somehow, I ended up here. It's one of the very few memories that stayed with me over the years." Sadness settled over her features as she remembered.

"How long were you here?"

"That first time? Two days. Clarissa and Lucius were the ones that found me after my mother sounded the alarm. I realize, now, how dangerous what I did that day was. How much she risked, they all risked."

Caid brushed the back of his hand over her cheek. "You didn't know."

"I know. She never yelled at me." She shook her head. "My parents were at Lucius's manor, waiting for me. They just took me in their arms, hugged me tightly. My father..." She laughed softly, a light, song-like sound that filled him with warmth. "He just said 'leave a note next time sweetheart so we don't worry.'"

"Lucius and Clarissa knew?"

"They all did. I know now that even Nanette knew. It had to have been so hard for her to play the part of loyal friend to Aoife over those centuries. To keep herself safe, her Coven safe. Trying to glean any information that would put any of us in danger. What they all risk with the council, going against the vote. We can all be judged for treason."

He winked at her. "They'd have to catch us first."

"We could have an adventure."

"Oh, babe, I think we're already having that adventure." He chuckled deeply.

Róisín brought a leg over his hip, using the momentum to flip him on his back beneath her. Sitting astride him, she tipped her head back, soaking in the calmness of the valley. "I came here that day you first kissed me. The beginning of all this, I didn't—" Her body trembled. "I didn't handle it well at all. Especially the more I learned about Aoife, or the sacrifices my mother made for me. It felt like with every secret I discovered, everything I learned, I lost a piece of my soul. That day, I needed the open space. So many times in my life I sought out this valley. It's heard a lot of my own confessions, soothed tears, let me scream, let me purge my power."

"Now?" he asked quietly from below her. His hands at her hips, thumbs stroking soft circles over her skin.

When she brought her eyes back to him, they contained the same stars inside of them that blinked above them. "I want it to feel my love, witness my freedom. Feel that light that's lit inside my soul."

Caid lay still, studying her for a moment—the wind blew her hair over her shoulders, along her bare chest. Sitting up, he then cupped her face in his hands before bringing their mouths together, feasting.

She rocked her hips over the hard length of him, sucking his tongue into her mouth, drawing a sound from his chest that sounded raw, primal. He gripped her hips, shifting her back some. She trailed a hand over his chest, then reached between them, gripping his cock in her hands.

They both watched her bring him to her entrance, then stroking the swollen head of his cock along her folds before she slowly slid over the length of him until she was fully seated, their bodies joined.

"Let your power go," she said huskily.

"I'll either flood the valley or burn everything I can reach with it."

"No, you won't," she said. "Just trust me."

Before he could argue, hers rose around them, electrifying the air in the valley. The sensation almost brought him to his peak, making him squeeze his eyes closed to gather himself, hold back.

"Trust me." She rocked against him.

"Fuck." He reached for his control first, then he urged his magic up, pressing it out to join hers.

Her head fell back, and she released a long, low moan. Shifting them, he laid her back, hooking his arm under one of her legs, letting himself in deeper. All he could feel was pure ecstasy everywhere their bodies touched, everywhere his fingers caressed. Her skin sweeter than honey beneath his tongue as he used it to stroke and explore, working her body to its climax, trying to hold his own back.

Her breathy moans turned into desperate cries around her pants, her hips pumping frantically against him. The sky above shifting and dancing into the pinks and golds of the early morning. The start of a new day.

Róisín clenched around him, the orgasm exploding through her.

His name, a cry ripped from her lips that echoed across the valley. Before she could finish coming down from that high she was riding, he pulled out, moving down her body.

"But you're not," she said, her words coming between the gasps, and she tried to catch her breath.

"I'm not ready for whatever this is to be over yet." He pressed a kiss to the spot just above her clitoris. "If I stay inside of you, there's no way I'm lasting another second."

"Oh, Goddess," she moaned when he sucked on her. She fisted her hands in his hair, gripping tightly, and she ground herself against his face, coming again.

"Caid, I don't know if I..."

He used the flat of his tongue to stroke along her entrance, followed by the soft touch of his trailing fingers.

Caid could only grin, his face nearly buried in her sweet heat. "Just a little longer."

"Let me." She tried to reach for him.

He lazily moved his fingers, keeping her in her blissed-out state. "If you touch me, I'm completely undone. I could see the pain, the sadness when you started telling me about this place. It's not that anymore, got it? This is going to be the place your *mate* fucked your brains out. This valley is going to hear all those screams of lust and love. Okay?"

She whimpered, her body moved closer to his hands, writhing against his palm.

"Okay?" He repeated then nipped the skin just above her left hip.

Her eyes slowly opened and she looked down at him. "Okay." Then her body broke into pieces, shaking as the next orgasm crashed over her.

Rising back over her, he guided himself into her gently. "I love you, Róisín."

There was no time for her to respond. On his second thrust into her, they came together, sending birds scattering, and Caid swore speeding the sun's rise over the valley.

Chapter 84

THROUGH the patio doors at her house in Greens Glen Róisín saw Lina sitting with David in her lap, Thomas next to her with a handful of raspberries. Would David still stay in Maine if Róisín didn't make it through this? Would he stay if she moved to Ireland to live in her family's home? They would have to talk again the moment they had an opportunity for privacy. She wanted him to still stay, to remain and help Lina.

"Do you think he knows?" Caid nodded his head toward David and Thomas.

Róisín tapped a finger against her chin in thought. "I don't know if David would—" She blinked as Thomas spoke, followed by David's response. "Ah, shit? Yes?"

Caid smirked at her. "You've cursed more in the past four weeks than in the..."

"What?" She pulled her attention away from the doors. "What's wrong?"

He stared through the glass at the trio on the patio, wearing a confused expression. "We've been gone for what, two months? Why does it look like no time at all has passed? Are you?"

"No, I'm not using any of my magic. Time moves differently

throughout the realms. Each is at a different point in time of its life cycle."

"I just thought it was kind of like the northern versus southern hemisphere here. Molennius was winter, here it is summer. Roidon, that was in its summer too."

"Some realms, time moves slower than the others. Earth is perhaps one of the slowest. I think Shianshani is the only realm closest to Earth."

"So..." He glanced back at Lina. "She won't be pissed about how long we've been gone?"

"The combined time away between the realms we were in, to her..." She tapped a finger to her lips, running the math through her head. "It hasn't really been that long at all."

"Wait." He snatched her wrist before she could open the door. "The time you left for your work trips."

"I was gone for weeks sometimes," she replied.

"I... this is going to... yep, I've got nothing, so I'm going to stop now. Let's go tell Lina she can't have her baby in a regular hospital because she might be Glinda the Good Witch." He stalked toward the door. "This is so fucking wild," he mumbled under his breath.

Róisín chuckled. He was never mad, nor upset with every new door that opened in his new life. He had handled it all in the most Caid way he knew how, armed with sarcasm and wit. And love, and care. It was in the way his eyes softened when he paused at the door, his sister nuzzling David's fur between his ears.

Róisín stood behind him and placed a hand lightly on his shoulder blade. "We've got this," she whispered.

He straightened, gave a sharp nod, then shoved the door open.

Lina and Thomas were on their feet the moment Caid slid the door open, Thomas pointing to David, his eyes wide and bright. "A talking rabbit!"

Róisín smiled, pushing her magic out toward the plant pot he stood next to, urging the morning glory vines to grow up into the form of a person, then to embrace him. He jumped, yelping as he spun around.

"What..." He jerked back around to face her, eyes wide.

"Surprise!" She wiggled her fingers, nudging the vines back down.

"I'm gonna..." He motioned to the chair. "Sit back down."

"You should probably sit too," Caid told Lina.

"What? Why? What's happening?" She looked from him to Róisín. "Is this about Madigan?"

The hiss of a sharp exhale sounded from Caid, and the bottom of her world dropped out. Her attention shifted to David, where he was cradled in Lina's arms.

"She threatened me," David said flatly.

"With what?" Róisín shot back.

"A cage."

Now she lifted her eyes to Lina, seeing the guilt on her face.

"I knew something else was going on, I did what I felt I had to do," Lina said.

Pinching the bridge of her nose, Róisín closed her eyes. "Caid..."

Caid rocked back on his heels and clucked his tongue. She couldn't see him, but she would bet all her magic that he grinned, like a hungry cat watching a bird on a feeder, at Lina. "You sure?"

She groaned, nodding. "Yep. Consider the ease-into-it plan scrapped."

From beside her, his deep laugh rolled out of him. Perhaps, she should have held him to their ease-into-it part of the plan they'd come up with before leaving Rose Valley. She had seen the sibling dynamic between the two, and, from that menacing chuckle, knew this was going to go sideways, quickly.

"Plan?" Lina asked.

"She just said there is no plan," Caid replied with faux innocence.

"What do you... oh my, holy shit, you... you?!" Lina gasped and Róisín finally opened her eyes.

One of Caid's arms extended outward, growing a small forest along his forearm, while the fingers on his other hand were lit like candles on a birthday cake.

"I guess I get to say surprise now." He waved his lit fingers at Lina.

"But how?!" Lina moved to touch the small trees, stopping short, bringing her hand back to rest on her stomach.

"Apparently, in your line somewhere on either your mother's or father's side, there was a witch, or witches, who let their power go dormant. Most likely for protection during the hunt of their time," Róisín did her best to explain.

Lina reached out again, fingers brushing a tree. Bewilderment settled on her face. "How did you find out?"

The trees were puffed out by smoke. The heat radiating from Caid's body had them stepping away from him. Róisín could feel his power shifting into the shadows of his anger. She sent a cooling breeze to wrap around him and he spun to her, eyes filled with pain and dark rage.

They had agreed that they wouldn't tell Lina about what had happened when Madigan had come for Róisín. She needed to know about Madigan, that he was dangerous. That was all. Placing a hand on his forearm, she gave him a slight shake of her head. Slowly, he cooled.

"Okay, so, better question." Lina glanced over her shoulder at Thomas. "Do I?"

"Nanette wasn't one hundred percent sure. However, there is a possibility." Thomas rose and went to Lina's side. "Which is why we're actually here," Róisín continued. "Shasta has a midwife, Helen, who will arrive shortly. She's going to stay with you until the baby comes."

"Babies," Lina mumbled.

"What?" Caid straightened.

"You, uh, you were right, dammit. We found out yesterday that baby number two has been hiding behind baby number one. Now that they're bigger..." Her shoulders slumped. "Twins!"

Caid snorted and scratched at the back of his neck. He pressed his lips together, but not before Róisín heard the quick, quiet chuckle escape. "Well... shit."

Lina shrugged. "You were right."

"Could you repeat that? I couldn't quite hear you." He tapped his ear, leaning closer.

"You were right," she said louder.

"I'd really love to gloat more, except the current situation we find ourselves in"—Caid nodded to her stomach—"is more important. You can't go to the hospital to have them."

"Could labor, you know—" Thomas waved his hands in the air in front of him, then over his head, miming what Róisín guessed to be magic. "Make her?"

"It could," Róisín replied. "That's why Helen is going to come. She'll stay here in my house so you two can still have your space. She'll be close, yet not underfoot."

Lina bit her bottom lip. "She'll do all the checking, measuring, heartbeat, and stuff like my doctor has been doing?"

"Yes, she's been the midwife on Molennius for over four centuries," she said.

"Four hundred years?!" Thomas squeaked out.

"We live a bit longer."

"Wait." Thomas sobered. "If she? She'll? The babies?"

Heavy sadness rose inside of Róisín. She had been relieved, celebrated even, when she had been granted more than a few more decades with Caid, but she hadn't forgotten how much it had hurt when she tried to reconcile their time together, before.

"Shit." His face fell.

Lina turned to him and took his face in her hands. "We'll figure it out when we get there, if we get there, okay? We won't worry about it right now."

He blinked down at her; he clenched and unclenched his jaw. "Okay."

"What happens now?" Lina asked.

"That's a really good ques—"

There was a crash, punctuated by a heavy thud as Matthew seemingly, no, literally fell from the sky onto the patio. He sprung to his feet, face pale and eyes wide when he looked at them.

Lina and Thomas screamed in surprise. Caid moved in front of Róisín, knowing the news he carried was not good from the black, anxious energy that rolled off of Matthew.

"He's with the Seer," he gasped out as though he'd run all the way from Roidon.

Róisín eyes widened, her heart in her throat. "Fuck."

CHAPTER 85

"WHAT in the Rob Zombie movie is this place?" Caid asked.

"It's the Dead Forest." Róisín squinted into the darkness of the forest with its snarled, twisted, leafless black trees. They were massive, ominous shapes under Roidon's full moons. A chill ran over her. "It's meant to deter the humans from finding the Seer."

Caid shivered, moving closer to her. "Well, it certainly works. My skin is ready to crawl away."

She turned to Matthew. "We're sure he's in there?"

"I could confirm it," Lucius answered from next to him.

"We saw what happened on Earth, he'll be expecting us." Róisín frowned. "We need a plan."

"Go in there, magic blazing?" Matthew suggested.

Lucius sighed heavily. "And get us all killed."

"What about the others?"

"Right here," Shasta whisper-shouted from behind them.

Róisín saw the look of relief cross over Matthew's face at the sight of Lily. Róisín lifted a brow at him. With a grin, he nodded. She mirrored his expression, understanding.

"There needs to be a plan," Nanette demanded. "We can't just rush in there."

"See?" Róisín gave Matthew a pointed look.

"What? My plan would catch him off guard, give us an advantage."

"No, it wouldn't." Caid took a step forward, his eyes still on the forest before them. "I can't explain it, but I can feel it. He knows we're here."

"Question is, why hasn't he shown himself?" Róisín joined him, reaching for his hand, hooking their fingers together.

"Most likely, he wants us to come to him," Shasta supplied.

Róisín peered into the darkness again, feeling something unfamiliar skitter along her spine. She released Caid's hand and brought her arms around herself, trying to fight the urge to shiver. "Do you think he's killed the Seer already?"

Lucius moved closer to the group so that he could keep his voice low. "We'd have felt it."

"If we're going to make a plan, we should probably do it, instead of sitting here chatting like it's teatime," Nanette grumbled.

Matthew looked down the line, catching Caid's attention. Something unspoken passed between them.

Róisín caught the way the corner of Caid's mouth tipped up into a smirk, the flash of mischief in his eyes. "No."

"You know you want to," Matthew chided from where he stood.

"You first," Caid said.

Matthew rolled his shoulders, then bounced on the balls of his feet as he did when he was getting ready to spar with her. He looked down at Lily and winked. "You may want to give me a little room, love. What is it that the Torch says exactly? Oh!" He cackled maniacally. "Flame on!"

Matthew's body ignited. The ground beneath Róisín's feet grew slick, drawing her attention away from the human fireball. Caid's entire body was engulfed in ice, shimmering like silver beneath the moonlight.

"What?" He flashed her a boyish grin.

"This isn't a joke," she scolded.

Lucius rubbed his jaw and rocked back onto his heels, nodding. "Mm, but they may be on to something."

Shasta leaned closer to Róisín. "What's happening?"

"We're going to die while these dummies are trying to figure out which comic book character they want to be," she answered through clenched teeth.

"Comic book?" Lily's brow knotted.

"From Earth and Molennius. Stories about people with sort of superpowers, saving their worlds," Róisín said. She sighed and put her hands on her hips. "Matthew has read them for as long as I can remember. I really don't see how this can be them being on to something though," she raised her voice enough for Lucius to hear.

"He'll let his guard down if he thinks we're unprepared, not taking him, or the threat of him, seriously." Lucius focused on a gnarled tree near the path they had gathered on. The ground shuddered, the tree groaned. After a moment, the roots snapped free. Slowly, the tree rose.

Matthew nodded in appreciation. "Nice one, Professor Xavier."

"We go in, playing super heroes, distracting him," Lucius continued. "Nanette and Lily will get the Seer out, you and Shasta take advantage of the opening the three of us"—he gestured to Matthew and Caid —"create to finish this once and for all."

Róisín didn't want to openly admit it, but it was a sound plan. Before she could agree, Lily shrieked, then disappeared.

Matthew's fire sputtered out, his eyes wild.

"Where'd she go?!" He spun around.

"Lily!" Nanette screamed.

Moments later, she was gone as well.

Shasta soon followed.

"What just happened?" Róisín whispered, afraid by speaking too loudly, she would be next.

Chapter 86

With unfamiliar arms wrapped around her, Shasta tumbled into her house, plummeting to the floor of the living room.

"Get off me!" she shouted and shoved herself away. Whirling around, she sucked in a sharp breath. "Frederick."

"Always a pleasure, Shasta." He gave her a mock bow. His yellow, snake-like eyes glinted in amusement as he surveyed the trio. "You too, Nanette."

With fire blazing in her eyes, Nanette rose and straightened her jacket. "I should have known. Your votes on the council, you're working with him."

He scoffed. "Madigan? Never." Crossing to the kitchen, he paused at the basket of fruit Shasta had placed on the island. He took an apple and bit into it while his eyes roamed over Lily. "My, child, you have certainly grown."

"Eyes off my granddaughter," Nanette spat out.

"She's a treat, Nanette." He made to move closer to her, but Nanette stepped into his path.

"Don't touch her," Nanette warned coldly.

"Testy." He tsked and rolled his eyes.

"What do you want? Where are the others?" Shasta tracked his movements as he paced her kitchen and tossed the apple from hand to hand. It was like watching rope skippers, waiting for that perfect moment to hop over the swinging ropes, feet moving quickly. He needed to move closer to her so that she wouldn't have to use much of her physical strength and speed to grab him. The less she exhausted herself, the better she would be able to help the other when they got back to Roidon.

"What I want." He sighed heavily. "Is to eat this apple in peace."

"Then you should have left us where we were so we couldn't bother you," Shasta said.

"See, then I wouldn't be doing my part in this if I had done that."

"Part in what?" Shasta and Nanette demanded in unison.

Frederick ran a hand idly through his long, black tresses before biting into the apple again. He chewed slowly. Abruptly, he tossed the apple into the air. "Hate to dash so quickly, but I've been given my leave."

"Don't you dare." Nanette reached for him, but he vanished before she could grasp him.

"What's going on?" Lily asked from where Nanette had backed her into the corner between the pantry door and refrigerator.

"He says he's not with Madigan." Shasta stooped to pick up the apple. Studying the two chunks Frederick had taken out of it, she frowned. Molennius only had an apple harvest on odd years. They lasted longer than those that grew every year, but the crop was still rare and considered a delicacy in her realm. "Such a wasteful twat. Do you think he was working with Mildred and Aoife?"

Nanette rubbed a hand over her face, her mouth pinched. "If he was, he joined them in the last few years, after I was needed at home more."

Nanette's unspoken words of the death of her daughter, Moira, sat heavy among them.

"This means Mildred is moving forward with whatever plans Aoife had." Shasta scowled. "We were so distracted with Madigan, they were working right under our noses."

"It would make sense as to why he had those books from the library," Lily reasoned.

"What?" Nanette spun to her.

"This morning." She moved into the kitchen. "I could track down that Frederick was the last to have had access to those books Matthew and I could not locate in Alleyette. The ones still missing. Before I could tell anyone, Matthew found Madigan with the Seer, then everything sort of went..." She tipped her palms up, spreading her fingers wide.

"Sideways," Shasta finished.

"We need to get back there," Lily pressed.

Shasta propped open the trash can, dropping the apple inside. "Let's get the hell out of here. We need to let the others know. Lucius's plan may no longer work given this change of events."

"We don't have much time. Not if he's with the Seer," Nanette noted.

"No, we don't," Shasta agreed grimly.

"I can't go, I'm stuck." Lily gasped.

Panic rose on Nanette's face, her eyes wide, mouth open. "I can't either."

Shasta's palms grew clammy. Swallowing hard, she looked between them. "I can't."

"How?" Lily asked.

As Shasta pressed with her magic, the ward skittered along her skin. "It's a reverse ward. We're trapped."

Chapter 87

IT took them ten minutes to calm Matthew down and refocus the remaining group's efforts. He sat on the trail-edge with his head between his knees, grinding his molars so loudly, Róisín could hear them from where she stood. She rubbed at her temples, her body shaking with each breath she took did.

What had happened? Had it all been just a trap?

Wrapping her arms around herself, she tried to focus, to calm her racing heart. She turned back to the forest. Her ears strained to hear beyond the noises raging and clanging inside of her mind. The adrenaline that had spiked her system moments ago, now fading. A thin layer of sweat broke out over her skin.

"It wasn't Madigan." Lucius had stood back to them, shoulders tense.

She caught his eye when he glanced over his shoulder. "How do we know?"

"You felt the power in the air, it was familiar." He shook his head, moving to help Matthew to his feet. "But it wasn't his."

Caid came up behind her, removing the flannel shirt he wore and slid it over her shoulders. The smell of wood and bergamot surrounded her. His smell, and the gentle tug he gave their tether, brought a sense of calm over her.

"What now?" Matthew asked, his voice raspy from his earlier shouts for Lily.

Róisín studied Lucius, the determined set of his mouth and hard lines around his eyes. Despite what had just happened, she had to trust her gut and her gut was telling her that even down three people, the initial plan would still work with adjustment.. "We stick to Lucius's plan."

Caid paced away, cracking his knuckles. "Is it still going to work?"

She shoved her arms into the sleeves of Caid's shirt, steeling herself. While she buttoned the shirt, she explained, "At this point, we just try to keep the Seer out of any crossfire. We focus on Madigan. You three distract him, I'll take the window you make and shatter it."

Lucius rested a hand on her shoulder. "Are you sure?"

"We don't have a choice," she whispered.

Matthew looked down at his hands and flexed his fingers. "After we finish here, they're all mine."

"We go together," she said. "Strength in numbers. We'll get her back." She reached for his hand, linking their fingers. "All of them."

THEIR FOOTSTEPS WERE quiet as they wove around the trees, closing in on the Seer's house. The trees shifted, reaching out to them, trying to hold them back, unused to trespassers walking by so boldly.

As they neared the back door, they whispered directives to one another, sending Matthew and Caid to the side doors, Lucius around the front. Róisín was to slip in through the small hatch that led into the basement, then wait for Caid to tug down their bond.

Róisín had just cloaked her presence and slipped through the small basement door below the hatch, when she felt Caid. She didn't move at first, having not heard any noise from within the house. He tugged again, luring her to cautiously move toward the door. Slowly, she edged it open, revealing an unexpected sight.

"Ah, there she is. My beauty." Madigan sat, one leg crossed over the other, in one of the blue suede chairs that Róisín had sat in only months before. The Seer sat next to him, knobbed fingers moving needles deftly as they knit.

Butterflies took flight in her stomach, and fog began to settle in her mind. She looked from the Seer to Madigan, then to the others. From Lucius and Matthew's knotted eyebrows, she knew she wasn't alone in her feelings.

"Come in." He waved her over. "No one comes to the Seer without reason, isn't that right, cennend?"

Four sharp inhales of breath, including her own, sounded like a storm in her ears. Had she heard correctly? He had to be lying.

"Make sure you offer our guests something to drink, child." The Seer motioned toward the tray before them that held a teapot and cups.

Róisín's eyes darted to Lucius questioningly. He managed a shrug in response, but his eyes were wide, unblinking.

"Here, sit." Madigan motioned toward the chair he had vacated. "You look like you've had a rather rough evening, my love."

Caid stood like a mountain, fists tight at his sides. His power boiled within him, begging for release. Róisín could feel it. It reached down their line, like an outstretched hand, to her magic, pleading for it to join, to release.

"Well, isn't this just a sight for a painting," a voice said from behind Lucius.

The air left the room. A volcano erupted inside of her. Its lava exploded against the walls of her stomach and chest, singeing the fluttering wings of the butterflies on contact. Swallowing down the rising heat, the urge to react, she pinned her arms to her sides and pressed her clenched fists against her thighs.

They all turned to Aoife, who stood with Henry. Aoife's maroon eyes took in the group of witches before them. She patted a slender, olive-toned hand to her perfectly knotted auburn bun before stepping further into the room.

"I never thought I'd see the day where my granddaughter fraternized with her granduncle after I worked so hard to make her believe him to be the boogie man."

Aoife moved further into the room. She paused at the table next to the Seer and bent to take a teacup in her hand. "Ugh, they could never make a cup of tea to save their life." She squeezed her eyes closed and shivered. "Lucius." She nodded to him as she passed. "Matthew."

Matthew lifted a hand, his fire just under the skin of his fingertips, turning them deep red. Caid moved closer to take his wrist, stopping him.

"Oh." Aoife stopped; attention drawn to him. "You're new."

Róisín tamped down the power of their bond, pressed down the way their magic slowly wound together—hers responding to the urging and desperation of his, wanting to ignite and explode. Time slowed and she could hear the blood rushing through her veins when Aoife leaned in, inhaling deeply, then stepped back, studying him.

"One of Nanette's then. Wonder where she had you hidden away." Aoife smoothed a hand on his chest.

"What do you want?" Róisín bit out. "How are you here?"

"The Goddess thinks she has the power to hold me." Aoife huffed. "She is in for quite a surprise. Once I'm finished here, I'm coming for her. Henry." She beckoned him forward.

He took a step, nodded to her in a silent assent to her mental command, then vanished. Only, it wasn't just he who vanished. Róisín now found herself alone with her grandmother, Madigan, and the Seer.

Be smart. Róisín fought the urge to reach out to Caid. She had seen him use his powers, as though he had the ability for centuries instead of weeks. She had to trust that wherever he was, he was strong enough to come back to her.

Her grandmother expected the broken girl she was before. There would be no way for Aoife to know just how strong she had become, not just with her magic.

She caught the way Madigan's anger toward Aoife rose off him in faint wisps of smoke. The way his pitch-black eyes had shifted, simmering bright red as he stared at her from where he stood across the room.

It wasn't just Róisín that Aoife's secrets had changed. Róisín could see that; she could use that. Taking calming breaths, pushing down the shudder that threatened to roll through her as she remembered Madigan's touch, she squared her shoulders. Before facing him, she prayed to the Goddess that she didn't waver or break.

"What do you request of me, my love?" Her voice caught on the last word. "To rid our future of this"—she looked her grandmother over with the disdain she truly held for her—"waste."

<h1 style="text-align:center">CHAPTER 88</h1>

CAID and Matthew stood back-to-back in the middle of a room comparable to a dungeon with its windowless stone walls that were sharp and jagged. The room was dimly lit with torches that sat in holders along the floor. Standing before Matthew was a woman with hair the color of snow. Mildred was what Matthew had called her. The man Aoife had called Henry, with his perfectly coiffed strawberry blond hair, keen blue eyes, stalked circles around Caid.

Mildred had questioned Caid's presence when they arrived wherever they were.

One of Nanette's, Henry had said, as though the words were rotted fruit brushing his tongue.

His connection with Róisín went quiet the moment Aoife had appeared, and he'd swallowed down his frustration at her attempt to shield him.

Let me take care of you.

"Push it down," Matthew whispered from the corner of his mouth behind him. "If I can feel it, they can feel it. They'll feed off it. Their magic is dark."

Caid blinked and looked up from the ground at Henry. He watched the way Henry paced, like a predator on prey, waiting for the signal.

"Why haven't they done anything?" Caid whispered back.

"Partly because they don't know what you are to Nanette, partly because I'm guessing Aoife wants me alive. Have you ever been in a fight, McGrath?"

"Sure." He followed Henry's movements, back and forth, back and forth. "I've knocked a few fists around. Fists being the keyword. Something tells me I'm a little out of my element here, though."

Matthew snorted. "That's a good one. Element."

"I wouldn't consider this a laughing matter, Matthew," Mildred's raspy voice scolded.

"It's all the same principal," he went on to Caid, ignoring her. "You just sort of... punch the magic out with your fist, directing it where you want it to go, what you want it to do."

He sized up Henry. The man appeared to be only in his mid-fifties. However, Caid knew that most likely he was at least four times that, if not more. He had about a solid four inches on him and outweighed him by another sixty pounds. "You take Snow White, I'll take Prince Douche?"

Matthew barked out a laugh. "I wasn't sure if I'd like you or not that first day. Now, I can't wait to do birthday parties for our kids together."

"Yeah, well." Caid shifted his position "Let's just live long enough to get there."

"That, my friend, is a sound plan. Ready?"

"Go!" Caid shouted and leaped at Henry.

Mildred was almost a moment too late shifting to the other side of the room when Matthew pounced on her, leaving him with nothing but air to fall on. Recovering quickly, he tucked and rolled, springing to his feet.

"I thought I was your favorite," he chided her, his false disappointment ringing out in the stone room.

Caid took hold of Henry by the throat, shaping water into a large hand and lifting him almost to the room's ceiling. Something dark inside of him rising as he urged each watery finger tighter around his neck.

"Where's my father?"

Matthew's shout startled Caid, almost causing him to drop Henry.

Before Henry could gain the upper hand, he sent him sailing across the room, aiming for Mildred who hit the stone wall and let out a loud oomph when Henry crashed into her.

"Get off me!" She shouted at Henry.

Matthew jumped back, barely avoiding the tumbling mess that was Mildred and Henry. He looked over his shoulder to Caid, impressed at how well he wielded his new magic. Together, they closed in on the pair who quickly scrambled to their feet. Henry moved to shift across the room, but Matthew was close enough that he followed. Henry choked out a gasping breath when Matthew landed atop of him.

"I know about you and Lily." Henry tried to struggle to his feet. "She thought she was so secretive every time she was in the library. Her head is so much louder than she realizes."

Matthew punched him, satisfied at the cracking sound of Henry's nose on the impact and the blood that immediately began to pour down his face. "Goddess, you still talk too much. Fucking *shut up*."

"Or what? All your fates are sealed. Aoife has plans for you all. You especially. After you're gone, she's mine." He sneered. "Oh, do I have some fun ideas planned after hearing all the things she wanted to do with you."

Letting his rage rise was unwise, dangerous. The same for letting it take over him. Wrapping his hands around Henry's neck, he leaned in, letting his fire rise.

"You won't get to touch a hair on her head." Matthew's hot breath hit Henry's face as he spoke. "Because you will not see the day's end."

Then, he let the fire consume him, consume Henry. Mildred's frantic pelts of rain washed over them. He urged the fire hotter and hotter, its roar growing with the flames. Henry's screams echoing through the Council's Judgement Chamber where they had been brought. When the only sounds left were the soft hisses of the drops on the flames, Matthew released what was left of Henry's body.

"You will pay for that," Mildred spat.

He spun on her, rage still wild within. "She will defeat them. Róisín.

She will not lose. Not only will Madigan be gone, but Aoife too. Then what?"

Mildred stumbled back a step, crashing against the wall of Caid's chest. He wrapped her in thorny vines, holding her in place.

"What happens when your plan falls apart, Mildred?" Matthew asked, his voice like a rumble of thunder as he let that anger speak through him.

After a moment of struggling against the vines, she stopped, studying him. Then her eyes flashed white, and she laughed. With a burst of her power, she was free of the vines, Caid and Matthew sent scattering away from her.

"It's fine if Aoife can't handle her pretty little granddaughter, because her absence gave me plenty of time to come up with a backup plan."

Chapter 89

"Lucius," a voice prodded him in his sleep. "Lucius, you need to wake. You don't belong here."

His eyes flew open.

"Clarissa." Her name was a soft breath from his lips.

"Hi, love." She gave him a sad smile. "How did you get here?"

"That all depends on where here is," he said, taking in his surroundings. The air was warm, fragrant with hyacinth and wisteria, Clarissa's two most beloved blooms.

"This is my afterworld."

"Did I?"

"No." She shook her head, offering him a small smile, dimples dotting each of her cheeks. He stepped forward, ready to kiss them as he always did, but stopped when she shook her head and rose from the ground. "I was in the garden when I heard an awful racket, then you just fell from the sky."

"I fell from the sky." He looked up, the clear blue sky hovering over them. "Matthew, Caid?"

"Neither are here." She brushed garden soil from her slacks, then offered him her hand. "We need to get you out of here before you're trapped."

"That wouldn't be such a bad thing," he replied. They had their visits, but nothing would ever come close to being the same as being with her every moment. Falling to sleep and waking with her in his arms. That familiar longing ache stretched inside of him.

"Oh, Lucius." She rested her hand against his cheek.

His body felt like it was melting as he tipped his head, leaning into her touch.

"I miss you, but it is not our time. We can't change what has been woven without consequence."

"I know." He closed his eyes, covering her hand with his. "I just need a moment. Just a moment."

"You can have more than that if you take the easy option," Frederick called from the pathway through Clarissa's garden.

"Frederick." Lucius's voice was dark, cold.

Frederick lifted a hand to his chest, wincing. "Here I go out of my way for centuries to be the nice guy to you all, and this is the second time today I've been greeted like I'm asking folks to chew on glass."

"Because we know the snake you are, Frederick." Clarissa glared at him. "What have you done?"

"Oh, I have done nothing. I've made sure that all of this gets pinned on our favorite witchy rebel, Mildred."

"The Goddess will know of your transgressions. She is our final judge," Lucius warned.

"Do you really think that all of this"—he spread his arms out, turning in a circle—"is ever going to make it to the council table? There *is* no council anymore. That ended the moment you and your too-good-for-the-rest-of-us pals went against the council vote by working with Róisín."

Lucius seethed. "You voted against her because you wanted to see her dead. With Aoife returned, when Róisín dies, all that power, the magic of life and death, goes to her. There would be no stopping Aoife then."

"That was sort of the plan." Frederick shrugged. "Then everything got messy. Madigan took a liking to his grandniece, you were all helping her, Aoife hadn't returned when she said she would." He pursed his lips. "Plans changed."

"What do you mean about Madigan?" Clarissa asked. She moved to step around Lucius, but he held out his arm and smoothly tucked her behind him, shielding her.

Frederick picked at his nails for a moment, then sighed. "As it so turns out, Aoife sort of forgot to tell Madigan that she had a granddaughter. If he had known, he would've surely deduced our endgame. Things would've gone haywire, she reasoned. She was, in fact, right. He discovered sweet little Róisín, but instead of killing her before Aoife could return, which would have been bad, he's decided he wants to take her as his own."

For once, Lucius was thankful for Frederick's overtness, his inability to not gloat when he held information no one else had. He prodded further. "I'm going to take a guess here, that wouldn't bode well for Aoife either. Not with Madigan being a siphon. It gives him access to Róisín's power whenever he wants it."

"Precisely." Frederick sounded relieved Lucius had caught on to the dilemma without him needing to explain further.

"The problem is Róisín will block him."

"If only. Aoife tapped me on the mental shoulder, telling me to get here and hurry to finish up with you, then get back to her because it appears that Róisín has switched teams." Frederick shuddered and gagged.

"What do you mean?" Lucius stepped forward.

"He's thralled her, surely." Clarissa reached out to him to stop him.

"No, she's too strong. We've been working on this for months," Lucius insisted. He made sure that every session had been at the end of a long, physically and emotionally taxing day so that Róisín would have the skill to dredge up her defenses even when she was running on a thread of energy. He had wanted her to be as prepared as she could be, for anything.

"Oh, there's no thrall." Frederick tapped his forehead, bringing his connection with Aoife up, projecting it out to them. "You can't thrall this type of enthusiasm into anyone."

CHAPTER 90

Róisín slid down Madigan's body. Her toes touched the ground, and she coyly licked her lips. He didn't know that the image she'd pulled up in her mind had been of Caid. The soft green splashes among the browns and golds of his eyes. His mouth that she could feast on for hours if fate would ever be kind enough to give them time.

Keeping the heat of that thought banked in her eyes, her hands drifted over Madigan's chest. She let her fingers explore the lines and planes beneath the fabric of his suit shirt. Admiring outwardly, cataloging inwardly. Feeling the physical power she would face paired with his magic.

Aoife was held in place momentarily by her magic. Róisín had slowly let her siphoning magic wrap around his, getting a feel for it, using it. It had taken time to do it unnoticed, it was singing in her blood. It was powerful.

There had been a scuffle at first. Aoife's immediate reaction to Róisín's remark to Madigan had set into action complete chaos. The room they'd stood in had been ruined. Plaster crumbled from the walls where their bodies had fallen against them, taking hits from blasts of magic thrown at one another. The stone mantle over the fireplace lay shattered on the floor. The chairs and table reduced to piles of splinters.

A hot, electric smell permeated the air around them from the expended magic.

Róisín let Madigan brush a hand over her arms, his magic healing the cuts that littered them. Satisfaction wrapped around her when she heard Aoife's intake of breath. She couldn't stop the smug grin from spreading at the sound.

Róisín had switched that light, warm part of herself off with such ease, she should've been alarmed. She had let the dark, the cold, fill her, hollowing the rest of herself out. She had used her fire magic to warm her body, sending heat toward Madigan in soft pulses. A misdirect to lead him to believe he aroused her. She pulled up her intimate memories of Caid, using them to shift her scent.

When Madigan's nostrils flared, his eyes darkening with desire, she knew she had succeeded in her hastily made plan.

Once Aoife went to the pits, to the darkness, any bond that had been in place was severed. But her responses to both Róisín and Madigan clarified that she, despite her plans to destroy him, held feelings still for Madigan.

Róisín watched Aoife, thinking of how much it had to chafe at Aoife to return to find that her granddaughter was not only no longer the weak, broken, confused woman she'd left behind, but was now at the side of her enemy in the quest for power.

What bothered Róisín the most had been Aoife's ability to return to their plane. How had Aoife broken free not just from the pits, but returned to life? It worried Róisín. The longer Aoife was there, living, the more chance there was for the balance to demand a shift. The balance would return Aoife's magic, the magic of their entire Coven, to her.

Would Róisín still be strong enough on her own?

She ran out of time in more ways than one. Despite the way her skin crawled, mouth dried, being on Madigan's side was the only way to save herself.

To save the others.

"There is not much I consider unfair play." He pulled his gaze from Róisín's mouth to Aoife. "This would be first on the list, though."

"The others couldn't know about her," Aoife said.

"Ah, another lie." His voice was a murmur as he stroked the backs of his fingers over Róisín's cheek. "You appeared before the council over fifty years ago with her. They didn't want to let Brenna's power pass to her, so you fought valiantly for her right to wield it. You should have taken better care to ward your records from me, Aoife."

The air crackled with Aoife's magic.

"Your lies, Aoife." His black eyes simmered with flames of orange. "What shall we do with her, my love?" He turned to Róisín, eyes softening. "I can feel your contempt rising. That anger, that rightful rage weaving into your power."

She took a slow breath, her body trembling, trying to appear uncertain. She tipped her head to the side, contemplating Aoife. For a moment, she lifted the veil, letting Aoife see the truth in her eyes. The power, the knowledge, her strength. Red blossomed on Aoife's neck, rising to her face as it twisted in anger.

"You think I'm it?" Aoife spat. "I'm not the only one."

Madigan moved behind Róisín and placed his hands upon her shoulders. It took every ounce of effort to not recoil.

Disconnect. Disconnect from it all.

"You underestimated your granddaughter, who is not to say that you're underestimating the others? Do you trust them, Aoife? Truly?"

She gave him a tight smile in response.

Róisín leaned back against him. "My love, we'll go after the others, right?"

"Of course." He swept her hair aside and bent his head to press a kiss to the side of her neck. "Your little friends as well. We can make them an offer they can't refuse so that you will not have to say goodbye to them."

"What kind of offer?" She tipped her head more, giving him better access to her neck, closing her eyes in false desire as he licked. She let her heat return to her body, warming it as if it would with her ecstasy. All her training over the past several months had been tedious at times, leaving her unsure of just how she was to use it against him. She was not the only one that didn't imagine it would be this. She suppressed a shiver.

"Join us. We can create a new world for us all without the Goddess."

His breath was hot against her skin, smelling of brimstone. "You will rule at my side. My queen. They can all have positions of power above those who sign away this pitiful life of restricted power and follow us."

"You would have me as your queen?"

His hand slid over her chest, lightly cupping the front of her throat. "I will take you as my everything."

"He'll tell you anything to have your power, Róisín," Aoife said. "He's a siphon. Look at what he did to our children."

Her attention snapped forward, eyes narrowed at her. "You shared that responsibility, grandmother. You may not have had the siphon strength he has, but you had it. The things he showed me when we first met, before the others came."

Madigan rumbled his approval of her rush to defend him against her back.

"He showed me many things too." Aoife spat on the floor between them, rage twisted her face.

They had dallied too long. Aoife's magic grew in power and pressed harder against theirs. Sweat beaded along her spine from the effort to use hers and Madigan's power to hold her in place.

Pressing forward, she turned her back to Aoife, so that she was face to face with him again. "You never answered my question, love. What do you require of me to end her?"

"That depends." He brushed a strand of hair from her face. "Do we want to play with our food, or cut straight to the chase?"

"I feel the longer we take to decide, we may just end up playing, regardless. She's fighting against my bonds, I fear her age and experience will overcome mine." She used her honest worry to feign weakness to him.

"Such honesty and openness." He smiled down at her. "I can tell that she was not the one who raised you."

"Shall we?" She blinked at him.

"Do we give her a head start?" he mused.

"She did clothe and feed me after my mother died, it seems only fair," Róisín reasoned.

"This is far from over," Aoife snarled, struggling against the hold of their magic.

"Mm, yes. A few seconds?"

"Is that too many? She could shift away from the house."

"I can bind her within these walls," he offered.

Róisín looked over her shoulder at her grandmother, winking at her. "I have a better idea." Róisín pulled his head down to hers and sealed her mouth over his.

Instead of the hungry, heated kiss she'd given him before, this one was full of power. She dug down into the depths of her well, pulling up her mother's magic. It filled her, thrummed in her veins, beat in her heart. It became every breath she took, every stroke of her tongue against his.

Madigan reached for her mind to stop her. He tried to grasp, then fumbled his siphoning magic as she took and took and took. He struggled against her, his hard, muscled body pushing against her with every ounce of energy he could muster, his magic failing him.

The pressure built inside of her, feeling as though she were a bomb about to explode. She slid her tongue over the roof of his mouth, feeling him fight against his own desire that her touch ignited.

Then she pressed every drop of her magic's power outward.

The fire went out in the fireplace, plunging the room into total darkness. The windows of the house shattered. It creaked, groaning loudly as it shifted on its foundation.

Madigan fell limp in her arms, an empty husk of what once was. She released him, gasping, and her power surged, pulsing in the air around her.

The Seer sat, knitting away within the barrier Madigan's magic had created. She had supposed it was her own now that kept them safe as she stepped around a piece of fallen ceiling.

Aoife had collapsed, empty as Madigan, on the floor behind the sofa. The invisible vines Róisín had bound her with were now opaque and had withered when her magic had pulled all the life from the room. The sight of the brittle, gray vines made her think of what Madigan had done to Greens Glen. She stared, unblinking, at what remained of the woman who had changed her entire life, and no longer felt anything. Even the feelings of betrayal and anger had subsided.

With the house beginning to crumble around them, Róisín pulled her magic back to her, her life magic enveloping her. She needed to get herself and the Seer out of there before they joined Aoife and Madigan, wherever they were.

Róisín carefully dodged falling debris, maneuvering to where the Seer sat, and she prayed to the Goddess that she was unmerciful with her judgment against them.

CHAPTER 91

"Now?" Shasta asked. If the circumstances were different, she would march upstairs and sprawl across her bed, sleeping for months. She had to dig deep to pull the effort to even blink at that moment. They had spent the last several minutes, hours, maybe even days because they couldn't tell from the blackened windows how much time had passed, throwing everything they had for magic at her house in an attempt to free them.

"Still nothing," Nanette replied with a frown.

"This makes no sense." Shasta stepped back from the door. "How?!" She shouted to no one, to everyone. "I spent a decade creating this house. A decade! This is how you repay me?!"

They'd tried everything to break free of the prison they found themselves in. They couldn't transport away, the doors and windows were magically sealed. At one point, they had coaxed Lily into shimmying her way up the chimney. Just inches from freedom, Lily found herself against an unseen barrier.

"Can you feel Matthew?" Shasta asked.

"What?" Nanette asked at the same time Lily replied, "No."

"We haven't been able to tie our bond yet," Lily whispered.

"Bond?" Nanette nearly dropped the book she had been skimming the pages of.

"Oh, shit, you didn't know." Shasta pressed her lips together, sending Lily an apologetic look. It wasn't her place to tell Nanette, but needing to get out of this damn house was.

Nanette lowered herself into a chair. "You're bonded with Matthew?"

Lily nodded.

"Are you sure?"

She nodded again.

"How?"

"We were—" She cleared her throat, shifting in her seat. "One time we were digging through the books in Alleyette. We both felt that zing or snap next to our Coven lines."

Nanette slowly raised an eyebrow. "You were just sitting there, reading a book and, just like that, felt it?"

"Um..."

Shasta brought a hand to her mouth to hide her smile.

"Lily."

"No?"

"No? Are you asking or are you telling?" Nanette demanded.

Lily threw her hands up. "What difference does it make?"

"It makes a huge difference!" Nanette shouted.

"Okay, okay, enough," Shasta intervened. "They're bonded, Nanette. It's neither here nor there right now. Obviously, there's a reason for it. We'll never know that reason unless we can get the hell out of here." She faced Lily. "You can't feel him?"

"No, it's still only my Coven members. I can only feel our bond right now when we're sharing a space."

"Dammit." Shasta rubbed her temples, trying to soothe the growing headache that was there. "Helen! She's skirted all of this by my sending her to Lina for the baby."

"Will she be able to help, though?" Nanette asked.

"I don't know about you, but I'm all out of ideas. We don't know where everyone else is, or if they're okay. We don't know if Madigan is still alive. I'm willing to try anything, even selling my soul right now."

Nanette was silent for a moment, tapping her fingers atop her book. "It's worth a shot."

CHAPTER 92

Lucius looked down at his hands, the red of Frederick's blood glaring back at him, a reminder of what had happened in Clarissa's afterworld. It had become hard to breathe, his chest having grown tight, his lungs unable to get enough air, when he realized what Róisín did. The sacrifice she made. He chalked it up to fatherly instinct, knowing the day she'd told them what had transpired at the ravine with Madigan, there was more. There was a scar that Madigan had given her that no one could see. And to know she gave herself to Madigan in that way, for them...

Then that panic settled next to his fear for Matthew, and his control snapped. There wasn't much he remembered from that moment. Only Clarissa's soothing magic enveloping him and Frederick's broken, bloodied, lifeless body in the hibiscus of Clarissa's afterworld garden.

They stood at the end of the Dead Forest. Clarissa, a solid presence at his side. A reminder of his life before.

"I can't stay here long," Clarissa said.

"We need to find the others. Matthew and Caid were with Róisín at the Seer's."

"Lucius, wait." She grabbed hold of his wrist, stopping him from charging forward toward the forest.

"Clarissa." His tone strained.

"Matthew is..." She pressed her lips together and drew them in-between her teeth, biting down. "We need to..."

"Something is going to happen, isn't it?" He faced her now.

"I—"

"Where is he? What's happening?" He gripped her shoulders, shaking her lightly, searching for calm.

"His fate has been woven," she whispered, tears in her eyes. "Just as mine, just as yours. I was always meant to help you, even though they changed what was to be. You were never meant to come to the after-world. I was meant to come here. Then, we were meant to go to Shasta."

He tried to catch his breath, struggling with the weight that had settled on his chest. "Fuck fate. Fuck fate, fuck the Sisters, fuck the Goddess."

"Don't say that."

"They took you away from me, they're not taking my son!"

"Lucius..."

"I can't—" He broke with a cry. He liked to think himself a strong man, capable of handling whatever the Sisters or Goddess threw his way, but he knew. The way his eyes no longer saw as clearly, a haze filling the edges of his sight, and the way his heart would sometimes forget to beat after Clarissa had died. There would be no surviving it if Matthew didn't make it.

There were things he still needed to tell him. Things Matthew needed to know. They needed that time together so that Lucius could find that courage he needed to speak those words to Matthew.

The world was cracking and rumbling around him.

"Lucius," Clarissa whispered. She wrapped her arms around him and pressed her face against his chest. "It will be okay. He'll be okay."

"What am I supposed to do, here, alone?"

"You won't be alone." She stroked a hand over his back. "There are things happening right now. In our world, the human world, across the realms. Something is coming, I can feel it in the energy of the after-world. What others say and carry with them from visits with their fami-lies. I can't see it, it's so foggy here." She tapped a finger to her temple. "I can feel it. There will be choices, sacrifices. It's not over."

He squeezed his eyes shut, holding onto the frayed thread he could find in the dark that had settled inside of him.

"Is Matthew one of those sacrifices?"

"I don't know."

CHAPTER 93

MILDRED stood between Caid and Matthew, tossing a baseball sized fireball from hand to hand. The trio had spent the last hour trading physical and magical blows. The longer he and Matthew fought Mildred, the thicker the darkness in his core grew. It moved like mud now, reaching through him, wrapping around him.

He tried to shake it off and reach for his magic. No, he stopped himself when he remembered what Róisín had said about their magic. It was a part of him, he needed to trust his instincts and the instincts of whatever it was that drove his magic. Even if it was dark and grimy. Whatever got him out of there, alive. He needed to find Róisín.

"You could just fold the hand now." Mildred added two more balls of fire, juggling.

"Not in a million years, bitch." Matthew spit out a mouthful of blood at her feet.

She clucked her tongue. "Tsk, tsk, I know your mother taught you better than that."

He flicked his hand, and a gust of wind extinguished the flames.

"I suppose I could go another round." She sighed. "Are you boys ready?"

Matthew looked beyond her to where Caid stood, watching, waiting. Like Matthew, Caid's face and arms were littered with cuts and bruises already blooming from blows. A knee of Caid's jeans was torn open. Matthew's shirt was in tatters.

"What is it you're getting out of all of this? If Aoife's gone, Madigan's gone." Matthew tossed a quick glance over his shoulder to where Henry's body was a pile of ash. "He's gone. What's left?"

"Power."

"Have you not learned from your predecessors?" He took a subtle step forward. Caid didn't hesitate, mirroring the move at her back.

"I have, as a matter of fact. Aoife's mistake was removing her entire Coven. All that power, but no one to march under her if she succeeded."

Matthew lifted an eyebrow. "She had you, didn't she? Henry? Frederick."

"No one can get in," she said.

"I don't think we need the help," Caid said, and she turned to him.

"Help never hurts, sweetheart. Although, I will say, Nanette has taught you well. She certainly did right by hiding you away. If the council were still complete, I would revel in hammering that gavel in judgment of this glaring transgression of hers."

"What about your judgment, Mildred?" Matthew asked. "We all face the Goddess in the end. What will she say of you?"

"Oh." A wicked grin tipped up the corners of her mouth, and she spun back to Matthew. "The Goddess is going to bow to me."

"Bow to you?" Matthew laughed at her.

"There are things in place, things happening that you could never understand because you're so blind," she snapped.

Matthew lifted his brows, waving his hands in a circular motion when her pause drew out, becoming bloated. "Well? Do go on, I know how much you like hearing yourself talk."

"Some things are best left unsaid."

Caid snorted, taking a step forward, putting himself almost right behind her. "Sounds like something someone who doesn't actually have a leg to stand on but wants others to believe they have something of value to save their own ass."

"Caid does have a point. Mildred has never been very ambitious. Never a self-starter." He looked from Caid to her. "Always a follower."

"What you're saying is that she has no backup plan," Caid said.

"Nope." Matthew tilted his head off to the side. "I'd say she's figured out that she was left behind, now she's flying by the seat of her pants."

"That, boys, is where you're wrong. I have my place, I have my purpose. Even if I may be the last of us standing, I still get my reward. There's still one very, very key piece at play in the game."

Caid's eyes shot over her shoulder. He had the confirmation of his suspicion in the way Matthew's jaw bulged as he clenched it, the line of his eyebrows as they came down over his eyes. Mildred had meant Róisín.

"She will learn the truth. She will turn," Mildred said, her voice low and menacing.

"That's where you're wrong." Matthew replied.

Caid made to move closer to her.

Matthew stopped him with an almost imperceptible shake of the head then ran full speed at Mildred. Caid shouted, and Matthew leapt into the air, slamming into Mildred and shifting them away before she could do anything to stop him.

Then, the floor opened, swallowing Caid.

His body slammed against a cold slab of metal, knocking the air from his lungs. Gasping, he rolled to his side and pushed up on all fours. His body swayed, his stomach roiling from the waves of pain rolling through his body. Fighting the urge to vomit, he made his way toward what he hoped was a wall, feeling to his front and sides as he went.

His fingers brushed against something smooth and hard, and he stopped. Caid took a moment, preparing himself for what he was about to curl his fingers around. Despite never having been near a true skeleton, his brain already knew he'd found a bone. To what, he didn't know, but given the situation he currently found himself in, he felt pretty comfortable he was accurate in his assumption that it was human.

"Ah, shit," he muttered when he gripped the bone. He used his other hand to balance himself and turned his body to sit down. Then, he used both hands to gauge the length of what he held.

A femur bone. Would it hold long enough for him to use it to pound his way through the overhead door? Could he even reach the door?

With a groan, he rose to his feet. Stretching his left arm overhead, he hissed out a breath when his knuckles smashed against the door he'd fallen through. He ran his fingers along the cold metal, feeling for an edge or seam. There. His index finger found it first, the middle seam. Gripping the bone like a baseball bat, he swung.

CHAPTER 94

Róisín threw her shoulder against the front door of the Seer's house, grunting at the impact. The floor beneath her feet rumbled and shook as the house collapsed behind them.

"Dammit." She grit her teeth together, throwing herself against the door again. It swung open, revealing the purpling dawn sky over the Dead Forest. With the Seer tucked against her side, she quickly made her way down the stairs, into the dark of the forest.

The Seer shifted beneath her, their body quaking. Then, like they had been made of ash, their body began to break into pieces, floating away on a slight breeze.

"My daughter," the forest called out to her.

Róisín jerked to a stop, senses alert. She shouted into the air, "What did you do with the Seer?"

"I did nothing." The Goddess, dressed in pale blue, flowing linen that danced with each step she took around the trees toward Róisín. Her hair appeared to be its own light source, the long golden locks shining brightly in the dark forest. "Without the house, the Seer drifts."

"Are they—" She swallowed, collecting her bearings. "Are they really his?"

The Goddess nodded, moving closer, circling her. Her amethyst colored eyes looked Róisín over for a moment before she lifted a thumb and brushed it over one of the cuts on Róisín's face.

Fighting the urge to press away the cold hand at her face, Róisín swallowed and hoped her voice stayed steady and strong. "Will they?"

"No. I bound them from doing harm with their gift. Do not fret about the Seer, daughter, without the house, they are nothing." She turned toward the direction of the house, hard lines setting around her mouth as she stared into the darkness.

"Why are you here? My mother, she…"

"I know." She rested a hand on her shoulder and stepped around to face her. "I know all that Brenna did before she passed on."

"Is she?" Róisín's body trembled, her heart racing. Her mouth was dry, her chest was heavy.

"Brenna is not in the darkness, nor does she remain underworld. We have let her join your father in the afterworld."

Róisín covered her mouth, quieting her sob. "You're here for me."

"No, my daughter." She smoothed a hand over her hair, giving her a loving smile. "It is not your time. Your people need you, we all need you."

She straightened, brow wrinkling.

"Threads have been pulled from both our loom and the humans."

"Madigan, my grandmother."

"They were threats to our kind, yes." The Goddess nodded. "Even with their power, they could not have pulled threads from the humans' loom."

"Shit."

The Goddess lifted her brows.

"What in the Hells am I supposed to do? I could barely get my feet under myself to do this." She threw her hand up, gesturing behind her to where the Seer's house was now rubble.

"You are to unite the Covens."

Róisín snorted. "That's it, huh? Get everyone to come together like one, big happy family."

The Goddess didn't answer, and a weight settled in the pit of her stomach like a brick.

"Unite the Covens? I don't exactly see Trifoa or Baijiola joining forces with Ely, or Molennius."

"There are already things in place to assure uniting."

"Matthew and Lily." Something new built inside of Róisín. Her mind began to race, her adrenaline flooding her veins.

"Are only a part of this."

"What happens if I can't do this?"

Again, no answer.

Róisín changed tactics. "Why me?"

"You are the key, Róisín. You are *our* key."

She wrinkled her nose, squinting at the Goddess before letting out a frustrated groan, putting her hands on her hips. "Do you want to tell me what you know? Or are you going to keep giving me cryptic answers or just not answering at all?"

"Unite the Covens, Róisín," The Goddess said, fading.

"Then what do I do?!" she shouted at the empty space left in the Goddess's place.

Chapter 95

SHASTA slumped against the wall, groaning and laying on the floor. The clock on the wall in the kitchen read it was nearing the end of the day on Molennius, yet the windows remained black as pitch, reflecting night. They had deduced that it had also been a part of the spelling placed on the house.

Helen's efforts to get inside or get them out of the house had failed. After what felt like hours of trying, Shasta sent her back to Greens Glen to keep Lina safe.

"I hope the others are okay," Lily whispered from where she sat next to the fireplace.

"Oh, honey." Nanette dropped into the empty spot next to her and took her in her arms. "Why didn't you tell me?"

Lily curled against her. "It was new... and I was sort of a brat to him about it at first."

"A brat?" Nanette arched her brows.

Lily's cheeks grew pink. "He kissed me, and I ran away from him."

"The first time Evelyn kissed me, I did the same," Shasta recalled from her spot on the floor.

"They were also bonded," Nanette said.

"You were?" Lily perked up.

Shasta rose, dragging her exhausted body closer to them. The wing-back chair made a sound in protest against her weight when she all but crashed down upon it. "We were, and I knew it before she did."

"How? I've spent so much time near him over our years, but it wasn't until that moment just before that it woke inside of me."

"The bond ties when the Sisters deem us ready to receive it," Shasta said. "They decided, despite my actions, I was ready before Ev was."

Lily sat up and tucked her legs under her. "Why did you run?"

"I was terrified. I had watched Brenna fall headlong into love with Stephen, even knowing what she knew. I didn't know that I would lose Ev, but the thought of giving my heart to someone... That someone could have that much hold on something so important when anything could happen. But I did it. Then she was killed in The Blitz."

Lily looked from her, to Nanette. "Wha—"

The front door flew open.

"Clarissa?!" Shasta shot to her feet, her heart skipping like a happy child with an ice cream. She brought her hands to her chest where her breath had caught.

"Surprise?" Clarissa gave her a sheepish smile.

"How?" She rushed to her side and embraced her. "Oh, you're really here." She relished the solidness of her friend in her arms. "You're really here."

"I can't stay much longer," she said. "I need to return to the after-world. First, I needed to help Lucius break the spells and get you all out of here."

"Frederick apparently was busy under Mildred's spellage lessons," Shasta muttered.

"Frederick is no longer an issue," Lucius said darkly, entering the house. "All the warding and spells are clear."

"Where are the others?" Nanette joined them.

Lucius clenched his jaw, eyes flashing with anger. "Aoife returned. Henry, Frederick, and I can assume Mildred all worked with her."

"Róisín?" Shasta looked between them.

"I don't know," he whispered. "Henry took me to the afterworld. Matthew and Caid, I haven't been able to locate them yet. I felt Matthew moments ago, however, I couldn't pinpoint where he was."

"Caid?" Nanette asked.

"Brenna has his bond warded. We can't reach it, only Róisín can." Shasta said.

"What do we do now?" Lily sat frozen on the sofa, her voice small.

Shasta chewed on her lip. Her mind sped with thoughts like train cars on a track that ran into a wall. Even when she doubled down on her effort, she couldn't get a complete thought together before it crashed and broke into bits. She was considered an elder, a leader. How quickly she was falling apart in the face of the biggest danger had her mother's words echoing loudly back to her.

You're only being named my heir because there isn't anyone else. You'll never be fit to lead, and I can only hope you'll have a child who will be.

No. She would keep it together. After all she and Brenna had done to prepare for this moment, she would not, could not, fail.

"Where would they have gone?" Lucius asked.

"A neutral place," Clarissa said. "We don't know how corrupted their Covens are, leading me to guess that they wouldn't want to risk being outed by their people."

"Alleyette," Shasta said.

"Or," Nanette raised a hand, "Trifoa. We all know Mildred's Coven has itched for centuries to free themselves from being a council member."

Shasta inclined her head. "Trifoa would be the obvious if their coup were to be discovered. They would think we wouldn't dare to believe they'd do it on the castle grounds where this exact thing is forbidden."

"I agree. Triofa is too obvious," Lucius said. "But, if we cannot find the others, we go to Trifoa."

"Lucius," Clarissa whispered. "A moment?"

"We'll wait outside." Shasta waved Lily over, slipping an arm around her waist in support. As much as Shasta wanted to stay wrapped in her friend's arms, to soak in the love that Clarissa always had an abundance of, she knew that it was time for Clarissa to return to the afterworld and that Lucius, Clarissa's soul, more than deserved the quiet moment to say goodbye.

Chapter 96

Róisín was alive. Her thoughts hadn't calmed since leaving the forest. Instead, they had grown more legs, giving them the ability to spin faster and faster. Her body was heavy, every move caused her to wince or groan as the spears of pain shot through her. Each breath was a fight, struggling against the weight that had settled there. There should be relief filling her to the brim. Madigan and Aoife were gone. They had done it. She had done it.

She limped toward the castle in Alleyette, exhaustion pulling at her, urging her to stop. Her mind hadn't slowed since the Goddess had left. The throb in her head grew, and she tried to piece together any clues from the message she had brought her in the forest.

The others had been okay. When she had reached down her connection for them, everyone quickly tugged back, filling her with relief.

She still had grabbed hold of Caid's tether, but as she neared the doors to the castle, it had grown harder to grasp, like it was fading.

Like he was fading.

With her heart sinking into her stomach, she tried to swallow around the lump in her throat. Stopping at the door, she stared at the large bronze handle, fighting back tears.

She let her weight fall against the door, opening it. Gathering the scraps of power that remained, including the dredges of Madigan's that she'd taken within herself, she gave a firm pull against Caid's line. She sucked in a sharp breath, her footsteps stumbling with the force that hit her when he pulled back.

She fell to her knees, drained. Everything ached. She held her breath, trying to quiet the noise within her to hear the noises around her.

"Caid?" she called out.

A rumble echoed through the halls in response.

She sent out another tug, more frantic. He responded with a more desperate pull back.

"Caid!"

She clambered to stand, adrenaline pushing away the fog of fatigue. She sprinted.

"Caid!"

The rumble grew louder.

"Caid!"

She stopped in the gallery room at the center of the first floor, eight hallways surrounding her.

"Caid!" Her cry became more frenzied as she tugged again.

The rumbling she'd heard before was more of a pounding sound now. A faint shout punctuated it.

"Róisín!"

"Caid." His name was a breath from her lips, and she began racing toward the hallway that led to the lower level.

They kept shouting to one another, back and forth. His voice grew louder and louder. Until she reached the holding room where they voted on council judgments.

She drew in a deep breath, bellowing his name again.

"Róisín!" he called out.

Something slammed against the floor beneath her.

"What the hell?" She looked down. "Where are you?"

"The floor ate me."

She dropped to her knees, then felt along the floor for any crack or opening. "How?!"

"About how you'd imagine it. Opened up and swallowed me."

"Now isn't the time to be a wiseass," she muttered.

"Madigan? Aoife?"

"Gone and gone."

"Everyone else?"

"Okay, I think. When I checked the tether, they pulled back. Matthew? Where's Matthew?"

She was met with silence.

"Caid?"

"I'm here," his answer was quiet.

She felt markings on the floor near the wall edge. Shifting, she brought her head down to bring her line of sight closer. "That bitch."

"Róisín?"

"Hold on," she grumbled. Closing her eyes, she searched for everything she had ever learned from Shasta growing up. Mildred held practice with ancient rune stones, much like Shasta and her Coven had. Deep in the recesses of her memories, she found what she needed. Quietly, she read the words along the floor, sending it opening. Scrambling across the floor, she peered over the edge, relief flooding her seeing Caid alive. Battered, but alive.

"Is that..." She squinted into the darkness below. "A fucking bone?"

"Hm?" He looked down. "Oh, this." He lifted his hand, waving what appeared to be a large bone. "This is Bob. Apparently, the floor ate him too."

She blinked rapidly, eyebrows shooting up. "Bob? Never mind." She shook her head. "Bob's not the issue right now. Where is Matthew, Caid?"

He dropped his chin to his chest, rubbing the back of his neck with a bloodied hand.

"Caid..." Her voice shook with her nerves.

"I don't know." He shook his head. "One minute he was there. Then the next, they were gone."

"They?"

"He and Mildred. She rambled on and on about Aoife's plan, how Madigan was a distraction. And—" He hoisted himself up, grunting when he splayed on the ground next to where she still knelt. The bone he'd held clattered to the floor next to him. "There was something she said about you, how she could still get to you and use you. Something changed on Matthew's face, like an understanding. Before I could do anything to her, he charged her, and the next thing I know, they were gone and the floor was trying to kill me."

Róisín rocked back onto her heels, her eyes wide. "She just thought you were another witch. My mother must have shielded our bond from them. Mildred still thought Matthew and I avoided our bond."

Caid struggled into a sitting position next to her. "What do you mean?"

"Caid? Róisín?" Shasta's voice echoed to them.

Róisín rubbed a hand over her face, squeezing her eyes closed. "Where's Henry?"

"Matthew..." Caid drew his finger along his neck, then pointed to a charred spot along the far wall.

"Fuck." With the events that had unfolded that day, she knew the council held no ground over Matthew's actions, but taking another person, another witch's life, regardless of the situation, would effect Matthew.

"There you are." Nanette rushed into the room. Shasta, Lily, and Lucius close on her heels.

"How bad are your injuries?" Shasta knelt next to her.

"Just my leg, really. A beam caught me on the way out of the Seer's. I'll manage." Róisín tried to rise to her feet but couldn't.

Caid was up quickly, at her side, wrapping a supportive arm around her waist, holding her against his side.

Lucius looked at all of them, then around the room, his gaze first settling on Róisín's, reading the emotion she did not try to hide.

His attention turned to Caid. "May I?"

Caid nodded and stilled.

As Lucius moved through Caid's last moments with Matthew, his eyes grew darker, until the black had swallowed the white. He clenched his jaw and closed his eyes, nostrils flaring at the breath he exhaled.

Then he let out a roar that rattled all their bones and shook the realms.

Epilogue

MATTHEW stumbled, reaching out to grasp onto one of the palms near the head of the beach. His skin felt tight, his stomach gnawed at him in hunger. It'd been a week since he'd somehow brought himself and Mildred to Aunellion.

Leaning against the trunk of the tree, he looked toward the water where a figure in a flowing sundress with hair the color of autumn swung a small girl around in a circle. The child's laughter spread across the beach.

After a moment, the child was set down, and she looked toward the trees.

"Uncle Matthew!" she called out. "Come swim with me!"

Uncle Matthew.

"Uncle Matthew probably forgot his swim trunks again." The figure turned to look in his direction now. She lifted her hand to shield her eyes from the sun, with the other, she waved him over. Even from a distance, he could see Róisín's belly was swollen from another pregnancy.

"He would forget his head if it wasn't attached," another figure replied, stepping into his line of view.

Lily.

"Are you just going to hug that tree all day, handsome, or are you going to join us?" Lily called over to him.

He took a staggering step forward and stopped when his focus cleared. Lily's stomach was rounded. A baby. Theirs.

Lucius and Caid were on the far side of the beach where the sand met the rocks, casting fishing lines.

His throat felt like glass when he swallowed. This wasn't real, none of it was. He still laid outside of the castle, Mildred's broken, lifeless body next to his. No one came to Aunellion, not anymore. The Goddess had sealed it, cursed it.

None of this was real. He still wasn't sure how he had made it here, only that he knew he lay in the Fog Fields, the fog settling over his body. He had heard stories about the cursed fog, created by Madigan's ancestors to shield all Aunellion from those who were uninvited. Its hallucinations consumed minds, destroyed people.

Matthew struggled to move his legs another step. Lucius was safe. He had tugged frantically down their Coven line when he had realized where Frederick was. He had felt Róisín tugging through his connection with her, created between them when she became her Coven head. She was okay. He had to pray to the Goddess that Lily was okay, too. He wouldn't think of what could've happened to her, not here, not now.

No, none of this before him was real, but he would live in whatever moment this was. Because in this, Róisín was filled with joy and happiness, Lily's steady eyes were on him filled with love, and seeing her bearing his child was better than fighting it and letting his mind sit in darkness before his end came.

Acknowledgments

I don't even know where to start. This has been a lifelong dream of mine and so many people have supported, and encouraged me when I finally took this leap.

First, to my grandfather, Bert Sr., for whom my story-telling pales in comparison to, but from the tree my imagination and love for writing has grown.

To Justin, my rock. I don't know how many times I panic dumped during this process on you, but you never told me to shelve the idea for a rainy day. Instead, you kept pushing me forward.

My son, who is so ecstatic his mom is writing a book – even if he's a long way out from being able to ever read such a 'grown up' book. Don't worry kiddo, mom's got that fish story spawning in her head.

To Lauren, one of my Beta readers. Your commentary gave me that mid-process push I needed to dig back in and get this train back on its rails.

Lisa, Alexandria, Donna, Chris, and Sara – this book would't have even gotten off the ground and to my editor if it were not for all of you. I cannot express gratitude deep enough for your help.

Brit, my amazing editor. Thank you for pushing me in places that felt dark and icky, the ones I didn't want to touch with a 100 foot pole, with gloves on.

Wendy, because if it were not for you, I would have never even began to explore the idea of really doing this.

My mother for supporting my book habit by taking me to the library, and also being a book hoarder herself so that I had plenty to feed my inner book gremlin.

My sisters, because how else would I have thought to write a book about magic if we hadn't spent all of those afternoons making potions outside?

And lastly, my dad. Because he's the coolest.

About the Author

H.S. Sullivan comes from a long line of storytellers and poets, so it is of no surprise she has been scratching down stories of her own since she was a small child.

She holds a B.A. in Journalism and is an award winning journalist for feature writing and photography. Writing professionally for 16 years, she often moonlights as a ghost writer for fitness blogs and magazines.

Sullivan was born and raised on the northern New England coast, where she currently lives with her husband, son, and their rescued heeler mix. When she's not writing or reading, she is training for her next Masters weightlifting meet, tending to her gardens, or swimming in the Atlantic.

Daughters of Legianne is Sullivan's debut novel, and the first in the Realms of Covens series.

To stay up-to-date on the Realms of Covens series and other upcoming works, visit hssullivan.com or follow on Instagram at @themothermermaid.

www.ingramcontent.com/pod-product-compliance
Lightning Source LLC
Chambersburg PA
CBHW060609300726
48975CB00005B/1509